"What do you want?" he gasped.
His assailant looked at the Ghost.

"I want what you took from me," she croaked.

"I took nothing from you."

"When I came, I had possessions. You took them."

"That was years back—"

Amos prodded him gently with the knife.

"I don't remember. Who can remember that long ago?"

He sounded desperate. Near tears. Not a man. A boy about to blubber helplessly under the pressure of the knife and her relentless gaze.

"I do," she said. "I had a book. I had a chain around my neck. I had a pendant on a chain. And I had a ring."

The wife had said nothing. Amos looked at her and caught a guilty flicker in her eyes. He reached out to her mind and felt a kind of reptilian movement in her thoughts, as if there were thick coils slowly slithering against each other in the depths as the mind tried to hide something from even itself. And then he caught what she was thinking, the thing she was trying to find a way not to admit out loud. She was wondering how to keep her money and her goods and deciding whether she would say anything if they started cutting her husband. Because he, Amos saw in her thoughts, did not know where she hid what she had stolen. And she was now deciding she trusted her future to the hidden loot more than she trusted the man whimpering beside her in a puddle of his own piss. She was not going to say where she kept it concealed. She had looked at the hand fate had dealt her and decided her husband would have to go on the forfeit pile.

THE PARADOX

CHARLIE FLETCHER

orbit

www.orbitbooks.net

Copyright © 2015 by Man Sunday Ltd.
Excerpt from *Skyborn* copyright © 2015 by David Dalglish
Excerpt from *Age of Iron* copyright © 2014 by Angus Watson

Orbit
Hachette Book Group
1290 Avenue of the Americas
New York, NY 10104
www.orbitbooks.net

Printed in the United States of America

RRD-C

First U.S. edition: August 2015
Originally published in Great Britain in 2015 by Orbit

10 9 8 7 6 5 4 3 2 1

Orbit is an imprint of Hachette Book Group.
The Orbit name and logo are trademarks of Little, Brown Book Group Limited.

The Hachette Speakers Bureau provides a wide range of authors for speaking events. To find out more, go to www.hachettespeakersbureau.com or call (866) 376-6591.

The publisher is not responsible for websites (or their content) that are not owned by the publisher.

Library of Congress Control Number: 2015941233
ISBN: 978-0-316-27954-3

For Domenica, for ever the loveliest of paradoxes

DRAMATIS PERSONAE

THE OVERSIGHT

Cook — *once a pirate*
The Smith — *smith, ringmaker and counsellor*
Hodge the Terrier Man — *ratcatcher at the Tower of London, blinded*
Charlie Pyefinch — *apprentice ratcatcher*
Lucy Harker — *a Glint and a lost girl*
Emmet — *a golem*
Jed — *an Old English Terrier*

IN LONDON

Caitlin Sean ná Gaolaire — *a venatrix, from Skibbereen*
An amorous doctor — *unfaithful to his wife*
Young woman — *child thief and changeling*
A newborn baby — *her father, also a changeling*
Francis Blackdyke, Viscount Mountfellon — *man of science turned supranaturalist*
The Citizen — *a sea-green incorruptible, thought dead*
Issachar Templebane Esq. — *lawyer and broker*

Sherehog, Vintry, Jewry, Westcheap, Aldersgate, Backchurch, Pountney, Poultry, Outwich, Bothaw, Abchurch and Coram Templebane – *adopted sons (unimpaired)*
William George Bunyon – *innkeeper and gaoler of the Sly House*
Nell Bunyon – *his daughter*
Obadiah Tittensor – *owner and Master of Lady of Nantasket, out of Boston, Mass.*

RUTLANDSHIRE

Whitlowe – *a running boy*
A footman
Old Biles – *servant and nightwatchman*

AT THE ANDOVER WORKHOUSE

M'Gregor – *superintendent*
Mrs M'Gregor – *his wife*

IN THE COUNTRYSIDE

The Ghost of the Itch Ward – *formerly of the Andover Workhouse, real name unknown*
Amos Templebane – *adopted son of Issachar (mute but intelligent)*

BETWEEN THE WORLDS

Sara Falk – *keeper of the Safe House in Wellclose Square*
Mr Sharp – *protector and sentinel*
The Raven – *a wise old bird*
John Dee – *known as The Walker between the Worlds*
A cavalier – *a Mirror Wight*
A bowman – *a Mirror Wight*
The nun – *onetime Marianne de Rohan, now a Mirror Wight*

BEYOND LAW AND LORE

Badger Skull, Bull Tattoo, Raven Totem, Fore-and-Aft and others — *Sluagh*

ON THE STEINERNES MEER

Frau Wachman — *a grief-stricken mother*
Herr Wachman — *her husband*
Peter — *a boy*
Otto von Fleischl — Schattenjäger, *a hunter*
Ida Laemmel — Schattenjägersmesser, *his "knife"*

BOSTON, MASSACHUSETTS

Prudence Tittensor — *wife of Obadiah, holder of secrets*

"Wildfire Rules All"

Heraclitus, Fragment 64

"Fire lives the death of air, and air lives the death of fire; water lives the death of earth, earth that of water" . . . so says Heraclitus, the ancient philosopher of flux and flame so beloved of the Alchemists. He believed this eternal fire was the key to the cyclical process of transmutation, both the creative spark and the destructive conflagration, changing the elements into one another so that, as Diogenes Laertius attests, "the world is alternately born from fire and again resolved into fire in fixed cycles to all eternity, and this is determined by destiny". Finding themselves guardians of a fragment of the original Wildfire, the Free Company for The Oversight of London have not been satisfied with leaving so potentially destructive a force to the vagaries of that destiny, but have devoted great effort and cunning to keeping it safe and contained. Indeed, of all the arcane duties involved in The Oversight's responsibility for keeping the balance between the natural and the supranatural worlds, this has been the keystone or, as it were, the fulcrum on which the balance depends . . . there are those who believe the Wildfire did not come from this world at all, but from another sphere whence it escaped, and to which it is inexorably drawn back (whence its volatility) . . . a sphere now rendered dark

and hungry by its absence, but this is, so far as I know, conjecture
and little evidence has come to my attention . . .

from *The Great and Hidden History of the World* by the Rabbi Dr Hayyim
Samuel Falk (also known as the Ba'al Shem of London)

PROLOGUE

A DOUBLE JEOPARDY: FIRST PART

Issachar Templebane examined his own dead face with more disappointment than sorrow. He noted how surprised it looked at the sudden interruption of all the clever plans that had once boiled so vigorously through the lifeless brain already beginning to rot behind that high forehead. The rictus of shock frozen on the waxy skin gave the lie to those who claimed that death by drowning was a peaceful and a painless departure, though it did occur to him that the expression might merely be one of distress at the taste of the noxious mix of Thames water and sewer effluent that had been his final fatal inhalation.

"Well," he said, reaching his good hand down and thumbing open an eye which gave a slight sticky pop as the lid detached unwillingly from an eyeball now devoid of life or lubrication. "Well, brother, you are a fool to have fallen in so untimely a manner, and I shall have to carry on without you."

The eye stared gummily back at a spot on the ceiling over Issachar's shoulder. He in turn hung over the face that was – his dead brother being also his identical twin – notionally but not actually his own. The movement was awkward and made him wince as the broken arm that was hanging in a sling twisted uncomfortably.

"I was thinking that I might unman myself by looking at your dead face, but now that I do so I must admit my first reaction is one of determination, for sad and distressing though it is to see you thus, it chiefly makes me resolved never to be seen by my own survivors with such a surprised and disappointed expression. I have to say that for such a preternaturally bright and accomplished man, brother, you look shamefully taken aback."

He let the eyelid go and sucked his teeth.

"It won't do though, it won't do at all. I am diminished by your death. I feel like a . . ."

And here, unusually for Issachar, words quite left him. He waited for them to return, eyes turned to the ceiling, blinking more rapidly than normal. He took a deep breath, then released a long, calming exhalation, massaging his broken arm with his good hand as he did so.

"I feel something has been stolen from me," he said. And the snarl with which he said it made it clear that the flush beginning to pink the ridges of his cheekbones was not grief but anger. "Well, brother, the dissolution of the partnership does not signal the end of the enterprise. I will continue alone, and I will destroy them. The precious Oversight may be adept at fighting the insubstantial and the arcane; we shall see how they are guarded against an assault in the real world. They think they have stopped us, but they have not. They have simply confirmed my opinion that our future prosperity is only guaranteed by their eradication, root and branch. I shall grub up their vines, burn their storehouses and sow their fields with salt. Once gone they will stay gone for ever. Their last thought will be an agonised regret that they attempted to thwart the House of Templebane."

FIRST PART

THE BLOODY BOY

CHAPTER 1

THE FIRST STEP

Sara Falk had passed through the mirror in one decisive step. Behind her, she left the basement of the familiar Safe House and the support of people who had known her all her life, the tight-knit band of guardians and friends who would have died to protect her, just as much as she would have risked everything for them.

It was thus a hard first step to take away from them, but she took it boldly and decisively, and she did not go precisely alone, nor without means of self-preservation: she was armed to the teeth, carrying a bright candle in one hand and the Raven on her shoulder. She looked herself up and down in the reflection, taking a brief inventory: slender but stout top-boots visible beneath an oiled silk overskirt that emerged from a black riding jacket buttoned tight around her lean body, her hands bunched inside equally black gloves on top of which gleamed two gold rings. The difference she noticed about her appearance, apart from the unaccustomed weaponry, was that she had taken to wearing her rings on the left hand, her recent travails having involved losing the other one and the rings with it – leading her to nearly expire – until it had been miraculously returned and even more miraculously re-attached. Above all that was her face, taut with exhaustion but still, as ever, decades too young for the prematurely white hair pulled tight into a thick white plait which curled round her neck and hung over her right collarbone. The eyes that looked back at her from the mirror were the grey-green of a midwinter sea and, she was pleased to note, steady and determined, despite the tug of exhaustion and the drumming of her heart beneath the tight coat buttons.

"Right," she said so quietly that only the Raven heard. "Let us go."

And she took a firm pace forward into the mirror. She passed through the surface of the glass with less resistance than popping a soap bubble, and then she stopped dead.

She lifted the candle. It seemed to flare brighter as she did so. She stared ahead into the uniform corridor created by the endless reflections of the mirror stretching away to a vanishing point lost in the darkness beyond the throw of the candlelight. When she turned round she did not see the back of the mirror she had just walked through, but an identical tunnel of mirrors now stretching away in the opposite direction until it too became lost in the gloom beyond the light. When she looked down, she saw the mirrored ceiling reflected all the way up into eventual darkness, and when she looked to one side, the same endless multiplication of reflections stretched to right and left.

"So," she said, "a maze it is."

The Raven clacked its beak in her ear.

"I know," she replied. "We shall have to mark the starting point if we are to have any hope of returning. I shall——"

The Raven hopped to the ground and shuddered briefly. Then it lofted back on to her shoulder. Where it had stood was an impressive splatter of bird's mess.

". . . I'm sure that will do nicely," said Sara. "Or if not quite nicely, adequately."

CHAPTER 2

THE BLOODY BOY

Amos Templebane (mute by birth and Templebane by adoption) had blood on his hands. Figurative blood, since the man he had killed was weeks in the past, and possibly even justifiable blood since the tinker in question had been about to cut Amos's throat the instant before Amos had backhanded him with the man's own frying pan, knocking him into the turbid canal in which he had drowned. Amos had walked and thought himself across many leagues of English countryside since that desperate night and in the course of that journey had both come to terms with the slaying, and made a vow that he would never, ever take another life. But arguably unimpeachable though his actions may have been, and admirable though his subsequent resolution was, the fact is that Amos had certainly killed a man.

The cold, detailed murderousness radiating from the mind of the grey-haired woman he had freed from the Eel House as she strode ahead of him across the water meadow was a different order of thing: it was as disconcerting as the discovery that she could read his thoughts just as well as he himself could hear what went on in other people's heads. Until she had spoken to him in his mind as he passed the little brick building in the dark and persuaded him to unlock it and release her, he had until now thought his ability was unique.

Where are you going? he thought.

She answered him in a voice hoarse and reedy from long disuse.

"To the poorhouse. To the Warden's bedroom."

The poorhouse. The words reminded him of his own early years in a similar institution in London. The memories were far from happy ones.

What will you do?

"Take what is mine," she said.

He had no memory of possessions in his own poorhouse. His memories were of being smaller than everyone else, and having nothing except fear and discomfort.

What is that?

"Revenge," she said. "For a start, revenge."

Why must you do violence?

She stopped and looked at him, her face implacable in the silvered moonlight.

"Because I must, Bloody Boy, because I must."

Why do you call me that? I am not bloody, and I am a man.

"You cannot yet be more than eighteen years old, and you already reek of blood. It was the first thing I noticed about you: even before my eyes saw you, my nose found you."

Her smile was fragile and terrible.

"Death walks with you, before and behind," she said. "Life taken and life to be taken. It's on you like a stench."

I will not take life.

She snorted and turned away.

"Your will does not enter into it, Bloody Boy," she said. "Not when fate has other plans."

He wished he had not given her a knife.

As he followed her towards the squat barrack of the poorhouse, he could see her head was full of blood as she planned her actions: she would stop by a water butt and reach down into the inky depths to retrieve a piece of oval glass, a mirror that she had previously hidden there. And then she would enter the back door of the Warden's dwelling and slip through the kitchen and ascend the backstairs, keeping to the left-hand side of the treads close to the wall so that they would not creak and give her approach away. She would ease open the bedroom door and cross the floor in two or three fast steps to stand beside the large double bed and its hopefully still snoring occupants, M'Gregor the Warden and his wife. And then—

Why kill him?

"Stop looking at my thoughts," she said without slowing.

What has she done?

"She is worse than him," she said. "You will help me."

There was something in her manner, in her single-mindedness, that was not quite human. It was feral, focused and unthinking. It was as if she had been imagining this revenge for so long that it was now more instinct than plan.

Wait, he thought.

"I have been waiting for long enough," she said. "I have been waiting for longer than you have been alive."

She slipped through the hedge and into the small yard at the back of the poorhouse.

What is this place?

"I told you. A vale of tears. It is the Andover Workhouse. It is my prison."

Just as he had seen her imagine it, she retrieved the looking-glass from the bottom of the water butt, leaning right down into it so that her arm was wet to the shoulder and her hair stuck to her face in wet snakes. She shook the water off and slid it into the pocket of her shift.

Why do you need a mirror?

He was beginning to realise she was mad.

"Wait and see," she said, and turned to the back door.

She worried the lock with the thin blade of the knife in an intent, nimble-fingered way that told him she had done this before. There was a snicking noise and she eased the door open, revealing the shadowy passage within.

Wait.

She turned to look at him.

You don't have to do this. You could just leave. By dawn you can be miles from here.

"You have no idea what I have to do," she said. "You must help me."

He took her arm.

She looked at the knife in her other hand. She looked pointedly back at his fingers gripping her arm.

"It would be foolish and dangerous to stop me," she whispered, "and quite against your own interests."

My interests don't need the slaughter of innocents in their bed.

The thought jumped from him before he could cloak it. And before he could stop her she had the knife at his throat. She stared into his eyes. He felt assaulted by the intensity of her scrutiny as much as by the prick of the blade. She appeared to be devouring everything about him, scanning his face, smelling him, feral again, sensing his warmth, his strength, his vulnerabilities . . .

She pulled the knife back, her eyes still sharp. She pointed up the stairs with a jerk of her head.

"He rapes the boys in the foundling ward. Mostly the boys, the smaller the better. Sometimes it's the girls. She knows and says nothing. She keeps the books and steals the money the parish puts aside for food and medicine. People die of hunger here, while that milk-fat bitch sleeps on a chest full of money. More than that, she steals from the inmates if they're unlucky enough to arrive with anything of value: kerchiefs, boots, whatever – she takes them and sells them. She took my things."

She had not blinked as she listed the crimes of the M'Gregors. He did his best not to break eye contact and stared right back at her.

"He does what he does because he has disgusting urges he has not the strength or character to resist. She looks the other way just because she likes money. She is worse. She knows and she is a woman, and a woman should be a mother; even if she has no blood-kin, she should be a mother to poor children without their own parents . . ."

She blinked. And now she was shaking with anger. He could feel it coming off her like a hot vibration in the air between them.

"A mother should protect," she said. "A mother should fight. A mother should punish those who harm."

But slaughtering them in their beds? This is mad.

She grinned at him, showing her teeth but no hint of mirth.

"Oh, I know. I went mad a long time ago. They saw to that."

Then—

"Then nothing. They could lock me up and take away the things whose lack made me run mad with grief and worse, but they could not control what I did with that madness. They could not stop me making the madness my own weapon. And now they will meet the edge of that weapon. Now they will pay."

Don't kill them.

For some reason, a reason he could not yet fathom, it was important that she did not kill the people sleeping upstairs. Maybe it was because, whatever she said about herself being the weapon, the edge that the victims would actually meet was the one on the blade he had handed her earlier. Or maybe it was because he had not really bothered to think enough about the dead tinker, and perhaps the weight of that untallied death, pushed to one side as he had walked away from it, was now suddenly crushing down on him.

He shook his head emphatically.

Don't kill them.

"I do not forgive."

Don't kill them.

"They must be punished. I have told you why . . ."

Yes. But you lied.

She froze. Just for an instant, but long enough for him to pull the knife from his own belt and get it between them. Her lip curled back in a silent snarl, and then, as she controlled herself, dropped back over her exposed teeth in what was – given the circumstances – a reasonable facsimile of a genuine smile.

He does not rape boys. Or girls. Does he?

She said nothing.

She does steal. You did not lie about that.

Her head cocked infinitesimally. It might have been a nod of acknowledgement.

You told the truth about her. But you lied about him.

Again her head twitched.

You looked into my head. You thought you saw my memories. You thought you knew my past. So you tried to make me think he was a monster from my childhood. You tried to make me an accomplice to murder by lying to me.

"Yes," she said. "Stupid of me. I have been silent so long, alone for such a span of years that I had quite forgot myself . . ."

She dropped the knife to her side again and rubbed her hand across her face as if trying to wake properly.

"I have spent so many years without talking, just sitting and thinking and listening to snatches of other people's thoughts that I did not remember that others gifted or cursed like I – as you are – could read my own thoughts quite as easily. It was half-witted of me."

It sounded oddly like an apology. She shook herself and turned to the stairs.

Don't kill them.

"It is not that easy," she said, looking up at the ceiling and hissing quietly as she spoke. "You cannot leave evil unpunished."

For one as youthful as he was, Amos knew a lot about evil, and a lot about fear. Raised in a London workhouse as an orphan, singled out by the dark colour of his skin, he had been an obvious target for the bullies. He knew well what it was to get through days avoiding blows and ridicule only to find the nights were worse as all manner of indignities and viciousness were cloaked in the meagre blanket of the dark. Adopted by the Templebanes and moved to the comparative comfort of their counting house on Bishopsgate, his lot had in fact worsened. The indifferent, institutionalised viciousness of the workhouse had been general. The cruelty of his new position as youngest of an artificially assembled barracks of adopted brothers, all encouraged to vie against each other in an atmosphere of competition and betrayal, was specific, personal and focused directly on him. He was young but the imposition of terror and the anticipation of worse was a subject he was already a master at. He had been beaten regularly enough to know exactly how and where to apply the blows to another.

Punish them by not killing them. Punish them by making them live in fear and captivity.

She snorted.

"You suggest I go to the Justices of the Peace? You think they are not all hugger-mugger with each other? You think they will believe a madwoman and imprison them?"

No.

"Well then," she said, and turned towards the stairs, the blade held low at her side, flashing dully in the last beam of moonlight that penetrated the dark maw of the house.

I think you can imprison them in their own minds. Kill them and their suffering stops. Lock them in fear inside their own skulls and they will suffer as you have suffered.

"And how would I do that?" she spat.

And so he told her. And as he told her she smiled.

"I can do better than that," she said. "I can do something even more incomprehensible to them, something they will think is so impossible that it will make them think they are run madder than I . . ."

What?

"You'll see it too. Come."

CHAPTER 3

A NEW BEGINNING

Cook's kitchen was heart and hearth of the Safe House on Wellclose Square. Almost an entire wall was taken up by the sprawling brass-bound behemoth of the Dreadnought Patent Range, a vast cast-iron oven at the centre of which was a grate containing a well-riddled pile of coals burning red-hot. The gas globes had not been lit, though outside it was long past dark, so the fire-glow and a single candle at the centre of the great pine table were the only illumination. A lifetime of repeated scrubbing had whitened the deal tabletop so that it reflected the candlelight up onto the three faces gathered around it.

Lucy Harker and Charlie Pyefinch, the newest recruits to The Oversight, had been shown beds upstairs, where it was hoped they were restoring their energies and resting their minds after their journey to London and the consequent drama of the events that had greeted them on arrival. They were absent not merely because they were tired and bewildered: they were too new to be part of the conversation between the three remaining members of the Last Hand.

The Smith sat with his fingers clasped round a tall pint mug full of spiced hot chocolate. His eyes were fixed on Cook and Hodge. Lit from below, his iron-hard eyes staring out from beneath a thunderous brow through the steam rising from the mug, he looked both still and catastrophically dangerous, as if he might start hurling lightning bolts at the slightest provocation.

Cook had discarded her normal mob-cap for the moment and replaced it with a green spotted kerchief that she wore sailor-style, knotted at the back to keep her hair out of her way. This, coupled with the old scar that ran down her cheek, made her look more than usually like a pirate than a practitioner of the culinary arts. Despite this precaution, a rogue strand of grey-blonde had escaped the bandana, and she kept having to blow it out of her eye as she worked steadily on the third member of the trio.

Hodge looked neither dangerous nor piratical. He looked ruined. His face was speckled with black powder-burns, some of which would now remain with him for life. He had thrown himself in front of a gun to save his colleagues, and though the ball had not hit him as he deflected the barrel, the powder flash had burnt and tattooed his face and, worse than that, blinded him.

He sat patiently as Cook very gently bathed his wounds with soft cloths and a warm decoction of her own devising, held in an earthenware bowl on the table in front of him.

His terrier, Jed, sat on his lap and allowed himself to be stroked, something the normally self-sufficient dog would not abide for more than a moment, preferring a short scratch behind the ears or, if the day's work was done, a longer and in-depth scratch of his chest and stomach, ideally taken on his back in front of a fire as his right leg jigged automatically in answering pleasure. It was the dog's only real indulgence, but in this case he knew that Hodge, his friend and defender, was in trouble. And so the terrier allowed this petting, aware that the ruined man was making himself calm by feeling the life and the familiar rough texture of the broken fur beneath his hands. Hodge avoided disturbing the salve on the wound Jed himself had taken on his right flank, having insisted that Cook deal with the dog first. In his own way the Terrier Man had as nice a sense of priorities as his dog.

"Hold steady," said Cook severely as she thumbed back Hodge's right eyelid. She looked into the milky, bloodshot orb it revealed. The Smith cocked his head at her. She shook hers back at him.

"You can talk, you know," said Hodge. "I may be blind but Jed can see you pantomiming away at each other quite clearly."

And it was true. His gift was to run his mind alongside and within his animals, and though his own eyes were now – literally – shot, Jed's were sharp enough for the both of them, and Hodge saw what he saw.

Cook turned his face and repeated her examination of the other eye.

"You're right," she said. "You'll not see anything out of the left eye again. This eye . . . I don't know."

"I do," said Hodge. "I can't see a damned thing out of it."

"Maybe not now," said Cook. "But it's not as badly damaged as the other. It might come back a bit if you're lucky."

"Do I look lucky?" said Hodge, turning the wreckage of his face towards her.

"Yes," growled The Smith. "You look like a man who avoided having his head blown apart by a pistol ball by the narrowest of inches. You look like a man blinded, but who has access to other sets of eyes. You look like a man with work in front of him and friends to support him in doing it. But you *sound* like a man who's sorry for himself."

Cook looked at him sharply.

"He doesn't have time for self-pity. None of us do," said The Smith. "We have, as I see it, only three things in our favour at what is, by anything I can recall, the lowest ebb of this Free Company's fortunes."

He pointed at the plain candle at the table's centre, its base standing in an innocent-looking wreath of twigs which a perceptive eye might notice was of five different trees.

"We have the Wildfire, which is both a strength and a responsibility."

He held up a second finger.

"We have the Warrandice, and that is more than a strength – it is a lifesaver, for without the Iron Law that it imposes on the Sluagh and others like them, we should be overwhelmed. Our blades would not have the power against them that we enjoy, and we would be hard put to keep them in check . . ."

"We would be swamped," said Hodge.

"We have other powers against them," protested Cook. "And many other enemies than the Sluagh."

"No enemies as numerous or as well organised," said The Smith. "And no powers as simple and immediate as their antipathy to Cold Iron. Without it and the repellent power of running water, this city would be a hunting ground for them."

"Have I mentioned before that in my estimate you have always over-stressed the Sluagh?" said Cook.

"You have," said The Smith, bridling. "And repetition does not make your observation any truer. I have known them longer than you. I have seen where they draw their foul strength. I have seen—"

"You said three," said Hodge, cutting in with the decisive air of a man stamping on a fuse before it reached the powder keg.

"What?" said The Smith after a moment's silence.

"You said we have three things in our favour. I'd like to hear what the last one is. I could do with some good news, all things considered," said Hodge. He had stopped scratching the ears of the dog in his lap. Jed nudged him with his nose, and he began again.

"Go on then," said Cook. "Don't mind me. What else do we have going for us?"

"By the skin of our teeth we still have a full Hand," said The Smith. "Though in truth while we notionally have five last members of The Oversight, two of this Hand are unproven and one of them is also—"

"Is what?" said Cook.

"Lucy Harker is an unknown quantity," said The Smith. "She is an unknown quantity and our enemies are thwarted but not departed. Whatever happened on the Thames is not an end of anything but the start of what will be a long and dangerous passage in our history. And because of that, we do not have the luxury of self-pity."

"He's right," said Hodge.

"He may be right but you hold still. I'm going to make a poultice and then you're going to wear it beneath a bandage," said Cook. "And then you will rest."

"That I will not argue with," said the Terrier Man. "I feel like following Jed's habit after a fight, just curling up by the fire and going into myself for a while."

"That dog's got sense," said Cook.

The Smith took a swig of hot chocolate and grimaced.

"What is that?" he said.

"Chilli and brandy," said Cook. "And some blackstrap molasses."

He took another sip, smaller this time.

"What's wrong?" said Cook in a tone that contained the faintest warning edge, as if her professional credentials were being questioned.

"Nothing," said The Smith carefully. "It was just a little . . . unexpected. Rather jolts, as it were."

"Thought we all needed a little gingering up after the day's events," she said. "Get the wretched river damp out of our bones."

"Well, it's certainly a . . . striking combination," he said, and took another swig. "No. I think it's growing on me."

"Good," she said, with the air of someone carefully resheathing a half-drawn sword. "I'm sure I'm very glad that it meets your approval."

She turned to the range and removed a pot from the simmering oven.

"We'll let this cool," she said as she spooned a thick, green porridge-like substance onto a square of muslin. "And then we'll bandage you."

Hodge wrinkled his nose.

"Smells like a pond."

"Eyebright, mallow, willow bark, wild garlic and some of my Chinese root and what-nots," she said.

"It's the what-nots that worry me," said Hodge. "I've seen your medicine box. What some of the dried stuff in there is, no normal person would want to know."

"Lucky you're not a normal person then, isn't it?" said Cook.

"Don't know where you acquired such a chest full of foreign noxiousness," he grumbled.

"Effective, practical noxiousness," she corrected. "The Chinese know more about medicine than most of our jumped-up barber-surgeons do, Royal Society or no Royal Society. I took it from the bowels of a pirate junk that made the mistake of trying to board us in the mouth of the Yalu River. I thought it would be useful, and so it has proved. All the river pirates were very healthy."

"Were they?" said The Smith.

"Undoubtedly," she said, her eyes drifting happily upwards to the ceiling to where a notched cutlass hung next to an equally battered colander. "They fought with commendable vigour, and I later had the opportunity of examining their bodies before we burnt their junk. Strong as oxen, to a man."

"And you learned how to use the foul contents of the chest how?" said Hodge.

"Instinct," she said airily. "It's like cooking. Only a blockhead or one of these new-fangled male 'chefs' need a recipe: a true cook uses instinct and a feel for ingredients and suitable combinations."

"So you've been healing us all these years by randomly applying these strange barks and dried animal parts according to mere whim?" said Hodge, drawing away from the smell of the cooling poultice in front of him.

"Whim, and the year of training I received from the very useful young pirate girl we spared and took with us," she said. "She was a lovely thing and once she had stopped trying to kill us in our sleep she became a good friend. She had the way of these herbs and I taught her English in return. Jumped ship in Macau in the end and we never saw her again, more's the pity."

She ran her hand unconsciously over the small lacquered chest on the table beside her.

"I wish she was here now."

"Always fascinating to add another glimpse of your colourful past to the mosaic," said The Smith, "but now is not the time for romantic reminiscences."

"Nothing to do with romance," said Cook. "She was one of us. Had Sharp's speed and ability with the eyes. If she was here now we'd have another member of The Oversight."

He grunted and watched as she gently pushed the soft wodge of muslin and poultice into place, carefully making sure it filled the indentation of Hodge's eye socket before beginning to secure it with a bandage wrapped tightly round his head.

"Your plan?" said Hodge. "You always have a plan."

The Smith nodded. Then remembered his friend's blindness.

"Yes," he said. "The boy Pyefinch knows the city, and more than that his family is known to us. He will be useful and he can be trained quickly. I have few reservations about the boy."

"But the girl?" said Cook.

"Yes," said Hodge, cocking his head at The Smith, who grimaced before carefully continuing.

"But the girl is an unknown quantity who has at the very least been worked on to act against us."

"She made amends—" said Cook.

"She was brought here pretending to be French, pretending to be mute, pretending to be a prisoner. Sara Falk gave her sanctuary which she repaid by sneaking through the house at night and attempting to steal from us, a crime she had clearly been placed here with the express intention of committing. In the course of our discovery of her treachery she escaped through a mirror, breaking the connection so sharply that Sara's hand, reaching into the mirror to save her, was sheared clean off, and with it the rings that allow her to control her gift."

Here Cook attempted to interrupt, perhaps to say that she knew all this, but The Smith, now he had started, seemed determined to list the girl's crimes in full. "Without her rings, Sara wasted away, and we lost Sharp to the mirrors as he endeavoured to retrieve them. So, though the girl Harker is a largely unknown quantity, the one thing we know for certain is that she has acted against us and weakened us, whether by her own will or another's. And—"

"And we know she made amends by bringing Sara's hand back," Cook said.

"And then *apparently* made amends by bringing Sara's hand back," agreed The Smith.

"You don't trust her," said Hodge.

"I am going to take her to live with me on the Isle of Dogs. I do not think she should sleep in the Safe House again until she is . . . trained."

"You're going to test her," said Cook.

"I am going to train her. And yes, I am going to test her."

"And then?" said Hodge.

"And then we are going to take this fight to our enemies before they can come back to us. We will find out who they are. We will find out what they want. We will find out how they are connected. And then . . ."

"We will destroy them," said Cook, tying the bandage off. "That is your plan?"

"You have a better one?"

"No," she admitted. "But if the Disaster teaches us anything it is that we are better at protection than destruction. We are guards, not soldiers."

"Then perhaps I have phrased it badly, old friend," he said. "Think of this as a medical procedure. The healthy body that we are sworn to protect is assailed by a virulent and malicious canker that has whittled us down to a shadow of our former strength. I am not advocating a war. I am preparing a calm and determined excision of an invasive and potentially fatal tumour."

She looked down the corridor towards the hidden door behind which lay the Murano Cabinet that had swallowed up both Mr Sharp and Sara Falk.

"But our sharpest blades are both gone into the mirrors," she said.

The Smith followed her gaze.

"I am The Smith," he said. "I would not be much of one if I couldn't fashion new weapons."

"The girl?" she said again. "But the girl—"

"But the girl is not the only option," he said. "I have a sense something is changing."

CHAPTER 4

A DOUBLE JEOPARDY: SECOND PART

Further west, in the crooked house on Chandos Place, Francis Blackdyke, Viscount Mountfellon, was on the verge of falling out with his co-conspirator and guest, the aged Frenchman known as The Citizen. Mountfellon was still irked by the balking of his plans and the near-drowning he had suffered as he and Templebane sought to bring about the demise of the meddling society known as The Oversight on the cold waters of Blackwater Reach. The Citizen was irritatingly unmoved by the inconveniences thus visited on the noble Lord, and was much more concerned with the death of the Green Man upon whom he had been experimenting on in the soundproofed basement of the house. The Green Man, a supranatural variant who was – like many supranatural creatures – hypersensitive and violently allergic to iron, had been subjected to a long and painful process whereby The Citizen tried to overcome his mortal antipathy by giving transfusions of blood into which were mixed solutions of green vitriol, or iron sulphate.

Ultimately The Citizen's enthusiasm for increasing the concentration of the solutions had been stronger than the Green Man's constitution, and though he had shown a small but promising initial desensitisation to iron, after weeks of rising doses his heart had simply burst.

The Citizen had just confirmed this through a precise dissection of the cadaver and was standing over it in a leather apron, his arms bloodied to the elbows as he conversed with the nobleman whose hospitality he relied upon.

"I merely said that although they had won a round, we would undoubtedly win the bout," said Mountfellon. "And the trophies that go with it."

He had brought a decanter of brandy and two glasses. He poured drinks for them both and slid one towards The Citizen as he drank his own down in two fast gulps. He looked at the eviscerated corpse of the Green Man lying on the slab between them with a dispassionate interest.

"Everything is a game to you British," said The Citizen, reaching for a towel. "It is an infantile obsession."

"Infantile, sir?" said Mountfellon, bridling.

The Citizen waved a hand airily as if no insult were intended.

"I speak as one who was once similarly illusioned, Milord. When I was younger, in my prime, full of the follies of youth, mistaking my strength and vigour for actual experience, I relished having strong enemies against which to test my own merit. Very much like your British compulsion, it was, I suppose, a kind of sensibility that I had picked up from the *ancien régime* under whose yoke I had been educated. That I broke that very regime and extirpated it, root and branch, does not hide the ironic fact that I was formed by the thing we revolted so successfully against . . ."

"And yet there is a king again in France, so your extirpation can only be seen as partial," said Mountfellon sourly.

The Citizen turned his head to look at him in slow surprise.

"You are very out of sorts, Milord, to be contradicting me so bluntly."

Mountfellon waved a hand in what was perhaps an unconscious mimicry of his earlier airy dismissal, and reached for the decanter.

"I was nearly shot to blazes and then drowned. But please continue . . ."

The Citizen stared at him without blinking, his parchment-white face unnaturally still and unreadable. Then he exhaled, as if having decided not to spring across the table and attack Mountfellon directly, and took a sip from the other glass.

"I was only going to observe that once upon a time I liked to test my strength against a strong enemy. It was conceited and it was a kind of faux chivalric urge that made me think so. What I NOW think is that I prefer my enemies bled white and powerless. I have no energy or interest in the struggle or the game. I only wish to exterminate and destroy. They are not adversaries; they are mere obstacles, and I now know, from my studies, that power is the only thing that matters at all. Chivalry, testing oneself, the very illusion of individual will: all a mirage that is obliterated by the bright cleansing light of pure power."

"So you would bleed The Oversight?" scowled Mountfellon.

"They are bled already," he said with a dismissive shrug. "That they were moving their precious artefacts from the Safe House by the river is a sign of desperation. And however much they mauled your hired bravos, they will have taken further hurt too. So we must now eradicate them for ever."

Mountfellon carefully placed his glass back on the table.

"I do not wish to eradicate them before we have those artefacts or the contents of that damned Red Library in our hands, my dear Citizen. I will not countenance a wholesale destruction of that valuable storehouse of knowledge," he said. "We have spoken of this."

"Of course," purred The Citizen. "Why? Do you think I do not remember every conversation we have ever had? Do you begin to mistrust me?"

"You have a bloodthirsty streak," said Mountfellon. "It is the only thing I mistrust in you, if I might be blunt."

"If you were truly being polite, Milord, you should perhaps have asked if you might be blunt before you were so," said The Citizen, his lips twisting into a smile like a withered rose. "But I have no shame about it. There is something profoundly cleansing in the flow of blood. And there is power in it. As you yourself know from your experimental practice."

"There is a difference between a lack of false sentiment about blood-letting consequent on valid experimentation, and an actual appetite for it," said Mountfellon.

"Are we falling out, Milord?" said The Citizen, the smile beginning to curdle a little.

"Not at all," said Mountfellon. "We are speaking frankly to one another as equals should. I do not want your enthusiasm to precipitate a bloodbath that would deprive us of treasures which a slower and more methodical assault might assure us of."

"And yet only moments ago you were seething and saying they had nearly shot you to blazes!" said The Citizen.

"A loss of dignity and my life briefly in peril does not mean they can unman my mind," said Mountfellon. "I am a Natural Philosopher and a Man of Science. That they cannot change. I will have their chattels and their knowledge, and then as much blood can flow as you like."

He sank another brandy and pointed at the open chest cavity, and the flaps of green-tinged flesh that had been expertly flensed back like pages in a folio to expose the organs within.

"Now, sir, now that we are fast friends again, do pray tell me precisely how its heart burst."

CHAPTER 5

THE NEXT STEP

Having taken her first pace through the mirror, Sara Falk did not take the subsequent step without careful thought. Instead, once the Raven had comprehensively marked the point of their ingress for future reference, she closed her eyes and stood there, trying to clear her mind and feel the atmosphere of the long corridor. The truth is that she had no detailed plan: all she knew she had to do was to find Mr Sharp. He had gone into the mirrors in order to find her hand because on it was the ring containing her heart-stone, the absence of which had been causing her to sicken and fade away. It had been an heroically doomed gesture, a measure born of desperation, since his chance of finding the hand was remote in the extreme. The hand had been returned to her by other means, and now she was honour-bound to follow him into the wilderness of mirrors and try and bring him home. And in truth it was more than honour that bound her to this, she knew: it was affection, a connection that had grown between them as they themselves had grown up together, an attachment that had increased and strengthened in intensity all the more for being unvoiced over the years, much as a banked-up fire will burn longer and hotter than one that quickly expends its energy in wild and demonstrative flames. She had known her quest for him was quite as quixotic as his for her, but that had not stopped her from embarking on it.

Indeed hers was more liable to failure since he had taken the Coburg Ivory into the mirrors with him, a device known as a "get-you-home", to enable him to navigate the maze with some small chance of success. She had no such get-you-home beyond the signature of the Raven, so casually squittered across the glass at her feet. It was because her quest was so desperate that she had embarked on it so quickly, without giving herself time for second thoughts – the very thoughts that were now preventing her taking the second step.

"I can't feel anything," she said. "I thought I would perhaps . . . sense him. I thought I would."

The Raven clattered its beak again. Sara looked at it, and raised an eyebrow.

"I remember many games," she said. "Which one do you mean?"

The Raven did not answer. Instead it dropped daintily to the floor in front of her, neatly avoiding the mess, and pecked pointedly at her boots.

"Oh," said Sara after a moment. "That game."

Sara was a Glint. She wore gloves most of the time because when she touched things like walls and buildings she could draw the past out of them, like a recording she felt as strongly as if she was living it herself. The most traumatic events left the strongest signatures in stone, and because of that Glinting was not for the faint of heart. Indeed many who had the gift thought themselves mad or accursed until they learned to control it. As a young girl, Sara had been trained to it. She had mastered her ability until it became a gift and not the blight she had initially assumed. And one of the ways she had gained control over her glinting was in a game called "follow-my-leader". She had played it with The Smith when she was no taller than his hip, and she had played it with Hodge when she was a little older, and the game would begin like this: she would take off her shoes and close her eyes. The other would then walk away into the backstreets around Wellclose Square, and lose themselves in the milling populace of the neighbourhood. Sara would wait for them to disappear, count to a hundred and then follow them. To begin with she just got lost, confused and footsore. Those early games ended with The Smith turning back and finding her. And then he told her what to do: he told her to keep her eyes closed and trust her feet.

The first time she did this it was terrifying. She had once tried to explain to Cook what it felt like, but it was almost impossible to put into coherent sentences, because it was a kind of synaesthesia, a sensation that she could only express in terms of an unrelated sense, like coloured hearing or a perfumed sound. It was like feeling a strain of music beneath her feet and then walking down it as it unravelled in a narrow ribbon through the warp and weft of the much larger fabric woven by all the other people on the street. Hodge had told her it must be very like what the dog Jed experienced when following a scent trail through the competing stinks of the city. Sara knew Sharp's trace as if it was colour and smell and sound all together: it was the admixture, along with Cook's, that she most closely associated with home; it was like a warm, held note on a cello, something solid that she could cleave to through the competing melodies of an orchestra playing a symphony all around it. Often, in the more crowded parts of London, it actually felt as if several different symphonies were being performed by rival orchestras trying to drown each other out, but as she played the game more and more she began to get the hang of it, and developed a kind of sensory concentration that enabled her to track her quarry through the tangled distractions, even with her eyes open.

In time she became very good at follow-my-leader, so good that she would quickly work out where The Smith or Hodge was headed, and conspire to arrive before they did by taking a shortcut. This trick was enabled by their habit of ending at a pie shop or a bakery in order to reward the young girl for hunting them, and with enough training she came to know their favourite purveyors of treats and eatables. Following with her feet was different to feeling the past with her hands. She had wondered if it was something to do with the thickness of skin on her soles, but on this neither The Smith nor Hodge could enlighten her.

"Always been like that," said The Smith. "Most Glints can't do it, and those that can feel with their feet don't feel the same way with the rest of their body. It just happens that way."

Sara had not played the game for a long time, not much at all since she had grown to womanhood: any time The Oversight had required tracking skills, Jed and Hodge had provided them. A grown woman walking barefoot through London's questionable alleys drew attention to herself in a way a child would not.

"Well," said Sara. "There's no one watching us now."

And with that she bent, put the candle on the ground and took off her boots. She added the knife she had carried in one hand to the knife in her belt, and then closed her eyes. The Raven watched her flex her feet. They were long and elegant, and she rippled her toes like a pianist stretching her fingers.

"This will take a moment," she said. "Bear with me." .

The Raven shrugged and looked around. Sara's face became calm as she steadied her breathing and reached out with her mind, trying to grasp what her feet were reading. The first thing she had to do was to steel herself against feeling ridiculous and unexpectedly vulnerable. She had chosen her clothes and boots and weapons with a view to feeling protected and ready for anything that might come her way, and now that she had taken her boots off and was barefoot on the cold glass floor, she felt both childlike and considerably less guarded than she had expected to. At some level she felt naked. She tried to banish the thought, but failed. And then remembering that the trick to not thinking about a thing was to think of something else, she concentrated on the unusually smooth surface beneath the soles of her feet, and that led to her noticing what overlaid the smoothness and then she smelled something like a coloured noise, something impossible and familiar, and before she realised that she was sorting out things beneath her feet, she had relaxed.

"Oh," she said.

And a smile flicked up the corners of her mouth.

"This is going to be simpler than I thought."

The Raven, attuned as it habitually was to things ordinary ravens did not bother themselves with, noted that her breathing was slowing down and her pulse was starting to ease off the trip-hammer rapidity it had been climbing towards. It noted she was feeling relief. It heard her stifle something that might even have been a stillborn chuckle.

Sara was, behind her closed eyes, exultant. The mirrors were not like an alley through the East End of London: they felt much more like forgotten corridors, disregarded parts of a great house down which very few people had ever ventured. The strands meshed beneath her feet were few and easily differentiated: if the musical analogy was held to, she was going to have to keep track of one instrument in a small group, a trio or a quartet perhaps, not a series of competing orchestras, and better than that she could sense Sharp's strong, rounded note very clearly.

She opened her eyes and looked ahead. Although the passage through the repeated mirrors was only as visible as far as the light thrown by the candle she held, she now felt less fear of what lay ahead, because whatever it was, Mr Sharp was there too.

"This way," she said.

And she reached out her foot and silently took the second step. And then the next. And though her eyes were open, they were unfocused in the way she had learned to master while playing the game as a child: she saw but did not look. She was, however, vaguely buoyed by the light she carried banishing the shadows ahead.

It was perhaps good for her morale that she did not notice how, as she moved forward with that cheering candle held high, the darkness closed in solidly behind her.

CHAPTER 6

THE IMPOSSIBLE THING

M'Gregor woke with a hand over his mouth and a knife at his throat. The Warden of the Andover Workhouse gurgled and bucked and then, as he felt the sharp bite of steel on his neck, he stilled.

A match flared and he saw a young man with dark skin looming over him, staring into his eyes. When his attacker was sure M'Gregor was not going to struggle any more, he jerked his head sideways and pointed with his chin.

M'Gregor was too dulled by sleep and the previous evening's brandy, and too horrified by the rude manner of his wakening, to understand what he was being told.

"He wants you to look at me," said a scratchy and unfamiliar woman's voice. "He wants you to see what will happen to her if you cry out."

He looked into the eyes above him. The young man nodded. M'Gregor looked towards the spot where his wife habitually snored away the long hours of the night.

She was lying very still, eyes bulged out in terror as she was pressed down into the feather bed by a madwoman. The Ghost of the Itch Ward, long labelled by him as one of the deeply resented Useless Mouths that he had to feed on account of her being too soft-witted to work at bone-grinding or stone-breaking, was straddling her with a knife resting point-first on her windpipe.

His wife's eye strained sideways and found his. A tear leaked out of it and slid down the unfortunately porcine curve of her cheek.

The man took his hand away from his mouth. M'Gregor gasped and breathed in, trying to calm himself.

It was useless. His heart was beating nineteen to the dozen and there was a shamefully warm wetness leaking over his thigh and puddling around his buttocks.

"What do you want?" he gasped.

His assailant looked at the Ghost.

"I want what you took from me," she croaked.

"I took nothing from you."

"When I came, I had possessions. You took them."

"That was years back—"

Amos prodded him gently with the knife.

"I don't remember. Who can remember that long ago?"

He sounded desperate. Near tears. Not a man. A boy about to blubber helplessly under the pressure of the knife and her relentless gaze.

"I do," she said. "I had a book. I had a chain around my neck. I had a pendant on a chain. And I had a ring."

The wife had said nothing. Amos looked at her and caught a guilty flicker in her eyes. He reached out to her mind and felt a kind of reptilian movement in her thoughts, as if there were thick coils slowly slithering against each other in the depths as the mind tried to hide something from even itself. And then he caught what she was thinking, the thing she was trying to find a way not to admit out loud. She was wondering how to keep her money and her goods and deciding whether she would say anything if they started cutting her husband. Because he, Amos saw in her thoughts, did not know where she hid what she had stolen. And she was now deciding she trusted her future to the hidden loot more than she trusted the man whimpering beside her in a puddle of his own piss. She was not going to say where she kept it concealed. She had looked at the hand fate had dealt her and decided her husband would have to go on the forfeit pile.

She keeps what she has stolen in a small casket under the floorboard under the left front leg of the linen press.

The Ghost nodded.

"I heard." She looked down at the woman pinned beneath her.

"If you tell me where you have hidden what you steal, I will spare your husband. If you do not, we will slit him from ear to ear. What do you want? Plunder or husband?"

"There is no plunder!" squealed M'Gregor. "Not here!"

The Ghost stared into the eyes of the woman.

"Please God!" M'Gregor choked. "Yes, there may be some mistake in the accounting! Perhaps there is a small overage in our bank account that should perhaps be in the account of the poorhouse itself, but I cannot give that to you now. I can get you gold tomorrow if you spare us or, if not gold, a draft—"

"I do not want a draft. Or gold. I want what is mine. I am not a thief. I am not like you. I am vengeance."

She cocked her head at the woman beneath her. The small eyes had hardened.

"Love or money?" said the Ghost. "Which is it to be?"

"There is nothing," said the woman. "If there was, do you not think I would tell you to save my husband's life?"

There was a beat of silence.

"So. Not love then." The Ghost shrugged.

"She's telling the truth!" blubbered M'Gregor. "Can't you see . . . ?"

"No," said the Ghost. "She's lying."

She nodded to Amos.

"Get it. I will keep her quiet. He is too unmanned now to do anything but she would scream for help if I took the blade from her throat, wouldn't you, my piggy darling?"

Mrs M'Gregor's eyes tried to say no, but they were distracted by Amos's movements as he stepped off the bed and began to move the leg of the linen press across the bare floorboards. The sound of wood scraping on wood was punctuated by a gasp.

"How did—?" began Mrs M'Gregor, sounding more outraged than scared.

"I looked into the foul stew of your mind, piggy dear," said the Ghost.

Amos pried the floorboard up and retrieved a small ironbound casket, about a foot in length by half that across. It was secured by a padlock.

"You bitch," gasped M'Gregor in disbelief, staring at his wife. "You'd have let them cut my throat for what—?"

She looked away.

"Where is the key?" said the Ghost.

Mrs M'Gregor clamped her mouth shut. The Ghost laughed.

"You don't understand, do you? We can read your thoughts. You will never be alone. You will never be unwatched. You will never be safe from us. EVER!"

Mrs M'Gregor flinched. But to do her credit, she had one last spark of rebellion left in her, perhaps all she had now that her venality was fully exposed, or perhaps it was merely a despairing clutch at the last straw of sanity being whirled beyond her reach by the storm of circumstance assailing her on every side.

"You cannot read my mind."

"Of course not," said the Ghost. "Why, if I could read your mind, then up would be down, the real would be artifice, the shadows peopled by concrete things and not mere insubstantial fears and you – you would be haunted by more than the spectre of vengeance for the rest of your days. And I would know where you hid the key . . ."

"But you don't," said Mrs M'Gregor.

"Of course not," said the Ghost. "That would be impossible."

She stabbed the knife viciously downwards.

Mrs M'Gregor grunted in terror. The knife ripped into the bolster beside her head. The Ghost angled the knife and ripped upwards, gutting it in a cloud of goose feathers. She reached in, found a sewn-in pocket and cut it open. She retrieved a small iron key and held it out to Amos.

Mrs M'Gregor's eyes were wide and twitching. Where they had been sharp with resolution they now became oddly blunted and unmoored.

"Oh yes," said the Ghost with a grim smile. "The ghoulies, the ghosties and the long-leggedy beasties and all the unhallowed things that go bump in the night? We're real. And from us, nothing can deliver you!"

Mrs M'Gregor's eyes rolled back, white as twin moons in the abundant folds of her eyelids.

"Fainted clean away," said the Ghost, sounding disappointed, looking at M'Gregor who was now staring back at her from beneath a light sprinkling of goose-feathers. "Thought she had more in her, seeing as how she was willing to sacrifice you for a . . . for what?"

Amos brought the casket to her, holding the lid open.

She tipped it onto the bed. Three gold sovereigns, some silver, a lot of copper, some cheap jewellery, six wedding bands of dubious metal and some chains, equally dubious. It was not a king's ransom.

M'Gregor choked at the sight, despite himself.

"You fucking whore-bitch!" he rasped at his wife.

"Why, Warden M'Gregor! You should thank us," said the Ghost. "It is not many who know precisely how much they are valued by their loved ones . . ."

She was scrabbling through the mess, looking for something. Her voice became tighter.

"It's not there."

She slapped Mrs M'Gregor. Twice. Then again as her eyes came back down and into focus. She held the better-looking of all the chains in front of her face.

"The pendant?"

Mrs M'Gregor fishmouthed at her. Unable to speak. Amos caught the unvoiced thought.

It was just glass. Not an emerald. She had it tested at a jeweller in Salisbury. He gave her money for the gold band it was mounted in. It's gone.

The Ghost slapped the woman again, in fury this time.

Don't. It wasn't a real jewel . . .

"But it was MINE!" she shouted, drawing her knife hand back for a murderous slash across Mrs M'Gregor's throat.

Amos grabbed her wrist, twisted it and caught the knife as it fell from her spasming fingers.

You agreed. No killing.

"I didn't know they'd lost everything they stole!"

She only stole the chain. The book and the ring were taken by the man who left you here.

"I didn't see that," she said.

I did.

"What kind of man?"

Tall. A blue coat. A fine carriage. That's all she remembers.

She looked at him, appraising as her breathing came back under control.

You saw that?

He nodded.

"You can see deeper into her mind than I. Come. We must go then."

And as simply as that she scissored off the bed, took the candlestick from the bedside table, an ebony-handled hand mirror from the dresser, and walked through the smaller of the two doors into the bedroom, the one they had not entered by. He followed her, backing in, keeping his eyes on the two stunned M'Gregors, making sure that they in turn kept their eyes on his knives.

There was a flare of light behind him as the Ghost lit the candle, and in the same moment he caught a flash of surprise and intent from M'Gregor's mind.

This is a dead end!

He turned and found it to be so. She pulled the door to before he could back out, and then moved swiftly past him with a grim smile on her face. They stood in what was no more than a long attic space angled beneath the mansard roof. She placed the hand mirror on a small shelf and then held the one she had retrieved from the water butt in her hand so its plane was parallel with it, about three feet away. She bent her head and looked at the infinity of reflections thus revealed.

Amos heard both M'Gregor's thoughts and the shift and scrape as the big man came off the bed in the next room.

There is no exit! This is a dead end.

"We're still leaving. They'll eventually look in and we'll be gone and the impossibility of it will drive them quite mad."

He has a pair of horse-pistols under the bed. He is priming one now!

"A horse-pistol?"

The Ghost was alarmingly unconcerned by this new development, he felt.

He has a horse-pistol. Like a blunderbuss.

In the bedroom, Mrs M'Gregor watched her husband fumbling with the large and ancient wide-bored pistol he had retrieved from its hiding place under the mattress.

"Hurry up, you fool!" she hissed.

He lashed out sideways without looking.

The heavy metal barrel swung into her temple with a nasty crunch. Her hand reflexively clutched air as she fell backwards, but nothing could stop her as she toppled back off the bed, and by the time her head hit the wall and the weight of her following body snapped her neck, she was already mercifully unconscious.

Inside the attic they heard the thump and the crack and the muttered "bitch" that was all M'Gregor could manage by way of epitaph for his wife.

He hit her.

"You were right. This was better than killing them. Having a conscience seems to be . . . diverting"

She smiled.

"Give me your hand," said the Ghost.

He is going to shoot us in here. Like rats in a barrel!

"Your hand. Come with me."

There was a creak and some muttering from outside the door.

Amos looked at the madwoman.

Come with you how? We are stuck in a dead end.

"Then I hope I remember how to do this," she said.

Do what?

"Hold my wrist," she said. "We're going into the mirrors."

There was a scraping noise and a double click of metal on metal from outside.

Amos grabbed her wrist as she reached out and put her hand on the surface of the mirror.

It stayed there.

"Oh," she said.

What?

"Oh dear . . ."

Oh dear what?

She turned her face to him, a look of childish incomprehension washing across it that made her look younger and madder than she had before.

"I thought we would go into the mirrors."

Into the mirrors?

Mad as a March hare.

"It doesn't seem to work."

There was a crash as M'Gregor kicked the door in and filled the space, outlined by the moonlit room behind him.

"You bastards are dead," he said flatly. "Dunno what else you are and what trickery you're up to, but it don't matter a tuppenny fart. Dead as yesterday's fucking mutton is what you are . . ."

Amos stepped in front of the Ghost. He did not know why. He stared into M'Gregor's mad, shamed eyes and saw nothing but death.

The sound of the gun firing in the confined space was deafening, the percussion so loud that it jolted one of the loose diamonds of glass out of the lead window and sent it falling to the path below where it smashed as a sharp tinkling counterpoint to the gunshot itself.

Outside the M'Gregor's bedroom, the sound was loud enough to wake the under-warden in the gatehouse and send him searching for his clubbed stick and night lantern.

Inside the attic-closet, the blood was dripping off the ceiling, along with thicker gobbets of something more substantial. The gory matter splashed to the floor on either side of M'Gregor's feet, which were still planted firmly in the doorway.

The Ghost stared at Amos.

How did you do that?

Do what?

What you did. You looked into his eyes and . . . did something.

I didn't want him to shoot us.

So you made him put the gun under his chin and pull the trigger.

I just—

They were both too deafened to hear so they were talking in their heads.

Amos bent over and retched. The Ghost stared at M'Gregor's body in the doorway, legs locked in death, still upright, the top of his head blown into the roof above.

As she looked, the first death tremor spasmed through the half-headless corpse and then gravity took over as equilibrium was disturbed, and M'Gregor joined his wife on the floor.

I have never seen anyone do that.

I didn't know I could do it.

I didn't know anyone *could do it.*

She yanked him upright. She looked at the dripping ceiling and the soaked floor.

"So. I was right. And you were wrong. You should trust me: you are the Bloody Boy after all. Come. We must go now, and go fast."

Amos wanted to scream. He also wanted to fold in on himself and close his eyes and sleep because then he would not have to think or see all this blood, all this death he seemed to have caused by trying to stop it happening. But most of all he wanted to scream. But Amos was mute by birth, and could make no noise at all, even in his own defence. And because he was a Templebane by adoption, he was trained to think first and foremost about his own survival. So he followed the Ghost into the night, the unvoiced howl of protest and horror trapped for ever inside the confines of his own skull.

CHAPTER 7

SHARP, BLUNTED

Mr Sharp was not used to being bested, or lost, and he was not at all in the habit of going barefoot. He was, above all, absolutely not accustomed to being a victim. Duty, practice and the warranted degree of personal pride he took in controlling his more violent competencies had long inured him to the sensation of being the most dangerous thing in the dark streets down which his duties as a member of The Oversight conspired to send him. The passage through the mirrors had, however, clearly undone him.

That was it, he thought: it was the mirrors. He was used to the shadows. There was altogether too much light in the wilderness of repeating images in which he had now gone deeply and irrevocably astray. Everywhere he looked revealed a lesser version of himself disappearing up an infinite tunnel of reflections: too much light, too little variation, nowhere to hide, nowhere to truly rest. Certainly there was nowhere to get a bearing. He knew he had slept at least twice since he had woken from the attack that had deprived him of his get-you-home, the Coburg Ivory and his knives and – most humiliatingly of all – his boots.

Being bested was one thing. Being robbed another. But stripping a man of his boots was an entirely different order of humiliation. Taking a man's boots was to mark him as an impotent discard in the great game of life.

The man Dee – if he was indeed Dee – had gulled him like the most callow dupe, and his bare feet were a badge of his humiliation. Head down, he watched them stumble along the mirrored floor, his brain still woolly and disconcertingly unrefreshed by his last sleep.

These unsatisfactory sleeps were worrying to him because he was normally blessed with the soldier's knack of taking five-minute naps whenever he could and waking from them promptly and revived. The mirror-bound sleeps – he was almost sure there had only been two but was not even convinced of that, so muzzy was his head – were different: he had no sense of how much time had passed while he was insensible and thus vulnerable. In fact he woke more tired than when he had let his head drop in the first place. Sleeping in the mirrors was draining him, sapping him not only of the very energy that repose was meant to restore, but also somehow enfeebling his ability to think straight. There was no doubt about it: he was losing track of time, just as surely as he had lost any sense of place and direction.

It was all this damned light.

And just when this thought came to him, he saw the black mirror. It came so conveniently that he wondered – fuzzily – if he had somehow called it into being as a respite from the unrelenting glare of the mirrored world. He stopped and turned at ninety degrees to stare in relief at the dark blankness.

It was the precise opposite of all the repetitive brightness in which he had been beset. It was nullity; it was void; it was a sovereign relief as relaxing to his eyes as it was to his mind, and he leant forward, hands splayed against it, and stared into the welcome lacuna, drinking it in with his eyes, greedy as a man in the desert who had stumbled on a well full of clear, cool water.

The blackness was not merely calming and refreshing, it was intoxicating. The longer he looked into it, the more he felt the tense muscles of his shoulders begin to relax, and with time his stiff back slackened enough to allow him to sway forward a little, almost as if swooning with relief.

He hung there for a very long time, staring deeply into the vacancy. Just gazing into it and allowing the void to fill his field of vision seemed to revivify him more than any of the unsatisfactory sleeps had done.

He would stop staring at it in a moment, when he was quite refreshed. He was certain he would do so. There was no urgency in the matter: he had not, he told himself in a voice that seemed to be getting fainter, been looking at the dark for so very long after all. He deserved respite, and his quest would indeed be easier and more prone to success if he allowed himself this brief interlude of replenishment.

He would definitely stop looking into the black mirror in a moment. He was determined on this. It was just so very . . . pleasant, looking into the featureless void. It demanded nothing of him. There was no harm in it. No harm at all. No harm in . . . and then his mind drifted away, briefly wondering exactly what it had been that there was no harm in . . . and then asking himself what he meant by harm . . . and then forgetting that question too.

CHAPTER 8

TO THE ISLE OF DOGS BY GOLEM

The second time Lucy Harker went to sleep in the Safe House she slept better than she had on the first occasion. This was partly because she was exhausted by the journey and adventures that had brought her back to the very house she had attempted to plunder at the outset of that whole series of small disasters. But mostly it was because, having been bitten once and thus deciding to be at least twice shy, Cook had tripled the sleeping draught in the hot milk she had been given before being sent to bed.

Her sleep was deep but not dreamless.

She was so tightly wrapped in slumber that she was unaware of the large figure in the high-collared coachman's cloak which entered the room, his dark face shadowed by the tricorn hat he wore day and night, inside or out. She did not feel the very careful bundling of bed sheets and blankets as he wrapped them across her, cocooning her still-sleeping body in a way that both kept her warm, insensible and – perhaps accidentally – bound. She only shifted a little as he lifted her in his arms and carried her down the stairs without a sound. The night air did not wake her as he bore her to the carriage he had prepared at the rear of the house, and she did not notice him lay her gently on the rugs spread on the floor between the two seats. He climbed to the driver's bench where The Smith sat waiting.

"Isle of Dogs," was all that The Smith said, and he gently eased the horse into motion. The rocking sensation of the well-sprung coach actually deepened Lucy's sleep and made her dreams flow more smoothly. And so, as the carriage passed along the Ratcliffe Highway, she dreamed of a life beyond the sea in France and, in the way of dreams, some of what came to her was what was, and some was what might have been.

When Lucy finally woke, hours later, she stayed very still, immediately aware that she was regaining consciousness somewhere entirely different from the place in which she had gone to sleep. This was not as distressing to her as it might have been to another person since she had become used to the worrying blanks in her mind. True, she had recently been able to maintain a clear continuum of recollection, but she had a history of unexplained holes in her memory that she had learned to live with. They came and went, and it was her practice, whenever she had quiet time to herself, to audit the ragged fabric of her past and see if, as occasionally happened, one of those holes had been patched as she slept. This morning she found she did indeed seem to remember more. She closed her eyes as she performed her review since experience had taught her it was best to keep as close to the dream state as possible when doing this. Waking too sharply led to the wisps of new memory dissolving, like dawn mist evaporated by the full sunlight of morning.

She saw the house in Paris, the blue door, the shutters, the dark hallway where she had glimpsed the very last of her mother as she was pulled inside by men whose uniforms matched the colour of the door. That hallway not only swallowed her mother, it seemed to have eaten a large chunk of Lucy's life too, because her next memories were of a farm and fields and she was bigger, big enough to carry water from the well in a heavy bucket, and after that was mainly sunshine, and no more city. The farm belonged to an Antoine and a Sylvie, and though she was encouraged to call them Aunt and Uncle, she always knew they weren't because Dagobert the farm-hand told her so, and they looked so different to her mother, dark where she was fair, angular where she was soft and rounded. They were, however, kind and though they may or may not have been blood, they were what she thought of as family as she grew and the seasons turned and the years whispered past like wind through the barley fields that surrounded the house.

It was Sylvie who gave her her mother's ring with the broken unicorn in it, and it was Sylvie who put it on the leather thong around her neck and told her to keep it beneath her clothes, hidden from strangers, in case greedy eyes saw the gold and tried to take it. The piece of sea-glass was the only other thing she had from her life in the city, and she didn't remember how she kept it, only that it was always in her pocket, always reassuringly close to hand.

Lucy remembered how much she had loved the countryside, and this was a fresh memory, covering a hole that had been there when she went to sleep. She was exhilarated by this. She now recalled how much she had loved the way the landscape changed through the year, each season containing the seeds of its opposite within it, always old beneath the gaudy spring, always new beneath the winter snow. It was in the woods beyond the farm that she discovered she had a skill that others didn't. At the time she thought that the reason she could move so quietly and yet so fast was because she was a child and thus smaller and nimbler than the grown-ups who surrounded her. She believed she was like the fish she saw when hunting for frogs beneath the overhanging ferns in the stream by the watermill, the tiny sticklebacks darting away so much faster than the fat, brown trout. She reasoned, in her childlike way, that smaller meant faster.

It was Antoine's reaction when she walked into the stable one afternoon to show him a live rabbit that she had plucked from a patch of cow-parsley that made her realise that she had done something unusual. He had not believed her when she told him she had just seen the rabbit and then gone and picked it up. So she'd let the rabbit go and then gone and fetched a partridge from beneath the hedge in the field by the mill-race. This time he'd taken her in to Sylvie and made her explain what she'd done. After a lot of questioning, all she had been able to say was that she had gone very slow and very fast at the same time. A look had flickered between the two adults, and then Antoine had laughed and ruffled her hair and told her she would be useful when he went hunting for the pot. He never did take her hunting, however, and when he walked into the woods with his old gun bumping on his shoulder he went alone. So her ability to go slow-yet-fast was something she only used for catching frogs and in delicately capturing butterflies that she would take to show Sylvie before releasing them back into a sky that was, in those memories, always blue and cloudless.

Lucy was big enough to harness the plough horse and lead it to and from work by the time she hit another blank, and after that one it seemed to be always rain, and Antoine was gone and Sylvie was full of sadness and something else as her stomach swelled through a wet and blustery autumn, and when the baby came just before Christmas, snow was definitely in the air as Lucy saddled the plough horse and rode into the small town for a doctor.

It was when she dismounted and touched the newly plastered wall by the doctor's house that she first glinted. The past slammed into her and she saw three men in torn velvet and silk with their hands tied behind them put against the wall and shot down as a crowd hooted and mocked behind the ragged firing squad. The force of the thing knocked her off her feet, and the doctor found her on his doorstep twitching as if having a fit. She'd managed to tell him that Tante Sylvie was in labour and some distress, and then he'd given her a foul-tasting draught of something that had made her sleep, and then she remembered nothing more of the farm and sunshine, and all happy memories ceased, washed out by the greyness of her next period of clear recollection in the convent school for pauper children, a place so soaked in unhappiness and tragedy that she became scared to touch anything in case the past bit her again and sent her into another fit.

In the convent school she began to wrap her hands in rags to protect herself from the past. The nuns would unwrap her hands and take away the rags, and she would find more and do it again. When there were no rags, she tore her clothes and used strips of her dress instead. Eventually they left her to it, but it was a rare victory for her. In the convent she had nothing. Her ring was taken from her as was her lump of glass, and when she asked where they were the Mother Superior told her it was kept safe in the locked drawer in the heavy oak desk in her office, in case it was of use one day as proof of her identity should someone come looking for her. Something in her smile made Lucy angry, and she had insisted on seeing it. She had not been allowed to. Instead she was beaten for her insolence.

The nuns were not patient with Lucy, perhaps because they too feared the Mother Superior, and when she told them of what she had seen of the past they shrilly told her she was a liar, or that a demon was already in her causing the visions of what was not there. It didn't matter much which, because the remedy for demons or lying was an identical beating from the same whippy birch followed by the insistence that she thanked and prayed for a blessing on the sister who had wielded the rod for doing so.

It was in the convent that she discovered another use for her ability to go slow-yet-fast: there were no butterflies to catch, no rabbits to pluck warm and surprised from cushioning clumps of cow-parsley and no clear blue skies at all, but there was a kitchen, and a constant hollow in her stomach that the bread and scrapings they were given to eat did not even begin to fill. So Lucy became the thing she was, the thing she had thought of herself as before Sara Falk had told her she was a Glint: she became a thief.

The first things she stole in the convent were the dry heel of a French loaf and three tomatoes. The second-to-last things she stole were her mother's ring, her sea-glass and the birch rod that hung in the corner of the Mother Superior's room. And the very last thing she stole was the key to the gate in the high convent walls.

She remembered unlocking the gate at midnight and slipping out onto the moonlit road to freedom, leaving the broken halves of the rod in the hallway inside. She remembered that the silvery road led past a millpond, because she had a very clear memory of shattering the perfect moon on its mirrored surface into a thousand pieces as she flung the heavy key

– with which she had of course conscientiously re-locked the gate from the outside – far out into the muddy depths beneath.

No further new memories revealed themselves as she sped over the familiar ragged landscape of the past that followed this, the oft-recalled incidents and the well-known holes that punctuated the broken chain of recollection which led from the hated convent to London and the present. Nevertheless she opened her eyes again, both excited by the fact she at least regained some memories and newly saddened by the immediacy of loss and betrayal that came with them.

She was on her side with half of her face sunk into a well-stuffed feather pillow, but the unobstructed eye took in a wall entirely lacking the pattern of the wallpaper that had lined the room she had gone to sleep in. This wall had no paper on it at all, being instead whitewashed and deckled with reflected sunlight that was constantly in motion in a way that told her the sea or a river was close by. She listened carefully. For a mad moment, for no other reason than that her head had been full of it all night, and just recently so, she wondered if she were back in France. It did not feel like she was in the city, and if not in London, why, she might be anywhere . . .

She could hear a light wind rattling the casement behind her, and felt the hint of a breeze on her neck. She could hear the lap of water in the mid-distance, but no waves, which made her think she must be by a river, or perhaps a lake. And then she heard someone moving in the room below. She turned on her back and looked at the ceiling. More rippled sunlight and one spider slowly moving from corner to corner. She flexed her hands, aware of the tight kidskin gloves she had been given the previous evening in the other house.

The room was spartan but clean. She looked down at herself and was surprised – given that she was in an entirely new room – to find the distinctive lemon-coloured blanket she remembered from the night before was still covering her. She sat up, swung her legs over the side of a bed that was half the width of the one she'd gone to sleep in, and then became very still again.

The casement window looked out on a broadly curving reach of river with marshy land on the distant shore. Sun glistered off the water, and three sailing barges were working their way from left to right against the flow.

It was not the riverine activity that stopped her moving. It was the golem sitting calmly against the wall beside the window, looking at her.

She recognised him. He was still dressed like an antiquated coachman and the empty eye sockets atop the well-defined cheekbones in the skilfully made clay face seemed pointed right at her. His mouth was set in a firm line that was neither grim nor quite a smile. The last time she had really seen him she had opened a door while trying to escape the Safe House and had run into him. He had not moved and she had bounced back into the room she had been trying to exit. It had been like running into a brick wall which, since bricks were made out of clay and so was he, was not so surprising.

She did not know how to address a golem so she settled for raising a hand in greeting.

"Hello," she said.

And then, after a suitable pause.

"Where am I?"

The golem cocked his head as if thinking, then made a wide and expansive sweep of his arm. The meaning, though unvoiced, was clear.

"I know I'm here," she said. "But where is here? And why?"

Something was wrong. More wrong than merely waking up in a different house from the one she'd dozed off in: she couldn't put her finger on it, maybe because she was dislocated and woozy from such a deep slumber and the confusing dreams that had peopled it, but the wrongness was there, like a bad tooth about to flare into pain.

"Am I a prisoner?" she said.

The golem shook his head.

"I was told I would be safe," she said.

The golem nodded and patted his chest. Clearly not only did he think she was safe, but claimed credit for ensuring that was the case by his watchful presence.

"So I can get up?" she said. She wanted to see Charlie Pyefinch and find out what was going on.

The golem nodded, but when she said, "Is Charlie Pyefinch here too?" he shook his head decisively.

"I'm going to find him," she announced, and stepped onto the cold floorboards. As she walked to the door she felt herself gently stopped by a large hand on her shoulder.

She rounded on the towering clay man.

"I thought I wasn't a prisoner—" she began, and then closed her mouth.

The golem was holding something out for her.

Boots.

He pointed at her feet.

"Oh," she said.

He stepped back and pointed at the clothes hung over the top of the bedrail at the foot of the mattress. He pointed out of the window and mimed a shiver.

"Cold," she said unbidden. "Oh. You're saying get dressed, it's cold." He nodded.

"Right," she said. "Good idea, but I'm not going to get und—"

He was already walking to the door, which he exited with the hint of a bow. She wondered if it was a trick of the light, but the severe line of his mouth seemed to have twitched upwards a fraction at one end.

"Er . . . thank you," she said. "I'll be quick."

He closed the door behind him, and she tore off the nightshirt and began pulling on the clothes left for her. It was only when she was cinching the laces on her second boot that the cause of the wrongness hit her.

She dropped the untied lace and sat bolt upright.

"My sea-glass!" she gasped. And then underlined her distress in the rural French dialect that instinctively overtook her in such moments. "*Merde* . . ."

She patted her pockets, looked beneath the narrow trundle bed and then ripped the bedclothes off the mattress, shaking them but finding nothing.

She sat on the stripped bed, heart hammering.

She was a Glint. She'd always been one but it had taken Sara Falk's gentle explanation to make her understand that the capacity she had to touch stone and relive events recorded therein was not a torment but a skill that could be mastered. The gloves she wore were Sara's own, to protect her from accidentally glinting against her will. All this was newish knowledge: what was old news to her was that her safety was inextricably tied up in always staying in possession of the piece of wave-tumbled sea-glass that she had been given by her scarcely remembered mother a lifetime ago. Sara had called it her heart-stone and told her all Glints were preserved in their health and sanity by their own glass: it was to return Sara's glass that she had risked everything by coming back to London. And it was her own heart-stone, the lump of glass that perfectly matched the shade of her eyes, that was now so alarmingly absent. And not just that, but the ring, the broken ring she also had from her mother, was missing.

She ran for the door and tore it open.

The golem was not there. There was nothing but a well-swept length of corridor with the angle of a staircase visible at the far end. She ran for it, boots clomping hollowly on the uncarpeted boards as she went, and swung herself one-handed on the worn newel post at the head of the stairs before careering downhill without losing much speed.

It was the untied bootlace that tripped her before she reached the floor. Her right foot trod heavily on it, and when the left tried to move she was suddenly self-hobbled into a stomach-lurching trip as gravity and forward velocity combined to hurl her headfirst towards the waiting flagstones below.

She had no time to scream, no time to organise her arms into reaching out to try and grab something or just soften the severe impact heading towards her face with sickening speed . . .

. . . but she did have a very fast-moving golem waiting at the bottom of the stairs. Emmet streaked forwards, his greatcoat snapping like a thunderclap as it whipped behind him, and he caught her and cushioned the impact so that her face found itself a bare three inches from the waiting slab of stone.

"Good morning," said the owner of the feet who stepped into view just ahead of her nose.

She craned her head upwards.

It was The Smith.

He held her heart-stone between his finger and thumb.

"You must have been looking for this."

Emmet lifted her right way up and placed her back on her unsteady feet.

She nodded at The Smith, winded and unsure of her voice. She looked around at the room. It was the most crowded and ancient workshop she had ever seen, even though it contained machinery such as lathes and drill presses that were clearly of very recent manufacture. At the centre of it was an old forge with a fire glowing within it.

She reached for her heart-stone.

"Oh no," he said. "This is not an offer. This is a lesson." And without looking he tossed it carelessly over his shoulder.

Into the fire.

Lucy's heart-stone spun over The Smith's shoulder and bounced off the lip of the furnace, towards which he had so casually tossed it.

Again Lucy didn't have time to cry out. She didn't have time to protest. She didn't have any time at all, not even time to think before the precious lump of sea-glass, the very thing on which her safety and sanity so precariously rested, had landed right in the heart of the fire, coming to rest on top of the white hot coals.

Something happened. She felt like she'd lurched and been hit and the world around her blurred like a spinning wheel and then jolted back into focus and she was looking down at her hand and there it was.

Her stone.

She registered what she'd done and dropped it, anticipating the searing heat about to blister the skin off her hand.

The Smith caught it. She stared at him. Everything was wrong. He had been between her and the fire. Now she was between him and it. She had no memory of moving. The slap of furnace heat that she'd been ignoring made her step away from the fire. He held out the stone.

"It's not hot. You moved too fast for that."

"I didn't . . ." she began. "I mean, I didn't know I was going to do that. I didn't mean to . . ."

"Yes, you did," he said. "You just moved too fast for the thought to catch up. I'll wager you already knew you could move fast when you wanted to, even if you did not know you could move even faster when you really needed to. We shall have to make that capacity a little more consciously available to you, Lucy Harker. What else can you do?"

She reached out for the stone. He pulled his hand away.

"What else?" he repeated.

"Can I have the stone?"

He cocked his head at her, peering deeply into her eyes.

"Yes," he said. "Of course. But not yet."

She felt her jaw clench and her fists bunch. If she hadn't felt so suddenly woozy from moving so unthinkingly fast she'd have argued with him. But then the thought came that if she moved fast enough there was no need to argue at all . . .

Her hand snapped out, fast as a whiplash. Her fingers closed over empty air.

The Smith was still smiling at her. A very annoying smile, the kind of adult smile that made her feel like a frustrated child again.

"Lesson one," he said. "Know you are fast, but don't think you're faster than your opponents until you know better. Overconfidence will get you into big trouble. Worse still, it may get others hurt."

She killed the sharp retort that was rising behind her teeth by closing them and swallowing it. She made a big effort to relax.

"May I have my heart-stone?" she said. "Please."

"You may have it when I have made a setting for it. It will be safer for you if you wear it."

She stared at him.

"It's what I do," he said. "I am The Smith. I make things. Useful things. Rings. Weapons. Jewellery. Tools – members of The Oversight."

"You make them?" she said.

"When I have the right raw materials, yes," he said. "Are you made of the right material?"

She wanted the security of that stone in her hand. In the midst of all this strangeness, here in this jumbled workshop beneath the festoons of unnameable tools and the machinery ranged around the walls, she wanted the cool familiarity of the one thing that had always calmed her. She closed her eyes and tried to quench the tide of bitterness rising inside her.

"I don't know," she said.

In the darkness behind her eyelids, she heard the wicker and hiss of the fire whose heat she could still feel on her back. She heard the water birds on the marshy riverbank beyond the doors to the workshop. And she heard a low rumbling chuckle.

She opened her eyes to see The Smith's austere face transformed by a smile.

"That was the right answer, Lucy Harker."

He handed her the heart-stone.

"Hold this for me until we have chosen a setting and I have made it. What would you prefer? A pendant that you can wear on a chain round your neck, or a ring? Sara Falk favours a ring, I know, but I have always wondered if that is the best way. After all, a ring presents itself to the eye, and also stands proud on the hand, making it liable to catch on things in the heat of the moment. A pendant on a chain keeps the stone as close as a ring and has the added advantage that you may wear it within your clothing next to the skin where none may know you carry it. And, tucked out of harm's way, it is not subject to snagging or catching."

He shrugged.

"But you may choose what you will. I would point out, however, that if you are to remain with us, the business of The Oversight has a tendency to involve a certain amount of vigorous action not entirely suited to obviously protuberant jewellery."

"You think I should have a pendant," she said.

"It is your choice," he said. "But yes. It is safer and more sensible."

"But Sara Falk chose a ring?"

"Sara Falk is a law unto herself," he said, "and possibly you are quite wilful as she."

"No," she said. "I'd like a pendant. It makes more sense. It keeps it safer, out of sight, like you said. And it leaves my hands freer. But I have no chain to wear it on."

"I make chains too," he said. "Chains are never a problem."

CHAPTER 9

THE WHITE TOWER

Hodge, despite Cook's reservations, had been determined to return to his lodgings within the Tower of London as soon as he could. Charlie was sent with him. At first Charlie thought he was there at Cook's behest, to keep an eye on the injured Terrier Man, but it soon became apparent that, blinded or no, Hodge was more than capable of both discharging his duties within the rambling precincts of the castle walls and looking after himself within the tidy confines of the ratcatcher's lodgings.

The first time that Charlie accompanied him he did not use the underground passage that led from the Safe House, but insisted they walk the long way round on the city streets.

"If you're to understand the Tower and what it means, then you should approach it as others do," he said. "And if you're to start a new job, you got to know the right way to do things before you find your own short-cuts."

Charlie was still blurry on the nature of the "new job" Hodge was referring to, but he followed him through the streets, marvelling at how well Hodge walked, using Jed the dog's eyes as his own, so that if you had not seen the ruin of his face and the kerchief tied across his eyes you would not have known he was blind. Clearly the man and the dog were used to working with each other from long before the recent injury, and this ease was now serving him well.

Hodge had paused and turned as they walked the narrow bridge towards the main gate. He jerked a thumb over his head at the large coat of arms carved into the stonework on the flat wall above the entrance. The portcullis was down, blocking the arch, and the defensive curves of the middle tower's twin turrets loomed on either side of it, making Charlie feel both small and vulnerable. He imagined in earlier days that there would have been an arrow tracking every person who proceeded up the causeway they now stood on. It was narrow for a reason. It was a killing ground.

"Notice anything?" said Hodge.

"Not the most welcoming-looking place I've seen," said Charlie.

"So I should hope," said Hodge. "Designed to keep ill-wishers out, first and foremost."

"Does the job, I should say," admitted Charlie.

"Not what I meant," said Hodge. "Look again. And see how to get in."

Charlie scanned the ominous façade. He wondered if he was meant to be looking for secret entrances hidden in the ancient stonework. Jed barked at him and wagged his tail. Then, having got his attention, the dog turned away and looked up at the arch, raising his chin pointedly, as if trying to give Charlie a hint.

"Don't help him," warned Hodge. "The boy's got to learn to notice things for himself."

Jed barked at him.

"That's different," said Hodge. "He's got good young eyes of his own. I've buggered mine up, haven't I?"

He turned his head back towards Charlie.

"Right," he said. "Smith says you're a sharp one. Stay here and count to thirty. Then meet me on the other side of that gate."

He strode towards the entrance. Jed watched him, tail still wagging. Then the dog turned, jumped up, licked Charlie's hand in farewell and ran after his partner. Hodge had reached the portcullis. A military-looking silhouette appeared on the other side of the massive oak grille, nodded and then waved to a hidden confederate. The portcullis rose smoothly, and when it was about four feet off the ground Hodge ducked beneath the spikes with Jed at his heels. The barrier then stopped rising and lowered with equal smoothness, landing with a very final thump.

Charlie stared at the impenetrable façade louring over him. He had no idea how to get in. Then he felt the wetness from Jed's farewell lick and looked down at this hand.

The dog had licked his ring finger. He looked at the ring, then back at the royal coat of arms, saw the similarity that he had missed, and smiled.

He marched up to the portcullis, conscious of the two pairs of eyes watching him from the other side: Jed's and the steely gaze of the waiting Beefeater.

"Clear off," said the guard. "We don't want your sort here."

Charlie swallowed and hoped he was right.

"Yes, you do," he said, and held out his ring. "I think."

The Beefeater squinted at it for long enough to make Charlie begin to wonder if he'd made a mistake, but then he stepped straight back and waved to his confederate.

The heavy wooden grating rose into the air and Charlie ducked under as soon as there was space to do so. Jed barked a greeting. Hodge extended a hand towards him as he spoke to the guard.

"Warden Marriot, this is Charlie Pyefinch. He'll be helping me from now on. Least till my eyes is better."

The Beefeater unbent and nodded, his eye now considerably less steely.

"Terrier Boy, are you?" he said with a distinctly unmilitary wink. "Well then, welcome aboard, younker."

And with that he swivelled smartly on his heels and marched back into the warmth of the waiting guardhouse.

Charlie had to jog to catch up with Hodge and the dog who were striding along the inner bridge to the next gate.

"Good work," said Hodge. "Saw the shield did you?"

"And the lion and the unicorn," said Charlie.

"Like the ones on your ring," said Hodge. "Says we been defending this mound of earth since before it was even a tower, so don't let anyone make you think this place ain't your place. If you're Oversight, there's nowhere that's more yours than this."

"Do the Beefeaters know about The Oversight then?" said Charlie.

"No," said Hodge. "Wouldn't be much of a secret if they did. Soldiers gossip worse than seamstresses. No, all they know is the ring is a sovereign *laissez-passez*, which is French for *carte blanche* to go anywhere you like."

He grinned at Charlie, who followed him through the next gate, which was not barred and only manned by another friendly Beefeater sitting on a bench enjoying the thin sunlight in his black and red uniform and strange squashed-pie hat. He exchanged pleasantries with Hodge and expressed sympathy about his wounds in such an unconcerned and amiably chaffing way that Charlie could see the guards at the Tower were used to Hodge returning knocked about from his other life beyond the walls.

Hodge walked across the swathe of clean green grass in the shadow of the White Tower itself, the imposingly tall block at the centre of the ring of fortifications, and showed Charlie the way to his official lodgings, which were a surprisingly clean and bright set of rooms approached by a narrow vennel between the workshops and the armoury on the east side of the castle.

The rooms had scrubbed floorboards and wooden panelling painted a faded green. There was little clutter, a box-bed with the panels drawn closed and, Charlie noted, just one of everything: one cup, one plate, one table with one stool pulled up to it, one chair in front of the fire. It was clean and wholesome and airy, but also aggressively the home of a bachelor. The only softness in the room was a large and much-mended cushion lying on the floor by the fire, and it was on this that Jed took up station while Hodge disappeared into another room to change. He emerged wearing clothes that were, to Charlie's eyes, considerably dirtier than the ones he had changed out of. He threw a pair of old nankeen sailor's trousers at Charlie.

"Put 'em on over your own clothes," he said. "Should be big enough for you to use as overalls for now, keep the muck off you."

"Muck?" said Charlie.

"Follow and learn," said Hodge. "You're one of the Last Hand now. There's important stuff you need to know."

And with that he swept a shuttered bull's-eye lantern off the table and walked to the door.

Five minutes later, Charlie was crouched double, walking awkwardly behind Hodge who was feeling his way through a low-built undercroft deep beneath the White Tower itself, an extremity they had reached by scrambling and crawling down a bewildering warren of passages, stairs and, in one memorable case, a slide that had taken Charlie by surprise and tumbled him straight down onto the earth floor they were now traversing.

"Smell that?" said Hodge, his voice betraying a happiness Charlie had not heard before. "Fresh rat piss. We'll catch some big bastard or I'm a Chinaman."

"Rat-catching?" said Charlie. "We're rat-catching?"

His question was met with silence.

"But . . . isn't The Oversight in dire peril?"

Hodge grunted.

"Peril and shorthanded doesn't mean we don't take care of the day-to-day," he said. "And these rats aren't going to kill themselves."

This didn't make any sense to Charlie, given everything he had heard about The Oversight and how thinly stretched they now were.

"But shouldn't we be watching these Templebanes and that Mountfellon fellow?" he said. "From what you been saying . . ."

"Cook stays and guards the Safe House," said Hodge. "Smith's got Lucy Harker out on the Isle of Dogs and ain't ready to let her out of his sight more'n he has to, which leaves you and I. And you don't know much about anything, not yet, you don't."

"I know enough to watch and report back," said Charlie. "I could keep an eye on the Templebanes, you could watch Mountfellon . . ."

"And who'd keep the rats down?" said Hodge.

"How can that be as important as watching our enemies?" said Charlie.

Hodge squatted on his haunches and peered into the darkness beyond the throw of the lantern. He was seeing through Jed's eyes, fifty feet ahead, tight in below the undercroft where the ground rose towards the roof leaving a space maybe two feet high.

"I'm not Terrier Man and ratcatcher by mistake, Charlie Pyefinch," he said. "The Oversight's always been pretty loosely associated, being a Free Company and all. It ain't had much truck with hierarchies and officials and any of that humbug, but as long as there's been an Oversight, there have been two positions that are always filled, and one's The Smith, and the other's the Terrier Man."

He thumbed upwards.

"The Tower's here to protect the ravens, not the other way round, whatever rumours you might hear to the contrary. And rats like raven's eggs more than anything, and seeing as how the ravens have their wings clipped, they're vulnerable too: some of the rats that get in here are big enough to kill a raven, easy. We've had some come in off the river through Traitors' Gate that were big as Jed himself."

Jed had stiffened and stopped. From the darkness Charlie could hear a warning growl.

"So that's why we're a-ratcatching. All you need know for now is that the ravens being here keep the old darkness at bay, and of all the things we're sworn to protect the city from it's that darkness that's first among foes. It's more important to keep the vermin in here down. The vermin out there will have to wait. Because . . ."

He stopped.

"What?" said Charlie.

"Because I got a feeling," said Hodge. "And tell you the truth it's bearing down on me heavier than the tons of stone above us."

"A feeling?" said Charlie.

"A premonition," said Hodge, grimacing.

"Is that something you have?" said Charlie. "Like, is that one of your gifts?"

"Gifts?" said Hodge. "What do you mean gifts?"

"You know," said Charlie. "Like a special power. The Sight?"

"Do I look like someone gifted with the Sight?" snorted Hodge bitterly, turning his blindfolded face towards him. "Or are you having a laugh?"

"No," said Charlie. "No, sorry, I wasn't . . ."

"Relax, Charlie," smiled Hodge. "I'm the one having a laugh. No. I ain't got the Sight, and truth to tell, I ain't never met a seer, nor met anyone I trust what has done, neither. People what can tell the future is just old wives' tales, you know?"

"What?" said Charlie. "Like golems? Or the Sluagh?"

"Is that you cheeking your elders and betters?" said Hodge.

"My mum says old wives get things right a lot more than people think," said Charlie.

"Well, she's no fool," said Hodge. "But I ain't got the Sight. Just a feeling in my bones. Like a storm coming in. And premonition might be too strong a word for it and all, but the long and the short of it is, I think it might be just as well that someone else knows the drill up here."

"In the Tower?" said Charlie.

Hodge nodded.

"Normally, when there was enough of us, the ratcatcher's always had an apprentice. I was one in my day . . ."

Charlie looked round at the dank undercroft. He felt the weight of earth and stone pressing down on his shoulders. He felt a similar pressure from the darkness that ringed them on all sides. He grimaced.

"I don't mean any offence, but I don't think I'm who you're looking for. I mean, I'm more of an outside, on-the-move kind of person . . ."

"No one likes tight spots," said Hodge as if he could read Charlie's thoughts. "But it ain't a question of me looking for anything, son. The job has its own way of doing the choosing . . ."

Charlie was about to protest further when Jed went mad in the darkness ahead. Hodge stiffened as they listened to a shrill crescendo of sharp excited yelps, then a barrelling, snarling noise followed by a squeal and then silence.

"Good dog," said Hodge. "That's a monster . . ."

Jed trotted out of the gloom, his jaws locked around the neck of a dead black rat that was almost as long as he was. His tail was wagging proudly as he dropped the corpse at Hodge's boots.

"That's as big a brute as I seen in years," said Hodge. "I'd say that's a good omen for you, Charlie Pyefinch. You're going to bring good luck to this enterprise, I reckon."

Charlie looked down at the bundle of torn black fur and the long pink whiplash of a tail curling out from beneath it like a question mark, and wondered if Hodge was really just whistling in the dark, cheerily talking about good luck to hide the fact he feared that something much less fortunate was hanging over all their futures, like an anvil, ready to drop.

CHAPTER 10

THE EMPTY CHAIR

Zebulon Templebane attended his last breakfast in the counting house that bore his and his brother's name as the centrepiece of a long, groaning table laid down the centre of the clerk's room.

He lay in a closed coffin, topped by a massive pillar candle of beeswax, his unseeing eyes beneath the lid each topped with a gold sovereign, his slack jaw bound shut by a clean, white kerchief carefully tied around the top of his head. The coffin was stained black and polished to such a high gloss that the assembled company of adopted sons could see both them-selves and the multitude of other candles arranged around the shuttered room. More than that, they could see the extraordinary feast that spread from the coffin as if it were some morbid cornucopia that had para-doxically spilled a profusion of lively delights down the long table.

It was the most remarkable superabundance of food and drink the found-ling sons had ever seen, more of a princely debauch than a funereal breakfast: the groaning board included hams, chickens, sponge cakes, potted shrimp, potted salmon, ginger cream, wine jelly, tartlets, lemon cake, caramel custard, raised pies, lobster salad, potted pigeons, tongue, all manner of fruit and boiled eggs, hot rolls, muffins and toast. There were steaming jugs of cocoa and there was, most extraordinary of all the anomalous luxuries, two jero-boams of champagne, standing like sentries at each end of the table.

The counting desks and the high stools which normally occupied the central space had been banished to the walls and there was one ominously empty chair at the end of the table where Zebulon, when alive, was wont to sit.

Issachar sat at the other end of the board, broken arm strapped to his chest with a black silk sling. The pain of the injury was disconcertingly growing rather than decreasing with the passage of time, but he had taken a small and precautionary dose of laudanum so as not to betray any weakness in the face of his "sons".

He looked slowly up and down the ranks of his foundling family, running them through his head as he took a quiet muster roll. Named for the city parishes from whose orphanages and poorhouses they had been taken, the roll made an odd assemblage of names. There was the burly Sherehog, with his newly broken jaw to match Issachar's arm, both presents from The Oversight; and avoiding his eyes further down the table was Coram, who had once been perhaps his favourite. Between them sat Vintry, Jewry, Westcheap, Aldersgate and Backchurch Templebane, while on the other side of the coffin were ranged Pountney and the often confused Poultry, Outwich, Bothaw and Abchurch Templebane. The only names absent were those who had perished on the river, and the mysteriously disappeared mute, Amos, who had been the youngest of the crew.

They were all poised between elation at the feast spread before them, and confusion, lest it was a trick. It was, after all, a funeral and not a bridal breakfast. Issachar drank a full bumper of champagne from brim to bottom, taking his time as he did so, letting them hang in the balance. It had ever been his and his brother's practice to keep the "children" in a state of permanent competition and insecurity, this being the best way to both control them and develop a very specific kind of toughness and obedience. The torn nature of the glances they kept giving the food and then the coffin amused him more than he had imagined it would. He had not, however, had this extravagance laid on to torture them. He had more serious reasons, and felt his brother's life should be celebrated by some uncharacteristic and memorable gesture. He put down his glass, wiped his mouth and spoke.

"Why are we here?" he asked.

"Funeral feast," said Sherehog, grinding the words out between gritted teeth, his broken jaw having been wired and bound in place by a bone-setter who had obligingly also removed a tooth in order that he might eat and drink via a straw while his face healed. Of all the brothers here, he was the drunkest, since only liquids came easy to him.

"A wake," said Westcheap.

"Show our respects," said Outwich and Poultry simultaneously.

Templebane shook his head. He pointed at the vacant seat at the other end of the table.

"We are here to fill an empty chair," he said. "For death not only diminishes – it provides. And in this case it provides a vacancy."

The boys all looked at each other, eyes glinting in the candlelight. Issachar and Zebulon had trained them well. They could smell an opportunity being dangled in front of them, even if they could not yet discern exactly what it was. Issachar swept his hand around at the table, all the treats and fancies laid out around the coffin.

"This food. This drink. All today's unwonted comforts are nothing to the future luxuries that will be available to whoever sits in that chair. All you have to do is take it—"

More looks flashed back and forth across the table. And then Sherehog, who invariably preferred a physical solution to a problem rather than one involving too much thought (which always confused him) leapt from his seat. As soon as he moved, at least half of the other brothers followed suit, clawing each other out of the way as they leapt for the chair—

"SIT DOWN!"

Issachar's voice lashed through the air. The mêlée disentangled itself and seats were resumed with a lot of embarrassed coughing.

Issachar's eye swept balefully over them, making each one feel it had taken a precise and damning tally of their worth.

"To sit in that chair you have to earn it," he said with menacing silkiness.

One of the few brothers who had remained in their seats raised a finger.

Issachar stared at him.

"Coram. You have a question?"

"How, Father?"

Issachar sat back and sucked his teeth, lip curled as he did so, as if he had just encountered some unpleasant taste within his mouth. He looked at the coffin, and then his gaze travelled up the pillar of beeswax to the flame burning at the top and rested there.

"Coram," he sighed. "Coram."

The other brothers exchanged that particular look that passes between people who know a punishment is about to be delivered, but not, happily, to themselves. Abchurch even sniggered until Westcheap mashed a heel into his toes to silence him.

"Coram," said Issachar, "of all here, you have the furthest to go to achieve that chair."

Sherehog kicked Coram under the table, the toe of his boot striking his shins with a malicious sharpness. Coram ignored it. His eyes were locked on Issachar's face. There were two reasons that his father could be angry with him. One was survivable, with a little nerve. The other was the kind of betrayal that would only end with him being found face down in the Thames one cold morning. And because he was certain that Issachar could not possibly know that he had agreed to be the eyes and ears of the nobleman Mountfellon, he realised he had to deal with the other displeasure directly.

Not for nothing had he been one of the more favoured sons prior to the debacle at Blackwater Reach. Sometimes, only very rarely, but certainly sometimes it was possible to impress the fathers by a show of strength rather than of unthinking obedience. And in this moment, even though he had no precise idea what the test actually was, he knew that to blink was to fail completely.

"Because I came back," he said clearly and without a shake in his voice.

Issachar's eyes dropped from the top of the funeral taper and locked on his.

"Because you came back alive."

"And the Night Father did not," said Coram.

Every eye in the room saw the muscles twitch on the side of Issachar's jaw.

"And my brother did not," he said.

The silence hung in the air like an axe about to fall.

Coram stood. The scrape of his chair raised one of Issachar's eyebrows, but other than that no one else moved.

"If I had been in the Night Father's boat instead of dearly departed Bassetshaw, who was a fool, or poor Garlickhythe, who was merely vicious but not overly courageous, then maybe he would have returned unscathed," he said. "But he put me on a boat with Mountfellon. It was his choice, not mine. Had I been on his boat, I could have saved him. And if not, I would not have returned."

There was a quiet wheeze of intaken breaths around the table.

"You speak ill of the dead and think to commend yourself to me?" said Issachar.

Coram didn't flinch. He knew that to do so was to lose everything.

"No. I speak the truth about them and you know it. You should blame the dead brothers, because that is fair. But if you blame me, you not only do wrong – which in your present and very understandable grief you may or may not care much about – but you also deprive yourself and the House of Templebane of a loyal and resourceful servant. And that I know you do care about."

"Do I?" said Issachar.

"You do," said Coram. "But if I'm mistaken and you have no use for me, just say so and I will go from here and never return."

Issachar stared at him. And then he inclined his head.

"Sit down," he said.

Coram took his seat. Only then did his leg betray his heightened nerves by shaking, but the movement was hidden by the table. To the rest of the room, he appeared cool and calm.

"One thing," said Issachar. "I do not need you to understand my grief. For you cannot encompass the merest portion of it."

Coram inclined his head. And when he raised it again he fancied he saw the faintest flicker of an approving smile move across Templebane's face before he turned to the others.

"So," he said, "this is how that chair, which will be the chair of my deputy can be won . . ."

They all sat forward eagerly.

"I want a plan for the eradication of The Oversight and the destruction of their headquarters in Wellclose Square. If the House of Templebane is to prosper, I am now convinced it must be in a London stripped of their unhelpful scrutiny. There are allies in the shadows whose powers can help us achieve great things, allies The Oversight would like to prevent us using under the pretext of some antiquated niceties, some secret 'laws' that they take it upon themselves alone to both know and enforce. They are busybodies with an archaic pedigree no one cares about, nothing more than an obstacle to trade. And trade is progress, boys, and mankind must travel forward, and so all obstacles to that great enterprise must be eradicated. I want a plan that looks like an accident, just in case we do not succeed at first strike, since they remain resourceful and nothing is certain, but I do not want a plan that will not succeed. Further to that, I want a permanent surveillance on them and reports twice a day, when I wake and when I go to bed. Whoever comes up with the best stratagem—"

He waved at the empty chair. Then he picked up his glass.

"Glasses, boys: to the memory of my brother – and to the destruction of The Oversight."

Behind the Wainscot
of the World

Just like as in a nest of boxes round,
Degrees of sizes in each box are found:
So, in this world, may many others be
Thinner and less, and less still by degree . . .

by Margaret Cavendish,
Duchess of Newcastle-upon-Tyne (1623–1653)

. . . it is conjectured that there are other worlds within the world, as close
as a paper-width but unreachable to us. What is certain is that there exists
a network of interconnected passages that link similarly appointed places
within our single world, allowing of shortcuts spanning hundreds of
leagues that may be taken in instants, and that the portals into these
tunnels are doubled looking-glasses.

For those with the ability, it is possible to enter these passages through
the very surface of the primary reflector, and move behind the surface
of the palpable sphere as effortlessly as a mouse scuttling unseen behind
the very wainscoting of the world . . . this mirror'd realm is not a blessing
or a boon to man, rather it is a new territory, perhaps sandwiched between
dimensions imperceptible to us, which contains as much danger as it does

miraculous opportunities for swift travel . . . notably there are Black Mirrors, whose operation I know naught of other than the horror they arouse in those that have travelled the mirror'd world, and there are "mirror-wights" or, as they are known colloquially, hop-toads. It is my belief that "wight" in this context does not carry the meaning of "man" as much as its older sense of "swift", in that it refers to the ability of these people to move quickly between places by the use of the looking-glass highway. A hop-toad is a common name, and must refer to the similar ability to spring nimbly from one location to another, seemingly without effort. Hop-toad also carries a base connotation, which perhaps refers to the rumoured use of the mirrors as a place where supranatural malfeasants can hide from the forces of order which operate on the other, normal side of the mirror. In this respect, the mirror'd world can act as a variety of infinite priest's hole for the hiding of fugitives who may well do or have done much harm beyond the mirrors, and who are hunted by those charged with policing such offences.

from *The Great and Hidden History of the World* by the Rabbi Dr Hayyim Samuel Falk (also known as the Ba'al Shem of London)

CHAPTER 11

THE BLOOD TOLL

Sara strode relentlessly onwards through the mirrors. Her progress was steady and repetitive as she walked in an increasingly trance-like state until she found she had somehow lost track of time in a sensation more acute than merely not being sure what hour it was, or even whether it was now night or day. It felt more uncanny than that: the deeper she delved into the mirrored maze, the shallower her connection with the outside world became, and the looser the grip and dictates of its temporal pull seemed to be. In fact it felt both as if time had lost track of her and that she had been moving inexorably away from the tug of some great magnet, its power decreasing with every step until the point came when she had become unhitched from something that had previously moored her to the concrete world. She now felt cast adrift in a way that made her somewhat nauseous. It was no longer a matter of not knowing whether it was night or day: it was increasingly unclear to her whether she had been walking for minutes, hours, days, weeks or seasons. The sensation made her head spin with something like vertigo.

The Raven rode her shoulder, curiously comforting in its proximity, head tucked under its wing as if asleep.

"How long have we been walking?" she said.

The bird lifted its head, shook it, peered around and then tucked it away again.

"You too?" she said. "I can't tell if it's today or next week. But I don't feel tired."

The Raven had nothing to add to this.

She scratched the wrist of the hand that had been severed, flexing its fingers as she did so.

"My wrist itches though. It's been getting worse."

She peeled back the leather glove and revealed the paper-thin silver band that now circled her arm.

The Raven opened an eye and clacked its beak.

"I don't know," Sara said. "I haven't tried."

The Raven looked at her.

"I'm not scared," she said. "I just hadn't thought of it."

She took her errant hand in the other and twisted.

"No," she said.

The Raven clacked.

"I'm not resisting," she said. "Look, I'm willing it to . . . oh."

The hand came off her arm, cleanly sheared away at the silver join which now revealed itself to be the meeting place of two mirrored stump surfaces. Although the wounds had looked this way when the hand was originally lopped from her arm and lost in the mirrors, to see the cut ends of the severed limb still mirrored in this fashion – and detachable no less – was disconcerting. She looked down at her disembodied fist. The fingers opened and flexed and wiggled.

"Well," she said. "I did not know I could do that."

She replaced it, mirrored stump to mirrored stump, and found herself once again two-handed.

"That," she said to the Raven, "is interesting. But it's still itchy . . ."

She took the hand off again and looked down into the roughly oval glassy surface on the wrist stump.

If she had not been looking down she would not have seen them. The mirror reflected the glass ceiling beneath which she passed. As she stepped from reflection to reflection, she noted that a new but unvarying vertical passage opened up like a series of identical mirrored chimneys heading to the invisible sky above her head.

It was the break in the pattern that warned her, the non-identical chimney, the regularity broken by the bulk of the Mirror Wight hanging overhead, waiting to drop.

There was a blur of descending motion. Without thinking she leapt away, snapping her hand back onto her wrist and drawing the longest blade from her belt as she did so. The Raven tumbled off her shoulder and flapped untidily into the air.

The Wight landed softly in front of her, crouched and ready with a black obsidian knife held in front of it. The stone dagger was the thing that caught her attention, not just because it was sharp and definitely pointed right at her, but because its uncompromising deep blackness was a complete counterpoint to the blanched man holding it.

He was almost monochrome, his facial pallor matched by the clothes he wore, clothes from which the original hues had faded almost entirely, like material left out in a merciless tropical sun, although in truth the colour had been leeched away by the light-hungry mirrors. The clothes were, however, distinctive in style if not depth of tint. He was barefoot, with naked, unstockinged calves above which knee breeches were laced, disappearing under the overhang of a long waistcoat of a style that had last been modish at the time of the Restoration, more than a century and a half ago. The long tousled wig the Wight wore confirmed the cavalier look, an ancient thing whose grey curls hung down on either side of his long and strangely pouchy face.

The deep-set eyes had pendulous bags under them, and the cheeks they sat on were saggy, the jawline dewlapped with slack flesh, as if the whole pale face itself was beginning to flow slowly downhill like a forgotten candle softened by too much time spent in an overwarm room.

But the eyes were sharp, pointed right at her.

"Mirror Wight," said Sara.

The Raven cawed in agreement and flapped back a couple of feet to hang unnaturally still in the air behind her shoulder.

Naming her assailant was just a reflex, not the most intelligent or considered thing she might have said – as meaningless as saying "cow" when surprised by one on a walk through a farmyard – but naming a thing had some power to it. And naming something she had only read about made her feel strangely less alone, for if someone had met Mirror Wights and written about them, then it stood to reason that it was possible to walk away from such a meeting unharmed.

"Lady," said the Wight. The eyes glittered as it made what might have been the smallest of courtly bows, more of a reflexive tremor than an intended gesture of respect.

Sara tentatively lowered her blade a little. She did not want to fight if talking could avoid the need for it. The Wight was a big man, a look exaggerated by the curls piled on top of the wig, but even without that artificial advantage, and slightly crouched and ready to spring though he was, he was still much taller than her. And quite apart from that, Sara was a talker and a listener and a thinker, not a born fighter.

"What do you want?" said Sara. "I mean no harm. I would just like to be on my way."

"Then on your way may you go," smiled the Wight.

She wished he hadn't smiled. His teeth were black. Not black as in rotten and neglected, but black as in exactly like the shiny stone dagger that he still hadn't lowered even slightly. The unnaturally pale gums that cushioned them only served to highlight their strangeness.

"Thank you," she said. She should have felt relieved, but she was already thinking ahead as to how she would pass him, and whether – assuming he was not lying and let her go ahead of him – she would be able to proceed without the crippling dread that he would then be padding along somewhere behind her all the time. Walking in the mirrors was bad enough, quite apart from the spectre of being stalked through them. What had seemed like a strange but sterile environment was now going to be haunted by fear.

"But you must pay," he said, just as she took a pace forward.

"Pay what?" said Sara, stopping and tightening her grip on the knife.

"Blood," he said. "The Blood Toll. None may pass through our domain without paying it."

The Raven snapped its beak in disapproval.

So, thought Sara, a fight it was going to be after all. She felt sadness and the lack of Mr Sharp in equal, pungent measure.

"I give you fair warning," she said, holding out the glove on top of which she wore her rings. "By Law and Lore, let me pass. We are The Oversight."

The Wight looked unimpressed.

"Oversight you may be, but whatever else you are, you are not a 'we', my lady, for I can see only one of you, and behind your pet bird, down the long chain of mirrors, an infinity of nobody else . . . Pay the toll."

"It is a form of words," she said, "customarily used by those who bear this ring. It means harm one of us, harm all, and that if you do so, all will avenge."

"Pretty words too," he said. "Very lovely in troth, but 'customarily', in *my* usage, those who pass must pay the toll by providing a gentleman of the mirrors with a small and refreshing beverage."

And he reached inside the hanging pockets on the skirt of his waistcoat and produced a well-worn pewter mug from the depths within.

"Or in simpler terms, for I apprehend that a mere untutored woman may require plainer elucidation: bleed yourself or let me bleed you, for what I want is your red, my pretty."

He placed the battered mug on the glass floor between them and nudged it towards her with his toe with an encouraging wave of his knife.

"You wish to milk me of my blood?" she said.

"Life in the mirrors thins the vital fluid," he said. "Takes the vigour quite from it, so it does, much as it takes pigment from us. But it is life. And if you would pass through the realm we have made our home, then you must pay the toll."

And he nudged the tankard another inch towards her.

"That's a half-pint mug," said Sara. "That's a lot of blood."

Sara had once been bled by her grandfather, when a child, to cure a fever. He had taken no more than an eggcup full and that had left her feeling pained and weak for days. A half-pint of blood, especially in her reduced state, was not an option she relished at all. She was not sure that she could spare even half that.

"Fill it twice and you may pass." He shrugged, flashing black teeth in a nasty smile.

"Twice?" she said. "You said beverage, not beverages."

"Ah yes, but whereas you are demonstrably not presently part of a 'we', I am," he said, nodding at something behind her.

The Raven cawed an urgent warning. Sara turned in time to see a second Wight flicker through the mirrored wall two mirrors back and to the left of her.

This new Wight carried a longbow, the arrow nocked and held ready. He had evidently been in the mirrors even longer than the cavalier. He wore tight leggings, a codpiece and a leather jerkin, all so etiolated by his chosen habitat that he seemed to be a uniform dirty white colour – except for the whites of his eyes which were disconcertingly as black as his bared teeth and the obsidian chip that tipped the arrow pointed straight at Sara's heart.

"A mug for me, a mug for him, bind yourself up and be on your way," said the cavalier.

"I cannot spare it," she said.

"You cannot *not* spare it, my dear, for if you do not give it freely, we shall take it anyway," he said. "I am trying to be a gentleman about this but we do not have all day, and if another of my companions appears, then that will be three half-pints and things get messy."

"Messy?" she said, playing for time. She would have to try and step out of the mirrors, but she didn't know if she could do it fast enough to avoid the arrow. And even if she did step out of the mirrors, she had no idea what she would be walking into, other than some unfamiliar room into which the Mirror Wights could in fact follow her.

Wights lived in the mirrors but could emerge momentarily. As long as they didn't spend too much time out of the protection of the mirrored realm, they remained untouched by time. At least that is what Sara had read. Looking at them, with their leeched skin and black teeth, it was however clear *something* was touching them, even if time did not have them fully in its grasp.

She felt a jab in her back. The bowman had barefooted up behind her and was prodding her with the tip of the arrow.

"Messy means blood on the mirrors. Us don't like blood on the mirrors. A blooded mirror's a fell thing, my flower," he said in a deep ruined voice that sounded like each word was being dragged through sharp gravel. "A blooded mirror, blooded on this side – why, that's a world of pain . . ."

"And not necessarily *this* world," laughed the cavalier, voice dry as tinder. "A blooded mirror becomes a blackened mirror, and what lies beyond a Black Mirror . . ."

He shook his head. The grey curls swung pendulously back and forth as he did so.

"What lies beyond the Black Mirrors is horrors we as best not talk of in case they has ears as well as eyes," said the bowman, echoing the unpleasant laugh with a dispiriting snigger of his own.

She turned to look at him again. He was about her height, and as she moved he stepped carefully back and raised the arrow so that it was aimed right at her eye.

"The Black Mirrors watch us," he spat. "It ain't good. Us don't want to make more of them." He squinted at her down the length of the shaft. "Now you stay very still, for if I put this arrow clean and gentle in your little peeper here, you won't bleed much. So why don't you do as I say, my coney?"

Sara Falk stared back at him, unblinking, trying to clear her mind. What was going to happen next was not going to be about thinking. It was going to be about moving very, very fast.

"Very well," she said, taking a deep calming breath. "I will do exactly as you say—"

And she did. She didn't move an inch out of place. She maintained eye contact, staring at him down the length of the arrow shaft; his aiming eye at the other end of it locked on hers, a hard man determined not to lose even something as little as a staring contest with a mere woman. Which suited her entirely, since while he focused on her eye and not blinking his own, he wasn't watching the rest of her, so he didn't register her hand blurring upwards until it was too late.

She grabbed the shaft of the arrow before he could let fly. As the command to loose it was still racing from his brain to his fingers, she jerked it off the taut bowstring.

As his fingers opened to release, she punched the arrow straight backwards with all her strength.

The bowstring snapped forward, shredding the fletches on an arrow now going at speed in the opposite direction. The string smacked painfully into the side of her fist just as the back of the arrow punched through the bowman's eye and on into the brain beyond with a sickening popping sensation.

She heard a roar of anger from behind and felt rather than saw the cavalier leap at her. She kept hold of the arrow shaft and spun out of the way, stabbing into the space she had just vacated, hoping to meet her assailant and impale him by his own momentum. The arrow instead met the stone dagger and skittered sideways into the cavalier's shoulder. He yelped and stumbled into the falling corpse of the bowman. The two of them went down in a snarled tangle of limbs.

Sara knew this was her moment of choice – stay and try and finish him off, or run and put distance between them. It wasn't really a choice. She shifted the knife to her right hand.

He saw her coming and rolled sideways and then just flickered and disappeared.

"Damn," gasped Sara.

He had gone into a mirror.

She hurdled the dead bowman, unable to stop fast enough, and then spun around, looking front and back. If the cavalier had flickered out of one mirror, he could as easily appear out of another at any moment.

She caught the movement with the tail of her eye and threw the knife without knowing she'd done it, running on instinct. She turned and saw the whirling blade heading right for the cavalier who just flickered through another mirror and disappeared, leaving the knife to clatter to the ground a hundred feet down the empty glass corridor.

Sensing he'd try and come through a mirror behind her, she ran to retrieve it, pulling another knife from her boot as she did so. She got halfway there before she was proved wrong. He stepped out of a mirror beside her, crouched low and ready to fight. Thankfully he was looking past where she was to where she had been, and their eyes met as she sprinted past.

He cut at her, too wide and too late, and then he glimmered through a mirror and, before she could stop her pell-mell dash for the thrown knife, appeared between her and it.

He slashed another wicked blow across her path, which she would have run into had she not thrown herself backwards and slid beneath it. The obsidian blade razored air particles in half just above her face, so close she could feel the wind of its passage. She reached her thrown knife and grabbed it as she rolled back to her feet.

The cavalier blinked away through a mirror again. Clearly he had no problem getting in and out of them, and knowing exactly where he would emerge.

Sara stood still and listened. The Raven flapped over and landed on her shoulder, then shuffled around so it could keep watch on her back.

"Good idea," she said, breathing hard, trying to control her adrenalin and slow her speeding pulse. "Thank you."

For a long beat they were alone in the glass corridor, with no company other than the dead bowman bleeding quietly out in a heap about a hundred feet away.

The cavalier suddenly stepped back into the corridor between them. She hadn't even had time to raise the knife to throw it before he flickered away again.

She realised she felt a tingle through her bare feet, like the faintest of tremors, each time he went in or out of the mirrors. It came again and there he was on the other side of her. Again he disappeared before she could throw a knife at him. The next time he appeared he was actually smiling, showing his unnerving obsidian teeth as he played a very lethal game of cat and mouse with her.

He disappeared, she moved, he reappeared, this time dropping out of a mirror, smile getting larger.

"Only a matter of time," he said, and then was gone.

The game was making her disorientated as he flicked back in and out, but then she noticed he never now came quite close enough to strike her, and that's what saved her – not her speed or her tenacity, but her thinking.

Why was he doing that? The answer stopped her in her tracks. He was trying to achieve the disorientation, to make her dizzy and tired. He was just wearing her out. But in doing so, in flickering in and out of the mirrors, he had made her aware that she could sense his transition by the vibrations resonating through the soles of her feet.

She knew what to do.

She closed her eyes and crossed her arms over her chest, a knife poised between the fingers of each hand. The moment she felt the vibration she threw her arms violently sideways, opening out into a crucifix as the blades flew left and right down the corridor. Her eyes opened and she saw one blade spinning futilely down the mirrored channel to her left. She heard a chunking impact as she turned fast to her right.

The Raven cawed in approval and lofted into the air.

"Damn you," swore the cavalier, looking down at the blade buried in his thigh. From the gush of blood it was clear the femoral artery was severed. He reached for the mirrored wall beside him but fell suddenly backwards, landing in a stunned sitting position before he could escape again.

Sara drew her last knife. His eyes found hers and he shook his head.

"Nay, lady. I am done. Save your blade."

He stared down at the blood pooling around him. It was dark red, so dark as to almost match his teeth, and it seemed thicker than normal blood.

He reached a hand into it and pulled it out, looking with a kind of dumbfounded fascination at the viscous strands that remained attached, like half-set glue. He shook his head again.

"The fault was mine. I had not thought so fair a flower would conceal such ruthlessly sharp thorns. But come closer, for my strength is failing and there is something I must tell you . . ."

Sara kept her distance, conscious that he had not let go of the obsidian dagger.

"Well," he sighed disappointedly. "I should have killed you straight away."

Sara nodded.

"It would have been better for you," she agreed.

"I always had a weakness for the handsome ones," he said. "So fair thou seemed . . ."

He smiled a terrible black-toothed grimace at her.

". . . so fell thou wert. And so fell I, never to rise . . . etcetera, etcetera. You have quite killed my capacity to epigrammatise, I fear . . ."

He made a tired, flowery gesture with his hand and something sly seemed to shrug in resignation behind his eyes.

"I took you to be a lady . . ."

He dropped the knife into the pool of blackening gore surrounding his legs like treacle. Sara just watched, hard-eyed, as he began to cough gobbets of blackness onto the front of his waistcoat. He pulled off his wig and ran a tired hand up over his eyes and across the cropped white stubble of his skull.

". . . but you took us for a pair of fools. And poor Ned the Bowman didn't even like wenches . . ."

Sara looked down at him and showed him the rings on her finger.

"As I said, we are The Oversight. We do not get to be The Oversight by being unprepared. Or untrained. Or unwilling to shed blood."

He looked down at the blackness surrounding his splayed legs. It might have been a trick of the light but she noticed one thing that was certainly true and another that may have been her imagination. The certain thing was that the black pool of blood did not overlap more than the mirrored rectangle he sat in. It filled right up to the straight edges but did not overspill to the next mirror. And the second thing was that he appeared to be sinking slightly.

"You would not shed blood so carelessly if you heeded my words," he said.

"No," she said. "If I heeded your prattle I would be dead or dying."

"I just wanted a little blood," he sighed. "Just the Blood Toll."

"You had plenty of your own," she said. "Look at it all."

"You are hard," he croaked.

"Thank you," she said, and walked back down the mirrors to retrieve her knives, keeping an eye on him as he coughed and twitched, and then, as she took her eye off him just for a moment while she bent to retrieve the last one, he jerked and disappeared.

Or rather, what she thought she saw was something black rear up and engulf him, before dragging him down into the floor. It was a thing whose shape her mind was unable to let her eyes make sense of. The infinite "wrongness" of it was somehow much too large for the space it momentarily invaded, and it juddered distressingly in and out of vision, both there and not there at the same time, as if it could not keep its purchase on the "here" and kept being tugged back into a "there" it was trying to escape from. She was halfway to telling herself that she had imagined it when her body rebelled at what she had seen and she had to control an impulse to retch, as if the thing had left a psychic stench or stain behind it, having tainted this world just by shuddering in and out of it for a mere moment.

All that was left was a black mirror with the obsidian dagger resting on it.

When she turned to look at the dead bowman, she found the second Mirror Wight had also disappeared. All that remained was his bow and a scrabble of arrows which had fallen out of his quiver as he himself had dropped to the ground. The mirror he had sprawled on, and more significantly bled on, was now black, as black as the obsidian dagger, as black as the arrow tips she knelt slowly to gather up. It was so black that she realised she was making a point of not looking directly at it, in the way that at the other end of the scale of brightness you did not look directly at the sun.

She looked at the arrows in her hand, and the bow at her feet. After a moment she put them down in a neat pile.

Having more weapons was theoretically a good idea, but she knew having a weapon she had no expertise with was going to be more of a problem than a help. False confidence could be fatal.

She walked back to the spot where the cavalier had disappeared. Another black mirror had replaced the silvered one that had been there, like a missing tooth in a perfect smile. The stone dagger sat on the surface, almost invisibly blending in when viewed from on top. Something made her not want to reach for it, so she went back and picked up the bow and used it to snag the obsidian blade and drag it within reach, off the jet-black rectangle. It felt ice-cold in her gloved hand, and she was about to drop it when it warmed, almost fast enough to make her think she had imagined it. It was unexpectedly heavy yet it did not feel cumbersome. She stuck it in her belt. True, she had never touched a blade like it other than the ancient stone knife that The Smith kept in his workshop, but a blade was a blade, and she was comfortable with it in a way that she wasn't with the bow, which she skittered back across the glass to rest with the arrows.

Then, because she had always made it a point of honour to face things that scared her, she tried to look down into the black mirror. For a moment she saw her own reflection, but something seemed to swim in the depths beneath it which was impossible of course since the black was perfect and unrelieved. Nevertheless she felt the urge to retch again and look away, and so she did, not least because she had the distressingly rank feeling something polluted was looking back out at her.

She knew she was going to hate crossing the mirror, so she took a run up and jumped it. She felt relief on landing safely on the other side, but found herself looking quickly back to make sure the surface was still glassy and not writhing up and reaching after her.

The Raven hovered over the black mirror and peered down at it, its sable feathers and hard, shiny eyes matching the darkness beneath. It did not blink, and it did not hurry. Instead it released another prodigious squitter of bird's mess that splattered contemptuously across the window, partially obliterating the darkness beyond, before flapping unconcernedly after Sara.

She grinned.

"Tough bird, aren't you?" she said with something dangerously close to affection.

The Raven landed on her shoulder and clacked its beak.

"Thank you," said Sara. "From you, that's a compliment . . ."

It was only then that she noticed something had changed beneath her feet. She could no longer feel Sharp's trail resonating beneath them.

In fact she could feel nothing.

It was as if no one had ever passed down this passage before.

Either the black mirror had cut the flow and erased all trace of what had gone before, or Sharp had taken a turn she had missed. It took backtracking across the two black mirrors a couple of heart-stopping times to confirm what she feared. The trail remained strong up until the first black mirror, which sheared it cleanly off.

She had lost the trail, eradicating it with her acts of violence. Either that or, even worse, Sharp had made a turn into one of the mirrors that had turned black with the Mirror Wight's blood.

Everything – the trail, Sharp – and Sara herself – was lost.

CHAPTER 12

GHOST BY DAYLIGHT

Amos had washed the blood off in the chalk stream running through the water meadow as they had hurried from the Andover Workhouse, but days later he was still tainted by the feel of it, as if his hands were still sticky and besmirched. He had not left the madwoman yet, though he had the strong feeling he should do so before too long.

The trouble was that she knew things about him that he wished to understand better, and was able to talk directly to his mind, and he back to her: for the first time in his life his muteness was no obstacle and the speed of conversation was exhilarating enough in itself for someone who had previously had to communicate in writing or by dumb show. The things she was able to talk to him about were what really hooked him though, he knew that. She knew about his gifts, and though he resented her for calling him the Bloody Boy and then having so gleefully enjoyed the way her gory prophecy had come true, the glimpse of the world she had revealed to him was addictive.

He knew he ought to leave her soon because there was a malignity and a danger hanging about her like a fizz in the air, but before they parted he wanted to learn as much as he could of what she had to teach him. And so as they walked they talked, though more often there were no audible words since they thought to each other, or occasionally, when she was tired of thinking her side of the conversation, there were only words on her side, which made her seem all the madder to any of the few people they passed on the way.

Amos had returned to his habit of keeping off the better travelled roads and where possible took to the woods and the downland, following the old drovers' paths. He had to hold her elbow as they walked because she was tiring fast. Indeed if she became any more exhausted he knew he would have to carry her or leave her. And the trouble with leaving her somewhere out of the way was that he was certain she would die, and then her blood too would be on his hands. And so, having begun the journey, he steeled himself to its completion, as much in defiance of her certainty that he was the Bloody Boy as out of any instinctive kindness.

She had said they should walk to the sea. He didn't know where the sea was, and neither did she, but he decided that if they followed the general flow of the rivers and kept on a southerly bearing, they would get there soon enough.

The other reason they kept off the more heavily travelled roads was in case a hue and cry had been raised on discovery of the gory events at Andover, but in truth there was no need for caution: the discovery of the dead husband and wife, the one with the self-administered gunshot wound and the other with the distinctive bruising of a domestic beating, had persuaded the local magistrate that M'Gregor, after a long and provoking marriage to an admitted termagant and virago, had finally snapped. He had clearly beaten his wife and then, consumed by an excess of remorse at her death, intended or accidental, taken his own life. Messy, it was agreed, but conveniently neat.

The disappearance of the Ghost of the Itch Ward was not connected with the events at all. Her absence was almost unremarked by the under-wardens, who decided she must have wandered off in the uproar that had followed the discovery of the M'Gregors' bodies. Her demise had been long anticipated, her affectless demeanour being consistent with other inmates who had turned their faces to the wall and faded away, the only difference being that, face to the wall or no, she had inexplicably and somewhat provokingly remained. Somehow she had escaped the Eel House and wandered off. No one asked after her, she had no family and after a while the under-wardens, already a little unwilling to admit they had been in the habit of disciplining a frail old charge by locking her in the dank building overnight, marked her as "deceased" and forgot her.

So the only things that actually pursued the Ghost and Amos were the memories of the blood dripping from the ceiling and Amos's sense he had made some avoidable and fatal mistake which had led to the carnage, an error whose precise shape he could not quite clearly ascertain.

They were not uncomfortable as they travelled, the Ghost having taken Mrs M'Gregor's best weatherproof cloak from the closet when they left, and he had blankets and an oilskin in the tinker's pack he was already travelling with. And they had the contents of the chest Mrs M'Gregor had used to store up her stolen goods. As noted, it was not a king's ransom, but neither of them was used to a regal lifestyle, and it was more than enough to buy food and milk and suchlike from the occasional farms or hamlets they allowed themselves to visit on their way across the countryside.

At night they would find a dry spot in the woodland and Amos would make a fire, and though he always wanted to ask her more questions, the tiredness that attended their day-long walks usually only allowed a brief moment of unguarded calm while he heated some food before they'd both wrap themselves up and let the warmth of the crackling flames lull them quickly to sleep. And then dawn would wake them once more, stiff and cold, backs to the now extinguished fire.

There was something in the relish with which she called him the Bloody Boy that fascinated him horribly: she had been impressed by what he had done to M'Gregor's mind, and as surprised at it as he had been. She had also been deeply disappointed at her own inability to effect an escape from the dead end via the mirrors, a trick she claimed once to have thought no more of than stepping through a normal doorway. He would have been able to dismiss her claims as delusions, were it not for his inability to discount the truths she told him about his past, truths that were linked by the thing that gave him his unwelcome nickname: blood.

I have been mad a long time, she admitted on the second night, as he stirred an improvised pease porridge in one of the tinker's battered pannikins over a fragrant beechwood fire beneath the vaulting branches of an old oak. *I was wronged and pursued and after much torment and anguish, deposited by my persecutor at the door of the Andover Workhouse. I was in such a reduced state, physically and mentally that they thought I would die within the month. I certainly believe that was the plan: that I should die legally, defensibly but largely unremarked. They had taken from me what was most valuable, most precious, most loved. My children were torn from me. You will not know this, but the love a mother has for her children winds its roots tight around the heart. And I loved them both, though some might have thought I had reason to love the one less than the other since she came unbidden, and the seed from which she sprung was not of my choosing or consent. Nevertheless the love took root, deep and firm, twined around the core of me, unbreakable, that affection as much a part of my life as when the children had been when I carried them within my belly, buttressed from the unkind shocks of the outer world by my flesh and fed by my blood.*

And then they were taken, or rather I was taken from them.

What happened to them I do not know. It was long ago and a pall of unreason hangs between me and then. But I felt them snatched from me, and the wounds of that savagery have never healed and smart just as sharply now as they did half a lifetime ago. And like a sentry who puts a sharp stone in his boot so as not to fall asleep through too much comfort, that pain has stopped me slipping away into oblivion. I spent years in a fog, and in that fog only two things allowed me to endure. The first was a determination to be avenged. And the second was the lingering vestige of a trick I once had the way of. It is a trick of which I was almost as summarily and completely dispossessed of as I was of the little lost ones ripped away from me, but I retained one aspect of it, and that was the blood link. And it was the blood link that brought you to me, whether you credit it or not.

Her eyes had sparkled as she spoke of the trick and the "blood link", and he had understandably pressed her on it, but she had turned away from the fire and gone to sleep, holding her secret close to her as she did so, curled round it like a miser in the dark.

She told him the same story the next morning, as if unaware she had spoken of it the night before, and then the following afternoon as they had walked up a long downland slope, open to a warm and cleansing wind that scoured over the sheep-cropped grass and smelled, he realised when they reached the crest and saw the distant flash of water far below, of the sea.

Seeing the Channel raised her spirits, but she did not hurry forward. Instead she sat and looked out at the immensity stretching to the horizon ahead. It was a sun-deckled expanse of water over which the shadows of the clouds moved like the passing silhouettes of sky-bound leviathans.

However much I could travel in my head, she said, *I could never achieve something as nourishing to the soul as this. To walk hard, to tame a relentless slope with all its false horizons, and then to gain such a breathtaking expanse of the world by the action of aching leg muscles, that is something I could never do. Oh, I remember this, when I was free and wild and my body was vigorous and the world was my joy! Oh, I have missed this . . . !*

And he heard a strange noise, so strange that he thought someone must have crept up on them, for it was the sound of laughter, a young woman's laughter. And once he had looked wildly around to find whoever it might be and ascertained that they were, as he had thought, alone, he focused on her face and saw it was she who was laughing, her eyes shining and tears streaking down her cheeks.

He looked away before she caught him looking, and left her to it. He listened to the wind nickering past as he watched two distant boats plough past each other close to the horizon, one under full sail, its white canvas brightly reflecting the sunlight, the other a thin, funnelled steam packet streaking the air behind it with a grimy smudge as it passed. Not speaking was the right thing to do, because she eventually filled the silence in his head.

I could travel outside my body. With my mind. When I was small I thought it was a kind of waking dream or an act of the imagination. I even worried then that I might be a little mad, little knowing that later in life I would taste the bitter reality of true madness. I was found out by one who knew all about such things, and was told that there was a kind of blood, supranatural blood, that runs strong in some people and gives them abilities that once were much more common than they are now. And so I was trained in this ability to travel in my head. And it was glorious and exhilarating, because once I realised that what I saw was real, and more, that I could control how and where I went to see it, the world became vast to me. To be able to do this was tiring, and so I did not do it all the time, but at night, knowing there were long hours of bedrest ahead of me, I would go. And the things and the people I saw were as much an education as the books my father bombarded me with.

She paused and he thought she was going to stop talking of this, but she asked for water, which he gave her, and then she continued.

Those ships out there on the trackless sea, they navigate by compass and stars, using charts and sextants and all manner of devices to get from port to port. When you travel the wide world beyond your body, travelling with your mind, you also need to keep bearings. Otherwise you cannot control where you go, although you can always return home to your head, however lost you may be, since there is a chain of belonging that will snap you back like a stretched spring, because the self likes its home more than it does the outer wilds. So to keep bearings you develop waymarkers, milestones of the mind. These can be events or people or places, sometimes all three. Do you understand?

He didn't, not fully, but he nodded, not wanting to break the flow of her explanation.

"Ha," she said out loud, as if reading his thoughts. "Well, when I was separated from my children and my things and the other objects that kept me moored in place, then all those waymarkers were swept from me. It was as if I lost the map of the world, and could no longer travel in my mind, beyond myself. So that was added to the total of all that I had lost. And then one day, one cold winter's day when the M'Gregors had grudgingly allowed that a fire might be lit in the women's dayroom in order that we might not freeze to death and thus bring the workhouse into disrepute, I fell off my stool as the under-wardens brushed past with a begrudged basket of sea-coal. And I cut my head. And the knock and the blood wakened something within me, and I found I had one shard of a waymarker left inside my brain, buried like a long-forgotten splinter. And that waymarker gave me two things, Bloody Boy. It gave me a way to walk beyond my body again, and in time, it gave me you."

He looked at her. Their eyes met. And she nodded with a kind of savage glee.

You didn't know that, did you? That I called you?

He shook his head. Not only did he not know that, he didn't believe her. This was another of her imaginings. Like walking behind the world in the mirrors.

You know my waymarker? The one that stayed with me?

No.

You don't believe me, do you?

I believe you believe it.

Her eyes remained locked on his.

A bloody thing happened to me once. A bad thing. It happened in sunlight, in a field. The blood was part of the waymarker, part of what imprinted it in my mind. That and the persecutor and the place. And that's where I found you.

His throat was unaccountably dry. He took a swig from the tin flask he had shared with her. The water tasted sour, or maybe he was him tasting his own mouth, his own rising fear at what she was clearly so eager to have him believe.

You are scared.

I am not.

You feel you are standing on the edge of a great abyss, a chasm that is hidden from you by a curtain. You think as long as you do not see the abyss you will be free from the impulse it exerts, the horrible tug that will unmoor you and make you liable to cast yourself into it.

I don't feel anything like that, he lied.

Then ask where the place is.

He couldn't. He did not want to think that his passage across the country, the seemingly random journey that had ended at the Eel House and the carnage in the M'Gregor's closet had been destined. Most of all, he had the horrible certainty that the place was the canalside where he had bloodied the murderous tinker's head with his own frying pan as he killed him. He did not want to talk of it, or have her rootle around in whatever memories of the manslaughter he was suppressing. Perhaps the tinker was the persecutor who had wronged her in the sunshine. He tried to remember how old the tinker had been, to work out if the ages coincided or made this conjecture an impossibility. He realised the tinker had been one of those weather-beaten men of indeterminate age who might have been anywhere between forty and sixty. It was all too possible, and all too terrible that she might know of this, that she might in some measure have been responsible for it . . .

I believe you. You don't need to prove it.

He didn't want to touch on the tinker's death. She smiled at him. He realised with an inexorable dread that she was going to tell him anyway.

Bowland's Gibbet.

His mind blanked. He knew the name, but could not, for an instant, remember where it was. It was not the canalside. It was—

She reached for his hand. It was so unexpectedly personal and gentle a gesture that he found he had put his in hers before thinking not to. She traced a small scar, the one that Mountfellon had given him.

"Bowland's Gibbet," she said. "At the gates to Gallstaine Hall. You were cut by him in a thunderstorm, in his coach. He is easy and liberal with others' pain. That was the blood. That was the place. That was the persecutor. I saw you at my waymarker and I saw you bled, and I stayed with you. I showed you the Shadowgangers waiting to take you from the back of the coach, and I pointed your feet towards the running water that they could not follow you over as you ran. And then I found you at the canalside and called you to me across all the lost and lonely miles. I brought you to the Eel House. I brought you here."

He retrieved his hand and looked at the scar.

Why?

She stood and stretched and began walking downhill, towards the distant shore below.

Because you can help.

He stumbled to his feet, shouldered his pack and clattered after her. His thoughts were unexpectedly panicked and almost incoherent. He shaped a question for her.

Why?

She didn't stop or turn, but seemed to pick up speed with every step. Her answer came through like an exultant shout.

Because Mountfellon must die!

CHAPTER 13

PLAYING WITH FIRE

Charlie and Lucy's education swiftly fell into a routine. Charlie would go out with Hodge and patrol the deepest and darkest extremities of the Tower, prosecuting the unending war on rats. Lucy would spend that morning time with The Smith; it was not initially clear to her what she was supposed to be learning, but he gave her small tasks about the workshop, not domestic things like cleaning or sweeping which he took care of himself, but other practical things like stacking wood, or sorting through jumbled drawers and boxes, or just holding things for him as he worked on them. And as they worked alongside each other she realised he was actually telling her important things about The Oversight and the realities of the strange world being opened up to her, but without lecturing. It was almost as if by doing something manual together, he was allowing the top layer of her consciousness to calm down and ingest facts without noticing, in a way it might not have done had she been tensely receiving a more formal lesson. When she mentioned this to Charlie, he admitted that Hodge had been following the same process of education-by-misdirection with him as they ratted, but that he had not been sharp enough to notice it.

"Haven't got your brains, see, Lucy Harker," he grinned.

She was also bright enough to know this wasn't true. What it was was that Charlie had grown up with a different kind of brains, within a family and an exotic but regular world that required certain ways of thinking. She'd been looking after herself for much longer, without the buttressing of a family to watch over her too. She envied him of course, but she also valued her own independent cast of mind. It might make her seem overly suspicious of others, but she couldn't see that as a bad thing. And because her mind was shaped to respond in such a way, she began to also suspect that The Smith was drawing parts of her story from her in the most subtle and seemingly accidental of interrogations. And that just put her on her guard again.

The Smith remained an unsettling enigma to her: he was gruff and kind enough, and he could even on occasion surprise her into laughter, but he also had a darkness in him that made her never quite comfortable. It was like the tension she remembered from the great bull on Sylvie and Antoine's farm all those years ago – a feeling that the normally docile nature of the huge beast could snap at any minute and then the fury and power of its brute strength would turn it into an unstoppable destructive force. The sense she got from him was like that of a thunderhead which might look its most beautiful in a sunlit sky just before it blotted out that same sun and unleashed the titanic storm within.

She would discuss this with Charlie, whom she trusted as much as she trusted anyone, in the afternoons when they were together being taught by Hodge and Cook. Again these afternoons didn't seem quite like any lessons she expected, but would take the form of "Go to Goodbehere's shop and get such-and-such, then go to Eschalaz's in Wapping and fetch some Smyrna Figs – oh, and on the way, see if you see anything unusual that might be of interest to us". Or again "Go to Josiah Blam's pie shop and fetch a tuppenny belly-buster – but don't touch ground except in Cable Street, and try not to be seen as you go. Or fall off anything too high". Or again "Go to the West India Docks and give dock master Mashiter my respects and ask him when the next ship on the China trade is due to up anchor – and see how many times you see Hodge on the way". In this way, the city was made both a playground and a schoolroom

for them, and they began to know their way around its streets and its
rooftops too.

Another danger occurred to Lucy as Emmet was driving her back to
the Isle of Dogs one late evening after a full day and a bracingly good
pie supper which Cook had made for them all. (Cook never allowed
them to eat the belly-busters they were sent for, declaring them inferior
things filled with questionable meat, and gave them to Jed instead, who
had no such qualms.) This other danger was simply that she was enjoying
herself. She was liking people. Especially Charlie and Cook. Liking people,
in the way Lucy's mind worked, was undoubtedly weakness, not because
you lowered your guard with them, but because it opened up a softness
that time or ill-wishers would inevitably exploit.

So between her naturally suspicious bent, her mistrust of liking people
and her reflexive aversion towards being told what to do or not to do,
it was not surprising that when The Smith told her not to touch something in the workshop, her fingers immediately itched with the desire
to do so.

She had been looking at the tools spread around the bewilderingly
crowded room as she waited for the battered black kettle to boil on the
forge fire, and had reached for what was, he had told her, the oldest tool
in the place. It sat on a shelf just above the modern brass-rosetted
complexity of the Holtzapffel Rose Engine, and it was such an unrelieved
black that it seemed to suck light into itself.

She lifted it carefully, surprised at its weight which was more like lead
than stone. And even though she was wearing her thin leather gloves,
she sensed a tiny shudder in the black stone, as if there was a power in
it longing to escape.

"Ah," said The Smith from behind her. He didn't tell her to put it
down, or forbid her to examine it or anything like that. He just said,
"Ah."

She looked up at him.

"It's very heavy," she said.

"You have no idea," he said. He was smiling but his eyes were elsewhere for a moment. "Sometimes I think it's the heaviest thing in the world."

And then his eyes returned from a long way off and his smile tightened a little.

"I think it would be really good if you were to remember not to touch that particular tool without your gloves on," he said. "By which I mean that not only is that a stone you might not enjoy glinting, but the force of the past stacked up in the obsidian might be permanently damaging to any Glint who unwittingly channelled it."

And then his smile came back to full strength.

"Touch it with gloves, examine it all you will. And if you ever see a similar weapon? Leave the place you see it and come and tell me immediately, without delay, even if it means leaving something you think is more important undone."

She looked at the knife and the way the black stone seemed to hungrily suck light into itself, and then she put it carefully back where she had found it.

"Mind your fingers," said The Smith.

She withdrew them sharply as the knife swivelled like a compass needle answering to a magnetic pull.

The Smith pointed to the glowing coals at the centre of the forge.

"And the other thing about it is that it always points towards Wildfire if close enough," he said.

"I thought that was in the Safe House," she said. They'd been shown the inextinguishable candle at the centre of the scrubbed pine table in Cook's kitchen.

"That's the original flame," he said. "But there's some in everything it kindles. Cook's range has some in its coals, this forge has some in it – and then again, so do I."

He picked up a candle from the workbench and tossed it to her. He snapped his fingers as it was in mid-flight and it ignited, landing in her hand with a full flame engulfing the wick.

"See you started without us," said Hodge from the doorway. Jed was at his feet, wagging his tail, eyes bright. Charlie appeared at his shoulder.

"What?" said Lucy.

"They're going to teach us how to make light," said Charlie with a grin. "Since I seem to spend half the day in the dark, it seemed like a good idea."

"Controlling the Wildfire is always a good idea," said The Smith. "Come and put these on."

He produced a pair of bracelets made from five twigs plaited together, like miniature versions of the wreath surrounding the candle in the Safe House. The Smith took the candle from her grasp and slid one over her wrist.

"Good," he said. "Now take off your glove."

Charlie, with no glove to slow him up, went first. Lucy watched as The Smith held the candle out to him.

"Close your hand slowly around the flame," he said. "Don't flinch. Whatever you do, don't flinch at all, and keep it steady. You're going to crush the flame."

Lucy watched him do so.

"Ouch," he said, looking accusingly at Hodge. "I thought the brace-lets were protection."

"You're not on fire, are you?" said Hodge.

"No," said Charlie. "But my hand hurts. A lot."

"That's the fire gone into you. Wouldn't do so if you didn't have the blood," said The Smith. "All members of The Oversight have to do this. It's useful."

"And it's a way of making sure you're made of the right stuff," added Hodge.

"Light the candle," said The Smith. "Then it's Miss Harker's turn."

Lucy had peeled her glove back but, having seen the sweat break out on Charlie's face, was in no hurry to follow his example.

Charlie took a step towards the forge. The Smith's hand stopped him.

"By yourself," he said. "Wildfire's in you. Just let it out."

"How?" said Charlie.

"Feel it, think it, kindle it," said Hodge.

"Just make it so," said The Smith. "There's no trick to it really, though some like to snap their fingers, or snap their wrists to trigger it. Some find it makes them sneeze a bit to start with."

As it turned out, Charlie was a good sneezer but not, despite his initial enthusiasm, a natural kindler. Lucy, on the other hand, was immediately able to light a candle every second or third try. Greatly to Charlie's chagrin, she had lit the candle a score of times before he produced a single sputtering ignition.

"Try it like this," said The Smith after a lot more failed attempts. "Think of the fire being there all the time. In you. It's about you – it's your fire now: it's nothing to do with the candle – candle's just a convenience to hold your fire."

In the end what solved it for Charlie was a game. He and Lucy were set up in a corner of the workshop with a half dozen candles each. The first to light all their candles won, and the one who won the most games by the time the sausages which Hodge and Charlie had brought with them were cooked would get supper, and the other would get the leftover bread from breakfast.

Lucy kept winning, but Charlie began to catch up as the forge filled with the sizzle and smell of frying saveloy, and by the time the food was ready he was almost as fast as her.

"Almost," said The Smith, "but not quite."

Charlie watched in rising horror as the sausages were divided into three plates, and he was passed the fourth, containing no more than a heel of stale bread.

"We're The Oversight," said Hodge. "We don't get prizes for coming second."

"But—" said Charlie.

"But nothing," said Lucy, biting into her first sausage. "We just learned how to make fire, Charlie! And you're whining about a few sausages?"

He stared at her. She grinned at him. She knew she'd share her sausages in a minute, but was enjoying having won something for a change. A little teasing wouldn't do him any harm.

She lifted the sausage to her mouth. It caught fire, singing her nose. She dropped it on the floor with a gasp. Charlie's face split in a wide grin of its own as Jed pounced on the windfall and ate it in two bites.

"I see it's not just candles we can light," he said. "I reckon we could have some fun with that . . ."

"Charlie Pyefinch!" said The Smith, sounding harsh but inexpertly hiding a smile. "Control yourself! There's enough chance of harm out there in the dark without us injuring each other!"

CHAPTER 14

ABCHURCH'S APPLE

Coram Templebane was determined to repair his fortunes and achieve the previously unimagined promotion to become his extant father's deputy. He had a shrewd and realistic view of the competition, and though his "brothers" were all in their own way resourceful and ruthless, he was only really worried about Pountney and Abchurch providing any serious competition. Both were naturally clever with wide, retentive memories; each was cunning and neither would have any scruples about doing the other or Coram down at the very first opportunity.

The other brothers were dangerous in certain circumstances – physically stronger, more vicious and so on – but Coram was not especially worried about anyone he could outthink. He moved quickly and decisively following the funeral breakfast, and after Coram had made an unobserved visit to a pill-grinder in an apothecary shop just off Bleeding Hart Lane, Pountney was taken gravely ill with an indelicate, persistent and debilitating complaint that the local physician called a Galloping Black Flux, and which the other brothers called Shitting Himself to Death. Pountney's illness followed so closely on the heels of the unprecedented gorging that had attended Zebulon's testimonial meal that it was ascribed to overindulgence in previously unencountered rich foods. Coram, knowing that Issachar was probably just as clear in his assessment of which three sons were the frontrunners in the race to be his deputy, did not dose Abchurch since the removal of his two competitors by identical means could only implicate him as the *fons et origo* of their discomfiture. And he was unsure as to how Issachar would react to having a poisoner in his house: poison was a very particular kind of threat, and one that people – even ruthless people – had qualms about. Issachar himself might feel unduly threatened if he had to suspect every mouthful he ate.

Coram was presently occupying a bench outside the sugar refinery on Wellclose Square. He had been watching the Safe House since dawn, taking turns with a rotating roster of his brothers, two of whom were even now watching the rear door and the discreet river gate beyond. It was a pleasant place to sit, and favoured by the neighbourhood as such, since the caramel smell of the sugar boiling in the giant vats within the manufactory wafted over it in a warm miasma. For Coram, however, this smell was not pleasant, and he was quite looking forward to being relieved from his watch. When he had been small, before being taken into the protection of the foundling hospital at Coram's Fields, from which he derived his name, he had witnessed a disaster at a sugar baker's. In fact it had been the same disaster that had orphaned him, since his parents had both worked in the place, and he had been being babysat at a neighbour's rooms close by. He had little exact memory about it other than a great alarm raised across the parish, the night being lit by a roaring inferno and, most memorable of all, as he was carried away on the shoulder of the fleeing neighbour, he had looked down and seen streams of burning sugar, molten like lava, running along the road behind them. Twelve people had died in the fire, eight buildings including a church had burnt or been so badly damaged they had to be demolished, and Coram had been deposited in the care of the orphanage before the burning lake of sugar had cooled enough for the rescuers to remove – with picks and crowbars – the bodies of his family and their co-workers. As a result, he had what his brothers considered to be an irrational dislike of toffee apples and a lifelong aversion to the smell of burnt sugar.

He was thinking of this when Abchurch appeared at his shoulder with the alarming news that "Poor ol' Pountney's squittering nuffink but blood now". Coram grimaced sympathetically and made room on the bench.

"Can't fink how Pounters is going to see out the week if he goes on like this," said Abchurch, choosing to remain standing. "It's a wery wicious flux as 'as got him in its grip and no mistake."

He squinted down the long cobbled slope towards the Safe House and rummaged in a brown paper bag of apples he had obviously purchased on the way over. Abchurch squinted at everything since his eyes worked independently of each other, the legacy of untreated childhood strabismus ensuring they were always out of step. This, taken in tandem with his lisp, part affected, part natural, made some less perspicacious people think he was not as bright as he actually was.

"Poor ol' Pounters, eh?" he repeated. "Can't fink how he can 'ave got taken so low, and all the rest of us right as trivets. Pippin?"

He rummaged in the bag and hooked out a shiny apple which he offered Coram. Despite or maybe because of him accompanying this invitation with as innocent and engaging a smile as a boss-eyed young man with little chin could muster, Coram declined.

"You have it," he said. "I'm not in the mood for apples."

Abchurch looked at the apple. Coram watched him with hidden amusement from the corner of his eye, interested to see if he would bite into it. A horse trotted round the corner pulling a milk cart, wheels trundling noisily on the granite setts. Abchurch flinched at the noise and stepped back.

"Oh blast," he said.

The apple bounced on the pavement and then rolled into the road. It bobbled away on the cobbles, gathering speed as gravity pulled it down the incline. Halfway towards the Safe House, the camber on the road on that side of the square had pulled it into the gutter where it accelerated until it met the angle at the corner of the square and bounced over the lip of the pavement, rolling across the paving stones and disappearing into the area in front of the Safe House.

"Blast," repeated Abchurch. "What a waste of a werry good Pippin."

Coram stood, hiding his amusement. Perhaps it was all an accident. But either way, Abchurch's apple had just given him the germ of an idea.

"Don't worry, old son. Nothing's ever truly wasted," he said, clapping his skew-eyed rival on the shoulder. "Not if you look at it straight."

He allowed his smile to appear once he was safely round the corner. He would cloak it again once he reached his father because it never did to let on that one was pleased with oneself in front of Issachar, but in his heart he knew he had a plan for them that would not only confound his rivals, but would put an end to The Oversight once and for all, with never a clue as to who or what had been behind it other than mere accident and unfortunate topography.

SECOND PART
THE DEATH OF AIR

On Solitary Agents

It is not only the Free Companies who police the border between the canny and the uncanny. There are some who do not avail themselves of the benefits of shared endeavour, and prefer to act independently in the pursuit of balance and protection. Their motives are often the same as those in The Oversight, or The Remnant of the Americas, or the French Paladin, but equally they are sometimes acting for mere personal enrichment as an unlicensed thief-taker might. They are known as *seeker*, or *venator* (from the Latin for "hunter") or, if female, *venatrix*.

The venatrix operates as a local wise woman might, except with a roving disposition. Strong and independent women with natural and supranatural blood in their veins have made an unconventional and self-supporting life for themselves on the fringes of more normally patriarchal communities by using their gifts as healers or seers, providing valuable succour, support and protection in exchange for food, services or money. The venatrix, however, works beyond the confines of a single community. Often ills are visited on one location by malign forces that then move on beyond the ambit of the local protectress, if the neighbourhood is lucky to have one. The venatrix undertakes to hunt the perpetrators down and to do whatever they can to ensure restitution is made. They do not like the constraint of the Free Companies for obvious reasons, in that the unpaid provision of the services they charge for is a serious impediment to their well-being. As a result they are more likely to operate in remote rural areas, and are almost never seen in heavily populated areas like London itself.

from *The Great and Hidden History of the World*
by the Rabbi Dr Hayyim Samuel Falk (also known as the Ba'al Shem of
London)

CHAPTER 15

THE CHANGE

There are as many ways to steal a child as there are children, but there is only one way to do so and be absolutely undetected, and the young woman on the edge of Upper Rathbone Place had the trick of it. She stood in the lee of a mews house, her eyes fixed on the lights on the back of the tall building that overhung it.

She knew which of the windows were bedrooms, and indeed she knew who bedded whom behind the topmost window, the small one below the eaves, where the servants lived. She knew the room below it was the child's room, the night nursery. She knew the night nurse and the father of the house had an assignation every Thursday night in the room above. And it was Thursday. The little bundle in her own arms shifted and gurgled, and she stroked it calmingly, without taking her eyes off the story the lights were telling her in case she missed the opportunity for which she was waiting.

The father of the house was a medical man. The night nurse was an accommodating young Irishwoman from Skibbereen with a tight waist, a high bust and a dangerous twinkle in her eye. The woman in the shadows knew the twinkle was dangerous because she had put it there, or if not precisely applied a twinkle where none had previously existed, she had looked into the eyes of the medical gentleman and left him with the impression that this was so. She had that skill too, as well as the secret of stealing children undetected: she could suggest things to people without them remembering she had done so. She could do this and then make them forget they had ever even met, let alone been worked on by her. She had done this often, through many bodies but only one unconscionably long life. She was a changeling.

She was also a watcher in the shadows, and while she watched undetected, she planned. She knew the medical gentleman was in the habit of administering a calming draught of his own concoction to still the jangled nerves of his wife. The wife's nerves had, the wife herself felt, been particularly set on edge by the discordant and messy business of childbirth, but the truth is that she had always been of a highly strung – not to say delicate – disposition, and had she not been an heiress, the medical man might not have been so keen to wed her. Bedding her was another thing altogether, and the procreative exertions had occasioned so many tears and so much silently exacted post-coital recrimination that he had subsequently made other arrangements for quenching that particular fire, arrangements involving the taut waist from Skibbereen.

The marital consummation had, however, had one other consequence, and it was that particular child that was the subject of the changeling's plans. She knew that on Thursday nights the medical gentleman increased the proportion of laudanum in the draught he prepared for his wife with the result that she slept early and deeply, rendering her unaware of the movements of her husband in the intervening hours as he made his way up the narrow back stair to the night nurse's bed. She heard neither suspicious creaks, nor the unattended noises of her child in the night nursery above her.

The husband and the high bust from Skibbereen were too mutually occupied to pay much attention to the intermittent grizzling of the infant in the room below them. And it was this gap in attention – partly cultivated by her own actions – that the changeling was waiting to take advantage of.

The light in the uppermost room dimmed. And with that the watcher moved. She flitted across the slick cobbles and swung herself up onto the roof of the mews house with startling ease, seeming to swarm up the wall without pausing to select handholds, and then she was nimbly running across the sloped tile roof before jumping to the narrow top of a garden wall that took her all the way to the back of the tall house. Reaching the looming cliff of brick, she stretched an arm up for the nearest window-ledge and scaled the façade with the fluid ease of a piece of smoke made flesh. In less than a minute she had transferred herself from the shadows in the alley to the window of the third-storey nursery, and then she ducked her head below the sash and disappeared inside.

The small child was chuntering unhappily in the cot, not quite exhausted enough to stop. The woman bent over him and placed a hand on his cheek. Despite the darkness, she could see a gleam as the infant eyes searched for hers and then, as they found them, the grizzling dwindled and then petered out.

The interloper made a low cooing noise, and the previously unhappy noises were replaced by a gentle gurgle of contentment. The changeling lifted him out of the cot and looked at his face in the shaft of moonlight lancing through the window behind her. It was a distinctive face, with a strong brow overhung by a tangle of short dark curls and a single mole just to the left of perfect rosebud lips.

She put the child on the floor and leant over the cot, pulling something out of the bundle tied close to her body which she tucked beneath the covers. Then she bent down, picked up the child from the carpet and in two steps had reached the window. An instant later she was gone without a backward look, and the room was silent, and only a very sharp pair of ears would have caught the only other noise which was the rustling and scraping that marked the child thief's descent back to the street.

Then there was a cough and a squeal. And though there was no one to see it, an identical child with rosebud lips and a mole began to wail in the cot.

In the room above, the father of the house was lying on top of the night nurse, his face buried in the crook of her neck, cushioned by the soft abundance of her red hair. He breathed in deeply, bewitched by the smell of her which was to him the clean salt-tang of the sea above the sweet smell of sun-warmed gorse that he remembered from his childhood long ago.

This, he knew, this is what drew him to her and though what they did was undoubtedly wrong, it felt right: it was in truth both beautifully, exhilaratingly wrong and badly and addictively right, because the flat stomach and the perfect skin beneath his hands felt and smelled like home. His hands circled her waist indecisively, as if unsure whether to venture upwards to the rising curve of her breast, or to slide downwards to find the tantalisingly forbidden warmth waiting to welcome him between her legs.

As his fingers made their own decision and headed south, the girl stiffened and raised her head from the pillow, ears cocked.

"Now did you hear that?"

He froze, groggy between guilt and frustration.

"What?"

He watched her listen, the clean cut of her jaw, the curve of her neck, the bright eyes softened by the grey-dark of the unlit room but still, to him, intoxicating.

"Nothing," she said and turned to him. "It was nothing."

Her smile was more than reassuring. It was, in that moment, everything to him. He could not tear his eyes from hers. He wanted to tumble into them, he wanted to lose himself, he wanted to be inside her, deep inside, hidden inside, safe-home inside, so deep that nothing could . . .

Her cool hand gently paused the urgent resumption his fingers had made on their downward journey.

"Now, mister, I think you're done . . ."

Momentary confusion ploughed a shallow furrow across his brow.

"But I . . ."

Her other hand came up to his face and just as gently smoothed the creases away.

"Arrah no, sure but you've had a lovely time, and are you not powerful sleepy now?" Her voice was naturally sweet and softened by the gentle accent of her native County Cork. "So you are, so drift away now, and all the naughty fun you'll be wanting of me will be had in your dreams and will seem quite as real to you when you wake as if we had done it anyway, so no one's the poorer, and I'll be a sight less discommoded . . ."

He smiled as he felt the warmth of her hand move to his waiting tumescence and closed his eyes in beatific anticipation. And then sank face forward into the pillows and began to snore.

The girl from Skibbereen neatly slipped out from beneath him as he descended, a smile on her face as she looked at the side of his head, the greying hair and the thick mutton-chop whiskers now wedged into her pillow. She turned his head so that he wasn't stifled, had one last look at his slumbering face and patted him on his back. There was no malice in the gesture; it seemed like a friendly farewell of sorts.

"No, no, there you go. Sleep like a baby, big strong man . . . I'm far too nasty for you anyway."

And with that she twisted out of the bed and headed for the door.

She entered the night nursery and crossed straight to the cot. She twitched back the covers. The child lay happily on its back, arms sprawled in the abandonment of sleep, one flung wide, the other curved behind its back, breathing easy through the distinctive rosebud mouth.

The night nurse reached down and pulled out the arm trapped beneath the child. She turned its wrist, as if expecting to find something there.

The child opened its eyes and looked at her, bleary with waking. The mouth began to twist into an unhappy grimace and it took a deep breath.

The gentle girl from Skibbereen slapped it, and slapped it hard.

"One keek out of you, you little monster, and I'll be after tying a brace of flat-irons round your neck and throwing you into the deep dark waters of the Fleet Ditch with the rest of the filth that flows through it."

The tears began to flow from the shocked child's eyes. It took another breath, face red with shock and indignation.

The girl slapped it again.

"Nary a squeak. I'm not joking. I'll do it. By the Lady Stone at Drombeg, you have my oath I'll do it, so I will. It's not like I haven't done it to your sort before."

The child became silent, lip quivering, little hands opening and closing in frustration. The night nurse picked the child up by the arm and calmly put it in the carpet bag.

"Not a single keek, boyo," she repeated as she quickly tied back her hair. Then she picked up the bag and quietly left the room.

The girl from Skibbereen walks calmly through the night streets. In one hand she swings the child-laden bag. In the other she holds something small that she rubs between her finger and thumb, like a pebble.

Whenever she comes to a junction or a cross-alley she pauses and closes her eyes, the only movement being the repetitive rolling of the pebble, which seems unconscious.

She doesn't stop long and when she does, on two occasions, men of dubious appearance emerge from doorways and ask if she is lost or requires help, offers which, given the late hour and the demeanour of the men, contain more promise of trouble than actual succour.

She doesn't speak to either of them, but the look she returns seems to satisfy something in each, and they leave her to pass on into the narrower streets of the city unharmed.

She finds the child thief in a basement room on the edge of a rookery in Endell Street. She stops in the narrow roadway and lifts her head as if sniffing the wind. And then she walks backwards a few paces and turns slowly, face blank, the hand rotating the pebble casting vaguely to right and left in a distinctive and almost hypnotic motion as if she was dowsing for something.

It is a thin house at the fork of two alleys that led past it on either side into the darker recesses of the rookery proper. It had once been painted white, but that was long ago, and presumably although it had also been built with the use of a try square and plumb-line, age had not only mottled and discoloured it, but had also combined forces with a local subsidence which had encouraged its ancient walls to belly and sway alarmingly out of true, so that it stood akimbo in the black maw of the rookery like a single tooth, crooked and rotten.

She found the rickety steps leading into the narrow and gloomy area in front of the basement. She stepped over the two drunks on the ground in front of the door and pushed inside.

It was a drinking den, but at this hour the tables were empty except for another pair of sleeping inebriates, and the child thief with the baby, sitting at a table in the corner, rocking it gently.

"Is that your baby?" said the girl from Skibbereen.

"It is," she answered without looking up.

"Well, he's a beauty and no mistake. How old is he?"

"He's young," she said.

"Young, is it?" smiled the night nurse. "And there's you no Methuselah either, to be sure."

The child thief continued rocking the baby.

"And how old are you?" said the night nurse, looking closely at her. "Why, you can't be more than fourteen or fifteen, though you're tall for your age."

"I'm old enough," said the girl, a hint of defiance creeping into her voice.

"Sure you are, *mavourneen*," said the night nurse. "And when the baby is grown, you'll be what – thirty and a bit and he'll be a strapping lusty lad of sixteen or so, is that the size of it?"

"I don't know what you mean," said the child thief, looking up at the smiling night nurse and seeing her properly for the first time. Her eyes widened in recognition.

"I'm Caitlin Sean ná Gaolaire. I'm from Skibbereen. My family call me Cait, but here's the thing of it: I have two things that you don't know I have. I have a straight razor just here, in my sleeve. And I have *your* family there, in the bag."

The girl's eyes slid around Cait, looking for an escape route.

"Now you can keep quiet as you like, but lie to me again and I'm as like to use that razor just so you can tell people the Cait really does have your tongue."

She paused, thinking.

"Mind you, you'd have to write to tell them, wouldn't you?" she mused. "But maybe that won't make the joke any less funny."

"How did you find me?" said the changeling.

"That would be telling," said Caitlin Sean ná Gaolaire. "Give me the child."

The girl kept hold of the bundle.

"You're thinking you still have a chance. You're trying to work out the play. But you see the thing is, the game's over. There was a trap. You fell in it."

"Who are you?"

"Law and Lore."

"You are The Oversight?" said the changeling, eyeing the door.

Caitlin threw back her head and laughed. One of the drunks woke and looked at her.

"Go back to sleep," she said looking right back at him. He closed his eyes and put his cheek back down into the warm pool of gin drool on the tabletop.

"I'm not a joiner. I work alone. I'm *fiagaí*."

"I don't know what that is—"

"I'm a hunter. I've tracked you all the way here."

The girl nodded slowly, her pallor increasing.

"You're a venatrix."

Caitlin shrugged her assent.

"Same rose, different name. I've been following your trail all the long winding way from Skibbereen," she said.

The girl swallowed thickly, as if she was resisting the urge to vomit.

"Skibbereen?"

"Arrah, surely you remember it: halfway between Ballydehoy and the Stones at Drombeg? It's the loveliest spot in all of County Cork, and Cork's a little green slice of heaven itself, if you believe in such things. I'm sure you remember it – faith, it's the place you stole the Factor's baby two summers ago."

The girl looked at her. Mouth slack.

"Carroty hair, not as dark as mine, lovely green eyes, scatter of freckles just where they should be and a birthmark shaped like the Heir Islands on the underside of her left upper arm, nothing big, but pale and distinctive. Where is she?"

"I don't know what you're talking—" began the girl, and then her eyes were caught by the flash of steel that Caitlin revealed by a seemingly unconscious flick of her wrist, the distinctive lever shape on the end of a bone-handled straight razor tucked snugly into her cuff.

"Your family is in the bag, changeling. You are free to leave, but if you do, I've already promised to drown him in the Fleet Ditch, along with the two flat-irons that are in the bag with him. But whatever you choose, you leave the true child here. I must have it back in its bed before it is missed."

"One thing," gulped the girl. "I don't understand this: I made the man of the house want you. I did it to make him drug the wife and be . . . distracted with you. I don't understand."

Caitlin Sean ná Gaolaire no longer looked soft and gentle as she shook her head sadly.

"I'm not here to give you a lesson, girl. I hunt. I remedy. Occasionally, if it feels right to me, I punish. But, to be quick, because the night is half over and there are things to be done, what you don't understand is that in any game the best thing to do is make your opponent make her mistakes for you. And the easiest way to do that is to let them think they have control. Confidence is a double-edged blade, sure enough: it'll cut back and kill you if you let it."

She held out her hand for the baby.

"I'm not confident that you're not going to kill us," swallowed the girl.

"Well, I'm not a savage or a monster," said Caitlin. "But that depends on whether you take me to the true baby from the Factor at Skibbereen."

"I can't," said the changeling.

"No," said Caitlin. "You just think you can't. You haven't thought hard enough on it. A night in the Sly House will put you right. And if not, we shall have another talk about it. Put the baby on the table."

Still the girl wouldn't quite let herself put the stolen child down.

"It's not your last card – stop trying to think how to play it. I'm a nice enough girl myself, but if you don't do what I say I'd as soon cut your head off and be done with you. And however fast you think you are, I'm ten times quicker. I'd have to be in my line of work, wouldn't I, dear?"

The girl nodded. She put the baby bundle on the table amid the dirty glasses. Caitlin Sean ná Gaolaire was not lying. Her hand flashed silver and there was a click. The girl gasped and sat down, trying to staunch the blood she knew must be gushing from her wrist.

"No, no, no," said Cait. "I have not cut you at all. It's just the cuffs, see?"

The girl looked down and before she could fully raise her hand off the wound that was not there, Cait had snapped the thin iron manacle around her other wrist too.

"It burns," hissed the girl.

"Then hurry up," said Caitlin. "Pick up your brother in that bag and let's be returning the true babby to the poor doctor and his wife, and then off to the Sly House with you. I've a favour to ask The Oversight, and like anything unpleasant I'd as soon get it over with quickly."

CHAPTER 16

SHARP

He did not know how long the small nun had been watching him, because he seemed not to quite hear the polite clearing of her throat, neither the first time she did it, nor indeed the fourth.

He only noticed her when she reached a tentative hand out and tugged insistently at his sleeve.

Even then he did not move with his customary speed and decisiveness: he remained as he had been, leaning across the passage of mirrors in a kind of slumped diagonal, the black mirror less than a foot from his nose.

He blinked, less in surprise than at the harsh brightness he had been avoiding but because, catching sight of himself again in the hated multiplicity of mirrors, Sharp was shocked to see how groggy and unshaven he looked, like a man waking up from a deep slumber. He was almost more shocked by that than by the unexplained and unnoticed appearance of the nun.

"*Vous ne pouvez pas rester dans les miroirs!*" she hissed urgently from behind a hand that covered her mouth. "*Vous allez mourir!*"

She was not just short – in fact, little as a child – but was small-boned and birdlike, delicate as a wren, the victim of some deficiency in nature or nutrition. Unlike a child, her pale flesh, where it emerged from the dusty grey-white of her habit, was wrinkled with age. The skin stretched across the back of the hand covering her mouth was almost translucent, like parchment. The deep hood of her wimple overhung her eyes, and indeed her whole tiny body was in danger of being overwhelmed by the comparative bulk of her robes. Her feet, just visible beneath the hem of her garment were bare like his own and painfully thin, with the bones clearly outlined, more akin to birds' feet than human ones.

"*Vous ne pouvez pas rester ici!*" she repeated. "*Vous allez mourir!*"

Sharp had shared Sara Falk's education as they had grown up together. He understood French well and spoke it passably, but it was not a skill he had anticipated using when he had set off into the mirrors on his quest for Sara.

She tugged again at his sleeve.

"*Les ténèbres viendront pour vous!*"

"I'm sorry," he said in French. "I do not . . . I cannot . . ."

The words seemed to be locked in treacle, and would not come easily.

"The darkness will come for you," she repeated, "if you stay."

She tugged at him, harder this time. His hands seemed reluctant to unglue themselves from the black mirror. His muscles protested, his feet ached, his back was sore and he realised that he had been stuck in one position for considerably longer than he had thought. He pulled his hands away from the mirror surface, fighting an almost magnetic pull that wanted to keep them there. He rubbed his eyes and cleared his throat.

"I am searching for someone," he said, stumbling to find the right French words. "Do you speak English?"

"No," she said. "You are lost."

"I am searching for a young woman – her name is Lucy," he said. "With a hand. An extra hand. That is, who has stolen a hand . . ."

He was aware that he was sounding quite as incoherent as the jumbled thoughts inside his head. Tiredness was part of it, but there was more.

"The hand has rings on it. And a glove. It . . . they . . . my friend needs them. Sara. That is why I must find her. Not my friend. The French girl who stole the hand."

He sounded worse than incoherent. He sounded mad.

The little nun looked around him and then turned to check behind herself in a bobbing and sharply alert movement which amplified her likeness to a bird.

"You are worse than lost. You are drawn to the darkness."

He shook his head.

"No. Indeed I am sworn against it." He bunched his hand and showed her his ring. "I am of The Oversight of London."

The words gave him a moment's strength, reminding him of who he was. The ring made no impression on her that he could tell, but then her eyes remained hidden and unreadable in the shadow of her wimple. She stretched out her other hand and pointed at the black mirror.

"Sworn you may be, monsieur, but you have been staring into that mirror for an age."

"Nonsense," he said. "It was a moment . . ."

She shook her head.

"You are not attuned to the mirrors. You have lost hold on time already. You think you have been in them for minutes, hours, yes? You may well have been in them for days, weeks, months even."

"No," he said.

"Yes," she insisted. "You have lost the ability to judge this. It will not be long before you lose everything else."

He felt vomitous and hungry at the same time. His head was pounding and it seemed as if he were having to strain his thoughts through several thick layers of flannel. He knew there were things he should be doing, and questions he should already have asked.

"Who are you?" he said.

"I am no one," she said. "When I was someone, I had a name. Now I am just myself. You must leave the mirrors."

"I cannot," he said. The flannel in his head was getting more and more impenetrable. It was as if drinking the blackness from the mirror had

left him with a colossal and growing hangover. He held out his ring
again. "I seek a hand that wears this ring. A gloved hand. A woman's
hand."

She pecked her head forward and went momentarily still. Then she
bobbed back.

"I have seen a ring like this," she said.

"Can you take me to it?" he asked, the words tumbling out before he
could consider them.

"I can take you to the last place I saw it," she said with a shrug. "If
I told you I could do more, I would be lying."

Sharp could tell a liar by instinct. He could also look deep into their
eyes and turn their minds so that anything hiding beneath their words
was visible to him. The tone of her voice told him she was telling the
truth. But that truth seemed so unlikely, so opportune, so convenient
that the part of him that mistrusted everything, even his own judgement,
struggled to make itself heard through the clothiness in his head.

"May I see your face, sister?" he said.

"My eyes, you mean?" she said. "You would read my mind, Mr
Oversight, to see if I am lying?" She held out the simple cross that hung
round her neck. "Is not it enough that I swear on this cross?"

"Without meaning to give offence, sister, I have encountered as many
men who hide their sins behind their religious paraphernalia as I have
those who live up to what their crosses or stars or what-not are meant
to represent." He smiled. He felt more like his old self.

"If you could look into my true eyes, you would see they were blue
and clear and innocent, though a little clouded by sadness and betrayal,
I fear," she said, still keeping her head down and the eyes in question
in the shadow of her hood. "You would find nothing to object to in
them."

"Then please be so kind as to look at me," he said. "I mean no harm
by it."

He knelt in front of her, bringing his head down to her level. She
looked away, her hand clamped over her mouth.

"And I mean you no harm," she said. "But you cannot look into those eyes. Those eyes are lost to me."

"Lost?" he said, reaching a hand gently towards her shoulder, intending to turn her towards him. She flinched away, as if sensing his movement.

"Lost and long gone," she said. "I am not the woman I was. But I am still not a liar. I am, however, what you see—" She turned her head towards him. "—an abomination. Please forgive me."

Her face was taut with age, the skin stretched over a delicacy of bone and sinew that would always have been frail but once would have been beautiful too. The eyes that looked out of the somehow still gentle face were not blue or clear or saddened. They were black. As black and shiny as the teeth she revealed as she took her hand away from her mouth and reached into the folds of her robe.

"You are a Mirror Wight," he said in English, as his hand instinctively made its own journey inside his coat to find the comforting handle of his last knife.

She shrugged.

"What you call me does not matter. What I am is this, and being this I have my own needs and customs." Her hand emerged from her garment with a flash of metal that made Sharp step back and draw his own blade.

The black eyes fixed on him, her face caught between understanding and reproach. She crouched and placed the thing she had taken from her habit on the mirrored floor, then hopped back away from it.

It was a small tin beaker, battered and worn, no larger than an egg-cup.

Sharp thought of all he had been told about Mirror Wights and looked around him in case there were more surprises waiting beyond the ambit of his vision.

She twitched her head towards the cup.

"I don't need much, sir, but I do need some. You do not have to fill the cup, but the small amount that you can well spare will benefit me more than I can say. And in return I will take you to the place I last saw that ring."

Sharp looked at her. Though better than it had been, his head still felt claggy and thick, and his thoughts moved sluggishly and with unaccustomed difficulty.

"Measure twice, cut once," he said in English.

"Sir?" said the nun, head twitching towards him, the black eyes as beady as a crow's.

"Something a friend once told me," he said in French. "It means: make a decision and then examine it again to make sure it is the right one."

"There are others like me in the mirrors," she said. "None of them would ask for so little blood. And many of them would not ask at all. They would just take it."

"They could try," he said, spinning the knife in his hands.

He bungled it, his thumb closing too soon and knocking the blade to the floor where it spun and clattered against the mirrors, coming to rest at her feet.

He couldn't believe he'd dropped his knife. He never fumbled. Deftness was part of who he was.

She bent and stood again, his knife in her hands. She turned it over and looked at it with interest.

"Pretty," she said, and looked up at him with a smile. He knew it was a measure of just how far gone he was that his last blade was now in her hands.

He had no doubt he could best her, blade or no blade, if it came to it. He could imagine how easily her bones would crack and snap, but he shuddered at the thought of it.

She spun the knife, checked it and then held it out, haft first, towards him.

"It is your choice. I will not force you. I am an abomination through necessity, not inclination. I remember what it was to be like you."

He took the knife from her, conscious that he snatched at it a little too eagerly. He felt disconcertingly clumsy. He felt worse when he saw he was standing over her with the blade pointing towards her throat. He stepped back, smiled apologetically and then slipped the blade back into his belt with as little awkwardness as he could manage.

She stooped and retrieved her cup. Even clasped in her small hands, it looked pitiably small.

"Whatever you do," she said, "get out of the mirrors. They are killing you."

She disappeared the cup back inside whatever pocket was hidden within her robe and turned to walk away.

He watched the myriad identical reflections of her begin to diminish as the distance between them increased, and then with a twitching movement, like a bird ruffling its feathers, she stopped and turned at a right angle, about to walk out of view.

He felt a strange tug in his breastbone.

"Wait," he called in English, and then corrected himself. "*Attendez, s'il vous plaît.*"

He drew his knife again and began to walk towards her. It had been a very small cup, he thought. And it wasn't like he had a better plan. It wasn't as if he had any plan at all. So what harm could it do?

CHAPTER 17

THE NIGHT VISITOR

A knocking on the door after midnight is never good news. The Safe House was slumbering: Cook asleep in her feather bed, Charlie on his horsehair mattress under the eaves and Emmet still as a statue in the wood-lined room by the side-door to the half basement.

The sound of the knocker banging imperiously woke them all. By the time Charlie had hurtled down the stairs and Cook had strode purposefully from her room trying to tie the sash of her dressing-gown without dropping the precautionary boarding axe she'd picked up on her way out, Emmet was at the front door.

He did not open it until Cook arrived and tapped his shoulder.

"Go on then," she said.

Charlie looked at her axe.

"What?" she said as Emmet began unlatching locks and sliding bolts.

"Nothing," said Charlie.

She followed his eyes to the weapon in her hand.

"We get some strange night callers in our way of business," she said, hefting the hatchet then dropping it so that it hung less obviously against the billowing folds of her dressing-gown.

"And don't you be giving me the old fish-eye," she said. "You'll have a blade somewhere you can get to it in a hurry, I'll be bound," she said.

He grinned at her.

Emmet opened the door.

"I'll be looking for Jack Sharp or the woman of the house," said a dry Irish voice. "And it's sorry I am for the lateness of the hour."

Charlie peered over Emmet's mountainous shoulder.

Caitlin stood confidently on the top step while next to her, one step lower, a young woman scarcely more than a girl stood with her hands cuffed in front of her, fingers curled round the handle of a heavy-looking bag which hung to her knees. The girl looked sick.

"I'm the woman of the house," said Cook, sniffing the air.

"Sara Falk you are not," said Caitlin with a laugh in her voice. "That or Sharp Jack is a liar . . ."

"Sara Falk is away," said Cook coolly.

They looked each other up and down, and as they did so Charlie understood that though they could not be more different in almost every fashion, in one crucial respect they were evenly matched, and that was in the easy way each projected a sense of coiled threat behind perfectly polite exteriors.

"So you'd be the Cook," said Caitlin. "And a pleasure to make your acquaintance, so it is."

"Just Cook," said the older woman. "And likewise, I'm sure."

They nodded at each other.

"I like your axe," said Caitlin.

"And I *don't* like the smell of your friend," said Cook. "Who are you and why have you brought her here?"

"I'm Caitlin Sean ná Gaolaire. Her name doesn't matter a field of beans, and truth is I clear forgot to ask it. What's to the point though is that, as your nose probably tells you, she's a changeling. As is the one in the bag. She switched it with a real baby earlier, and I've just returned the rightful child to its own cot, and now I'm tired and after the loan of one of your cells in the Sly House."

Cook just stared at her. Charlie knew when she went that still it meant she was getting angry.

"You know about the Sly House?" she said. "But you are not one of us."

"Sure and doesn't that fine feller Jack Sharp owe me a favour," said Cait. "No mystery there. Old friends is me and Jack."

"You are not old friends," said Cook emphatically. "I have known the boy all his life and he was never friends with any young lady, indeed he's never been so."

"He's been to Bristol, Cook dear," smiled Cait. "Chasing a bad couple off a Baltic trader who'd done a little mischief in the Port o' London before slipping their moorings and looking to repeat the nastiness in the next port visited, a *Neck* and a *Klabautermann* it was, a couple of years back, you'll remember?"

Cook twirled the axe and then stopped it dead when she caught herself doing it.

"You're the one."

"We had a shared quarry," said Cait.

"You're the venatrix," said Cook.

"That I am," said Cait.

"He said you as good as saved his life," said Cook. 'He didn't say you were so . . . young."

"Well, he's a modest one," grinned Cait. "Was as much the other way round, truth to tell. I was in a tight spot and pleased for the help."

Cook put the axe down carefully, leaning it against the wall.

"You'd better come in and warm yourself," she said. "It's a cold night."

"Not to look a gift horse in the mouth, but I'd as soon get these two under a safe lock first," said Cait.

"Emmet and Charlie can do it," said Cook. "If you're happy to trust them."

"What's a venatrix?" said Charlie.

Cait looked at him as if only just noticing he was there. The slow smile she greeted him with lurched somewhere low in his stomach. She turned to Cook.

"He looks trustworthy enough," she said. "But I'd like the golem to keep a tight grip on her. She's fast and fly, this one. And the one in the bag's a pure streak of venomous swelter."

She looked up at Emmet.

"Never seen a golem before. A fine-looking thing it is, to be sure."

"He's not a thing," said Charlie. "He's Emmet."

Cait nodded and smiled at the clay face looming above her.

"Fair do's to you, big man, I meant no offence."

And she stuck out her hand. After a moment of pause, Emmet reached out and shook it. Cook raised an eyebrow at Charlie.

"Well, that's a first," she said. "Now you go across and lock 'em away in the same cell."

She turned to Caitlin.

"How old's the one in the bag?"

"Baby," she said.

"Teeth yet?" said Cook.

"Maybe four," said Caitlin. "And he'd use them."

"So mind when you open the bag," said Cook, "or let Emmet do it."

Caitlin let Emmet take the changeling by the shoulder and steer her out into the square, heading for the tavern and the hidden cells beneath. Charlie stepped aside to let Caitlin enter.

"Is there really a baby in that bag?" he said.

She nodded.

"And it would bite your eyes out too, soon as spit," she said. "So watch your fingers."

By the time Bunyon had been woken and the warded Sly House cells had been opened and closed again on the changelings, Cook had tea and warmed-over pie in front of Caitlin, who lost no time in helping herself. Charlie came back into the Safe House and found them in the kitchen, facing each other across the table. Cook was sliding what was at least a second wedge of pie onto Cait's plate.

She tucked into it as if it was the first food after a long famine.

"Jack Sharp said you were the most dangerous thing in the Safe House," she said around a full mouth. "And if I was living here I think I'd die of pie. This is glorious stuff here, faith – even the pastry itself's magic."

Cook's nose pinked with pride.

"I've made better," she said.

"Well, don't show it to me," said Caitlin, "or I'll never leave. Ambrosia this is."

Cook slid Charlie a slice on a clean plate. It was larger than the others, perhaps to make up for the earlier missed sausages.

"You never said what a venatrix is," he said.

"You're looking at one," said Caitlin.

"She's a hunter. She's like us, but she's not part of any group," said Cook.

"Like a thief-taker?" said Charlie.

"Yes and no," said Caitlin. "I travel after mischief. And far as I can, I serve Law and Lore. But I'm a free agent."

"And why these changelings, here and now?" said Cook.

"Well, and here's me thinking you'd be as pleased as hook-nosed Punch himself to have two such things that were on your patch without you noticing it brought in and made safe," said Cait, raising an eyebrow. "And me thinking too that after a favour like that you'd maybe not be so interested in my affairs."

"Everything that happens in London is our affair," said Cook. "We are The Oversight."

"Arrah now, but you overlooked that nasty pair, didn't you?" said Cait, washing down the last of her pie with a deep swig of tea. She pushed back from the table and stretched comfortably. "And I'd wonder why, except it might be a rude question. Prying into *your* affairs . . ."

"What brings you to London all the way from . . . wherever it is you came from?" said Cook.

"Skibbereen," said Caitlin. "A lovely place it is too. And for another slice of that pie, sure I'll tell you a piece of my business."

Cook glanced at Charlie as she cut another pastry-covered wedge and slid it onto Caitlin's waiting plate.

"One thing a venatrix is," she said, "is mercenary. You seldom get something for nothing from them. What we do to uphold the balance, they do to profit."

Caitlin snorted.

"Rank prejudice, no offence to you. Do I look like a rich woman? I take a fee for my services but that makes me professional, not grasping."

She enjoyed a couple of mouthfuls.

"The Factor at Skibbereen had a lovely little daughter – he and his wife who's a kind, charitable woman though blighted by an unfortunate wall eye, though that's by the by. Pride and joy of the family, first child: a tiny morsel of sunshine and all that's good in the world, she was. And then she was stolen, and the babby she was swapped with looked just like her, but wasn't. And in any other family, they would just have noticed the character of the poor thing changing and taken on a slow sadness about it that they probably wouldn't have ever spoken of one to the other. But the Factor has the Sight, and he saw something was wrong, not with the child's spirits but with the child itself. So he came to me and told me his child had been changed and that his wife would die of a broken heart if she ever found out, and he gave me good coin, real sovereigns of gold, to put this right. And I gave him my word. And I have tracked this family of changelings for two years. And I will return his true daughter to him, for another thing that a venatrix is, Charlie, is honourable. Because if you do not have a group to support you, as you in the mighty Oversight do, then all you have is yourself. And if your own word's no good in this world – well, you have nothing at all."

Charlie nodded at her and grinned. Cook lent over and poked him with the end of a wooden spoon.

"If you're so interested in her business, then there's a passage in the book upstairs you might like to read that'll tell you all you need to know about changelings," she said. "Takes a lot to make my flesh creep, but you know what, Charlie Pyefinch, changelings do the job nicely."

"Which book?" he said, hoping she wasn't implying he'd been displaying too much interest in the new arrival. Or indeed, if he had, that the new arrival herself hadn't noticed.

"*The Great and Hidden History of the World*," she said. "Written by Sara's grandfather, it was. Was a man who never used one word where four or five would do, but if you cut your way through the fat there's good meat for learning on in there. I'll show you."

CHAPTER 18

THE HARM

Sharp squatted in front of the little nun. Her black eyes were fixed on him as she pulled the small tin cup from the bleached folds of her habit.

He held out his hand. She put the cup in it.

"Wait," she said. Her hand disappeared back inside the garment and re-emerged with a small box, about three inches long and one inch wide and the thickness of a finger in depth. It was made of ivory or perhaps bone, its colour matching that of her habit. Initials were picked out on the lid in tiny holes. Sharp read them upside down.

"'M de R,'" he said.

"Marianne de Rohan," she said. "The name means nothing. Just someone who once owned this box."

She opened the lid. Inside was a dirty-looking twist of some kind of diaphanous material. He looked at her.

She said a word in French that he did not understand. She repeated it. He shrugged.

"I do not know that word."

"From a spider? The net of a spider? For to catch flies?" she said.

"Spider-web," he said in English.

It was her turn to shrug.

"I do not speak your language," she said. "But this is from a spider and it will help stop the bleeding."

He put the cup on the ground and prepared to nick the edge of his palm with his blade. She reached out to stop him.

"Not there," she said. "It does not heal so well, and it stings every time you flex your hand."

Her finger pushed back his cuff. She pointed to a vein a couple of inches below the wrist.

"Here," she said. "Just a shallow nick here, where there are fewer nerves. It will smart less and it will close up easily afterwards if you keep pressure on it for a while."

His eyes met hers.

"I have been in these mirrors a long time," she said. "I made three vows in my life. And the last was to outlive my persecutors, whatever I became in the process."

"And?" he said.

"And my persecutors do not die like normal men," she said. "I did not know that when I vowed. Maybe if I'd known this I would not have sworn as I did. Maybe there are better forms of revenge, but at the time I thought this would do. I was very young. But a vow is a vow."

The glance she gave him caught him unguarded, and he looked away on reflex, but not before he had seen a flicker of something momentarily young and proud in the age-scored face.

"One cup," he said.

"What you can spare," she replied.

He cut himself and held the small wound over the cup, transferring the knife to his teeth and using his free hand to squeeze the blood into it. He was not squeamish about gore, but he did feel light-headed as he watched the inky blood collect, first a thimbleful, then another, then the cup was half full and what had seemed like a small container suddenly appeared much larger now that it was his vital fluid that was slowly moving up the inside wall.

Something – honour or perhaps stubbornness – made him fill the cup to the brim.

"Enough," she said sharply as the level top developed a slight bulging meniscus. "Don't bleed onto the mirrors."

She reached over and dobbed a wad of spider-web on the nick in his arm and pressed down on it.

"Just wait," she said. "Just a moment while the wound closes. Do you have a handkerchief?"

He nodded, conscious of the pressure on his arm and the unwanted intimacy of the moment.

"What were the other two vows?" he said.

"One was to this habit," she said. "The other was personal."

The way she said "personal" made him decide not to press her on the matter.

"Now you keep the pressure on and bind the cut with your kerchief," she said, moving back from him.

He did as she suggested, and almost missed seeing her take the cup and drink the blood. He didn't see it directly; rather he saw it in a reflection, unobserved by her. She dipped her tongue into the surface and took a first taste, savouring it, her face relaxing into a smile, and then she held the cup to her lips and took a long, slow pull on it, draining it in one draught.

She closed her eyes and allowed whatever the benefit of the blood was to course through her. Her smile widened and she shuddered in a manner so profound that he looked instinctively away, feeling that he was observing something too intimate and private for his own comfort and sense of propriety. Once he'd bound the cut on his forearm tight and pulled his cuffs back down over it, he risked looking at her again. This time his reaction was a more palpable shudder of distaste: she was running her finger around the inside of the metal canister and sucking the redness from it, like a greedy child licking the remnants of a mixing bowl.

He stood and looked away until she was finished and the cup had returned to its place within her habit.

"Good," she said. "Thank you."

"And now you will take me to where you saw the woman with this ring," he said.

"As we agreed," she said.

They walked a long way before she took a turn to the right and carried on walking. Once more, the repetitive monotony of the mirrored world began to dull Sharp's senses, and with increasing frequency he found himself stumbling along in a kind of walking sleep.

Again awareness of time passing totally eluded him, and he felt his thoughts slowing and beginning to fray at the edges. He again had the odd feeling of slow vertigo, as if he was walking through time instead of space.

Whenever he asked the little nun how much further they had to go, she would just wave her hand onwards and say they were getting closer but had distance to cover. He grew to hate the sight of her heels flashing back and forth beneath the hem of her habit, but kept his eyes locked on them, walking close behind, ever watchful in case she tricked him by suddenly darting into a mirror and disappearing if and when he nodded off. The prospect of falling asleep was a very real one since he was so footsore and exhausted that he now was stumbling along on the very cusp of unconsciousness.

And then she stopped, so suddenly that he bumped into her.

"Here," she said. "It was here. She went through here."

She pointed a finger at the mirror to her left.

To him it looked like every other mirror that he had walked past, another infinitely repeating reflection, another passage they could walk along for ever.

"How do we walk through the mirror and not just along the passageway of reflections?" he said, struggling again to find the right words to express himself.

"Did no one tell you how?" she said, her black eyes looking him up and down in disbelief.

He tried to remember. He must have known this once. His skull was full of thick flannel again.

"You have to see it again as a mirror and not part of an endless tunnel," she said. "You must do this in your head. You decide it is a mirror again, and it will be, and as a mirror it becomes a portal back into the normal world."

She stared at him.

"You understand this. I found you leaning against a solid mirror, did I not? A black mirror. You had decided not to walk through it, surely? If you had decided to walk on through it, you could have, you know. And then you would have been truly lost . . ."

The memory of the black mirror and the awareness that he could have fallen into it chilled and confused him.

"I had a device," he murmured. "I had an Ivory, a thing of spheres within spheres – it helped me traverse this looking-glass wasteland . . ."

He was very tired.

She shook her head, turned away and leant into the mirror. She made a little spy-glass of her fist and pressed her eye against it, peering through what was clearly and tangibly to her now a solid mirror.

"Here," she said. "Look."

He did as she had done, and squinted through his fist. There was just darkness beyond the mirror.

"I can see nothing," he said.

"It is an unlit room," she said. "So take one careful step in and then stop before proceeding further in case you stumble over something."

She reached into her habit and removed a stub of tallow and a small tinderbox.

"I will follow and light a candle," she said.

He felt the pressure of her hand on his back and found he was stepping forward without quite meaning to or indeed believing that he was crossing back out of the mirrored world. There was a faint popping sensation, as slight as if he had just walked through the membrane of a giant soap bubble, and in that instant all the brightness of the mirrors was gone and he was in darkness.

More than just darkness, he was in cold air that had a dank fustiness to it, a gut-wrenching mucid stink that assaulted his nose and coated the back of his throat at the same time, shockingly rekindling a sense – smell – that had atrophied through disuse as he had wandered lost in the odourless sterility of the mirror-maze. He gagged and stumbled forward, and as he stumbled his foot hit nothing and he fell further, retching, in a sudden horrid lurch that ended in a hard, crunching impact among an unseen tangle of iron-hard branches and twigs. He heard them crunch and snap beneath him, and felt the sharp jag as they poked and cut into his side.

He lay there, sprawled and winded, waiting for the nun to follow with her candle so that he could see how to extricate himself from the jumble he had clearly become ensnared in.

She did not come. He waited in darkness and pain and discomfort, but she never followed him through the looking-glass.

Back in the mirrored maze, the nun stood in front of the glass into which she had pushed him. She raised her eyes and examined herself. She did not look triumphant as she gazed at her face, the black orbs of her eyeballs scanning slowly up and down.

She shuddered.

"Father, forgive me," she muttered.

Then she stepped sideways and, after a deep breath, walked into the next mirror and disappeared.

Sharp had got unsteadily to his feet. The uncomfortable snarl of sticks and branches did not provide anything like a firm footing, slithering and cracking under him. Once more he cursed Dee for stealing his boots.

And then he saw a light, high above him – a small chink of dim candle-flame wavering through an opening in a high and unreachable ceiling to whatever room he had become trapped in. It wasn't enough light to show him what was the nature of his prison, but it was sufficient to illuminate the face of the nun peering down at him.

"Are you there?" she called.

He bit off a curse and tried to calm himself enough to think straight.

"What have you done?" he shouted back.

"I have trapped you," she said simply and without guile, satisfaction or indeed the faintest hint of guilt. "I am sorry."

Her apology was disconcerting, not least because her tone was quavering but sincere. Her face moved back from the hole and her hands flickered in and out of the candlelight in a movement that initially perplexed him until he saw she was reeling something in, pulling it up on a string. As it neared the hole in the roof, it caught the light beyond the opening and he understood in a cold flash both what it was and why she was pulling it out of his reach.

It was a wood-framed mirror, the very mirror he had come through, the only way in – and possibly out – of his prison.

"Wait!" he shouted, and the percussive strength of his yell was enough to stop her for a moment. The mirror swung uncertainly a couple of feet below the hole in the roof.

Enough of his normal self remained for his hand to be moving even as he shouted. He retrieved his last blade, the one the thief Dee had missed, the one that The Smith had made for him as a farewell gift, and without time to think, threw it with every ounce of strength left in his arm.

The knife whirred into the darkness, flying straight, fast and true. The Smith had sharpened it to a razor-like keenness, and it cut through the string three inches above the mirror.

The knife spanged into the stone curve of the roof, sending sparks, and the mirror dropped straight down.

The nun jerked the string an instant too late as Sharp realised that the mirror was going to smash unless he caught it, rendering his hastily improvised plan as dangerous as if she had taken the thing away. He leapt forward, hands stretching for where he estimated the now unseen mirror would land.

He sprawled painfully on the tangle, skittering and snapping more branches as he did so, and then received a sharp blow as the mirror glanced off the side of his head and hit his shoulder.

He twisted and grabbed for it in the dark, and was surprised and delighted, despite the pain he was in, to find he had broken its fall and stopped it shattering.

He stood shakily and looked up at the chink of light. The nun peered down at him, blinking.

"One mirror is no good to you, you know," she said sadly. "You can step out of any mirror, but to step into one you need another to open a passage."

He decided not to argue with her. One mirror was better than none, and there had to be a reason she had been retrieving it. He'd work out why later. As it was, frustrating her in something was a small victory and given the huge setback she had just inflicted on him, he would take it.

"You lied to me," he said.

"I did not lie," she replied, and he detected a surprising note of sadness in her voice. "I told the truth. You asked for a hand bearing a ring like yours. Feel around you. You will find a ring. You will find many rings, many hands too, I'm sorry to say, among the bones."

Bones.

He was not teetering on top of a sprawl of wood.

He was on a bone pile. He reached a hand down. The twigs he had snapped were ribs; the boulder he had banged his head against was a skull.

He found eye sockets, a jawbone.

Teeth.

"What have you done?" he growled.

"Many things," she said. "But not this. This was done by others a long time ago. And the multitude trapped here, killed here, they carried rings like yours. They were men and women. I did not lie to you."

A multitude of rings like his. His throat suddenly felt raw, as if he had been sobbing. He knew what the mucid stink was now, why it was familiar, why it was so bad. It was old rot, bodily rot, the rot of death, the smell of crypts broken open and defiled. And there was, of course, only one event that had led to such a wholesale and concentrated slaughter of The Oversight in its long and uncanny history. And he was standing in the evidence, knee deep in it.

He didn't want to see what he was amongst, who he was amongst. But he had to, even though he now knew the answer from what she had said. The Smith had been right warning him about the mirrors. They were lethally dangerous. And he must see the proof of it, the truth at the end of the great riddle that had decimated The Oversight a generation past, even though the prospect of holding that knowledge in his head filled him with sick dread.

"Give me the candle," he said. "Throw it down."

"No," she said. "I am sorry. But I have thought hard on this. I chose this trap with care. One mirror inside the cavern to let you in, only this small opening in the roof, too small for you to escape even if you could climb up here."

"Well, I have your mirror," he said icily. "I am most sorry to disoblige."

He was lying. The thing he was most sorry about was that he could not find his blade in the dark and send it whirring into her damned throat.

"I was taking the mirror for your own protection. So that nothing could follow you in there," she said. "For I am afraid you are stuck and so quite at my whim."

Her strange politeness was disconcerting. He strove to subdue the mind-killing rage that was rising in him like a dark, incoming wave of grief and frustration, and think clearly.

"What do you want?" he said.

"A new deal," she said. "Again I am sorry, but I need blood to drink from time to time, and I am quite frail and so must use guile rather than violence to survive. You, now you are out of the mirrors, will require water and food to survive. So I will feed you and you will feed me."

He thought of what she was saying, of what it would be like. It did not need much thought.

"No," he said. "I will not be your damn milch cow."

Now he was out of the mirrors, their influence on his head seemed to be evaporating. He felt bruised, cheated, exhausted and – knowing whom he had fallen among – despairing, but he also felt a familiar and sustaining edge of anger returning to him.

"But then you will die . . ." she said, and there was no threat in her voice as she spoke, rather a kind of tremulous disbelief. "You will starve here for there is no other way out."

He did not reply.

"But I did not lie," she said. "I have misled you but I did not lie."

Again he declined to answer. Sometimes, the only power one has is in withholding, in declining to join the fight. His decision not to engage seemed to bewilder her. Her voice, when it came again, had a new and peevish crack in it.

"But my word is good. If I say I will keep you alive, I will. I offer you life!"

He let the silence hang there in the fetid gulf of air that separated them.

"A life by itself is of no interest to me," he said. "For my word is as good as yours, and I gave it to another. If I cannot use my life to find her hand and save her, then as well to end it now."

"What are you saying?" she said.

"I am saying the life you offer to sustain for me is not my own, for I am sworn to find my friend's hand, one Sara Falk of the Free Company for The Oversight of London," he said. "She is not here. It is not here. It was severed by the mirrors and lost within them. And if you leave me imprisoned in this charnel house then that life has no purpose and I am happy enough – nay honoured – to die among the` remnants of better men and women than I."

He was standing on the remains of the Disaster. He had entered the mirrors to find the Harker girl, regain the hand and thereby save Sara, but had instead discovered the members of The Oversight who'd gone into the mirrors themselves decades earlier, to fight an unimaginable threat that had instead simply disappeared them from the face of the earth.

"Unless my word is true, I am nothing," he said. He was aware as he said it that he sounded stiff and sententious, but was surprised to find that he meant it. "And if I cannot save my friend, then the sooner I become that nothing the better. Keep your food and your water, and your pettifogging hair-splitting about whether you lied or just deceived me: I repeat, I will not be your damned milch cow."

This time the silence was hers.

"I do not need much blood," she said querulously. "You have seen that."

Her candle went out. He stood in the darkness and listened to her scumble about and fuss with her tinderbox until there was a scrape and a flare, and the chink of golden light overhead reappeared.

"I did not choose to become the abomination I am," she said. "I have tried to remain true to what I was, in that I have taken pride in not being as the other Mirror Wights. I have tried to keep myself human and kind."

"Then let me out," he said. "Help me."

Her face disappeared. He looked up at the chink. As far as he could see, the space beyond was a rough-hewn passage cut through bare rock. He could see no sign of blocks or bricks. Her face edged back into view.

"If you describe the girl who stole this hand to me, I will look for her and it for you. And I will bring them here. Or if you tell me where Sara Falk is, I will find her and bring her here," she said. "But you must let me have a little blood when I ask for it, to sustain me as I pursue your quest."

He thought about it and shook his head slowly.

"There is no point bringing Sara, for she is in London and her health has already tied her to her bed. And the deal is not a good one besides, for you would pretend to look for me and milk me as you intended," he said. "There is no incentive for you to fulfil your end of such a deal."

"I do not lie," she said. It was clear that she took pride in this. He would like to believe her. "But I do have an incentive: if I restore your friend to you, will you in turn give me your word that you will hunt out my enemy for me beyond the mirrors, you and The Oversight?"

"Why would you trust me if I agreed to that?" he said. "We are trapped in a hopeless loop of mistrust. I would say anything to get you to find Sara Falk's hand, and you know that . . . there is no point us talking further, because lie will pile upon lie and neither of us are fools."

"You will keep your side of the bargain," she said, "for my persecutor is one of the men who set this trap for those who died here before you."

Sharp went cold and still.

"Who is he?" he said.

She told him.

"The Citizen Robespierre is dead," he said after a long pause, his voice leaden with disappointment. "They cut his head off long before the Disaster. In sight of thousands. With a guillotine."

"No, monsieur," she said. "His death was a conjuring trick on a public and bloody stage. He lives. And though now beyond his natural span, he not only lives, but lives in your precious London."

Sharp looked up into the distant black eyes. Her look was level and true.

"Just as saving this Sara Falk is your reason for living, besting The Citizen is mine. You can find your friend. What he took from me can never be returned. Find him, destroy him and I will be as happy as you are to depart this life."

Sharp was not a man of inaction: he was better making decisions and adjusting later if they turned out to be wrong. And then again, she may have deceived him but there was truth in the fact she had not lied to do so.

Which is why, with care and great detail he began to tell her everything he could think of about Lucy Harker that might help her recognise her, and when he had exhausted that he told her about Sara Falk too, in case the hand thief proved unfindable.

Sometimes life was certain; most of the time, it was just a stab in the dark.

ON THE CHANGELING

. . . changelings work in "cells" of two or three and they operate together
to achieve what is, in very tangible terms, a barefaced cheat on death itself.
The whole mechanism of changelingry is designed and adapted to create a
continuum of life beyond the bodily decay that all flesh is heir to. Simply
put, changelings are able to move their consciousness into new bodies, and
then are able to make the physiognomies of the new vessel shift and "change"
to mimic another person. It is not clear why the changelings do not just
cuckoo their consciousness into someone else's baby, but they do not. It is
perhaps part of the unknown mechanism by which their blood operates that
minds can only be passed into bodies which are receptive to them by virtue
of being flesh of their flesh, fruit of their seed. Which is to say that as an
aged changeling nears the terminal decrepitude of its current body, it fathers
or mothers a child with the male or female member of its cell. If, say the
changeling about to die is male, then the mother gives birth after an unnaturally short term (at five and a half months, it is said by authorities such as
Henricus Khunrath) and the baby either has no mind of its own, or its mind
is pushed aside by the parent requiring use of the new body, very much in
the manner of the aforementioned cuckoo. Both Bernard of Treves and
Khunrath suggest that in fact the minds are swapped . . . so that the seeming
baby has a consciousness that is often centuries old, whereas the decrepit

body of the old man or woman ends its days with the confused and figuratively dribbling mind of an uncomprehending baby trapped in a senile body that dies in a matter of months, with consciousness that has never grown beyond a very unsteady grasp of bodily functions and linguistic skills that enable it only to mow and chatter at the cruel trick played on it by fate, through the agency of its parents. Who knows how many old worthies mumbling out the last days of their lives stuck away in the corner are in fact the victims of such a horror?

As to why changelings substitute their babies with those of normal people, there are several theories: some ascribe it to mere malice or a love of mischief. This can be discounted since there is no sense to it, and the trouble the changelings go to in order that they might pass their minds forward is too great an enterprise to be put at risk entirely on a whim or a love of malign discord. It would seem logical that leaving the changeling babies to the care of unsuspecting parents serves some practical purpose whose mechanism is at present opaque to us. It may be that changeling mothers cannot nurse their own offspring, and so require that others perform the service as unwitting wet-nurses. Or it may be that by putting a changeling baby into the crib of a well-favoured family, the changeling cell ensures that its members accrue wealth and power over time through inheritance, and thus do not have to toil for their keep and future security. In this they are very much human cuckoos . . . It is the opinion of this writer that the unnatural act of birthing a body and then shifting and discarding its original consciousness leaves some kind of taint upon the mother/child combination that requires the covert and enforced "fostering". Certainly the testimony of one changeling taken by The Oversight in the early 1600s was that "she would not on any account suckle the baby born to her, since the presence within it of the very man who had swived it into being made such an act unnatural to the mother and irreparably bitter to the child". That said, once the changeling baby has grown beyond puberty, the fleshes seem to have no repugnance to each other and by their subsequent conjunctions the cycle of procreation and vicious substitution continues . . . whatever the truth of it, it is certain that changelings do not raise their own children. Some do raise the stolen natural children; most, it is to be regretted, dispose of them in a variety of ways that range from abandonment, murder or sale. The incestuous cuckooing that characterises changeling practice makes them some of the most pernicious offenders against Law and Lore, since their very modus operandi and means of propagation axiomatically necessitate predation across the line between natural and unnatural.

from *The Great and Hidden History of the World* by the Rabbi Dr Hayyim Samuel Falk (also known as the Ba'al Shem of London)

CHAPTER 19

INTERROGATION

The interrogation of the changeling took place in the cells in the Sly House at noon the next day. Caitlin waited, as requested, until The Smith had been summoned from the Isle of Dogs, and it was agreed that Lucy and Charlie could observe, this being if nothing else a good opportunity for some education into the mysteries of their new vocation. Caitlin begged the use of an iron stew pot from Cook, with the promise that it should be thoroughly scoured before being returned, and Charlie found himself deputed to carry it for her as they proceeded along the subterranean passage linking the Safe House to the hidden cells. It was a big, ungainly thing, and banged against his knees as he walked. The second time he knocked the lid off, Lucy bent and took it for him.

"Thanks," he said.

"I just don't want you dropping it on my foot," she said. "This thing's heavy."

The Smith was gruffly formal with Caitlin, as if he were more worried about being correct and observing some hidden rituals of politeness than actually being welcoming. She in return was cheerful and direct. Lucy warmed to her instantly, responding to the challenging flash of her eyes as she gripped her gloved hand in greeting.

"Well, 'tis a Glint you are," said Cait. "And a burden that is to bear for one so young, I'm thinking, having to take the weight of all the nasty past on your shoulders when you least expect it, nastiness you've no responsibility for as well."

"It can be turned into a useful tool," said The Smith.

"Well, I'm sure it can," said Cait, grinning at Lucy, "but who wants to be a tool when they'd rather be a free person?"

"We are born with responsibilities," said The Smith.

"We are not, begging your pardon," said Cait. "We are born with freedom. Responsibilities only come later, when we have the experience to choose them and the strength to bear them."

"You are a philosopher," said The Smith. The way he said it didn't sound like a compliment.

"The devil I am," said Cait. "I'm a hunter. Simple trade for a simple girl. Point me at my prey and I catch it. Eventually. Philosophers spend their time weaving nets of words to catch ideas and just get themselves all snarled up in them instead."

"There's truth in that," admitted The Smith, unbending a little. "And you seem to have caught a changeling."

"Two of them," said Cait, leading the way along the passage to the cells. "I've righted the wrong they were doing here in your fine city, but I'm afraid I have some unfinished business with them. I'm obliged for any help you may be able to give me, and I'm certainly more than grateful for the use of your cells."

"If you've stopped them swapping a child here, then we owe you a debt, no doubt about that," growled The Smith. "Were we not so reduced in our numbers, I'm sure we would have found them ourselves."

"Arrah, I'm sure you would, sure as guns in the great heyday of the past, but no offence, it's not a secret that you've been powerful dwindled for a generation."

"Dwindled but effective," said The Smith. And he had, Lucy noted, the grace to *harrumph* and look a little embarrassed at the claim.

"So you are," said Caitlin, quite as if she believed him. She looked at Charlie and Lucy.

"This'll be your first dealing with changelings, yes?"

They nodded.

"Well, the thing to remember is nothing is as it seems, and what may look cruel to you is just necessity. They're both older than this building, and they've left a long trail of tears and misery behind them over the generations. Keep an eye on their faces and see if you can see them changing, trying to be something they're not, something you like more than what they really are. Which is murderous parasites and leeches."

And with that she opened the door, standing to one side and letting The Smith enter first.

The changeling girl was sitting on a bed against the back wall of the wood-lined cell, her knees raised defensively to her chin with the baby held in the wedge-shaped gap between her legs and torso. It was grizzling, quite quietly but determinedly.

"I know what you want," she said, glowering out at them from beneath the lock of hair that had fallen over her eyes.

Cait smiled breezily back at her.

"Well, I should hope so because I told you fair and square last night, just before you refused to tell me what I wanted to know."

"You want to eradicate us," spat the girl.

Cait shook her head and began rolling up her sleeves. The girl's eyes flickered as she followed this seemingly innocent action, and Lucy could see she was wondering why Cait was doing this, what future action necessitated such a workmanlike preparation. She was wondering the same.

"I've no such large ambitions," said Cait. "It's not my job like The Smith here to keep the whole wide world at peace. My job's just to keep the little scraps of my own bit of it together, where they should be. And my little piece of the world is in Cork, as I told you. And you've worked a mortal wrong on the Factor and his wife, stolen their child and replaced it with one of your kind."

"Why are you rolling up your sleeves?" said the girl. "What are you going to do?"

"Whatever's necessary," said Cait, hooking a stool out from under the table against the other wall and sitting on it. "All you need to do is tell me what you did with the Factor's child. If it's still alive. If it's not . . . well, that's another song, and let's not start it till we know the facts here."

The girl stared at her, eyes wide. Cait's calmness was terrifying her.

"If the child's alive . . ." began the girl carefully.

"If?" said Cait, dragging the stool two feet closer with a terrible squeal of wood on wood. "*If?*"

"No, it's alive," gulped the changeling.

The baby let out a complaining squall. She hugged it tight – more, Charlie thought, to silence than comfort it.

"Then all you need to do is to tell me where the true child is so I can return it."

"And then?" said the girl.

Cait spread her arms wide.

"And then our business is done, *acushla*."

The girl's eyes slid off Cait and found The Smith standing against the wall by the door. She hooked her chin at him.

"And what about their business?"

"Their business is none of mine," said Cait.

"But you put me in their hands," spat the girl.

"No, no, no," said Cait, calm as ever. "You did that all by your lonesome self, so you did, first by breaking Law and Lore and then by not telling me what I wanted to know. If you're feeling stitched up, young lady, sure but isn't it yourself did all the fine needlework in the first place?"

The baby growled. The girl crushed it tighter to her chest. Her face twisted into a surly fear-stained scowl.

"Well then, there's no reason to tell you anything, is there? I'm done for, sewn my own grave cloth is what you're telling me, right?"

"I'm sure there's accommodations can be reached," said Cait. "There always are."

"No. *You* may be done with me if I tell you what's what, but look at him—"

She pointed at The Smith again.

"He's just waiting like a thundercloud. He's not done with me."

"That's The Smith," said Cait. "And he always looks like his eyes are about to spit lightning, from what I'm told. But though I've just met the man, I've heard the stories since I was a little thing, and I'll tell you, I never heard anyone say he wasn't a fair man, true to his own lights . . ."

The girl spoke over Cait's shoulder, directly to The Smith.

"You're going to kill us, aren't you?"

"No," said The Smith. "We don't hold life as lightly as you. We have other means of . . . rectification."

"Rectification?" said the girl. "I don't even know what that means . . ."

"It means we'd rather extinguish your abilities, cauterise your mind and set you to make amends—"

"Means he's not going to be nearly as tough as I am if you don't help me," cut in Cait. "Because the talking's over."

She moved suddenly and the girl flinched, but all Cait was doing was turning to look at Charlie and Lucy.

"So. This thing that is going to happen now, it's going to happen and you won't like it. But the thing to remember is that the little pink babby there looks gentle and innocent and nice as pie, as all little morsels of life do. But he's older than this building, like I said, and he's mired in dark deeds and other people's misery, generations deep. He has killed babbies that look just like him again and again, and if not killed, then he has ripped them from their loving families and cast them alone in the world, lost for ever among strangers."

Something in her words, particularly the last ones, made Lucy's eyes sting. Her mouth was already dry with anticipation of whatever was to come next.

"Why are you telling them that?" said the girl on the bed.

Cait stretched out a hand and clicked her fingers without looking back.

"Charlie Pyefinch, may I have it now please?"

Charlie stumbled forward, exchanging a worried look with Lucy as he passed. He placed the bail of the iron pot in Cait's hand.

Her fingers closed on it and she held it at full arm's length, swinging with a slight creak of iron on iron. He realised that she must be much stronger than her lithe physique hinted at, because the pot was more than heavy. He didn't think he'd be able to hold it like that without bending his arm.

"Why are you telling them that?" said the girl again, eyes locked on the swinging pot as if it were a pendulum that was starting to hypnotise her.

Cait let it dangle for a couple more beats, then suddenly put the pot down on the floor between her feet with a thump and lifted the lid.

The girl jumped at the noise.

"Because I'm going to put your brother-son-father thing into this iron pot. And then I'm going to put the iron lid on the iron pot—"

There was a gasp of indrawn air from the girl.

"—and then the lid will hopefully muffle the worst of his screaming as all that nasty iron leaches the power from him. At least it starts by leaching the power and the abilities, but I've found it then goes on and starts to eat away at the mind. And by the mind, mind, I mean all the long ages of memories in there. All the lives it's stolen and cuckooed onto for its own selfish survival. So even if it keeps breathing, it'll come out as limp and useless as a dishrag. No sense of past or present. A husk. And all your years of tricking and stealing and harming gone for nothing, because your brother won't remember what or who he was or how he can go on being the very filth he is. And like enough he'll go to sleep and forget to wake up, soon enough. I'm told that's what happens to a changeling when the long passage of years is wiped from the mind. See, life's a long or a short journey over uncharted waters, and cheat as you might try to, everybody pays the tillerman in the end."

She reached gently for the baby.

The infant's eyes widened, and then its head twisted and its free hand slapped and clawed at the girl's face as it screamed at her with a shrill, ragged and above all venomous howl that seemed to tear the barely formed vocal chords as it came.

"TELLTHEMSTUPIDBITCH!"

The baby – the now horribly talking baby – had drawn blood on his sister-mother's face. Cait turned and raised an eyebrow at Charlie and Lucy.

"Do you hear the mouth on him? Charlie, pick him up and pop him in the pot . . ."

Charlie hesitated, but the brother-son was in too much of a frenzy of panic to notice. He jerked his head forward and bit the girl on the chin, worrying her as a terrier might. She yelped and held him at arm's length.

"TELL THEM!"

He yowled, eyes screwed so tight the tears started from them like little sprays.

"BITCHWHORESTUPIDBITCHWHORE! TELL THEM!"

"*Lady of Nantasket*," whimpered the girl, holding her face in shock.

"What?" said Cait.

"TELL HER STUPI—"

The girl slapped the baby. Hard. It quietened the spitting imp whose face puckered in shock, and it calmed the girl. She looked at Cait.

"*Lady of Nantasket*, out of Boston," she said. "Boston, Massachusetts."

"What about it?" said Cait.

"It's a ship on the American trade. Brings over lumber, dried fish, rum, goes back with finished goods."

"And why do I care about that?" said Cait.

"Because the owner and Master is called Obadiah Tittensor, and he and his wife, who travels aboard, by the way, being a half owner, wanted a child."

"They wanted a child."

"They couldn't have one the normal way," said the girl. Cait stared at her.

"And having swapped the poor Factor's baby with your own spawn in the unnatural way, you sold these Tittensors the real child. The real child that wasn't yours to sell."

The girl nodded, eyes wary, as if expecting a blow.

"They're kind, prosperous people," she said. "We haven't harmed the child!"

Cait's eyes shut her up.

"So," said Cait. "So, now *I* have to harm this kind, prosperous couple by taking away a child they will have grown to love, in order that I can fulfil my vow to the rightful parents."

There was a dangerous edge to her voice.

"Do you know what I wish?" she said, holding up the pot lid.

The girl shook her head.

Cait crashed the lid on the pot at her feet.

"I wish I had a pot big enough for the evil pair of you."

Something seemed to suddenly occur to her.

"Arrah now, but how do I know you're not lying?"

The girl shrugged and looked at the baby. He just spat at her.

"Charlie," said Cait, snapping her fingers. "One for the pot. Though mind yourself, he'll as like bite and scratch at you."

"TELL THEM!" shrilled the baby.

"I told the Tittensors my sister was having a baby soon, and didn't want it either," the girl said. "They wanted a baby brother for the one they had off me."

"And you're going to America to sell them a baby?" said Cait. "Now that sounds like altogether too much trouble even for such as you . . ."

"No," said the girl. "*Lady of Nantasket* docks five times a year in the Pool of London."

Cait sat back. Looked at The Smith.

"We can confirm that at the port office," he said. "Hodge has contacts . . ."

Cait turned back to the girl.

"And when might we be expecting it next?" she said sweetly.

The girl told her. Cait nodded and turned on her stool, stretching as she stood up.

"Smith, sir. Might I have the use of your cells until then?" she said. "I'll be happy to pay my way in cash or kind."

"What manner of 'kind' were you thinking of, Miss ná Gaolaire?" The Smith said.

She grinned at him.

"Well, as we were saying earlier, though I take you at your word, for sure who wouldn't, that you are dwindled but effective, it seems as if you didn't know either of these beauties was in your fair city and up to no good. So I'm thinking you could do with an extra pair of eyes, temporary like?"

"You want to join . . ." he began.

"No," she said. "No, no, no. Begging your pardon, but I'm no joiner at all. I am a helper though, and I'm more than happy to pay my way as a supernumerary friend of your enterprise, of my own free will."

The Smith looked back at her, face giving very little away.

"I'll talk to Cook," he said.

"Fair dos," said Cait, winking at Lucy. It was just a wink given in passing, but it produced a tiny and unexpected flutter in Lucy's stomach, as if a butterfly had just woken up.

"What are you going to do to us?" said the girl on the bed, voice flat now. Tears were rolling silently down her cheek, and she was staring in something close to shock at the small smear of blood on her fingertips where she had felt the wound on her chin left by the four sharp teeth in the malevolent baby's mouth.

"Now look at that," said Cait, poking the infant. "Is that any way to treat your sister. Or your mother. Or your lover, for that matter?"

The baby hissed at her.

"How do you get your heads round that nasty stew anyway?" said Cait.

The baby coiled on the mattress and stared balefully at her.

"IF I WAS GROWN I WOULD KILL YOU BUT NOT BEFORE I HAD—"

Cait raised a warning hand. The baby choked off its stream of bile.

"Well, you're not grown, little vileness," she said, "so keep a civil tongue in your head or I'll be having you over my knee and skelping you your bare bum till you learn better manners."

She turned to The Smith, and handed Charlie the pot.

"Now, sir, do you think Cook has any more of that delicious pie left?" she said as she rose.

"With Cook, pie is always a strong possibility," he said. "Now cut along, youngsters, for I believe Hodge is keen to take you out and about this afternoon, and you could do with some fresh air after all this fetidness in here."

Lucy fell in with Cait as they walked back along the passage.

"Would you really have put the changeling in the pot?" she said.

"Without a qualm," said Cait. "Well, maybe a bit of a qualm because it's a nice enough pot and Cook seems to prize it, and it seems a shame to dirty it up with one of them, because they do, you know, tend to lose control of their thingies when they're in there."

"What thingies?" asked Lucy.

"Faculties," said Charlie.

"And their bladders and bowels," said Cait. "They spew like fire hoses from both ends. That's why I always use a lid."

CHAPTER 20

A DISTINCT ABSENCE OF ALP

Although he took a pride in keeping an opaque veil over his true feelings and did not like to share his emotions with anyone, The Citizen did admit to himself that he had been more than a little deflated by the death of the Green Man. It had been a long and well-planned experiment, and had initially seemed promising. The sudden demise of its subject was irksome and sapped his energy – energy that he was especially rigorous about husbanding carefully. He had cheated death once, and though not by any means – not by any means that he was conscious of at least – a superstitious man, he did often wonder, strictly in a spirit of scientific contemplation, if the fact he had exceeded the normal span of years meant he had also outlived his bodily appetites. Power he was still hungry for, but food and drink seemed to revivify and nourish him less and less with each passing year.

It was this that had made him addicted to the effects of the Alps, and wherever he had travelled he had arranged that one of these breath-stealers would also make themselves available to him, for a fee paid to their family in the customary way. Breath-stealers, Alps (or maras as they were known across central Europe) had the ability to restore their own reserves of vital essence by bearing down on their unsuspecting victims – animal or human – as they slept and sucking the exhalations from their mouths.

From this, the belief that a bad dream or nightmare (night-*mara*) leaves the victim pale and exhausted from being "ridden" all night can be seen to have a very real antecedent. Alps have the added ability to store this vital breath and exhale it into the mouths of others, transferring the regenerative benefits of their activities.

The Citizen's latest Alp had been installed in an empty town house on Golden Square. The house was another of Mountfellon's properties, and there was a network of secret tunnels and untravelled alleys leading to an entrance so that The Citizen could move from Chandos Place to Golden Square without being seen on the city streets. Despite the fact that anyone who might have recognised the old Jacobin was long dead, he shunned public exposure and had become, through habit, a creature of tunnels and shadows. But sapped as he was by the death of the Green Man, and disappointed as he also was by the failure of Mountfellon's stratagem against The Oversight, he had determined that he needed another draught of energy from his tame Alp.

And so, on an afternoon when the sun was already low in the sky, a section of panelling in the dusty grandeur of the forgotten mansion on Golden Square cracked open, and The Citizen emerged into the silent house. He walked to the chaise-longue that stood at the centre of the room, stepping over the heavy stone weights that were scattered on the floor and trailing a hand along the board that was propped against it. By the use of those weights and that board, he had ridden the Alp, mouths sealed together, the pressure crushing the breath out the creature and into his own mouth. He felt a quickening of his vitals at the very thought of it. It had been a surge of life through his old frame that had an almost erotic charge to it, progenitive in its very essence, he supposed.

He wanted that now. But the house was empty. And as he looked around, he realised it was much more than emptiness he was feeling: it was a distinct absence of Alp. The house was abandoned. Something about the stillness told him the breath-stealer was gone and would not return. He tried to react scientifically to this sense, to see what the unnoticed and subliminal cues were that made him feel this. He looked at the patch of scrubbed floor where the Alp had cleaned blood from the sprung parquet, blood that The Citizen had spilled as he cut the unsuspecting throat of a hired helper. He walked slowly around the room, replaying that first meeting, remembering where everything had been. He walked into the dust-filled hall and noted that the only footsteps disturbing the dirty grey layer of stour went from the door into the main room and back. No sign of occupation. No sense that the Alp had returned after disposing of the hired man's body.

His face tightened. Despite himself he called out.

"Hello?" he cried.

And then to kill the hatefully empty echo, he spoke in the Alp's own tongue.

"*Bist du hier, mein Freund?*"

No reply. He grimaced. Even though there was clearly no one there to answer him he felt he had betrayed a weakness.

He moved to the front door and tried it. It was locked. He was about to turn away when he saw a movement in the light at the bottom of the door, and he became very still.

There was something outside. Something sniffing – more than sniffing: inhaling deeply – a dog, a damned dog trying to smell him, smelling him. He took a step backwards and heard a growl from the other side of the door. And then he heard the rough man's voice coming up the steps.

"Hoi, Jed, what you got there, boy?"

There was a spyhole in the door, and on instinct The Citizen reached out to move the swinging flap out of the way so he could see who it was on the front step. And then, just as he was about to touch it, there was a scratching noise and it moved.

On the other side of the door, Charlie stood with his eye to the spyhole, a long, thin knife blade in his hand at his ear, levering the trap open so he could squint into the building that had got Jed's attention.

He could see the empty hall, the dusty steps on the once grand staircase behind it, a door leading to a clearly derelict room and not much else.

Hodge and Lucy climbed the steps behind him.

"What is it?" said Hodge.

"Empty," said Charlie. "Grand. But derelict."

"Shouldn't we go in?" said Lucy.

Jed barked.

On the other side of the door, The Citizen was bent double, having ducked down the very instant he'd seen Charlie slide the spyhole cover out of the way. His eye was now level with the keyhole. He peered through it.

He could see no faces but there was a hand – Charlie's – right at the level of the hole.

And on the hand was a ring. The Citizen stared at it, eyes widening.

The wretched dog barked again.

"Are we going in?" said Charlie.

There was a pause.

"No," whispered Hodge. "Something in there Jed wants to get at, but his barking's likely drawn attention to itself, hasn't it?"

Jed dropped his head as if embarrassed.

"Terriers is always head-on and no back-off in them at that, but not so good for stratagem, is they?" sighed Hodge, reaching down to scratch him behind the ears. "We come back tonight, get in through the roof, see if there's more of the bastards, though an Alp's a solitary thing more often than not, and the one I killed didn't look like a sociable cove . . ."

The Citizen's blood, never particularly warm, ran colder at this. His Alp, his lifeline, gone. And more than that, if he could not contact the people who had provided him, the only other source of Alps he knew of was far away in Lower Canada, where a rump of his old associates from Paris had fled a long time ago. He was not even sure their successors would respond if he sent for an Alp, so he would have to get to Canada himself, and he had a horror of drowning, which made sea voyages unthinkable.

"Going in through the roof sounds fun," said Lucy.

"Not for you, missy," said Hodge. "You'll be tucked up nice and safe on the Isle of Dogs."

The Citizen heard them walk off, and only after a minute did he rise to full height and make his way back across the hall, over the floor of the great room and out through the secret door in the panelling.

And then he ran. Ten minutes later he was locked in his underground study, the door barred. He was writing a note, the steel nib of his pen providing the only sound as it scratched and slashed his message across the paper. He folded it into an envelope, melted sealing wax and sealed it with his ring.

Then he unlocked a trunk at the back of the room and removed a metal-bound chest. He unlocked that and took out what at first looked like a black japanned deed-box.

He stood the box upright on the narrow end and carefully unlatched one of the two largest sides, as if opening the cover of a book. This revealed that the top was pierced by a series of ventilation holes. More than that, it revealed a black wax candle set into the base beneath the holes, and a simple clockwork mechanism that was attached to a small bell and striker. He hurriedly wound the key to the mechanism, tightening the drive spring. Then he lit the candle and rested the letter against the inside of the box which was clearly, now the candlelight was reflecting it, mirrored. He took a small folding scalpel from his pocket, nicked his thumb with a grimace and splashed the resultant tiny droplets of blood against the inner glass. And then he pulled a small lever on the clockwork releasing the mechanism, which began to strike the small bell and emit a series of regularly spaced silvery chimes. Then he closed the cover of the box, making the two internal mirrors face each other as he did so.

He stood with a shudder, and left his study to the sound of the small silvery bell, locking the door behind him as he left.

CHAPTER 21

THE MATTER OF BOOTS AND THE PASSAGE OF IRON

Sara Falk found time strangely elastic within the mirrors. She walked and walked without ever getting tired enough to stop, and she didn't really even have the natural clock of her stomach working strongly enough to give her a sense of time passing. In some ways it felt as if she were out of time entirely, in a dream. All she had to keep her moored was the strong sense of purpose to find Sharp.

Having lost his trail, she had quailed at the immensity of the task, but had decided that her choice was simple: to be crushed by that immensity or to explore it. She chose the latter course, and was walking in what she visualised as a right-angled spiral. She walked ahead for fifty paces, then turned right for another fifty paces, then another right for fifty, then another for sixty and so on, gradually extending her spiral quartering of the maze in the hope that eventually she would cut Sharp's trail again. Keeping track of the counting was hard, and she was in the thousands when tiredness and perhaps desperation finally took their sudden and inevitable toll.

She simply sat down. So fast she was not sure if she had not actually fallen. She slumped against the mirror at her side and looked at the Raven.

"Three thousand, seven hundred and fifty," she said blankly. "I think. I'm losing count."

She yawned.

"Have I been walking for hours or days?" she said.

The Raven just blinked at her.

"I don't care," she said. Her eyes were dark shadows.

"If I sleep will you stand watch?"

The Raven clacked its beak and hopped closer as Sara drew her largest blade and laid it ready beside her.

"Just in case we have more unwelcome visitors while I sleep," she said. "I don't want to stop and rest. But I think I have to. I think I may feel less . . ."

She lost the word and shuddered. Her eyes felt moist but she was not going to wipe them in front of the Raven. It might misinterpret the gesture for sentiment.

"I may feel less hopeless," she said. "I may wake with a fresh plan. Three thousand, seven hundred and sixty perhaps it was. Remind me when I . . ."

Her eyes closed and she was gone. The Raven hopped a little closer, and then was still too.

Time passed.

Nothing moved.

Something changed.

No one noticed.

And more time passed.

Sara woke with the immediate certainty that she was being observed. She opened her eyes and found almost her entire field of vision was filled with a man's boot.

The boot was familiar and Sara's first sensation on seeing it was to be flushed with a potent but contradictory mixture of relief and disbelief.

"Jack!" she said, pushing herself up on her hands. "Why, Jack—"

"John," rasped an unfamiliar voice. "No one calls me Jack, and most call me 'doctor' . . ."

She looked at the man looming over her – the boots giving way to a long and unfamiliar coat and an even less familiar grey goatee and medieval-looking skull-cap.

She covered her confusion by looking round for her companion.

"Where has it gone?" she said.

"Where has what gone?" he said.

"The Raven," she said.

He looked around before he spoke.

"There is no Raven."

She stood up. He stepped back half a pace, suddenly tense, as if preparing to fight. Or flee.

Her gaze swiftly swept the repetitively sterile space.

"There's always a Raven," she said.

"Not here," he said. "Here, there's always just mirrors."

Her eyes finished their short tour of the limited horizon and rested on him.

"And you," she said.

"And me," he agreed.

"You are not a Mirror Wight," she said.

He smiled, whether from amusement or to confirm the truth of her statement by a mirthless display of his definitively white – and thus not black – teeth, it wasn't clear.

"And neither are you," he said. He pointed to her rings. "You are from The Oversight of London."

She kept her teeth hidden behind the taut line of her lips.

"I am Sara Falk."

"And I am John Dee."

"Doctor Dee was a member of The Oversight in the Elizabethan era," she said after a beat. "That is not possible."

"No," he said. "Not possible anywhere but here."

Sara's hand had found the handle of the knife beneath her coat and was resting on it. He looked at her as if he could see through the dark material and knew exactly what she was doing.

"If I may speak plainly, time is strange in the mirrors. It flows differently.

There are worlds within worlds, spheres within spheres, revolving at different speeds, perhaps."

"You cannot just 'survive' in the mirrors," said Sara. "Not if you are not a Mirror Wight."

He opened the neck of his coat and showed her the chain he wore beneath it. There was a ring on it. A gold ring with a bloodstone, incised with the familiar unicorn and lion. He inclined his head and raised his eyebrows as if to say, "I told you so," and then reached inside his shirt and pulled out another chain which ran through a hole drilled through a piece of rough white stone, and next to it a small silver bell, such as a cat might wear.

"I move in and out of the mirrored worlds. Judiciously. And I carry an amulet, a white counter-stone if you will, a thing that affords me protection from the lixivial effects of the glass."

"Lixivial?" she said. "If you think that is speaking plainly, sir, you delude yourself."

"Ah. It means 'leaching'. The mirrors leach colour and vigour from their inhabitants. The word is from the—"

"I do not care where the word is from," she said. "What are you doing here?"

"I am evading the pull of mortality by endeavouring to understand the currents of time as they are affected by the mirrors."

She shook her head.

"I know the history of The Oversight, sir. Dee is two and a half centuries gone from the world. You are not Dee—"

"But I am. Both gone from the world, and standing in front of you. Behind the world, as it were. I told you: time is elastic in the mirrors. Let me show you the trick of it," he said, reaching out a hand.

"Why would you do that?" she replied, stepping back.

"The Oversight is, among other things, a society given to mutual aid," he smiled. "Especially *in extremis*."

"If you were Dee, if you were a member of The Oversight, you would have stayed in touch."

He said nothing.

"If you are indeed John Dee," she repeated.

"Why would I not be?" he said.

"You could have taken his name. As easy as stealing someone's ring. Or someone's boots . . ."

"I did not steal the boots," he said. "I found them."

"The immemorial excuse of every thief since time began," she said.

"I am not sure time began. I begin to think it was always there. Or perhaps it is curved and cyclical," he mused, then waved his hand as if to banish the digression. "But that's another thing altogether. I found the boots on a black mirror. They were lying on top of this and these."

He pulled out the Coburg Ivory from the pocket of his coat, and flipped the coat back to reveal a belt full of knives. Knives that Sara recognised with a sick lurch in the pit of her stomach as Sharp's blades. Dee watched her keenly.

"A black mirror occurs where blood is spilt. It opens a door to quite another sphere than ours, I think. If these boots, these knives and this get-you-home belonged to friends of yours then I am afraid it is likely they are gone past any ability you may have to find them."

"Him," she said, the word tumbling out before she could bite it back.

"Him?" he said.

"Not they," she said. "Him. There was only one."

"And now I am afraid he is undoubtedly gone," he said. "I am sorry. But that is the honest and bitter likelihood of it."

His face was impenetrably bland, but his eyes were too sharp for her to do anything other than remain wary.

"Lady," he said, "if I were a liar, why would I tell you such a harsh truth? If I were a deceiver, be sure I would give you honeyed words and hope."

She did not trust herself to speak. The sight of Sharp's blades – blades which were as much a part of him as his slow smile or his serious eyes – had sucked all the vitality and urgency from her. The sight of his knives in another man's belt was, to her, the almost complete extinction of hope.

Almost.

"What did you do to the Raven?" she said.

"I am sorry?" he said, brow crinkling.

"You will likely be so if you lie to me again, sir," she said. "What is your business?"

His smile was feline and infuriating. Her hand loosened the blade in its sheath beneath her coat.

"I am what you might call a supranatural philosopher, a student of the arcane," he said. "I have confederates beyond the mirrors who help me, and who in return I render services to . . ."

"But not The Oversight, of which the real Dee was once a part," she said, "and that is curious, no?"

"I assure you The Oversight and I went on our parallel but separate ways after an amicable separation," he said. "What the history you may have read says of me I do not know, but that is the truth of it. The Free Company was ascendant, there was, if anything, a superfluity of members and I left it by mutual agreement in the rudest of health, in order to pursue my own studies."

"I do not think you are Dee. I think you are an imposter in a pair of stolen boots," she said. "And for all I know, that ring round your neck is something else you have robbed from its rightful owner. But whatever or whoever you are, by Law and Lore I require you to hand over those knives, that Ivory, the boots and above all that ring."

What she really wanted most of all was the Ivory, the get-you-home. Everything else was sentiment. The Ivory was a practical aid that might lead her to Sharp. Her mind was running clear again.

"Law and Lore," he said. "And how will you enforce that, Miss Falk?"

"By any means necessary," she said.

"Such as the one you are holding beneath the skirt of your jacket, for example?" He smiled, and suddenly he did not look so old or so well disposed towards her, as if a veil had just been discarded. And his hand was also beneath his own coat, where she now knew Sharp's blades were.

"I do not wish to harm you. Or fight you, Miss Falk," he said.

"That is wise," she said, "for it won't end well if you do."

He smiled again, and then, faster than she had imagined possible, he had a knife in both hands, and was crouched and ready with a litheness that belied his age.

"It didn't have to—" he began, when a high-pitched and persistent chime filled the space. He winced.

Sara took advantage of this to step away from him and draw her knife.

The chiming put her teeth on edge. He stood and, to her surprise, sheathed the knives. He put his hand around the bell on the chain round his neck as if trying to muffle the noise. It didn't work.

"Well," he said, the words clearly hurting him almost as much as the sound of the bell. "I am called elsewhere. This unpleasantness is postponed . . ."

And before she could move, he stepped out of the passage into the mirror behind him.

And Sara was alone again. But this time without even the companionship of the Raven.

She tried to remember how many steps she had got up to on her quartering of the mirrors. She wanted to get away from this spot as soon as she could, in case the unsettling Dr Dee returned.

CHAPTER 22

THE HUNGRY WORLD

On their return from the afternoon with Hodge in which they'd discovered the Alp's abandoned quarters, they found Cook complaining about the untidy state of her kitchen. A series of deliveries had all arrived at the same time, and her large scrubbed tabletop was invisible under all manner of sacks and brown-paper-wrapped parcels.

"Right," she said as soon as they entered the kitchen. "It's no use making those big hungry eyes at me, Charlie Pyefinch. There'll be no tea until this is packed away, and I have business at Goodbehere's, so I suggest you all fill the storerooms with this mess, and then when I return I shall no doubt be in a better frame of mind and attempt some pikelets or suchlike."

Lucy's sharp eyes had spotted pastry sitting beneath a damp towel on the sideboard, so she knew Cook was not really in the foul and thunderous temper she was affecting.

The Smith came in with a large dripping basket of eels while they were putting things away.

Cait caught him at the door appearing, as was her wont, from nowhere.

"Ah, see, I wouldn't be dribbling that wet creel into the lady's kitchen right now if I was you," she said. "She's a bit on the sensitive side today. I've been hiding from her all afternoon."

"Right. Thank you for the warning," he said, turning round. "Back pantry it is."

Lucy was already in the back pantry, putting a coarse sack of potatoes away. The dirt on the vegetables had seeped through the sack and her gloves were muddy as a result. So she'd gone to the sink and begun to wash them with a new bar of Caverhill's Patent Pine Tar soap. She washed the gloves on her hands, just as if washing the hands themselves, and as she did so inhaled the piny tang of the suds and somehow the smell and the coarse sacking filled one of the holes in her memories, and she found she was gripping the side of the sink very tightly so as not to fall over at the nastiness of it.

It was at that moment The Smith entered with his basket of eels. He put it on the ground over a drain grate, and then saw her face.

"What?" said The Smith.

"A memory," she said. "It. I . . ."

"You glinted something?" he said. Then looked at her gloved hands. "But how—?"

"No," she said.

She had to sit down; she moved a box off a barrel and lowered herself onto it. The Smith gave her a peculiar look, and then walked out of the door. She heard the screech and whoosh of the pump-handle, and then he returned with Cait and a cup full of cold water. She took a few sips and nodded. He leant back on the shelves and raised a shaggy eyebrow.

"I just remembered things I didn't know I'd forgotten," she said. She pointed at the hessian sack, then at the soap.

"It was the smell," she said. "This piny, tarry smell. And then the sacking. It just made me remember something . . ."

"Nothing good," Cait said. "Not from the way you reacted. You're white as a sheet."

She nodded.

"Tell me," said The Smith.

"Arrah now, come sit by the range and get your colour back first," said Cait. She put her arm round Lucy's shoulder and led her gently back into the kitchen proper.

Jed cocked his head at them. Charlie opened his mouth with a question that The Smith killed with one look before he could voice it.

Lucy sat at the table and sipped her water. She was conscious of them looking at her, of the heat at her back from the range, and most of all of the firm hand that the girl from Skibbereen kept companionably on her shoulder.

Clearly looks were exchanged that she wasn't privy to, because Charlie suddenly got very busy clearing the rest of the provisions off the table, and Hodge decided Jed wanted to go outside to take care of some canine needs better addressed in the street than inside a kitchen.

"Go on," said Cait. "If you've a mind. Better out than in."

"I was brought to the Safe House with a plaster put over my mouth," Lucy said. "It was a rough square of sacking like that potato sack and it smelled of pine, because of the pitch they'd used to stick it to my face."

"Yes," The Smith said. "Sara Falk was horrified that you'd been treated like that. Sharp too."

"Well, I remembered that well enough," she said, taking another sip from the tin cup. "But until I went in there . . ."

She nodded at the back pantry.

"I'd forgotten the people who did it to me."

"The plaster?" he said.

She nodded.

"Was a man called Ketch," said The Smith. "Sharp said. A sort of local drunk. Bill Ketch."

"No," said Lucy. "It wasn't Ketch. It was others."

"Others," said The Smith, raising an eyebrow. "What kind of others?"

"Others like the ones who tried to stop us on the way here. Charlie and me. On the canal. Others with faces covered in blue lines, wearing skins and bones – I mean clothes that looked sort of normal except they're made of hide and fur and use bits of dead things to fasten them."

"Sluagh," said The Smith.

"Yes," she said. Her heart was thudding at the memory of it. "Sluagh."

"Bad cess to 'em," said Cait, squeezing her shoulder encouragingly.

"Slow down," The Smith said. "Take your time."

She shook her head. She had to get this memory out of the way as fast as she could.

"They took me and they tied me up somewhere. I can't remember where they took me from except I was asleep and then I wasn't and they were carrying me away from the light into a wood. I think it was a wood: there were branches and brambles anyway. And then they held my head and they stared at me. And I tried to not look into their eyes because I knew that was what they were trying to make me do, so I concentrated on the patterns on their faces, the blue tattoos, and I just followed the lines like a maze, trying to lose myself in them and not hear what they were saying, but all the lines kept leading back to the eyes, and I think that's when they got in my head and started shutting bits of memory away and putting other bits and pieces in there."

She shuddered and felt sick and cold at the core of herself.

"Them going inside my mind," she said. "I don't know how to explain but it's . . . it leaves you feeling dirty and . . ."

"Violated," The Smith said gently. "It's like rape."

Cait stepped back and looked at him.

"Arrah now, and how would you be knowing what rape felt like, big strong man?"

Him saying the word didn't help. Putting a name to it wasn't the thing. Saying it made it worse. Made it public. Lucy felt sicker and more exposed.

"It's nothing like rape," she said. Though of course it was. "I mean, I've not been that unlucky, but I've had men try after me, bad men, and so far I've been faster and smarter than them."

She remembered breaking a bottle on a man's head by the sea in France. It wasn't a good memory either: she could remember his hands, his breath, hot and meaty and garlicky, and she could still feel the impact in her hand and the cracking sound. She'd run so fast she never knew if it was the bottle or his skull, or both.

"And you can fight, because you're strong," Cait said. "And I can—"

"But against the Sluagh, opening your mind and laying your innermost self bare – there's no power, no strength that you can use against it," said The Smith. "It's like they put a thing in you, a stain . . ."

"A blackness," Lucy said. He nodded.

"They put a blackness inside you and your brain freezes in terror and then they can do what they like because all the rest of you can do is concentrate on that blackness and watch it, in case it moves and hurts you."

She stared at him.

"Yes. How do you know?"

"I've been around a very long time, Lucy Harker," he said. As if that answered anything at all.

And then Cook returned and the tension in the room broke as she had to be filled in, and then Charlie miraculously reappeared, having finished pretending he was stacking things in the storeroom, and Lucy was sent to get dry gloves, and then tea, jam and buttery pikelets and pipe-smoking happened, and the world looked better again.

Except clearly Lucy's memory that the Sluagh had been involved in working on her mind had added evidently something to the equation that The Smith had been trying to solve as he tried to assess the sum of the enemies currently ranged against them. She noticed him talking quietly to Hodge and Cook when she was supposedly involved in conversation with Charlie and Cait, and when she asked again if she might to go back out with Hodge and Charlie to look more closely at the house on Golden Square, he forbad it. She had been looking forward to a break in the routine of going back to the Isle of Dogs each night and staying out with them, but she found herself back in the dog cart with The Smith, heading east as the evening lengthened.

He spoke little as they went, not even pointing useful and educative things as they passed them in the way he normally would. When they reached the house, he bade her a good night and went into the workshop.

She lay awake, thinking of the day's doings and trying to put them together, adding the new scrap of memory to the patchwork of her past, and most of all trying to parse the sudden tension she had felt between Cait and The Smith. And then she found she was just thinking of Cait and wishing she could be more like her, more direct and calm and then she started thinking she'd like wild, unruly hair like Cait's . . . and then she noticed the silence.

The Smith had stopped working in the room below.

And then she heard the ghost of a footstep on the ground outside, and perhaps because it was a footstep evidently trying not to be heard, she slipped out of bed and looked out of the window and saw The Smith walking carefully away from the house in the dark.

Of all the lessons that Lucy had enjoyed most, the ones involving tracking each other through the crowded city was her favourite. In part this was because she was so very good at it, naturally alert and gifted with the ability to go fast-yet-slow when she needed to. And she and Charlie had been told that since they were to be trained on the job, that no experience was to be wasted. Maybe this is why thirty seconds later she found herself beneath the starless sky, trailing The Smith as he picked up speed, striding across the rough ground, heading north. Or perhaps it was the unexpectedly furtive way he had left the house, carrying a bag she had never seen before. Maybe she just followed because she was inquisitive and thought if she could see where he went she might get to the bottom of why it was she was so deeply ambivalent about a man who should, by all rights, be a welcome protector.

The Smith was a very fast walker, his long strides eating up the mileage with no hint of slowing as they headed north, moving off the Isle of Dogs and following the course of the North London Railway line all the way to Bow Road, where he joined it, heading east on the high street until they crossed the turbid waters of the River Lea and doglegged north again via Pudding Mill Water, where she nearly got seen by him as she flitted over the mill race by the looming new flour works. Luckily she found a scrap of shadow in time as his head turned to look back at the city he was now leaving behind as he struck out across the wilds of Hackney Marsh itself. From then on it was more a matter of guessing where he was going and zigzagging an intersecting course, keeping to the cover of the scant hedges vegetation lining the drainage cuts as he made his way in a more easterly direction, until he crossed the last major water by a thin, single-plank footbridge and strode up and over the railbed of the Cambridge Line, his feet crunching the clinker as he went.

Lucy followed on his tail, making sure she kept low and only trod on the wooden ties as she crossed the iron tracks. And then, three and a half miles and less than an hour after they had left The Folley, he came to a halt at a crossroads on Ruckholt Lane. On the south side was a farm, on the east the silhouette of a grand mansion behind a wall spiked with railings. To the west stretched the flat water of the new reservoirs for the East London Waterworks, dull silver planes looking blankly up at the night sky above.

The Smith turned towards the copse of trees on the north quarter of the junction. Lucy was in a ditch to his west. And for a long time they stayed like that. Then The Smith walked forward and hung the bag on a gnarled tree, and stepped back, staring into the shadows.

"Take it," he said.

This far from the city his voice, though quiet, reached her ears quite clearly. And for a while it seemed only her ears. And then there was a barely discernible rustle in the shadows beneath the trees, and a hoarse voice replied.

"Smith."

The shadow resolved into a man with hair plaited into long pigtails that hung from beneath an ancient fore-and-aft hat decorated with limpet shells. His clothes were patched from rabbit fur and pinned in place with bones instead of buttons. And his face, as Lucy had somehow dreaded it might be, was scarified with a maze of dark ink. She dipped her head lower behind the band of dock leaves, sure the Sluagh's eyes were sharper in the dark than The Smith's. But what disturbed her more than the Sluagh was The Smith's ease with it.

"How did you know we are here?" said Fore-and-Aft.

"There's just one of you, so don't be playing games with me," said The Smith easily. "And I'll be straight enough with you."

"But how did you know one of us would be here?" said Fore-and-Aft. "For you wouldn't have seen me if I hadn't moved."

"Last crossroads before running water and the iron railway on the edge of the city?" said The Smith. "One of you would always be here."

"What's in the bag?" said Fore-and-Aft.

"A question," said The Smith. "Open it."

The Sluagh took the bag, shook it and opened the drawstring. He reached a hand in and took out a small scrabble of something Lucy couldn't make out.

"Bones?" said Fore-and-Aft.

"A bone pet. Sent to my cells. To kill one of your own," said The Smith.

"Ah," said the Sluagh. "That bone pet."

He drew himself to full height and tossed the bag back to The Smith.

"No interest to me. Its job is done, and it would have been tied to the man who made it."

"Who was working for a man called Mountfellon," said The Smith. "Why?"

"I know nothing that might help you," said the Sluagh.

"Why did you work on the minds of a girl and the man Ketch to insert her into our midst?" said The Smith. "Why are you allied with this Mountfellon?"

"We ally with no one," said the Sluagh, turning away.

"By Law and Lore I command you to answer!" snapped The Smith.

The Sluagh rounded on him, entirely uncowed by his tone. His lip curled in a sneer.

"Law and Lore? You, the great traitor, dare invoke Law and Lore? Law and Lore exist to stop two worlds from colliding. I know the words you use. It is not just you who study us. You look into the shadows but we look back at you," he spat. "You say there is a natural world and another one alongside it, a world you call supranatural. Well, we call it the old world, the Pure World. We call the other new and unnatural one the Hungry World."

"The Hungry World?" said The Smith. "What does that nonsense mean?"

Fore-and-Aft grunted in contempt as he began to stride back and forth in front of The Smith, becoming increasingly agitated as the words began to pour out of him in a dam-burst of pent-up anger.

"And is your new world not a hungry one, Smith? Does it not take our forests to build ships so that that can go beyond the great salt waters and bring back more things to sate that endless hunger? Are our trees not taken to make pit props for the holes you dig, grubbing out the coal you need for your smoke-belching machine-farms? Do you not take our very darkness with your gas lamps, the deep darkness we need as much as you need sunlight? And what of our great silences? The places where the only sound was the wind passing over the land and the cry of the birds? You have put your clanking steam machines with their whistles and their damned iron rails through our wastelands. You breed like rabbits in a landscape without foxes. Every month there are more of you. Every year's end there is less room for us than there was at the beginning. The new world is insatiable and you, the mighty Oversight, are partial and blinkered and hostile to us, to the old world. You turn a blind eye to the harm done to us by the new world, by the Hungry World. You were charged to patrol the borders between both. You do not. You look one way, you push one way, your hand is not even, your 'justice' is not fair. You have all lived so long within the Hungry World you have forgotten you have our blood as well as theirs! And when we defend ourselves, because you do not, we are punished and hounded and hurt. We are an affront to you, not because we are monsters, but because your own betrayal of Law and Lore is the true monstrosity, and we are but the living remnants who remind you of your failure and your perfidy, the mirror in which you see yourselves as you really are: lackeys and lick-spittles of the Hungry World."

The Smith had stood his ground in front of the tirade, like an oak tree facing down a gale, but now he took a step forward.

"Be very careful who you call lickspittle, Nightganger, for my hammer might remember the taste of Sluagh blood and get hungry again."

They stared each other down. Then The Smith relaxed, dismissing his moment of threat in a chuckle.

"Forgive me. I came for information. Not a lecture on your griev-ances."

"These are not grievances, Smith. These are atrocities," said Fore-and-Aft. "There is an old way that our people have travelled for twice a thousand years or more, between Wenlock Edge and Grimsby. And the hungry men have pinned iron rails across it, rails that go from London to Manchester and have no break in them. And now the old way cannot be used by us, or such as us, who cannot cross cold iron. Did The Oversight stop the rails? Did you enforce Law and Lore and stop them destroying our ancient landscape? No. You looked the other way. This web of iron is a cage. To pass over the land in our troops is a part of who we have always been, but now we wake up each morning to find another swathe of countryside is barred to us, or only accessible if we take a crazed meandering route that switches back and forth like a madman trying to escape a maze. You are mongrels. You have Pure blood mixed with that of the Hungry World, but I think you hate the Pure in you. I think that is why you betray us at every turn, ignoring our interests and letting the Hungry World eat at us like a wasting disease. You want us to die. You want us to leave, because the Hungry World is too greedy to share. It is a void that must fill itself at anyone's cost but its own."

"What do you want?" said The Smith.

"Law and Lore. Fairly applied. No more. No less."

"And what does that have to do with Mountfellon?" said The Smith sharply. "Is this avalanche of resentment what is behind your new loyalty to him?"

Fore-and-Aft shook his head, almost sadly.

"Who are you to speak of loyalty to us? You of all the people who walk beneath the sky? How can you hope to change your destiny, turn-coat," he sneered. "The mighty Smith who will always betray all you love, as you always have, when the darkness comes back in you."

The Smith's hands flexed, as if he wished he had his hammer to hand.

"Once I believed that," he said, voice rough and low.

"Once?" said the Sluagh.

"Once, yes," said The Smith. "But then I remembered I was a maker. I can turn a horseshoe into a knife or a sword into a ploughshare and back again. I can make or remake anything. Including my fate."

The Sluagh shook his head.

"My father's fathers were right. You have run mad with arrogance."

"Your father's fathers feared the darkness so they made themselves its pets. I went into the darkness. I looked it in the eye. And then I came back. Your father's fathers knew nothing . . ." said The Smith.

The Sluagh smiled nastily and leant in and whispered so that Lucy could only just make out what he said:

"The others, The Oversight, do they ever know – ever guess – what you were? What your true allegiance is? Do you even know?"

"They know who I am. They know I am true. And not even you can guess at my allegiance," said The Smith.

"None come back from beyond the dark mirror unless the powers that rule there allow it," said Fore-and-Aft.

"How would you know?"

The Sluagh waved a hand at the darkness of the night above.

"I am sworn to the night. I know its mysteries."

The Smith laughed, a deep-throated rumble of true mirth.

"The night? The night is nothing compared to the void beyond the mirrors. If dark was light then the darkness beyond is strong as a thousand suns, and the night you say you understand is no more than the sputtering flame on a ha'penny dip."

He picked up the bag of bones and emptied them onto the road. Then he trod on them, ground them to splinters and kicked the debris towards the Sluagh.

"Tell your chieftains. If you continue to work against me, this will be your fate. Ground to flinders and dust and lost in the night breeze. And if I hear of any of you working for Mountfellon or that damned lawyer Templebane we will come against you all with the full force of Lore and Law."

He turned on his heel and strode south.

"Smith," called the Sluagh. "One thing: the Black Knife."

The Smith stopped despite himself, and turned.

"Do you still have it?"

The Smith did not answer. The Sluagh laughed mirthlessly and nodded his head.

"Then I think we all know where your allegiance lies."

And he stepped back into the shadows and was gone. The Smith stared after him for a long time, so long that Lucy got cramp in her leg from not moving as she watched. And then he turned his back on the outer darkness and headed back for the scattered lights of the city beyond the marsh.

Lucy bit down on her lip to ride the cramp and keep herself still as she tried to both understand what she'd just heard, and work out what had not been quite right about it. Because it had not cleared up her mistrust of The Smith at all. In fact, it had posed more questions than she had set out in the night to answer.

As she waited for him to get far enough away before she risked moving to rub and stretch out the cramp, she wished she was going to return to the Safe House and not The Folley on the lonely Isle of Dogs. With Charlie and Cook and even – maybe especially – Cait she felt more secure. With The Smith and his solitary house, she felt too vulnerable and strange.

The Safe House was like a hidden castle within the city, a stronghold that could never fall.

CHAPTER 23

A DENIABLE RUSE

Issachar Templebane was unwell. Not only were his spirits understandably diminished by the death of his twin, the arm that the hellion Sara Falk had smashed was excruciatingly painful. She had not merely broken it, but done so by shattering his elbow. It was an injury that had clearly confounded the bone-setter because it was getting more, rather than less, agonising. He could not sleep properly because every time he moved it felt as if the joint were being dashed to splinters once again. He had returned to the bone-setter and terrified the man into a second attempt at putting him back together, but it had been so painful that he had passed out, and even now he had little confidence he would ever have the use of the joint again. In anticipation of this, he had insisted the arm be strapped to his chest in a sling that allowed him to reach his mouth with the hand by simple action of the wrist. There was, he felt dispassionately, no sense with being left with a functionless arm mended at an angle that didn't even allow him to feed himself with it.

This was about the last dispassionate thought he had, since the homemade variation of Sydenham's Tincture of Laudanum that he favoured for the pain (raw opium, saffron, cinnamon and cloves, bruised and then macerated in a little sherry wine and white honey according to an old family recipe) was having distinct effects on both his thinking and his bowels: where Pountney Templebane was clearly evacuating himself painfully into oblivion in the outhouse in the corner of the courtyard, Issachar was now severely constipated. He was also afflicted by a persistent itching all over his torso, which demented and frustrated him in equal measure, and which also made him suspect his un-emptied bowels were poisoning him from within which led him to send for increasingly strong emetics from the apothecary. His mouth was permanently dry, his eyes seemed to be weakening and his breathing felt shallower and reedier than he could ever remember. He spent a lot of time assembling and reassessing his symptoms and becoming unaccustomedly worried as he did so, which was a result of the overarching effect of his opiated state: unlike some who encounter the poppy and become euphoric, Issachar's constitution took the other path. He was increasingly dysphoric, prey to a deep unease and constantly nagging anxiety. He was, in short, not the Issachar Templebane he had been.

And to make things all the worse, the pain was not much helped by the regular dosing. One effect of this malaise was that Issachar was very keen that the forthcoming move against The Oversight should be entirely deniable, something that might best be seen as accidental. His desire for retribution was entirely personal. He had no desire to advertise, nor would it sweeten his vengeance if The Oversight knew he was the hand that moved against them. He simply wished them removed from the scene. And he was also concerned, increasingly so as the tincture sweated through him in ever larger doses, that if this plan went awry they would come after him and extract a vengeance he might be powerless to resist. There is something elementally unmanning to the psyche in having one of your arms put out of action, and this added to his desire for caution.

Coram's plan had the triple virtues of simplicity, guaranteed devastation and the appearance of a complete and tragic accident.

"Tell me again," he said, wincing as he adjusted his position in the high-backed Chesterfield in which he spent most of his days and nights.

"The sugar manufactory is directly up the slope from The Oversight's headquarters," said Coram. "There are two huge boiling vats, each as tall as a house, resting on hardened firebrick kilns, which provide the heat that melts the sugar. All that is needed is to ensure the kilns explode, making the vats topple, and then a river of flaming molten sugar descends the street and burns them to the ground. I should say that anyone in the house would be unable to escape the flow if not the flames. And if we were 'accidentally' to ensure that a wagon containing barrels of turpentine happened to be drawn up outside the house in the way of the fiery flow, why, I think the ensuing holocaust could be considerably exacerbated."

"Considerably," agreed Templebane, wincing as he reached for the tincture. Coram intercepted him, uncapped the bottle and held it out.

"Thank you, boy," he said, taking a swig. He closed his eyes and waited for the effect to dull the sharpness in his elbow. "And how will you ensure the kilns explode?"

"Grenadoes," Coram said. "I have already arranged to purchase some through the back door, as it were, of the Woolwich Arsenal. It'll be easy as bowling to roll them into the kilns, since the openings are large enough to admit big balks of wood and we don't even need to go to the danger of lighting the fuses. The fire'll do it for us. Just roll 'em in and bunk off sharpish."

Templebane opened his eyes which were, Coram noted, irissed down to pinpricks. Despite that, they swept approvingly over him.

"Fire has always served the Templebanes well, boy. Yes, fire, the cleansing fire is just what we need. Acquire the grenadoes."

THIRD PART
THE DEATH OF EARTH

CHAPTER 24

CONSEQUENTIAL DAMAGE

"The Alp has gone," snarled The Citizen.

"Gone where?" said Mountfellon.

"Gone to whatever hell fate has prepared for him," said The Citizen. "He is dead."

"You have seen the body?"

"I have seen the signs and I know he is dead. Dead and I need . . ."

His eyes smouldered with rage as he choked apoplectically. The bout passed and he wiped the spittle off the corners of his mouth with a cuff.

"This is The cursed Oversight," he said.

"There are other explanations," said Mountfellon.

The Citizen stood up and hurled the chair away from him. It cracked against the wall and knocked a picture frame to the floor, where it broke into shards of gilt and plaster.

"No, Milord. No! They are not only thwarting us and obstructing our experimentation – they are now threatening MY LIFE!"

He was shaking with affronted rage.

"And what have you done?" said Mountfellon, eyeing the damage to his furnishings.

"I have sent a message to bring another Alp to me," said The Citizen. "In the fastest way possible. What do you think I did?"

"In the fastest way possible, or the fastest way acceptable?" said Mountfellon.

"The fastest way possible is the only way acceptable in this case," spat The Citizen.

"You used the mirrors," said Mountfellon. "Despite our agreement not to take that chance again."

"Yes," said The Citizen simply, staring him down. "My life could depend on it."

"Well. You will not do so again," said Mountfellon.

"Or?"

"Or you will answer to me, sir," said Mountfellon coolly.

"And what is the exact question I shall be answering, Milord?" replied The Citizen, his voice suddenly keen and steely as a box of knives.

"I cannot say exactly, but it will doubtless touch on where else you would be more comfortable pursuing your endeavours, Citizen," said Mountfellon. "I take it very ill that you broke your word on the use of the mirrors, but I will countenance one infelicity between us for two reasons: firstly because we share a higher goal; and secondly because you felt your survival was imperilled."

"You are very . . . gracious."

"I am very practical. And as a practical man I should point out that with the advent of the cross-channel steam-packet and the bewildering extension of the locomotive railway network both here and on the continent, a letter may travel to your destination with a despatch that would satisfy both your needs and my strictures in future, and thus save a great deal of wear and tear on our friendship and my paintings."

"Milord. I apologise for my assault on your . . . Romney was it?"

"It is a Ramsay. And a damn fine picture for a Scot. But no harm. A frame can be replaced easily."

"I am relieved."

"As I will be when you re-confirm your undertaking that while we work together in this house, you will not prosecute any assault on The Oversight before we have found a way for me to avail myself of the contents of their library."

The Citizen worked his mouth violently, as if trying to swallow one forced pleasantry too many, and then bowed his head.

"You have my word again, Milord. I am sorry you had to ask a second time."

The dangerous sparkle in his eye as Mountfellon turned away from him hinted that the true sorrow was at Mountfellon asking, not at himself having provoked the question in the first place.

CHAPTER 25

SEA-CHANGE

So Amos and the Ghost had found their way to the English Channel. They descended the green oceanic swell of the ancient, sheep-cropped downland and skirted the white cliffs until they discovered a runnel that dipped down to a shingle beach.

The beach was lonely and untravelled, although there was one fishing boat pulled high above the tideline and turned upside down, wedged safely in the V-shaped depression created where the runnel met the beach. It was held down by ropes against the wind, but laid on rocks that allowed it to stand higher than the ground, so that it was possible to walk beneath it without stooping too much. In fact, it made a very effective roof, and the space below could be used as a sort of improvised hut. That it had been used as such by others was evidenced by the circle of larger stones which had been arranged like an open air hearth just outside it, and by the three driftwood logs which had been dragged around the fire ring as benches. That it was still a boat occasionally used was evidenced by the rolled-up nets at the back of the shelter.

There was no sign of anyone on the beach, and the blackened stones looked not to have been host to a live fire for quite some time, since the glaucous leaves of a sea-cabbage had grown up in the centre of the pit. It was a readymade camp for them, and they were too tired to do anything other than adopt it gratefully, eat a hurried meal of warmed-over porridge and then fall dreamlessly to sleep beneath the upturned vault of the boat hull, using the bundled fishing nets as a mattress.

Amos woke on that first morning to find himself alone, and lay there for a long while, wondering if he felt relieved or betrayed by the apparent disappearance of the Ghost. The slow hiss and sudden percussive thump of the waves hitting the banked-up shingle provided a strangely mesmerising and restful noise in the background, and he had felt little urgency about stirring himself. He watched the sunlight reflect up off the water and dance across a small section of the boat-roof above his head, a patch of rippling light that moved and changed shape as the sun traversed the sky and the sea withdrew towards low tide. Eventually the need to piss moved him out from under the turtle-backed shelter, and he stood facing the sea as he emptied his bladder into a blooming tuft of thrift that had begun to colonise its way from the grass down onto the upper reaches of the beach.

Once relieved, he crunched his way over the pebbles to the steep shelf that led down to the water. He looked right and left and saw no sign of the Ghost, or indeed of anyone, bar the sails of a distant ship, hull down on the horizon.

He felt wonderfully alone.

He also felt like he hadn't had a bath in an age, which was true.

He knew there was a heel of soap in the tinker's pack, and he went and got it. And then with no more ceremony than shucking out of his boots, he walked into the sea, finding a firm, sandy bottom that shelved slowly and made him walk a full fifty yards towards France before he was even knee deep. He kept going and only stopped when the water reached his shoulders. He could not swim. And so he dipped his head below the surface just for a moment, and then began to slowly walk back. He washed his clothes with the soap as they remained on him, lathering and dipping below the water from time to time as he went. Since there was no one on the beach or the clifftops beyond he peeled off the wet and soapy clothes when he was ankle-deep, and rinsed them.

He threw them ashore and then, on impulse, ran back into the water, free and naked as the day he was born, the glittering sea-spray kicking up round his high-stepping feet as he ran, the sun warm on his body. He made no noise, being mute, but inside his head he was laughing gloriously, like the happy and innocent child he had never been. He plunged into the deeper, colder water and then erupted skywards in a great and joyous explosion of exuberance, so full of life and liberty that he felt he might just be able to keep going until he was flying higher and higher, soaring above the water and the beach and the clifftops and the great frozen chalk wave of the Downs beyond—

And then he saw her.

The Ghost was crouched over his clothes, gathering them up, lifting his boots, and walking away up the slope of the beach.

He lost his footing as he landed and went down hard, gravity returning with a vengeance. He shipped a generous mouthful of brine as he did so, and by the time he had got his feet back under him, his head above water and the lungful of Channel back outside himself where it should be, she had disappeared.

Wait.

There was no reply. Maybe she was too far away to hear his panicked thought.

Wait please!

He tried to run against the suck of the sea around his chest, but it seemed to take for ever to get far enough back inshore to clear his hips, and even then his forward progress was awkward and lumbering, all the earlier weightless joy having evaporated from his limbs. By the time he was knee-deep again he was too tired to run effectively, and he staggered ashore to find that running up the shingle bank was so strength-sapping and treacherous that he fell over twice before he crested the rise and saw her again.

She was laying his clothes out on the hot pebbles so they could dry. He stopped.

What are you doing?

She raised her eyes and stared levelly at him. Only then did he consider that he was naked. His hands dropped and cupped, and where he had only minutes before felt as if he could almost fly, he now found himself wishing the ground would open up and swallow him.

He had never been naked in front of a woman, even an old woman, in his life. He had scarcely been naked in front of anyone, in fact.

She shook her head at him, amused.

The body is just a shell. And I had assisted at a dissection long before I was your age, boy. Your physique holds no surprises for me. Go and walk up and down the beach until the wind has dried you.

He turned back down the slope and did as she had bidden. The look she had given him and the tone of her thoughts were different. Not just amused at his dismay at being caught without benefit of clothing, but somehow . . . he could not find the right word for the new tone. But then he had never had a mother, and so he was hard put to find the word "maternal" in his personal lexicon.

By the time he was wind-dry, there was a wisp of smoke rising from above the crest of the shingle, and he ascended to the upper shelf to find she had a billycan heating over the fire-pit.

She did not trouble to look away as he approached his clothes, so he had to run the gauntlet of her eyes a second time as he pulled on his under-drawers, which were still wet.

He left the rest of the clothes to bake on the hot stones and came to sit on one of the driftwood logs as she made herself free with the contents of his pack, brewing up the tea. This was the first time she had done this, and somehow the unwonted domesticity of her actions further perturbed him. Power had somehow shifted. He could not work out if this was a benign or a dangerous thing. She looked happy enough as she worked, and indeed he heard her hum as she did so, a nursery rhyme he recognised from the meagre schoolroom in the workhouse, the one called "Do you know the Muffin Man?". She paused for a moment and caught his eye.

A nice warm and buttery muffin would be just the thing right now, would it not?

He nodded as the wind eddied and drove the thin smoke from the fire right into his eyes. He closed them and waited until it moved back to its original quarter.

"Sit by an open fire with a smirched conscience and smoke will follow you round the compass," she said. "It's nature's way of punishing the unrighteous."

What?

"Have some tea," she said, pouring from the billycan. "I'm just teasing."

She was just as disconcerting as before, but he detected an unusual, gentler edge to her. He sipped the hot tannic brew, careful not to burn his lips on the metal rim of the cup. It was sweet.

"Last of the sugar," she said.

He nodded and drank. After the bracing cold of the sea and the caressing warmth of wind and sun, the tea coursed through him, heating him through from the inside and making him feel strangely both relaxed and reinvigorated.

Where were you? he asked.

"Along the shore, around the far bend in the cliffs," she said.

What were you doing?

"Looking," she said. "Just looking."

But she wouldn't say what for.

They stayed for two more nights, loafing on the edge of the world, enjoying the sun and the charged air where the waves pounded ceaselessly but – given the mildness of the season – relatively amiably along the pebble rampart that protected this stretch of cliff-buttressed downland from the sea.

On the afternoon of Amos's first "swim", the owner of the boat came down the runnel with his son and an aged donkey loaded with another fishing net. He was a cheery, red-faced man who seemed unconcerned that they had been using his vessel as a shelter, and even was so generous as to allow it was a "sensible" measure. He and his son then took the roof and turned it back into a boat, loaded it with the net and had allowed Amos to help them drag it into the water. Amos had shaken his head when offered a berth for the afternoon's fishing expedition, but when they had returned with three baskets of fish, the Ghost acquired more goodwill from this friendly and accommodating fisherman by using some of their purloined coin to purchase both some fish and a thick plug of his tobacco. She had noticed a cutty pipe in the bottom of the tinker's pack, and when the fisherman and his offspring had upended the boat back into its original roof-like configuration and headed back up the runnel with the even more overloaded donkey, she had filled it and lit up.

They had eaten well of the fresh fish, and they sat back in the darkness, watching the sparks from the fire ascend towards a moon that was within a thin sliver of full. She caught him looking at her, and pointed at the great silvered disc that seemed to hang on the very tip of the cliff above them, like a plate.

Close now.

Close to what? he thought back.

Close to full. And then we shall be able to leave.

Until this point he had not thought of where or indeed why they would go. But a yawn drowned his next thought, and then he was asleep.

He woke to find she had laid the blankets across him, and that the moon had travelled halfway across the star-strewn immensity overhead. It was so clear a night that he felt no need to roll under the cover of the boat-roof, in the shadow of which he expected she was now slumbering. He closed his eyes and returned to the comfort of sleep.

He would have slept less soundly if he had known that the Ghost was not doing the same thing under the cover of the boat, but was in fact haunting the chalk highlands above him, striding up to the flattened tops with a purposeful gleam in her eye, and a sharp metal knife in her hand.

She found the intersection of two sheep trails on the crest of the downland and sat there for a while, eyes turned to the moon. Then she sniffed the air and bent, cutting a small square of turf from the ground which she carefully laid aside, revealing the bare chalk beneath. Without flinching, she ran the blade across her palm and squeezed dark blood into the hole so that it spattered the white below. Then she used the knife again to rip a strip of cloth from the bottom of her shift, and stanched and bound the wound. She spat into the hole three times, and then looked down into it. Anyone close by would have heard the following doggerel whispered into the night.

> By the blood in my veins, by the moon in the sky,
> By the free earth below, Mountfellon must die.

She replaced the trapdoor of turf over the bloodied chalk and pressed it back into place. And then she sat, facing away from the beach, alert and waiting.

She spoke no more out loud, but the thought sped away from her like an arrow, away from the sea and back into the dark heart of the countryside to her north.

Come.

CHAPTER 26

CALM BEFORE THE STORM

Hodge was taking time to adjust to his reduced state. Charlie never heard him complain once about his blindness, and in that regard he was as tough and philosophical about the injury as Jed had always been with his own hurts and wounds: like the terrier he just became quieter and went into himself until he had healed as much as he was going to heal, and then he got on with life.

Charlie spent the most time with him of anyone since, in the absence of Sharp and Sara, Cook was the immoveable cornerstone of the Safe House, and The Smith spent his nights at The Folley where Lucy remained billeted, which was not to say that Lucy and Charlie saw little of each other: the truth was quite the opposite since Lucy was driven by dog cart, or sculled downriver by Emmet to the Safe House, which she entered by the river gate, and their daily shared lessons would take place in the kitchen or the Red Library.

"The Law," said The Smith, one dim afternoon as they clustered round the scrubbed deal table with the range seeming to throw out less heat than normal. "The Law is the simple bit. It's common sense, and where it's not sense, it's common decency. Law says neither natural nor supranatural should predate one upon the other, nor should either side use its own particular advantages to the detriment of the other."

"It's fair play," said Charlie.

"Exactly," said The Smith. "There's a line between the two and The Oversight patrols it. We keep the balance."

"Except when we don't," said Cook quietly, riddling the grate to try and coax more fire from the coals, speaking so low that Lucy thought she must be the only one who heard her. She turned and looked a question at the older woman.

Jed was sitting by the door, looking meaningfully at it and then back at Hodge and anyone who could catch his eye, tail thumping hopefully.

"In a minute," said Hodge. "I'm having my tea."

Jed barked.

"Anything worth having's worth waiting for," said Hodge cryptically.

Jed whined and then slumped to the ground with his back to them and his nose to the gap beneath the door. Every now and then he sniffed deeply and his tail thumped the floorboards.

"Cook sometimes has qualms," said The Smith.

"What are qualms?" said Lucy. She was thinking of what she had heard The Smith and the Sluagh talk about on Ruckholt Lane. Somehow the fact that Cook also often differed from The Smith's view of things just added to that discomforting itch she felt about him.

"Qualms are luxuries the desperate can't afford," said The Smith with a finality that ended the conversation without answering the question at all.

One of the worst things about that itch was that ever since she'd heard the Sluagh fire his parting shot about the Black Knife and the matter of allegiances, she had been sure the way to scratch it was to examine it more closely, and glint the truth from it. The Smith's prohibition, telling her it would be too much for her mind to cope with, might be the perfect way for him to keep her away from his secret. Or he might be telling the truth. It was the fear of the latter that kept her fingers off it. But it was a growing temptation. And a part of that temptation was that she'd never thought of using glinting as a tool, on purpose: there was something quite liberating about the prospect of using what had once seemed like an affliction as an extra power. But for the moment, caution outshouted curiosity.

Hodge and The Smith were still locked in their discussion.

"There are things we just do not have the time or the luxury of examining in our reduced and parlous state," said The Smith, clearly keen to move on with the lesson, which in this case happened to be about the identification of malign entities. "Now tell me three characteristics of changelings."

Charlie and Lucy exchanged a smile. They had spent a large portion of the previous afternoon watching the changelings in the Sly House cell through the viewing window. They were particularly pleased with themselves because they had snuck away to do this, and had entered the hidden passage beneath the public house without either of the Bunyons noticing. They were both getting better at moving fast and not being seen.

"Their faces don't quite work," said Lucy.

The Smith exhaled in disappointment.

"I should say their faces work all too well, Lucy Harker. I should say their ability to manipulate themselves to mimic those they seek to replace is evidence of a profoundly overdeveloped facial facility . . ."

"No," said Charlie. "Lucy's got it. They don't actually look *exactly* like whoever they're mimicking. They just make people think they do. It's more clever than copying like a calotype picture or a waxwork . . ."

"Is it?" said The Smith, sounding irritable and sceptical in equal measure.

"They can adjust their looks, but it's almost more a thing of expressions and atmospheres than being a facsimile," said Lucy.

"Facsimile," said The Smith. "Now that's a fancy word."

"If you don't want me using fancy words, someone shouldn't put a dictionary on my bedside table," said Lucy. "Or have Emmet do so."

Cook harrumphed and looked a bit embarrassed.

"Nothing wrong with reading dictionaries. Nutritious things, dictionaries," she said. "Thought you'd like it."

"I do," said Lucy. "I sometimes get lost in it when I can't sleep—"

"Changelings!" snapped The Smith. "We are talking about identifying them. Concentrate—"

"Look closely and you see their faces never quite set," said Lucy. "Like junket that doesn't take."

"My junket always takes," said Cook. "But I know what you mean."

"Sure, and I'm partial to a spot of junket myself," said a familiar voice from the corner.

The Smith turned to peer into the shadows. Cait leant forward into the light and smiled innocently.

"Glory o' the day to you," she said.

"I didn't know you were there," said The Smith.

The innocent smile turned into a mischievous grin that made something flip again in Lucy's stomach.

"I wouldn't be much of a hunter if I wasn't able to be unnoticed when I wanted, now would I?" she said. "The youngsters are right about the changelings. They don't copy exactly, not once they're grown. What they do is part acting, part expressions and mimicry, but all of it pushed along by working on your mind as you look at them. They're like conjurers who can see what you expect to see and then stop you noticing that what you *do* see isn't quite the full sixpence. And the truth is they are forgettable in themselves. Your eyes will slide off them if you don't concentrate. It's slippery they are, and no mistake."

She stepped out of the chair she had been sitting in and dragged it up to the table. She spun it and straddled it, leaning forward and resting her arms on the back as she looked into Lucy's and then Charlie's eyes.

"You'll be wanting to know the trick of recognising them and stopping that slipperiness?"

They nodded. The Smith and Cook exchanged a look. Cait held her palms out.

"Put your hands against mine," she said. Lucy and Charlie each pressed a palm to Cait's. Charlie felt self-conscious about the dry warmth of her skin against his own. She moved her hands back so there was a half-inch gap between them.

"Now close your eyes. Clear your mind, and tell me what you notice."

Charlie could still feel the warmth of her hand across the gap. More than that, he could feel a kind of buzz, or a vibration.

"Feel it?" said Cait.

"There's a reverberation," said Lucy.

"Well, that's another fine word and if it means a hum in the air like a hive full of bees, you're spot on," said Cait. "But there's something else."

"I can only feel a warmth and the hum," said Charlie.

"It's not a feeling thing," said Cait. "You have other senses than touch, do you not? Why, as many as the fingers on your hand if you trouble to count them."

"Fish," said Lucy suddenly. "There's a smell of fish. Clean fish, fresh fish — not sea fish."

Charlie inhaled and smiled.

"Yes. Freshwater fish," he said. "Like a trout."

"There you go," said Cait. "Open your eyes. A changeling sends a vibration through the air as it walks, and when it's changing it's even stronger. And there's always that clean fish smell about them — nothing unpleasant, just . . ."

"Slippery," said Charlie.

"Like a salmon," agreed Cait.

"Wait," said Lucy. "Does that mean you're a changeling too?"

"Faith no, not a bit of it," said Cait with a wink. "Just good at pretending."

The Smith nodded.

"Like a salmon," he said. "That's a good lesson. They won't forget."

Cait looked almost pleased at his grudging approval.

"Arrah now, sometimes show works better than tell," she said.

"Most times, in fact," said The Smith. "You learn more by doing than listening. Anything you choose to teach them while you're with us would be gratefully accepted, I assure you. You have gifts to give, and though I accept your decision to walk the lone path as a venatrix, it always seems a shame to me that you solitary ones have no one to pass your wit and knowledge on to. For you clearly have both in abundance."

Cait inclined her head slightly, taking the compliment. Cook looked at The Smith and then at Lucy. She raised her eyebrows theatrically as if to indicate that she thought a certain man who should be old enough to know better was a bit taken with the girl from Skibbereen.

"Well, teaching's an honourable thing and an undervalued thing," Cait said, "and sure, wouldn't I have been lost and floundering had I not had a wise old soul who took me under her wing as a mentor when I was green as new mown grass? I'm happy to share any useful scraps with these two while I'm enjoying your hospitality, and small thanks it is by comparison with all the delicious meals I'm getting used to. Going to quite spoil me for anyone else's cooking for the rest of my life, I can see that now, and what I can't see the waistband of my skirt's telling me, and no mistake."

Cook harrumphed, and looked embarrassed and pleased in equal measure.

"How do you do that?" said Charlie. "With the changelings?"

"Do what?" Cait said.

"Make yourself seem like them – I mean, send out vibrations and their smell. I mean . . . are you sure you're not some kind of . . . Are you a changeling?"

Cait snorted back a laugh.

"I'm a hunter, Charlie boy. And so it helps to be good at disguise and mimicry. It's like other trackers have birdcalls to bring in their prey, it's just a trick. I've the knack of sending out a resonance. The fish smell?"

She reached back and pulled a newspaper wrapped package into view.

"Two trout from Billingsgate market this morning. For my tea. And your education . . ."

The passage of time seemed to accelerate for both Lucy and Charlie as the late and lazy summer began to feel more like autumn. In part this was because they were both kept busy learning and doing what Cook described as "getting good and seasoned". Once it became apparent that the venatrix now had her own reasons for staying in London, awaiting the return of *Lady of Nantasket*, the ship that had taken the object of her hunt across the Atlantic, The Smith and the others seemed to relax about her. The two younger members of the Hand enjoyed walking the city with Cait almost as much as they liked doing so with Hodge. She was sharp and observant, and had the knack of alerting them to anomalies in such a way that made them feel partners in the enterprise, rather than mere students. She was, in simple terms, fun. Partly this was her nature, partly it was perhaps because she was so much closer to their own age than the other members of the Hand. And partly she was herself diverted by the great teeming variety the city presented them with, being herself, as she said, "no more than a simple country girl from the rolling green", and some of her wonder and mirth at the city was passed on to them. She was also a steadying influence on Lucy, who was able to talk to her about her misgivings about The Smith. When she first broached it, she had felt she was betraying a confidence, maybe even being needlessly open about a fear she would more normally have kept to herself, but Cait had listened to her carefully and seriously. And then she had said that in her mind, misgivings were always useful, and that she should listen to them and be willing to change her views if experience added new information to the picture.

"It's important to have strong beliefs and opinions," she said, "because you want to steer your own life according to your own lights. But the other side of being strong like that is you have to be open to the fact that you might be wrong, and be willing to change those opinions if the evidence rises up and smacks you in the eye."

And because Cait had doubts about being part of a group like The Oversight but was willing enough to work with them on a temporary basis, Lucy decided she was, for the moment, in the right place, where the benefits outweighed the dangers. And the education she was getting was undoubtedly both strange and useful.

Hodge was a good teacher in a wholly different way to Cait. He knew the city from rooftop to riverbed with the compendious detail of a true native. London was in his blood, and indeed the scars on his body attested to the fact that, like the pugnacious Jed who was now always at his side, quite a lot of his blood was spread around London in return.

What Charlie and Lucy didn't fully pick up on was the fact that the three other members of the Hand were exhausted and worried. They were all attuned to something lurking around them without being able to fully apprehend the shape of it. They knew the Safe House was being watched, and were sure that the eyes turned towards it from the shadows belonged to the House of Templebane, but since watching was not a transgression of Law or Lore, they were unable to act fully against it. Hodge did suggest that they should confront Issachar but the others dissuaded him, since not knowing the full extent of his interest or indeed his powers made this, for them, an unchancy thing to do.

"You're scared," Hodge said to The Smith one evening when they were alone, except for Charlie who was sitting in a corner determinedly practising igniting candles without a match, a skill he was still irritatingly less adept at than Lucy.

The Smith just looked at him.

"Standing still in a fight is a good way to lose it," said Hodge.

"We are not in a fight," said The Smith after a long silence. "We are in a war. We have always been in conflict, but things are changing. The Sluagh send one of their own into the city to help work out a stratagem directly against us in concert with other 'normal' enemies. Think how painstakingly that Sluagh, who died killed by his own bone pet, must have picked his way here through a maze of iron railway tracks and barriers of flowing water. Imagine the dedicated hatred necessary for one of them to do that."

"But still you are frightened," said Hodge. "You do not want to confront this Templebane because you fear his reach. And that is not worthy of us. Not worthy of Sharp. Or Sara. Or any that have gone before."

"If some of those who went before had been a little more frightened, it is likely they would not now be gone and we would not be in such a parlously reduced state," said The Smith. "So that argument cuts no ice with me, old friend. Fear is a perfectly good whetstone to keep us keen and ready."

"Those are just bloody words," said Hodge, who was at the core of his being a creature of action.

"More than words," said The Smith. "They are armour against folly. You know the saying . . . fools rush in . . . And we must think of the future."

Hodge snorted and tapped the handle of the knife at his belt.

"I'm no fool, Smith. And you know damn well that we are both far from what credulous folk who believe in such things call angels either."

He stood and made for the door.

"Where are you going?" said The Smith.

"The one bright spot on the horizon is that the Irish terrier bitch Jed's taken a spark to seems to be in season and is disposed to spend some time with him," said Hodge. "Only the uncooperative pimping bastard that thinks he owns her has got her shut up in a back closet behind a tall wall until it passes."

"And?" said Cook.

"And Jed would like a bit of a hand getting over," said Hodge, as if it was obvious. "Over the wall. They'll make some fierce, clever pups they will and all. And like you just said, Smith, got to think of the future."

He nodded at Charlie.

"And it's a crime for a growing boy not to have a dog of his own."

Charlie watched him leave, listening to the excited scrabbling of Jed's claws as he raced to the door, and realised that although he hadn't really considered it, a dog would indeed be a splendid thing to have at his side in whatever was to come in the years ahead.

CHAPTER 27

AMOS BOUND

Amos helped the Ghost search the shoreline the second day they were at the seaside. They trudged a mile and more along the beach, heads down, looking for sea-glass, glass with its original shininess frosted and its sharp edges smoothed and rounded by the action of the waves tumbling broken bottle shards back and forth among the stone pebbles. It was a strangely hypnotic thing to do, with the sound of the surf in his ears and the heat of the sun on his back. He scanned the endless variety of sea-shaped shingle ribboning away in front of him, trying to keep alert to the anomalies, the gleam of colour among the brown, white and grey of the flint pebbles. He found one piece that looked promising but the Ghost rejected it wordlessly, tossing it away into the salt water before continuing with her own perusal of the shoreline. He began collecting stones with holes in them instead, looping them on a piece of old twine he found tangled round a salt-bleached fragment of wood.

"Why are you collecting those?" said the Ghost.

He just shrugged and carried on.

"People used to think you could only see uncanny things by peering at them through a holed stone," she said. "It's not true though."

He knew this was right: he remembered the Sluagh, certainly the uncanniest things he had ever seen, materialising out of the darkness in the field behind the inn, just before he had run and fallen into the canal, the night he'd killed the tinker. He'd seen them straight, with no gimmick like a holed stone.

Why are you collecting sea-glass pebbles?

She didn't answer him. She just crunched ahead, looking at the line where the wet stones met the dry.

What do you need them for?

"I don't need them," she said quietly, after a while. "They're not for me."

Her eyes seemed to be sharper than his, because by the time they turned and headed back along the beach her pockets rattled with sea-glass in several shades of blue, green and orangey-brown. She rejected the two pieces he found because they were clear glass, now tumbled to a dull white.

"No one has white eyes," she sniffed, an explanation that clearly meant something to her but which left him none the wiser.

He carried on finding stones with holes worn in them, and by the time they got back to the boat he had a heavy loop of them swinging from his fist.

"Looks like a necklace," she said.

He nodded. He didn't tell her the swung weight of it also felt like a weapon. He hung it from the back of his pack and left it there.

They sat by the fire again as the sun dropped behind the edge of the world, and they talked about many things, but the one that stuck in his mind was the matter of The Oversight and their ongoing conflict with the Sluagh. She spoke of them with a strange mix of regret and something close to contempt, as if – he thought – she was talking of an old friend who had somehow betrayed her. He'd heard of the Free Company while listening in to conversations had behind closed doors in the counting house, but he'd never been quite sure what they did or why the Templebanes were opposed to them. Having himself had a terrifyingly close run with the Sluagh, he thought any people who were against them were probably more to be liked than feared, whatever the Ghost felt about them.

That night, for the first time since they stopped by the sea, he slept badly, gripped by a nightmare from which he woke groggy and disorientated, the kind of psychic fouling you make yourself stay awake after in order that the memory of it is washed away before closing your eyes and again risking sleep. Only when he was sure that the taste of the dream had faded entirely did he let himself drift off again. And then he had the dream all over again anyway: it was a gory replay of the death of Mr M'Gregor, a version where Amos was trapped in a great hall, full of doors, and he was chased by something, and each time he opened a door to escape there was someone from his past standing there with a horse-pistol like M'Gregor's, and no matter what he did – run away, try and slide past, plead, cajole, warn – they all just put the barrel beneath their chin and pulled the trigger happily, often laughing as they painted the door lintels and ceilings with the inside of their heads. It was the species of dream where you know it's a dream while you are bogged in it, and that the relief of consciousness is just a hair's breadth away, if only you could escape the inexorable tug of the illusion in which you're mired. He woke gasping, his hands clawing at the night air, as if he had pulled himself out of the pit of sleep by main force alone.

The Ghost was sitting in the moonlight, very still, looking at him.

I was trapped in a nightmare, he thought, sitting up.

"I saw," she said. "But it's all right now. We can go."

Go?

She stood and looked away back up the runnel towards the high chalk beyond.

"It's time," she said. "Full moon. It's not safe here any more."

Maybe he was still disorientated by the vividness of the carnage and the impotence and the guilt in his dreams, or perhaps it was the deep conviction in her tone, but he felt a chill shudder through him as he stood and looked around. Their safe haven did not look so welcoming somehow. The sea was too calm. The cliffs seemed to have grown taller while at the same time the moon appeared to have come unnaturally close, hanging over the water and silvering it from horizon to shore.

The intense reflection of its brightness made a thick streak of light which ran across the surface of the Channel from horizon to shore, a band of illumination that seemed to be ominously pointing directly at them.

Without much noticing how he got his boots on or hoisted the tinker's pack back onto his shoulders, Amos found himself hurrying away from the shingle, back up the slope towards the high chalk.

It felt as if it took longer to get back up to the top than it had to descend the sweep of land, not in that it took more energy, which it did, but more as if the ground had stretched in their absence. Much as the flat sea was rendered unworldly in the exceptional brightness of the low-hanging moon, the smoothness of the grass all around them no longer seemed at all familiar. There was not a whisper of wind, and all he could hear was the sound of their feet and the swing of the stones on the back of his pack, scuffing the canvas as they moved. He could also hear his heart pound and the noise of his breathing as they laboured upwards. For the longest time, he felt as if the arc of the slope ahead of them never changed, as if he was still dreaming, as if that dream was of walking ever onwards round a featureless grassy ball with no beginning or end, doomed to toil for ever over the endless curve, like a man trapped and tethered to a moon-washed treadmill. His eyes blinked in relief when he finally made out the shape of rocks breaking the featureless swell, humped round the sheep crossroads on the high ridge ahead.

The relief lasted until they reached the junction and the Ghost stopped and spoke to the rocks.

"I thought we would have to wait for you."

And then the rocks replied, standing up, revealing that they were not rocks at all, but men who had been crouched motionless in the moonlight.

"Why are you surprised?" the tallest one said. "You called us last moonrise."

He was a head taller than Amos. Even in the brightness of the night, it was hard to make out whether the expression on his face was kind or hostile because the normal, readable contours of his visage were broken up and obscured by the twisting tangle of dark tattoos that covered it. The tattoos extended up the shaven sides of his head to the crest of hair that ran down it, in the kind of long top-knot favoured by the distant Mohawk tribes of North America, a striking engraving of which Amos had once seen in the window of a printers in Cheapside. There was some kind of ornament or animal fixed to the very front of the hair, so that it squatted over the midpoint of his brow like the figurehead of a ship. Amos had the initial thought that it was some kind of giant beetle: it was humped and shiny enough with a kind of hard chitinous surface, but as the man angled his head to look back at him, he realised it was the skull of an animal, painted black. It was larger than a rabbit's skull. From the patchwork of black and white fur that made up the man's coat, he decided it must be a badger. It was an odd detail for him to be focusing on, he realised even as he made the thought, because that was not the most striking thing about the man, not the bones he wore plaited into his mohawk, nor the ones that fastened his clothes. Not even the sickle-shaped blade he held loose in one hand was the most striking thing, nor the tattoos. All of these were mere minutiae. The full horror of the thing was that the man that bore them was not a man. Nor was he, or at least his type, unknown to Amos. He was the thing he had been running from since he stepped off Mountfellon's coach.

He was the thing from whom Amos would even now, were it possible, run back into the blood-soaked horror of his recent dream to avoid.

He was worse than nightmare, because he walked the shadows and the darknesses of the real world, the same tattooed darkness that writhed across his face.

He was not a man.

He was Sluagh.

And Amos would have shucked his pack and run, run faster than he had ever run in his life, faster than anyone had ever run in all the long and fear-drenched history of the world, had he not sensed the Sluagh was ready for this and would casually hamstring him the moment he moved, flicking the ugly recurved blade at the straining tendons at the back of his knees in a crippling cut that would come swifter than thought.

The tattoos squirmed as Badger Skull exposed broken teeth in a smile.

"You can hear what I am thinking," he said, voice scratchy and hoarse. "Can't you?"

"He is mute," said the Ghost.

The other Sluagh rose and moved in to encircle Amos completely, looking and poking at him as if he were a sheep at a market. He was surrounded by tattooed faces and rank-smelling animal skins, worn with age and fastened by bones instead of buttons.

"Who is he?"

"He is the Bloody Boy," she replied. And there was something in the sharp look she threw sideways at him that made him keep silent and not say his true name.

And then someone grabbed him from behind and a sack was thrown over his head and cinched tight round his throat, and a boot kicked into the back of his knee, hinging it forward and chopping him helplessly into a kneeling position, and as he threw his hands forward to stop himself falling further, they were expertly looped into a noose that trapped them and bound them together.

He was helpless, blind and trussed up like a chicken for the slaughter in less time than it takes to sneeze.

CHAPTER 28

EX TENEBRIS LUX

It took Sharp some days to find his knife. It had bounced off the side of the cell when he had thrown it to sever the string with which the nun had tried to retrieve the mirror, and had landed somewhere in the dark, lost in the vast bone pile which covered the floor.

He had found someone else's knife within the hour, however.

Once the nun had disappeared from the high chink of light, and taken the candle with her, he had stood in the fetid blackness and tried to think what to do. He had no idea what kind of cavern he was penned in, other than the scant glimpse he had snatched before the candle went out, and given the unfathomable relationship between the topography of the mirrors and the actual geography of the world beyond, even less idea of where on earth it might be. Blind and without much hope as he was, it would have been easy to succumb to gloom or claustrophobia. Instead he thought of Sara Falk. He found himself wondering what she would do if she found herself in such an impossible pass. He decided she would not give up but would begin to organise herself. He set out on a shaky and treacherous journey across the tangle of bones to find the wall. A wall would be a good start. With a wall he would have something solid to lean on, something to sit against and rest.

He found the wall by slipping over and banging his head on it. For a moment the darkness was lit with stars, and the silence broken by a muffled curse.

Then, having found the wall, he decided to try and clear a small space to sit. Sightless and so by touch alone, he began to move bones out of the way. The floor was hard to find. For a long time, he moved ribs and vertebrae and femurs and skulls and who knows what else without finding anything beneath except more of the same. In the darkness, it felt like bones all the way down. Except every now and then the osseous remains were tangled in shreds of what had once been clothes – shirts and jackets and dresses and boots. Again, it was the kind of work that could easily have unhinged him had he let his mind wander on the matter of exactly whose skeletons he was handling because, if his surmise was correct, he would certainly have known and liked some of the dead when he was still a child. Indeed, he was shifting the bones of hands that might have held him with kindness, and knee bones on which a happier and much smaller version of himself might have sat. Because of this, he steeled himself not to succumb to the sadness all around him by speculating on the "who" of the bones, but instead on the more general "what": he used touch to identify the general types, and by concentrating on the individual components – a femur, a scapula, a jaw – he was able to avoid focusing on whose once familiar flesh they might have underpinned.

The boots were the first good thing that happened to him in the dark. There was a moment of qualm when he found the first pair, which he dispelled immediately, knowing the owners were long gone and would undoubtedly wish him well in his present extremity. But that pair did not fit him; the second pair must have been a woman's and were even smaller, but the third boot he tried on fit well enough, once he had removed the bony foot and shinbones, but finding its mate was impossible.

Still, one boot was better than no boots, and he dug on, using his protectively shod foot to shove the bone tangle aside as he went.

He had got used enough to grubbing among the fragmented skeletons and handling the bones not to feel queasy about it any more, and then his hand found skin.

The feeling of taut leathery hide beneath his hand made him retch, that and the thought that this might be the remains of someone he had known. He stopped working for a while and leant against the rough stone wall until he was able to steel himself to his task again. He bent and gripped what he now took to be a torso with both hands – and then his hand found a pocket. Not skin, he realised with relief. A leather jerkin.

He coughed out a short laugh, and then stopped, suddenly breathless with hope as he felt something else: in the pocket were three regularly shaped tubes, too uniform to be bones. He pulled one out and felt it. It had a flat bottom, a smooth cylindrical body about two hand breadths long, which tapered to a blunt dome at the end, out of which poked a tuft of something. String perhaps. Or . . .

"A wick."

He heard the wonder in his voice echo off the walls in the darkness. Then he flicked his wrist and the darkness was gone, banished and pushed to the very edges of his prison by the light blazing from the candle held in his hand.

"*Ex tenebris lux*," he said, and smiled, both at the banishment of the dark and the unbidden memory of Cook, sitting at a scrubbed deal table lit by a very similar candle, teaching a much younger version of himself Latin. In his mind's eye he could also see his fellow pupil, a young girl with raven-black tresses, sticking her tongue out at him, unseen by their unlikely Classical tutor. He had forgotten how Sara's face looked framed in dark hair, in the time before shock had turned it white. "Out of darkness, light."

He looked around the ceiling above him. He looked up first because he wanted to leave looking at the bone pile until last.

It was hard to see all the way, and he snapped a flame onto the two other candles and held all three over his head. The first thing he realised was that he was definitely not in a room. He was in a cave. The walls encircled him in a continuous overhanging curve, unclimbable and dwindling in circumference as they rose upwards, penning him at the base of a rock-bound void the shape of an irregular cone, wider at the bottom and narrowing to a flattened dome at the apex. It was a strangely smooth and organic shape, as if it had been formed by a bubble in the once molten rock, or perhaps by some unseen and aeons-long process of subterranean water erosion: certainly he saw irregularly spaced dark rings around the walls which marked the differing tidemarks of age-old water levels. Just below the apex of the roof, at the small end of the cone, was a paler ring, and offset to one side of it was a small hole, clearly the chink through which the nun had observed him.

He turned slowly, hoping to see another fissure which might hold a second way out of the natural bottle-dungeon at the bottom of which he stood, but the walls were dishearteningly regular.

He braced himself and looked around the floor to each side. It was a boneyard, as he had felt it to be. The skeletons were strewn haphazardly across each other, limbs splayed every which way in a great sprawling jumble of death. The bones were mostly dull and tallow-coloured, not bleached, and where they were not they were darker brown and shiny like old horn. Some were on their backs, some were face down, some were bent awkwardly in positions that made no sense to him, contorted in death and jammed in topsy-turvy wherever they fitted. Mostly the flesh was long gone, but there were some leathery remnants: hands like gloved talons, withered legs and one cocked skull pulled quizzically askance by an unrotted rawhide of tendons and skin still tethering one side of its neck to its shoulder. The clothes had mostly gone the way of the flesh and disintegrated to rags and dust, but there were tatterdemalion remnants here and there, mainly hats, boots and belts which survived, often more or less intact. And where there were belts, there were, he was pleased to see, blades.

He reached across and pulled a cutlass from a scabbard. The scabbard cracked and fell off what had once been a sword but was now a pitted shank of rust. He discarded it and looked for another.

They were all shaling arcs of corrosion, each as bad or worse than the last. By the time he found one that might, with weeks of grinding against the stone walls, be capable of retaining an edge, he had formed a nasty suspicion as to how all the people around him had died.

He sat back on his haunches and surveyed the charnel house floor.

"You drowned . . ." he said. "You all drowned. I'm sorry . . ."

He looked up again, his eyes rising above the aged, high watermarks until it found the paler ring close to the top.

"Brighter," he whispered.

The candles in his fist flared and started to burn stronger and faster. Melting wax began to ribbon down and spill over his fingers but he didn't flinch. Instead he stared at the pale ring. With more light he saw it for what it was — a circumference of desperate scratches and panicked gouges hacked there by the men and women, trapped by rising water which jammed them in against the unforgiving roof of the cavern, made in a last desperate attempt to break through the adamantine stone dome that had ultimately drowned them.

"Out," he said.

The candle flames extinguished themselves. He remained staring sightlessly at the roof, unable to clear his mind of the imagined end of The Oversight, the men and women kicking to stay afloat in the darkness as the water rose, becoming jammed in closer and closer to each other as the cavern roof narrowed to its blunt point, then chopping and slashing at the rock in final desperation as the air pocket got smaller and shallower. He did not want to know what that had looked like. They had had candles and his own ability to make them stay alight. They would have seen the end coming. The space above would not have been wide enough at the end for all that had been trapped in here to stay above the water, so at what point had they started drowning each other, submerging their comrades by mistake as each tried to boost his or her head above water? Had there been discipline? Honour? Sacrifice?

"It was a dog's death," he said to the void. "Someone drowned them. Like puppies in a bag."

He imagined the thrashing and the screams. He really did not want to know what that had sounded like, what had been shouted, who had said what to whom . . .

. . . but he imagined it anyway. He was used to life or death struggles, but rarely at odds of more than one or two to one. This was a different order of killing. And it had not been a fight, fair or foul. It had just been a trap, a fatal mechanism. It had been death wholesale, murder in bulk, an eradication, not a battle.

He stood there a long time. And because it was dark nothing saw him wipe his eyes, and nothing saw him set his jaw.

"Right," he said.

He put two candles in his pocket and flicked the remaining one into life. He looked around. There would be more candles, and other things that might be useful hidden in the tangled boneyard around him. If Fortune chose to smile, he might even find a mirror, though he was painfully aware Fortune had recently only favoured him with her absence. Though he could not make this right, he could still put things in order. And in doing so, who knew what he might find that might be useful? Even now he saw the remains of a barrel, and remembered that the ones who had bravely gone through the mirrors to destroy the great evil threatening the nation had taken gunpowder with them. From the parlous state of the barrel, it was clear that the powder had long been washed away, but there might be unbroken barrels beneath the bone pile. He would have to start digging.

But before he began, he saw himself in the mirror that he had saved. He remembered the nun's warning about other things following him in here, and shuddered. He didn't even like the idea of anything watching him from the other side. Now that he had walked in the world behind the mirrors, he knew he would never quite trust a looking-glass not to be observing him right back. Maybe that's why they were called looking-glasses, because they did the looking too. He turned it to the wall.

"Very well," he said, stretching. "I believe it is time to tidy up."

CHAPTER 29

THE WHITE TATTOO

Amos lay face down on the grass, his head in a rough hessian bag, power-less to extricate himself from the rope cuffing his hands, powerless to do anything other than listen to the words and thoughts passing back and forth in the night air above him. He had missed a passage of time, but did not know how. He assumed from the throb in his temples that he had fallen forward and stunned himself, or that he had been purpose-fully knocked out with a blow to the head.

The damp sack smelled terrible, as if dead things had been carried in it. Breathing was hard, and when he tried to move he realised at least one person and possibly two were actually sitting on him. He stopped strug-gling and concentrated on breathing and slowing his racing heart. As he did so, he was able to clear his mind enough to listen to the conversation going on beyond the limited world of his sack-wrapped head.

"He is a tool," said the Ghost. "A weapon."

"We have no need of more weapons," said a voice he took to be the one he had christened Badger Skull, who seemed to be the leader of the band of Sluagh.

"I know of what you have need," she said. "And better than that, I know how to get it, if you can be patient."

"You know nothing of our needs," he said.

"I know Mountfellon," she said. "And I know he must die."

Badger Skull paused. Amos heard the silence and somehow felt the freight it carried, but he did not see his captor turn and look pointedly at the other Sluagh before turning to peer even more closely at the Ghost, sniffing deeply as he did so, as if learning her scent.

"What do you know of us, you who calls us through blood and chalk and uses a name that is hateful to all the Pure who walk the clean darkness of night?" he said.

"I know you want the flag that was once yours," she said. One of the Sluagh sitting on Amos's back shifted and the sharp-set buttock bones dug painfully into the unprotected area over his kidneys.

"The flag is still ours," hissed another Sluagh, perhaps the one sitting on his legs. "It was stolen and iron-bound and stolen again, passed between our enemies and ill-wishers, its true power over us forgotten by them, but it is still ours!"

"I know it is," said the Ghost calmly. "I know it is a map of your world and a guarantor of free passage through it. I know it holds the oath-lock that binds all Sluagh and gives cold iron its power over you – a warrandice put on your own banner by your conquerors millennia past."

The Sluagh were suddenly quiet. Amos could almost see the looks being exchanged between his captors.

"How do you know this?" said Badger Skull. "Who are you?"

"I am no one," she said. "Once I was someone, once I knew things. Now I am vengeance. Now I am a weapon and a tool like the Bloody Boy there."

You betrayed me, thought Amos. *I helped you and you betrayed me.*

Yes, she replied. *What of it? It had to be done.*

And before he could reply she was talking again, almost as if she wanted to shut him up.

"I know where it is," she said.

"Gallstaine Hall," sneered Badger Skull. "The whereabouts is not unknown to us."

"But you do not know how to penetrate the defences that ward the building," she said. "Ironstone built and ringed and wrapped with iron, it is forbidden to you."

"We will find a way," he replied after a brief silence. "We have waited centuries. Everything fails in the end, even the plans and devices of cunning men."

"Especially the devices of men, cunning or no," she agreed. "But I can help you now. If I tell you how to use the Bloody Boy, you will have the flag within the next cycle of the moon. I have seen it."

"You cannot know that," said the Sluagh on Amos's back.

"She cannot see the future," said the one on his legs.

"No one can see the future," said Badger Skull. "Much is possible, many things that light-drenched folk cannot or do not dare to imagine. But not that."

"I can feel it though," she said. "I can feel the future."

"It is not possible," he said. "You are mad."

"She looks mad," chuckled the sharp-bottomed Sluagh, shifting again.

"Can a Glint survive without a heart-stone?" she said.

Badger Skull grunted.

"For a time," he said, "and then she becomes depleted. Then disordered. Then crazed. And then she dies."

"How long a time?" asked the Ghost.

"Three years, four years maybe, not much more," said Badger Skull. "There was a gang of monks up Lindisfarne way once put a Glint in a cell for her own good, thinking she was possessed but not wanting to burn her. Being 'kind' men. Was said she screamed solid for close to five years before she died. Monks took to suffering her cries as part of their penance. Such is the kindness of the light-dwellers. But we never heard of a Glint living stoneless longer than that."

"You're sure of that?" she said.

"Sure as the moon is silver, and that darkness swallows light," said the Sluagh.

"I was a Glint," she said. "I am a Glint. And my heart-stone was taken from me, with much else, fifteen years ago."

"That's not possible," said Badger Skull.

"Yet here I am," she said. "Not the girl I was. Not possible. Not the Glint I was. Something different. Something beyond. Something that feels the future tugging at me like the pull of an outgoing tide."

"So what are you?" said Badger Skull.

"I told you," she said. "I am vengeance."

"And you would be revenged upon Mountfellon," he said.

"Mountfellon must die," she replied. "I will show you how to take the flag he holds, and in return you will bring him to me."

"You wish to kill him yourself."

"Never send a man to do a woman's job," she replied. "I will not believe he is dead until I see the life run out of his eyes. This I have felt so strongly that yes, I have almost seen it."

"And the boy?"

"The boy is the key that will unlock everything. He is already linked by blood and place to Mountfellon. He is a weapon. I will tell you how to use him."

"Why will he do what we want?" said Badger Skull. "He is not vengeance. He is just a mute, dark-skinned boy with his head in a bag."

"He is the Bloody Boy," she repeated. "I have felt it."

The Sluagh snorted again.

"I know nothing of your 'Bloody Boys'. Madness."

"No," she said. "Once I was a Glint. Then my heart-stone was taken. Instead of dying I endured. I don't know why. But maybe through the crucible of madness I changed. Once, what happened in the past left a magnetic tug that I was able to attach to, like a lodestone. Now, what is going to happen exerts its own attraction, a disturbance in the ether, as if I am glinting forward rather than backward in time . . ."

"Enough," said Badger Skull. "Too much talk clouds things. I have decided. It shall be done. There is too much to be gained not to attempt it. And if it fails, then only time is lost. Time, and your life. And his."

"It will not fail," said the Ghost. "I have felt it."

The Sluagh looped a noose around Amos's forehead, tightening it so that the rope bit in to the depression below his brow, forcing his eyes closed, seeming to push the eyeballs back into their sockets. That was painful enough, but then they pulled the end of the rope down his back, through his legs and fed it up through the rope tying his hands together in front of him, and tugged it tight. His back arched, the rope cut painfully between his legs, and they tied it off so that he was kneeling with his head held backwards and his neck unprotected and open to whatever weapon they had prepared for it.

He felt like a bull at the slaughterhouse.

He grunted at them in protest, but all that got was laughter and a shove that sent him over on his side. Then, as he regained the breath that had been jarred from him, one of the Sluagh straddled him and sat on his side.

"Be still and thole it, boy," he said, "for this will hurt."

He bucked in terror as he felt the sharp cut of the razor at his neck. But he did not feel the following tug of a blade through veins and tendons, spilling his life away into the grass below. There was no cut. He felt the sting and then the withdrawal and then another sting, and then another. It was not a blade. It was a pin. Or a needle. Or a thorn. He was being slowly and deliberately pricked in a line around his neck. Once he realised they were not going to cut his throat, or at least not now, he relaxed as much as he could and tried to think.

"Thole it", he thought. *What is "thole"?*

Endure. Abide. Survive, answered the Ghost. *This will not kill you.*

What is it? He winced as the sharp pricking continued around his neck.

It is a tattoo. They are marking you.

Why?

He had a horror of finding himself with a writhing face covered in interlocked curlicues like the Sluagh.

"He wants to know what you are doing to him," said the Ghost. "He does not want a face like yours."

The Sluagh sitting astride him answered. It was Badger Skull. Amos heard him spit in contempt.

"He does not merit a face like ours. A face like ours is earned." He leant down and cuffed the back of Amos's head, sending it forward, making the rope across his eyes dig in and sending simultaneous shafts of pain between his legs and flashes of light behind his eyelids.

"It is old power, boy. It is not a shadow-mark, for you have not repudiated the light. It is a mark of ownership, a tithe on your future, a guarantor, if you will, of your subservience and compliance to our will."

"The white tattoo," said the Ghost, a note of wonder in her voice.

"You have heard of it?"

"I must have," she said. "Long ago, when I knew things."

"It is a warrandice," said the Sluagh, carrying on with the painful perforation of Amos's neck. "An oath-lock, if you will. And if you won't, in fact. When the band is finished you will take a vow to do as we ask, and to do so for a fixed term. The tattoo is white, which on most is next to invisible. On you it will be a noticeable band. As the term nears completion the tattoo will begin to blacken from first prick to last. If you do as you have sworn before blackness meets blackness, the tattoo will fade without harm. But if you fail or break your word and the black band completes itself, whatever hangs below it will shrivel and die. And since in your case that is your whole body, I suggest you try very hard to do as we ask."

Badger Skull slopped something wet into his hand, and then smeared it in Amos's neck. For a moment he thought it was a balm, something to take away the sting of the needle and whatever it was they were using as ink. It was an unexpected kindness, the soothing, cooling wetness against the rawness. Amos reached out with his mind for the Ghost, but she was suddenly closed to him as the line of the tattoo began to burn with a flaring intensity that stunned him rigid, and then dropped him into the dark well of unconsciousness.

CHAPTER 30

A FORTUITOUS CONVERGENCE

That Sara and the nun eventually crossed paths within the vastness of the mirrored maze was providential, but not entirely the result of luck, or rather, if it was luck, then it was the happy accident of Sara's doggedness and education, for she had been trained to deal with chaos or complexity by being methodical. Alone, Raven-less and lost, she had kept hold of that initial plan to quarter the mirrors by walking in a slowly expanding square spiral made by keeping point of her paces and always turning in the same direction. And eventually her feet found his trail again.

She strode past it, so desperately involved in counting – and not losing count – that she didn't realise what had happened until several paces later. Then she had stopped, scarcely believing her plan had – so many, many tens of thousands of paces later – actually worked. She walked carefully backwards, subtracting steps from her tally as she went in case what she had felt was a false trail, in order that she could get back on track if it were so. At this stage, the careful husbanding of the sum of her paces had become so important and relentless that the fact she was doing it to find Sharp had almost escaped her. The walking and counting and turning were almost all she could remember.

And then she found his trail a second time. She just stood there, letting the familiarity of his trace note resonate up through her, spreading warmth and vitality up the length of her body until it reached her face, where it emerged in a wide smile.

"There you are," she said. "There you are." She had almost forgotten how much the sense of Sharp was folded around her life, something that had always been there, something that felt like home. She wiped her eyes and began to follow the trail.

Only after she had got to a hundred and thirty did she realise she no longer needed to keep count of her paces any more. She grinned wider and picked up the pace.

The nun had not told Sharp how little she expected to find a disembodied hand in the mirrors. She thought it was – as had in fact happened – much more likely to have found itself separated by a mirror breaking as it was transitioning from one location in the outer world to another, and thus to be outside the mirrors entirely.

With that in mind, she had determined that it would be useful to retrace Sharp's passage through the mirrors in order perhaps to find this elusive girl who had stolen a hand, but more expediently to find her way back to his point of entry to the mirrored world, and so contact the woman he spoke of, this Sarah Falk, to ask her to come and show herself to Sharp. Finding the hand thief seemed a much more unlikely prospect since the nun felt sure the girl would only have used the mirrors as a means of escape, not as a hiding place, and so would now be far beyond the looking-glass realm. Much easier to find this Falk, she thought. Her head was full of her new plan, a kind of secret elation that she had serendipitously found a way to enlist a powerful group such as The Oversight in prosecuting the vengeance she sought. And it was not only vengeance, for she still retained a small corner of her heart that was not entirely wighted, where a sympathy with the normal world and its inhabitants remained alive. The Citizen, architect of the Disaster, executioner of so many thousands more than just those of The Oversight who he had conspired to drown as they had come to stop him was a living peril to humanity. He was, in his perversion, the definition of inhumanity.

The little nun hated him, but still some part of her also still loved the world from which she was banished.

She was thinking on this as she retraced Sharp's steps, and then suddenly found the passage ahead was occupied. She backed up on instinct. She was, after all, the most timid of the Mirror Wights, and had stayed safe by relying on her caution.

But then she spotted the rings and the gloves on the advancing woman, and as the woman stopped as she in turn saw the nun, she also noticed the long white plait of her hair whip as Sara turned quickly to see if she had just walked into another ambush, and she knew her. Sharp's description had been precise and vivid.

"You are Sara Falk," she said.

Sara had already produced a knife in each hand and was crouched in anticipation of attack.

"Mr Sharp sent me to find you."

"To find me?" said Sara. "Who are you?"

"To find your hand, in fact," said the nun. "But I see you have already recovered it."

Sara stared at her.

"I am a Mirror Wight, as you see," said the nun. "But I do not lie."

"Where is Sharp?" said Sara, still trying to work out what the ambush was.

"He is trapped but I can take you to him," said the nun. "Follow me if you would see him."

"I would," said Sara. She sheathed one knife back in her belt, but she kept the other in her right hand. "And I will cut your damned head off if you try to trick me."

"I do not lie," said the nun with a shrug.

"Neither do I," said Sara as she followed her down the passage of reflections. "Neither do I."

CHAPTER 31

NIGHTWALKERS ALL

Amos, mute then betrayed and now marked, travelled with the Sluagh and the Ghost. They rode with them on small, tough little ponies whose manes clattered with the bones and bird skulls plaited into them. He found the first few hours hard and painful on parts of himself that were not used to taking such a consistent pummelling, but he soon adjusted to the way of riding and was beginning to feel easier on a horse, although he was far from comfortable about anything else.

The warrandice scribed on his neck was sufficient coercion that he was neither bound nor hobbled to ensure that he didn't escape. The itching tattoo round his neck was sufficient reminder of what lay ahead for him if he tried to run, and the truth of it is that even if he had taken flight, he wouldn't have begun to know where to flee to for help.

He did think of running to London and throwing himself on the mercy of his fathers, but neither Issachar nor Zebulon had ever shown any sign of supranatural abilities, their power being based on knowledge and stratagem and an ability to influence others by more mundane methods. He knew of The Oversight, but didn't think for a moment they would help him even if they could. It wasn't that he shared the Ghost's equivocal view of them; it was that he was too clearly of the other party, being a notional Templebane. He knew that by now his fathers' latest move against them, taken in conjunction with Mountfellon, would have come to fruition, which would either have reduced the Free Company's effectiveness, erased it entirely – or failed. And if it had failed, then there could be no worse introduction to them than the name of Templebane.

So he travelled as the Sluagh travelled: by night and along forgotten paths which wound through the landscape with as much complexity as the dark markings on their bodies, avoiding running water and railways, keeping where possible to the watersheds and ridgelines of the country. His days became nights and his world slowly began to stand on its head. The Ghost, once her treachery was made plain, seemed to give it no further thought and accompanied him as before, almost as a friend and mentor rather than his very real persecutor.

She was clearly elated that a revenge she had spent a lifetime antici- pating was to be hers, and hers so very soon. He heard her talk quite openly about this to the Sluagh, who were, despite their habitual air of disdain for mere daywalkers, clearly fascinated by what she told them he had done to M'Gregor's mind.

"He is the perfect weapon, this boy," she said. "He has already proved himself to Mountfellon. Iron is no obstacle to him, nor running water. He will penetrate the ironbound perimeter of Gallstaine, bending the mind of any who hold the gates and doors, and once inside he will exact my revenge on Francis, and then you may have the thing he has so securely hidden away from you for all these years."

Francis was, Amos knew, the given name of the austere Mountfellon. The way that the Ghost began calling him increasingly by the more intimate name the closer they got to Rutlandshire seemed to indicate to Amos that she was returning to the point in her history where the viscount had violated their one-time friendship so brutally. The betrayal of faith, coming from someone who had once clearly been close to her, had made it unforgiveable.

They spoke of this one night during a pause the progress of the troop as he was unbound and directed to enter a toll keeper's cottage where he stole – on her instructions – paper, pen and ink from a table they had spied through a window. She wanted to write a letter of introduction that he could present to the gatekeeper at Gallstaine, to get him on the premises, the only obstacle she could see being his frustrating inability to speak for himself.

Don't worry, she told him. *I will pen a letter stipulating that it can only be released from your hand to Francis's. That will pique his interest and guarantee you get close enough to work your power on his mind.*

Her grin in the moonlight was disturbingly hungry.

You call him Francis.

Do I?

You have begun to, yes.

Well, we were children together once.

Friends.

Friends, yes. And now we are to be intimates again. Perhaps that is why I am slipping into the old way of talking of him . . .

Intimates?

The smile she gave him in the moonlight was stark and terrible.

There is nothing more intimate than revenge. As he once saw the hope die in my eyes, I will lean in and see him see me, and know it is more than hope that will be dying in his eyes, and that I am the means of his punishment.

Amos didn't waste breath pointing out that he was going to be the one with blood on his hands. He had tried to talk his way out of his fate more than once as they travelled, and knew she saw him as no more than an instrument in the matter, a dagger or a vial of poison, and that she was the hand that wielded him. She had supreme confidence that, when faced with Mountfellon, Amos would make him turn his mind and then his own hand against himself in the way M'Gregor had done. It did not occur to her that he might not be able to do it.

You did what you did to M'Gregor because you thought you were going to die. You will do what you will do to Francis because you KNOW you will die if you cheat the warrandice around your throat. Fear of death will again unlock your power.

On another night, the troop of Sluagh paused at a field in what Amos thought was most likely a part of Gloucestershire. He had been picking up geographical hints from milestones and fingerposts which they passed along the way. He was a little surprised at how far west they had come, but then the Ghost explained that they were taking a crooked path across the country to get around the great and − to them − insurmountable obstacle of the Thames. He had just noticed a sign pointing towards a nearby hamlet reading Seven Springs when they diverted from their course which had, for that last few miles, been shadowing the Cirencester road, and paused.

The troop was, for the first time, almost merry. They slid off their ponies and gathered around a small copse of dwarfish willow trees. There was laughter, which was new and there was back-slapping and smiles for everyone.

What's happening?

I don't know.

Her lack of knowledge was strangely disconcerting to him. She was his enemy, his own betrayer, but she was at least familiar and had so far been able to parse the supranatural for him. This made the unsettling holiday mood being displayed by the nightwalkers seem like a threat.

"I've never heard of them being like this," she whispered. "So . . ."

He waited for her to find the word, but she couldn't.

Normal?

She nodded.

"I suppose that's it."

Badger Skull turned and looked at them.

"And why should we not be normal? And who are you to say we are not normal all the time?"

Amos had only recently realised that the Sluagh could hear at least some of his thoughts, and he was far from comfortable with it.

"I meant no offence," she said.

Badger Skull grinned.

"We are relieved. We are happy. We have come to one of the great slip points on the landscape, where the Thames rises. Here things intersect: the Old Straight Roads and the Winding Paths. In this field is the source of the river. Seven Springs. Here we may walk around the impassable barrier the river puts between north and south for us, just as someone can walk around the end of a wall and see both sides. This is a blithe spot for us."

And he sprang over and pulled Amos from his horse, not roughly, but amiably.

"Stay, lady," he said. "The boy may come and join in the ritual, but it is not for you."

He kept his arm on Amos's shoulder as he walked him through the meadow to where the rest of the Sluagh had gathered in a circle around the willows. He pushed him into the perimeter and smiled at him.

"Please," he said. "Join us."

He caught the eye of another Sluagh who was raising an eyebrow at him.

"He can't do any harm, and he has at least some old blood, so the more the merrier, I say, even if his contribution might be a little weaker than the Pure."

And they all nodded and smiled and laughed and busied themselves with the fixings of their trousers and britches.

And then in concert they began to urinate, making exaggerated groans of relief that provoked more laughter.

"Go on," said Badger Skull, his britches already around his knees as he added to the inundation. "For luck."

Amos began to fumble at his flies.

"The Thames as all flowing water is an enemy to us, and will always be," said the Sluagh, looking up at the moon as he voided his bladder in an impressively long-lasting and thunderous stream. "And so a long time ago the custom began of our adding to the source whenever we pass it. Some believe it was just so we could boast we had wetted the head of the river to show our disrespect, others say the old ones thought that in time we could dilute the river and make its hold against us weak. Whatever the reason, when we come to the source of a river . . ."

He made a grand gesture with his hand like an impresario, and then shrugged.

"We piss in it."

Amos felt the Ghost's voice in his head.

What are you doing over there?

Nothing.

He let go like the others and enjoyed, for a brief moment, a sense of freedom from the living prison the Ghost had trapped him in.

Are you doing what I think you're doing?

If you think I'm smiling, then yes.

He had ridden out of that meadow with two strong memories which he turned round and round in his mind as they travelled onwards. The first was of that mild perturbation she had displayed at being momentarily excluded from the band, which made her a little less infallible to him. And the second was the truly discomfiting sensation he had got standing among the Sluagh as they had laughed and pissed and made bawdy jokes – just as if they were normal blunt men the like of which he knew a hundred back in London: they had not seemed scary or eldritch, or representatives of some ancient other order of life; they had seemed ordinarily coarse and – for an instant – less cruel because of it.

As they continued their crooked way towards Rutlandshire, Badger Skull took to riding beside him more often. Though he had the ability to hear Amos's thoughts, since the Sluagh were practised at getting inside people's minds and influencing them, he quaintly insisted on talking out loud himself.

They were detouring alongside a new stretch of railway beneath a cloudless sky lit by a high crescent moon. The Sluagh could not cross bare iron any more than they could traverse flowing water, but they could pass under it if there was a bridge or viaduct. The landscape they were travelling across was relatively flat, so bridges were few and far between, and the Sluagh were visibly frustrated by the enforced dogleg.

Badger Skull turned to Amos.

"Can you do it? As she says you can? Can you bend Mountfellon's mind?"

I don't know.

The Sluagh grimaced and pointed at his neck.

"The warrandice cannot be undone, you know."

I still don't know.

"She says you can," said Badger Skull, looking back at the Ghost who was riding at the back of the troop with a dreamy look on her face, which was turned to the moon just as someone riding by day would soak in the healing warmth of the sun.

She's mad. You do realise that, yes?

The Sluagh nodded.

"Mad doesn't mean wrong."

There was a noise from their left, a rising insistency of percussive chuffs reverberating off the walls of a deep cutting as a locomotive laboured up a mild grade towards them, a bull's-eye lantern throwing a baleful glow ahead of it as it came.

The troop of Sluagh melted into the dappled shadows of the beech wood lining the road, and were still as the ancient trees around them.

It was the first time Amos had seen a train pass by at night in the countryside, though he was used to seeing them in the city. Here in the stillness, the sound of the steam engine seemed discordant, a harsh, straight-edged kind of noise in a gentler, more rounded world. It over-rode the night sounds as it approached, and then the oncoming bulk of the locomotive and following carriages was doubled in the clear air above them as the dirty plume billowing from the engine's smoke-stack left a thick smear to mark its progress.

There was a sense of power and velocity as the engine passed, the glow of the bull's-eye being replaced for an instant by a blazing glimpse of the open firebox as it went by, and then the lit windows of the carriages chopped the night into bands of yellow light that flowed over them, like the strips of candlelight from within a zoetrope.

Amos looked to his side and saw them pass over the gaunt features of the hidden riders — slices of modern gaslight strobing across grim faces inked in ancient patterns. He had the strangest sensation that he was seeing two worlds staring at one another and that he was, in a way he could not quite comprehend, lucky to be seeing it.

None of the Sluagh moved until the clattering monster had disappeared around the bend that hugged the edge of the rising scarp beyond.

When they were back on the road, Badger Skull spoke again.

"When we have the flag, we shall not have to dance attendance on iron abominations like that, hiding as they pass. We shall just cross the rails and put them behind us as if they were no more than a hedgerow."

What is the flag?

Badger Skull rode on for a while before speaking. Amos thought he had decided not to answer, but then they came to the dip in the road where the anticipated bridge provided a way beneath the rails, and once the whole troop had passed through onto the road beyond, the chief stopped his horse and pointed back at the rails.

"Once the land held no obstacle to us but flowing water. Then iron came and changed everything. The old ones rose against the iron bearers and tried to banish the cursed metal from the island. But the iron bearers were not Pure, as we are; they were a mixed and mongrel people, those of our own who had mingled their rich blood inheritance with weaker tribes. But this iron, it gave them power and the wise men among the old Pure saw it would win in the end, unless we remade our vows to the darkness that made us, the fell dark whence we drew our strength."

I don't understand.

It might have been a trick of the moonlight, but Amos thought he saw the Sluagh smile for a moment.

"It is not important that you do. It is old history, tales lost in the fog of long-past time. But all that matters, to answer your question, is that the iron-bearers triumphed. They won the day. And they imposed a terrible peace on the Pure. They took our pennants, each tribe they conquered, and they joined them into one huge victory flag. And then they made a warrandice of their own. They knew the true Pure were not susceptible to iron as other weaker bloods, as changelings or the mara or Green Men and the like were. But they imposed a warrandice, that the true Pure, the mighty Sluagh, would from henceforth also cringe at the dull grey metal and be burnt by it And so we let them have the day and retreated into the night. We became Nightgangers and Shadow-walkers and abjured the light. We became wanderers, and trooped the old winding ways of the land. And for centuries that was our lot and we had little to do with lesser breeds. And then this happened."

He spat towards the twin moon-silvered rails stretching away into the dark behind them.

"They would not even leave us the night. They cut the flowing lines of our old paths with more iron than we had seen in centuries, caging the land, stealing our ancient ways without thought or conscience. And who has protected us from them? No one. But all that will change now. When you get us the flag."

The flag will do what?

"The flag contains the warrandice that unmans us in the face of iron. And while it is in the world, while any trace of it remains we remain gelded and helpless," said Badger Skull.

So you are going to destroy it?

"More."

Burn it?

"Burning leaves ash, makes smoke – they stay in the world and the warrandice remains."

So what will you do?

The Sluagh definitely smiled this time. Amos saw the flash of his teeth as he leant over and slapped Amos's horse into motion, and the two of them trotted to catch up with the troop ahead.

"We will put the flag out of this world," said Badger Skull. "And then we will be free to go where we will, no matter how they try and stake their damned iron tracks across the free land."

CHAPTER 32

WHAT THE HAMMER SAW

The truth of it is that if The Smith had not hidden the Black Knife, Lucy would not have given in to the need to scratch the itch. That's what she told herself. The stone dagger had disappeared the morning after Lucy had heard the Sluagh taunt him about it, implying that it held the key to a conflicted allegiance. And of all the misgivings that she had about belonging to The Oversight the fact that one of the leaders had a questionable fidelity was the biggest by far.

So after one night too many spent studying *The Great and Hidden History of the World* by candlelight in the upstairs room at The Folley, with no companionship other than the sound of the wind coming straight off Blackwall Reach and rattling the windows with a promise of winter to come, she gave in. The itch would have to be scratched. Maybe she wouldn't glint the knife, but she would find it and examine it with her gloves on. It might provide a missing piece of the puzzle which was discomforting her. So she listened for the regular snores of The Smith in the room across the passage, and then crept downstairs, keeping to the risers and boards she knew were creak-free from careful prior observation.

Then she took a candle and, with a small spark of pride at a new skill acquired under Cook's careful instruction, concentrated on it, closed her eyes and flicked her wrist.

The candle lit itself. She smiled.

"Dimmer," she said. The light became less bright. "Good."

She didn't want The Smith to wake and see her moving around as she searched.

Searching was a challenge in such a large and jumbled workshop. But she knew her way around it well enough to have an idea where any space large enough to hide the dagger might be, and she worked methodically, starting in one corner and working outwards.

She was careful not to make any noise, which was not easy in a task that involved moving a lot of tools and opening cabinets and drawers that liked to squeak or jangle as they moved. After an hour she was still only a fraction of the way through the space. This, she realised, might be a job that took more than one night. She decided to get some sleep.

And then, as she turned to go up the stairs again, she saw it.

On the bottom step, where it had not been when she descended. And not the stone dagger, not the Black Knife.

The Smith's hammer.

"Not what you're looking for," he said.

She turned to find he was sitting on the anvil, watching her. She had not thought he could move so quickly or so quietly. She swallowed. She felt guilty. She did not like feeling guilty. It proved she had loyalties to others, and that was the weakness she tried to stay away from.

"I suppose you heard the Sluagh out on Hackney Marsh talking about the Black Knife," he said.

His eyes were flat and unreadable, as was his tone. And now she felt worse than guilty. She felt scared. He had known all this time.

"I didn't spot you," he said. "You did a good job."

"But how—?" she began.

"Charlie Pyefinch," he said. "Hodge gave him the task of watching my tail."

And now she felt betrayed on top of everything else.

"We swore him to secrecy," The Smith said. "He didn't like it, if that helps."

It didn't.

"Remove your gloves," he said.

She went cold. She looked at the door. She'd have to get past him to get out, but she was fast.

"No," he said. "If you run you'll always wonder. Don't be a coward now. Because I don't think you've been one yet, and that's served you pretty well."

His words stung enough to make her peel the gloves off and jut her jaw at him.

"Right," she said. "Fine. Where is it?"

He shook his head.

"Not the Black Knife, Lucy Harker. I told you. You don't want to touch it. It'd hollow you out."

"But—" she said.

"But you want to know about it."

He stared at her. She nodded.

"Then touch the hammer. The hammer knows. The hammer was there."

"I don't understand," she said. The flatness in his eyes was terrible.

"We do not have time to doubt your loyalty. Without you, there will be no Last Hand. So see what you need to see and make your own choice once and for all. This is no time for uncertainty. If you want to know about the knife, if you want to know about *my* true allegiance, you can see for yourself. You're a Glint, girl: you can see what the hammer saw."

She walked slowly to the steps. Her hands were clammy. The hammer was the most ordinary thing in the crowded workshop. It was just a well-used tool, dinged and nicked with a long lifetime of hard use, a blunt instrument, its wooden handle worn and shiny. It didn't look like anything. And then as she reached for it, holding her breath, steeling herself for the impact of the past, she noticed it did look like something else. It looked old. And then her fingers touched it and she jolted and felt the past slam into her – and maybe because she has chosen to glint, for the first time doing it as a matter of choice rather than accident, she found she has more time to think about what she's seeing, more control—

The hammer is the hammer in her hand but the metal is brighter and the scars and the scratches have not yet dulled its surface.

The hand on the hammer is not hers: it is a man's hand, a blacksmith's hand, massive, blunt-fingered and wet with sweat.

The back of the hand is unfamiliar, covered in interlaced coils of dark blue tattoos.

Not her hand but the tug of the past is so insistent and personal that she can still feel the hook and swing on her muscles as the hammer rises and then falls repeatedly.

Ding. Ding. Ding. Ding. Clink.

Beneath the hammer, an anvil.

Ding. Ding. Ding. Ding. Clink.

On the anvil, a long bar of metal, red-hot.

Ding. Ding. Ding. Ding.

Four times the hammer hits the metal, shaping it.

Clink.

The fifth time the hammer moves and smacks the surface of the anvil, clearing the grey-black shale that comes off the beaten iron.

Ding. Ding. Ding. Ding. Clink.

Hiss.

The red metal is quenched in a pail of water. The tattooed blacksmith carries the hammer into the sun.

This is not the Isle of Dogs. This is not London. Or at least it is not a London Lucy has ever seen.

There are no stone buildings, no streets, no river, no stink of coal fires or river reek or sewer smell.

Nothing rotten.

She inhales instead the clean smell of wood fires. She is high on the side of a hill. There is a wooden palisade. A ditch beyond, and further below stretches an unspoilt landscape of green upon green.

It's an older world.

There are two groups of men, one kind with rough homespun leggings and hair tied back from their faces. They carry weapons, grey iron swords catching the weak sun in dull silvery flashes, and shields slung over their shoulders. Their faces and arms are striped and whorled with thick blue patterns painted on the skin.

The other group wears animal skins, and the writhing blue shapes that decorate their faces are finer and more complicated, tattooed on, not daubed.

The men with the tattooed faces also carry swords, short wide-bladed things the dull gold colour of bronze. The axes some hold are double-headed and vicious-looking. Others carry spears.

They see Lucy. Or rather they see the blacksmith.

Their faces curdle.

She cannot understand what they say, but the shapes their mouths make and the sounds that come out are ugly and contemptuous. One comes up and spits into her/his face.

Time jerks and Lucy feels the cut of it as the vision slices forward.

The hammer in her hand is rising and falling again.

Ding. Ding. Ding. Ding. Clink.

Another day. Cold outside. Low winter sun now, beyond the gloom of the forge.

Ding. Ding. Ding. Ding. Clink.

A commotion. People hurrying past the sunlight, cutting it into strips.

The hammer stops.

The blacksmith walks out.

The sweep of green is gone. The land is white with hoar-frost on the far side of the palisade.

The commotion comes from the ditch.

The tattooed men are driving animals ahead of them.

Horses. Dogs.

The dogs trot with their heads low, tails between their legs, weaving in and out of the horses' legs. If one tries to turn back, it is hit or kicked and jabbed with spears. No dog tries to turn back twice.

The horses' flanks are slick and wet with sweat and sheeted with blood. A grey mare tries to stop. The jab of a spear sends her forward, a dark red stain blooming on the pale curve of her haunch.

Time jerks.

Lucy has moved. Higher ground. Behind the palisade.

Looking down. The end of the long ditch. A deep pit.

In the pit, there are things Lucy does not want to see. But her eyes are unblinking. She cannot close them any more than she can turn away and break this connection with the past, hooked into her mind like a barb.

The ditch ends in a drop to the bottom of the pit, twenty-five feet below it. The things Lucy does not want to look at writhe and spasm beneath her.

The things are dogs and horses.

They have been driven over the edge and are desperately trying to keep afloat. Their hooves and paws scrabble the sheer, dirty white of the pit walls, for the pit has been dug so deep that the earth has given way to the layer of chalk beneath, and then been filled with water. They are bloodied and broken-limbed, terrified and drowning. Dogs try to scrabble onto the broad backs of horses who turn round and bite at them.

The dogs snarl and yelp and bite back.

Flailing hooves cave in dog skulls, or scramble for purchase on the bodies of other drowning animals. Hounds thrash, their jaws locked on each other as they sink together beneath the water.

It is the worst thing Lucy has seen.

And she has, in another glinted shard of the past, seen a woman burnt as a witch.

The hammer-bearer who both is and is not Lucy shouts a protest and waves the hammer at the group of men standing at the very top of the pit, out of the ditch. They are the tattooed faces who carry the bronze weapons.

They stand amid a small hill of cages, cloche-shaped half-spheres of woven branches piled one on the other. Oily black feathers and dark beady eyes are visible behind the pale, interlaced willow wands.

Their leader turns to glare at the hammer-bearer.

He points a sickle-shaped bronze blade at him and the viewpoint bucks and shifts as he is surprised by hands that grab him from behind. As the hammer falls to the ground, Lucy sees the tattooed blacksmith dragged away through the crowd, towards the bird-cages and the man she has decided is some kind of priest on the lip of the pit. She sees the blacksmith buck and twist and try to free himself. He is strong. The six men holding him are trying to subdue a roiling lightning bolt of pure fury.

He will destroy them . . .

And then he goes limp and his eyes die a little.

And Lucy sees what he has seen. The red-headed girl dragged after him, a bronze blade at her throat.

Again she does not understand the language they shout at him, but the meaning is obvious: if he fights any more, the blade opens the girl's windpipe.

The girl says something, flat, cold, proud. Her eyes flash contempt at the tattooed men holding her. She tries to thrust her neck on to the blade, but one of them grabs the thick rope of her hair and yanks her back. The blacksmith opens his mouth to shout something but before Lucy can hear it

Time slices again

And

It is night.

It is night and the stars are scattered brightly overhead. It is cold, so cold the moon has a double halo of ice crystals around it.

The young tattooed blacksmith is staring at the stars. He has no choice. He is tied to a board, flat on his back. His hands are stretched straight out on either side, lashed to a sturdy cross-piece.

The leader of the skin-wearers (for this is how Lucy thinks of them) stands astride him, chanting into the night. The crowd now surrounds the pit, faces drawn and expectant in the light of the two bonfires that have been lit on the edge, between which the young blacksmith is spread-eagled on his board. Half are the skin-wearers; the others are the ones in homespun, the ones whose weapons are iron and not bronze.

The dagger the leader holds up to the moon is neither. It is a wicked arc of jagged flint or some even darker stone.

He pauses in the chanting and bends so he is nose to tattooed nose with the blacksmith. His grin is a skull's rictus, his pupils have shrunk down to black pinpricks no larger than the stars overhead. A drool of spittle loops out of his mouth and catches the firelight, glistening as it falls into the blacksmith's face.

The board is grabbed by other hands.

It is pushed between the fires, over the brink, held there, so the black-smith's head is lower than his feet.

The knife-carrier laughs as he straightens and watches. He reaches behind him. Something black and feathery is taken from one of the cages placed in his hand. He jerks the blade through it.

It was a raven. Its head falls onto the board next to the blacksmith. The body is held above him as the blood spurts then spatters all over his upper body. Then the lifeless bird is tossed into the pit.

The cages are opened. Skin-wearers push each other aside to grab more ravens.

One after another they are stabbed and slashed, their blood emptied onto the blacksmith, flowing off his body on the tilted board and splashing into the pit far below.

Time jerks.

A deluge of dead ravens tumbles down into the pit, joining the corpse-jam of horses and dogs. Some horses are still alive, and more than a few dogs, which gives the carpet of dead and dying animals a horrible twitching movement.

Time jerks again. The leader of the skin-wearers again straddles the blacksmith, holds a flat disc of polished stone by a handle, holds it between the blacksmith's eyes and the stars overhead. In the black mirror, the tied man sees his own reflection, unrecognisable beneath the thick layer of raven gore covering his face like a bloody caul.

That's not what makes his eyes widen, shockingly white in the bloodied face.

What startles and then appals him is what he sees reflected behind his head.

What makes him stop breathing and forget to blink is the surface of the water below, shown in the mirror. Either it is rising, as if it has a life of its own, or else the charnel-house jumble of the animal sacrifice is being pulled beneath the surface in one huge clump.

Before he needs to breathe again, the water is clear, rippled, then un-rippled, then still.

He is staring into a stone mirror and seeing the answering mirror-smooth surface below, black as obsidian. Unnaturally still.

Right at the end, just before the last tip of raven wing disappeared Lucy thought she saw something sinewy and fluid and wrong moving below the water, black on black, but then the last pinion feather slipped beneath the surface and it was gone.

All eyes slowly dragged away from the glassy bottom of the pit and focused on the stone knife held at the blacksmith's throat.

The knife-wielder said something, the tattoos on his face seeming to writhe and become part of the darkness behind him, like dark smoke.

A question.

The blacksmith spat up into his eye.

The knife-man roared in anger. Drew back the knife for the killing blow, the straining neck naked to the blade as it began its brutal descent.

The blacksmith broke the cross-pole. His hands, the broken parts of the pole still lashed to the wrists, smacked together on either side of the head, cupped on each ear.

The killing stroke lost momentum as the executioner's ear-drums burst and he shrieked in pain.

The knife sliced the blacksmith's shoulder instead of his neck, but he didn't seem to notice.

He bucked and kicked and caught his would-be killer between the legs.

But the bucking action made the board slip, and the two of them slid over the edge before the other skin-wearers could save their leader.

And as they fell, time slices, a razor cut, not a chunk

and one minute Lucy saw them tumbling – the blacksmith pulling the knife out of his shoulder and the executioner's hands flailing to find a handhold in the night air –

then they were twenty-five feet lower, inches from the flat surface, and Lucy's eyes seemed to squirm in her head because it seemed as if at the last moment, the mirror-flat surface of the dark water writhed up and leapt hungrily for them, engulfing them and yanking them into the depths beneath.

And then a bigger time-slice

And the horrorstruck faces of the watchers on the rim looked down, lit by the guttering bonfires, skin-wearers and normal folk, and there was silence broken only by the sound of breathing and the sizzle and crack of the flames.

The surface was glass-flat.

Unmoving as stone.

Except for one irregularity. One flaw. One knurled lump standing proud on the perfect smoothness.

The stone knife lay on the surface, not floating, but lying on it as if on a sheet of blackest ice.

And then someone shouted.

The girl with the red hair. She pointed at the knife.

Fingers were clenched around the handle.

And as the silence was broken, the knife and the hand holding it began to move.

The angle changed.

The knife-tip jagged into the black surface like an ice-pick. The hand flexed with the effort of the man below the surface and then the crowd shouted as one as a shoulder burst the surface, then another hand splayed flat on the black mirror. The arm holding the knife shot further out and stabbed a new hold with the knife point.

A head broke the surface and the shouting and the screaming turned to a buzz and then a rumble as the blacksmith used the stone knife to pull his way back into this world from whatever lay in the depths beneath the black mirror.

He came out on his hands and knees and hung there, panting, staring down at his face.

Then he stood slowly, the broken wood of the cross-pieces still hanging off his wrists. He cut the rawhide strips without looking and stared up into the faces looking back at him.

The blackness, the gore seemed to slide off him, starting with his head, draining down towards his feet. And stranger than that, so strange that it made the crowd shout and point once again, was the fact that his black hair drained of colour too, and the whorls and switchbacks of his facial tattoos drained out as he watched it take the ink from his arms as well.

The black mirror or whatever lay beyond it, cheated of his body, was taking the darkness out of him.

He turns and seems to look straight at Lucy.

She stopped breathing. Her turn now.

Without the tattooed face, he is recognisable.

He is not just a smith. Or rather, he is more than that.

He is The Smith.

He was The Smith.

He was always The Smith

And just as she was reeling with the truth and the impossibility of it, a final lurching jag of the past hit her, like a vicious punch on a new bruise.

They come out of the dawn, through the marsh.

Men and iron.

Rough woollen cloaks, blades and axes as grey as the mist they stride through.

They do not hurry.

The chest-high reeds rustle as the grim and silent battle horde filters through, making a sound gentle and constant as the wind.

The hand that carries the hammer goes with them. A hand now without tattoos.

They are below the palisade.

The skin-wearers are waiting for them behind the spiked logs. They have bows. They loose, all together.

The twang of bowstrings fills the sky with arrows.

The Smith shouts something.

As one, the men around him bunch closer, shields overlapping edge to edge, a wooden wall, a sky shield.

The arrows arc downwards, whistling in with an angry noise.

The shield wall buckles and gives as the arrows thunk home like a hundred axe blows, but it holds and the warriors surge forward until they hear the next salvo twang into the sky, and then they prepare to receive them again.

Three more times the arrows loose, three more times the shield wall lurches forward to receive them. Each time closer to the palisade.

They reach the palings and begin to dig them out under cover of their barrier.

On the mound above the skin-wearers shriek at them. They bring forward hostages, hands tied. They wave swords at them, shouting at the shield wall.

The message is clear. The warriors continue to dig out the palisade, swords and picks and hands.

The first hostages are killed. Their bodies fall like heavy sacks.

And then Lucy recognises one.

The girl with the red hair. The blacksmith's girl.

She stands there, held by two tattooed men, a bowman and a swordsman who holds his blade at her throat. Her eyes are closed. Her body is limp, held upright by the men. The swordsman roars at The Smith, his eyes finding him in the crowd.

The Smith shouts at the men behind the shield wall.

One turns, his shield now a hedgehog of arrow shafts.

Sees The Smith begin to run at him.

He shouts at the next man next as he spins the blade in his free hand and scythes the edge through the arrows, shaving his shield smooth.

He turns the shorn shield to the sky and bends his knees, ready to take the weight of the incoming Smith. His companion grabs the other end of the buckler as The Smith leaps onto it.

They hurl the shield heavenwards – a human springboard – hurdling him high over the palisade – a sky-born berserker – hammer hooking hungrily towards the horrified swordsman ahead.

Lucy sees it all.

The red stain already sheeting from the girl's neck

The battle fury dying in The Smith's eyes even as he takes the swordsman's head off his shoulders –

– too late.

Eyes that will now for ever be too late.

And the past releases its grip and drops her back in the now –

And in that now she is looking into the same pale, washed-out eyes.

Eyes that have been too late for a long, long time.

The Smith took the hammer gently from her hands and lowered her to sit on the steps as she got her equilibrium back. Her head is spinning.

"She was your love. The red-haired girl."

He nodded.

"Your wife?"

He looked away. Shook his head. Looked back at her.

"My daughter."

None of this made sense, except it was true.

"But . . . how have you lived this long?"

"I haven't," he said. "I stopped living when I went through the black mirror. Everyone does. What is on the other side is the Other, and the Other is not life."

"But you came back."

"Yes."

"How?"

He sat next to her on the step and took a deep breath, eyes closed, head tilted back, as if saying what came next was a heavy weight he needed to brace himself to carry and not drop.

"I am the Anomaly. The Deviant. The Aberration. The Paradox, the True Paradox because I am not only the antithesis of reason, my survival contradicts the mortal power of the unreason that dwells behind the black mirrors. I am the dead man that walks, and the living man that dies every day. Because every dawn I wake and at some point I remember she is not here. I remember her on the palisade. I remember what it felt like, that last moment I was truly alive, when I believed she too lived still, the moment I hurried the shield wall, the moment I hung there between heaven and earth with the cold fury of righteousness coursing through my veins, knowing that my strength and speed could save her. The moment just before I failed."

He opened his eyes and looked down at her.

"No man could have saved her," said Lucy. "I saw, remember? She was dead before you jumped."

"No man could have come back from behind the black mirror," he said, "but I did. I should have been able to."

He exhaled and stood.

"And so you see me as I am: the man who can explain everything . . . except himself."

"You were Sluagh," she said.

"They weren't Sluagh then, not really, not in those days. They didn't forswear the day and take to nightwalking until we had conquered them," he said, laying the hammer back on the anvil. "We took their flag and we killed their chieftains, and we buried that damned black well deep below the hill again, and we brought the ravens back to watch over it, and we made an oath-lock in their conquered flags and forbade them iron, and made them fear it."

"And then?"

"And then time happened. History happened. And what was a shrine became a temple, and then a different kind of temple, and then a castle with a White Tower with a town growing around it. And people lived and died and forgot and the world became both simpler in some ways and harder in others. And those sworn to protect the Tower became those sworn to protect the city the town had become, and so the trust was passed on down the generations, mixed blood patrolling the line, if there is a line, and here we are."

She shook her head. Something was still wrong.

"Why are you telling me this?" she said.

"Because I know metal and materials and what is true and what is not. And there's something broken in you, Lucy Harker," he said. "It's trust. You can't trust. That's something we can't mend or teach. That's something we can only earn. And there are some kinds of mistrust that are planted so deep by such violent and unforgiveable betrayals that they can never really be uprooted by anyone outside yourself. The only thing that can grub out that deep wariness is love. Not love given, not love taken, but both: love shared. And that's what I wish you, girl. Love, and the strength to be true to it when you find it."

And with that he walked past her, putting a firm hand on her shoulder as he did so, and then disappeared upstairs.

She sat there looking out at the workshop lit by her candle, which stood on the anvil.

Her eyes glittered with unwanted moisture. She wiped them. Her instinctive mistrust of The Smith had been correct. He had got in deep behind her defences. And it hurt.

CHAPTER 33

THE ROCK AND THE WHIRLPOOL

Raised a Templebane, but sworn to secret loyalty by a Mountfellon, and a terrifyingly vengeful Mountfellon at that, Coram was caught between Scylla and Charybdis, and like many sharp customers in a similar predicament had decided the best thing to do was rely on his wits, play both ends against the middle and hope that he could arrange things so that either the whirlpool swallowed the rock, or the rock plugged the maelstrom.

He was walking back to the counting house with three grenadoes, cast-iron balls filled with gunpowder in the bag looped over his shoulder. The balls were packed in straw wadding to stop them knocking against each other. With a crimped, brush-like fuse poking out of the top, they looked like unexpectedly lethal pomegranates. He had just paid a bibulous and habitually impecunious warrant officer stationed at the Woolwich Arsenal a sovereign apiece for them, and was looking forward to showing them to Issachar. He would not tell him how much he had handed over, because he had led his surviving father to believe the price was four sovereigns. Coram had pocketed the surplus coin as an investment in his future.

Issachar had begun to look a little better than previously, an improvement in his health he had been heard to opine was due to Coram's unexpected enterprise in pursuing the interests of the House of Templebane during his indisposition. Coram was gratified with this, especially as it made Abchurch look very green around the gills, but he privately suspected Issachar's better temper was connected with the doses of Sydenham's tincture, of which he was taking noticeably less. So much for adamantine Scylla.

The whirlpool that was Charybdis required more thought, but in the end Coram had decided there was no way Mountfellon would ever know it was he who had formulated Templebane's destructive assault on the Safe House, and thus that there was little reason not to warn the noble lord of the plan before it happened. If he then decided to "discover" the plot and intervene with Templebane, Coram had no particular objection. And indeed he had insurance against being suspected as the spy within Templebane's family, since he determined it would be in both his and Mountfellon's ongoing interest that he should remain undiscovered in case he could be of use in the future. So he had prepared a scapegoat, and was to suggest to Mountfellon that he should accidentally identify "a squinny-eyed boy with no chin" who had come and sold him the information for a sovereign.

He felt the weight of the swinging bombs at his back, and smiled.

He found he was a little thrilled at the prospect of blowing up the sugar manufactory and seeing the consequent conflagration destroying the house of The Oversight. He hoped all remaining members would be within. He had not forgiven them for unmanning him on the river in front of Mountfellon.

One way or another, he was going to be fine.

For unknown to the strabismatic unfortunate in question, Coram had secreted the extra sovereign that he had extracted for the grenadoes from Issachar right beneath Abchurch's mattress, where it might easily be discovered if further proof were needed.

It was, he thought, a good investment in his future.

CHAPTER 34

THE BUNG

Time passed in the dark cavern, and the nun did not return. Sharp found early on that he was hungry in a way that he had never been in the mirrors. Lack of hunger or thirst, or any need for food or water seemed to be a feature of the looking-glass dimension, but now that he was back in the "normal" world (or at least under it) he was finding himself prey to those bodily needs once more.

He had slipped hard ship's biscuits into his pockets, and two small slabs of pemmican that the thief Dee had either not found or not troubled himself to steal. He ate as sparingly as he could from these as he worked, but the real problem was water.

He worked by candlelight, sifting through the bone pile, initially clearing a space around the mirror that he had propped face to the cavern wall. The skeletons and other detritus were four or five deep, but he found the stone floor beneath, and began to create order out of chaos. Initially he had intended to lay the bodies out separately, but it quickly became clear that the skeletons were in such an advanced stage of decay that working out which tibia went with whose ribs or skull and so forth was not going to be possible. So he found himself following the ancient custom of those who tend to the disposal of the long dead in ossuaries the world over, which is that he stacked the bones by type and shape, rather than by individual ownership. A pile of skulls grew next to leg bones stacked like cordwood, while all the diminishing sizes of bones were arranged in graded heaps around the edge of the cavern as he cleared space for them. Among the bones, he found the remains of more powder kegs, broken into their constituent barrel staves, which he duly stacked alongside the newly neat bone piles. After a while, he ceased to find the handling of remains unpleasant or charged with any kind of grim association and in the absence of anything else to busy himself with, he found himself taking pride in the painstaking action of clearing and sorting.

When he got to the centre of the floor, or the bottom of the cone, as he thought of it, he discovered both the answer to something that had been worrying him, and also the solution to his growing problem with dehydration: he had been wondering how, if the void had filled with enough water to leave tidemarks in the past, it was now dry. He moved a pair of skeletons twisted together in the folds of an oilskin cape that had resisted rotting, and found a narrow gash in the stone floor. It was about four feet long and maybe eight inches wide at the most, tapered at both ends in a slightly kinked peapod shape. And when he reached down into it, his hand found water, moving gently past from left to right. It was an underground stream, and the water, when he cupped it greedily to his parched mouth was cold and clean, with a flat mineral taste that was not unpleasant at all. This then was the drain that had emptied the void in the past, and now it was a welcome source of drinking water for his future. The channel was about arm-deep as far as he could tell, since he could touch the bottom if he stretched. When he did so, he found a shoe that had fallen in and wedged itself in a narrow groove, and he retrieved it and added it to the relevant pile.

Of course he found much else in the charnel heap. There were many more candles, which were very welcome. There were boots, shoes and belts which he mounded against the wall. There were fragments of unrotted cloth, and some garments that remained more or less intact. These he laid out on the ground and used as a mattress for the times when he extinguished the candles and went to sleep. There were horse-pistols and swords rusted to uselessness, and there was a surprisingly large number of coins which had fallen through the bone pile to the floor as the pockets they had once been in had rotted away to nothing.

And of course there were rings. Of all the things he sorted into piles, it was the rings that touched him most, rings that were all variants of the one he wore, gold rings set with mottled bloodstones on which were incised lions and unicorns, rampant. There were also wedding rings, and he took care to keep them all safely, tied into a handkerchief. He maintained a close tally on the number of them, adding to it every time he found another. He knew that precisely eighty-five souls had gone into the mirrors on the occasion of the Disaster, since the ominous number had often been mentioned by The Smith and Cook when discussing the tragedy which had brought The Oversight to its current desperate state. And yet, by the time he had cleared the bone jumble and stacked every bone, he had only gathered eighty-four rings. He re-counted them several times, and then went back to the piles of small bones and checked them again to make sure there was not an overlooked finger bone encircled by the missing signet. When that failed, he went through the piles of bigger bones. And when that too failed he gave up and extinguished the candle and tried to go to sleep.

He tried to think of other things. He stared into the darkness and thought of Sara Falk, of where she might be, of whether there was any possibility that the nun might find her. Thinking of the nun made him think of the man whose name she had told him, the man he must kill for her if she did miraculously make good on her part of the bargain and reunite him with Sara Falk. Thinking of the man, and her claim that he had been responsible for all the dead men and women in this cavern led him back to the number of them, and the number drew him relentlessly to the fact he was one ring shy of eighty-five, and then sleep was impossible and he relit the candle and walked to the pile of skulls.

He felt foolish doing it, but he methodically took each skull and shook it, like a child rattling a piggy bank, just in case the missing ring had tumbled into someone's brain-pan in the muddle of broken skeletons, and was hidden there. He heard no tell-tale clatter of metal on bone however, and restacked the skulls. As he did so he found he was automatically counting them, and that was when he found out there was one skull missing too.

He picked up the candle, flared it to maximum brightness and slowly prowled round his newly ordered circumference to see if he had put it on the wrong pile.

He had not. There was no doubt. He was missing a skull too. And there was nowhere it could be hiding. Just ordered piles of human components, accessories and the barrel staves. He squatted and looked around thoughtfully.

Five minutes later found him counting tibias. He totalled them, divided by two, and confirmed that there were the right number of bodies but the wrong number of heads.

He sat on the floor to consider this dilemma, chewing a small portion of his dwindling pemmican as he did so. The dried beef made him thirsty, and so he went to the runnel in the centre of the floor.

He did not drink from it when he got there. Instead he stood and stared down at it. It was, he realised, the only place the skull might be hiding.

He retrieved the candle and lay on the floor. Then he stuck the candle under water and peered into the flowing water.

The candle did not go out. Instead it flickered in the current as a normal flame might waver in a draught of air.

"Brighter," he said.

The flame grew in intensity and lit the walls of the subterranean channel. He checked one end as far as he could see, his face mashed to the stone as he strained to look back along the course of the rivulet. Then, seeing nothing, he switched round and peered carefully down the other way. He did not see the skull, but instead saw the ends of two bones, a radius and an ulna, still wrapped in a fragment of sleeve. He reached in and grasped them, and tugged. They were wedged in a wrinkle in the stone channel and did not come easy.

He pulled harder and then harder again, until he realised something was locking them in place. He pushed the candle back underwater and managed to squint down the channel and see that what was wedging them was the missing skull. He tried to reach it, but his arm was not long enough, his fingertips brushing the curve of bone but unable to get any purchase. He gripped the arm bones and pulled with more strength, twisting and levering them as much as he could until something cracked and the skull came loose from the cranny it was wedged in and was swept permanently out of reach by the flow, as the bones broke free and came out of the water so suddenly that he fell backwards. He stared at his catch, a whole skeletal forearm and the bones of the attached hand, balled up in the twisted remnants of the sleeve end. And among them was the unmistakeable gold band of the last missing ring.

He was so surprised and strangely pleased by this small victory that he laughed in delight, his merriment ringing round the dome above him.

Below him, unseen under the cavern floor, the skull he had dislodged bounced and bobbled in its own merry way, tumbling blindly along the imperceptibly narrowing curves of the channel, like a ball carried by the current. And then it stopped, wedged again, now wholly unreachable and this time corked like a bung, blocking the subterranean stream at a tapering choke point. The pressure of the current held it in place.

And dammed behind the sudden obstruction, the stream backed up, bubbling and gurgling up out of the slit in the floor, stopping Sharp's laughter in an instant.

He stared at the thin puddle emerging from the hole and spreading in a dark stain across the floor.

Once he had worked out the implications of what he was seeing, he did not waste a moment. He looked up at the distant roof, the tide marks and the piles he had spent so much time organising.

The cavern was going to fill with water. It had done so before. Sometimes it clearly did not fill all the way to the top. So this was not necessarily fatal. But it was deadly serious, because although he could swim, he could not do so indefinitely. He needed something to hold on to, something that floated.

All he had were the barrel staves and the wooden frame of the mirror. He worked fast. Using the belts he'd reclaimed, and twisting rags into ropes, he lashed together the curved wooden slats, using the mirror as a base to tie them too. He ended up with an ungainly rectangular pallet, not big enough to call a raft, maybe four foot by three foot and eighteen inches in depth. It wasn't something to sit on, but it would do, he hoped, to cling to if the water kept rising.

He had taken the precaution of collecting his pile of candles and jamming them about his person, wedged into boot-tops, pockets and waistcoat. By the time he'd done this and built his diminutive liferaft, the water was as high as his calves. He thought perhaps it was slowing, but as he sat on the long end of the propped up raft, he realised it had only slowed because the walls of the pear-shaped cone were widening and the increased volume was having a consequent effect on the apparent rate of rise in the water level.

And worse than that, he realised, the water was very cold. He was quite as likely to succumb to exposure as drown.

He wished he hadn't laughed so merrily all those long minutes ago. Somehow the dark water rising around him felt like a punishment for that immoderate moment of optimism.

If Sharp had believed in gods (which he didn't, gods being much more mundane and imaginary things than the arcane realities he dealt with on a regular basis) he might have thought they were punishing him for his one unguarded flash of hubris.

He extinguished the candle and composed himself to wait and see if the water would stop.

There was a quiet and deceptively gentle burbling as the now unseen water kept welling out of the cut in the floor. The only other sound in the perfect darkness was a single word.

"Sara."

Which was either an apology or perhaps as close to a prayer as a man without a god could get.

CHAPTER 35

THE DEWPOND

Amos did not recognise the approach to Gallstaine Hall until the ominous scaffolding that gave the junction known as Bowland's Gibbet its name swung into view across the fields. The old gallows silhouetted against another bright moonlit night sky seemed to him a stark and ominous harbinger of the dark deed he was now expected to perform. He had not of course forgotten why he was being shepherded across the countryside night after night as a weapon for another's revenge, but he had pushed it to the side of his mind and tried not to look at it too closely, since there was little he could do about the fatal tattoo closing round his neck other than comply. Instead he had concentrated on the experience of being with so strange a troop as the Sluagh, noting everything about them: what made them so other, so different from the people he had grown up with in the great city and, perhaps most surprisingly, what they had in common with normal folk. The Sluagh were so proud and disdainful of those who were not "Pure" that they would have vociferously refuted any shared characteristics with the mundane populace, but the truth, Amos saw, was that they were human and not "creatures": each had his own character, be it phlegmatic, complaining, inquisitive, garrulous or foul-mouthed and so on, just as ordinary people did. Within the group there were tensions and friendships, old rivalries that would flare up into well-worn arguments as they travelled, and jokes shared that would have the whole company smiling and laughing, as much from familiarity as any real humour. They did have a sense of humour, albeit a cruel one, which was the thing that disconcerted Amos the most in some ways, since he often found himself grinning in concert with the wild-faced night-riders, a thing he would never have expected. They were tough, harsh and prone to brag, especially about their ruthlessness and cruelty, and particularly when talking of themselves to Amos or the Ghost, but he noted that while they talked a vicious and cruel game, they did not terrorise anyone as they passed, and in fact seemed to move cautiously through the nightscape as if more worried about being seen than anything else. The braggadocious stories of merciless inhumanity seemed as much an ornamentation to create an impression of ferocity as the facial tattoos and the festoons of animal bones with which they adorned their clothes and hair.

And then, just when he was beginning to wonder if they were quite as bad as they were painted, not least by themselves, they came to the dewpond, and he realised that familiarity had not bred contempt, but something much more dangerous to him: vulnerability.

The dewpond was a perfectly circular depression brimful of water on the top of the small hill just behind Bowland's Gibbet. He had thought they would proceed straight to the gate of Mountfellon's Gallstaine Hall beyond, but the troop had turned aside and climbed the slope, the quiet chatter of the road dying on their lips, so that by the time he crested the rise, the procession had become unmistakeably serious. The Sluagh ringed the pool, none dismounting. Not one of the horses tried to drink from the flat water, which surprised Amos.

What is this?

The Ghost answered him.

This is a mist pond. Some call them dewponds. Be silent now. Something is happening.

He stared at the mirror-smooth expanse of water, seeing the perfect reflection of the great eye of the moon staring back up at him as if it were trapped in a hole beneath the ground. He looked around at his strange travelling companions. Their eyes were all shut, their heads tilted back, as if partaking in some silent communion from which he and the Ghost were excluded.

He looked beyond the ring of horsemen and saw a distant light beyond the gibbet, beyond the high estate wall he could now make out in the moonlight. The light came from a window in the squat mass of what must, he realised, be Gallstaine itself, and he wondered with a shudder if the man he was being sent to kill was sitting up late by the light of that distant lamp.

Badger Skull broke the silence, pulling his horse around to look out over the farmland behind them. He pointed.

"There are cows in those fields. And in the two fields beyond the copse over there. A bull too, if my nose isn't playing tricks. Bring them."

Without another word, the Sluagh reined their ponies around and spread away into the distant fields.

Why do you need cows?

"I don't need cows especially, boy," said the Sluagh. "But cows are what are closest to hand."

Closest to hand for what?

"For blood," said the Ghost. "He needs blood."

Badger Skull nodded and looked at Amos.

"Lots of blood will be spilled before the moon sets, Bloody Boy. And you must start the dance. Come."

And with that he leant down and took the reins from Amos's hand and led the pony towards the gates to Gallstaine, as if he thought Amos could not be trusted, at the last, to follow instructions.

The plan was simple. Too simple to Amos's way of thinking, but the Sluagh and the Ghost were of the confirmed opinion that either his mind would be powerful enough to make any more complex stratagem redundant, or it would not work at all, in which case again there was no sense in confusing things.

"It will work or it won't work," said the Ghost. "And I've seen the power you have when your own survival is threatened. It will work."

He scratched at the band around his neck as they emerged from the field and the ponies clattered down the metalled road to the gate. When he had first come here, it had been in the teeth of a howling rainstorm on a night when the clouds had done their best to drown Rutlandshire and wash it away into the adjoining Lincolnshire fenlands. He had not seen much except by lightning flash, other than rain, darkness and mud.

They stopped and looked at the gatehouse. It was a curved indentation in the high, iron-spiked wall that guarded the perimeter of Mountfellon's parkland. The gatehouse was almost buried by an unchecked growth of ivy, and the gates were of iron, unadorned as a jailhouse door, except for a single shield that bore the Mountfellon arms embossed on it.

All the things that Amos had pushed to the side of his mind chose this moment to rise up and demand his attention. He was going to kill a man. He did not like the man, but the only thing that Mountfellon had done to harm him was to nick his thumb with a scalpel in order to test his blood. That, and treating him with the unsurprising aloofness and haughty disdain that one of his class would naturally feel towards one of Amos's lowly state, were the only demerits he had accrued. And yet he was expected to enter his well-guarded fastness and persuade him to kill himself, or if not to die by his own hand – and this was worse – to work on his mind so that he would not defend himself against Amos's fatal attack.

Amos was not the Bloody Boy. He had determined not to be the Bloody Boy ever since the Ghost had so gleefully given him the name, even though the sight and, worse, the sound of M'Gregor's brains dripping off the ceiling in the Andover Workhouse now reasserted themselves horribly in his mind to prove the contrary. He could feel his heart pounding unnaturally fast, and a nasty prickling heat seemed to have spread from the damned white tattoo and fanned out across his whole body. He tried once more to tell himself exactly why he wasn't the Bloody Boy, chapter and verse, but all the reasons he had gone over in his mind as they had wound their way across the dark countryside to reach this sharp point of decision came down to one thing: Amos could live with himself, was able to push the horror of who and how he had killed to one side of his mind because he had not meant to kill. He had defended himself on both occasions without thought, without time to develop a thinking, considered intent. The tinker had been about to cut his throat; M'Gregor had been about to empty a blunderbuss through his face. And Amos had instinctively defended himself. So far, so lucky. So far, in fact, so natural.

This thing lying ahead of him was not reflex. This was not instinct. It was of course self-preservation because the white tattoo unfulfilled would, he was quite sure, kill him. But it was not the same thing as the other deaths. He had had time – even though he had spent much of it trying not to do so – to think about the bargain he had been forced into. And having been forced into it, he had had to weigh his own life against another's. On the animal level there was no reason to think much about it: for Amos to survive, to just keep breathing, Mountfellon must die.

But betrayed and trapped though he was by the tattoo, Amos had been trapped for far longer by his muteness. That muteness had made him turn inwards and develop the habit of talking to himself for want of others. And this lifelong habit of reflection, of turning things over and over in his mind, was a double-edged thing. It made him look at things from all angles. And though he undoubtedly intended to survive, he had thought this through. The price of his survival was not killing Mountfellon. It was a price that he would only pay afterwards: the true price was that he would then have to live out the rest of his life as the one who had killed a man, and done so thoughtfully, with considered intent. He would have to live with himself, knowing he had valued his unsteady vital flame at higher rate than another human's. And so the price he would pay would be that of not being Amos any more. This coming murder would not just be the end of Mountfellon, it would be the death of Amos's innocence, of his essential sense of who he was. What it would be the birth of he could not know, but he had the nastiest feeling deep within him that the Amos he still was would not like the Amos he would emerge as. And if he did not like that future Amos, the true Bloody Boy, then would the game he was about to embark on be worth the candle?

"You think too much, Bloody Boy," said the Ghost.

"Live or die. Black or white. Night or day. The biggest decisions are the simplest," grunted Badger Skull.

And perhaps because the sense that they had both been inside his head observing his thoughts made him doubly nauseous, on top of the dread of the blood to come, his stomach rebelled and he vomited copiously into the road.

They sat and watched him, unmoving as he stumbled from the pony and retched up again into the ditch. He found a kerchief in his pocket and wiped his face. Remembering that it was one he had found in the tinker's pack, he balled it and threw it into the bushes. He felt childish doing it, as if it was a last act of rebellion that meant precisely nothing to anyone, not even really himself. Then he turned and looked at them.

"There is no choice," said the Ghost. And there was the faintest undertone of a gentler self in her cracked voice, a whisper, perhaps, of apology.

He waved her quiet and strode towards the gatehouse, rubbing the itch that was extending around his neck.

I know. Enough. Mountfellon must die.

Decisiveness is a wonderful thing. It banishes the destabilising mists of uncertainty and clears the mind, eliminates havering on the edge of something and restores a sense of direction and forward motion.

Amos grasped the bell pull at the side of the gate and yanked it resolutely, three firm pulls. The accompanying jangle of bells within the gatehouse produced not the barking dog, nor the angry and unpleasant gatekeeper he remembered from his first visit, but the diminutive figure of the Running Boy, the messenger servant whose name, Amos was surprised to remember, was Whitlowe. He also remembered that the Whitlowe he had glimpsed in the lamplight what seemed like a long lifetime ago had been a snivelling child with a persistent dewdrop of nasal drip hanging from the end of his nose. On second meeting, it was clear this drop was a permanent rather than a merely persistent feature.

Whitlowe sniffed it back into the inner mysteries of his nostrils and wiped the back of a much-used cuff across his nose as he peered out into the rain.

"'Oo is it?" he said, voice querulous and piping. "Only the gatekeeper's away and I 'as orders not to open the gates for any but 'isself and the master."

Amos held out the letter the Ghost had provided him with.

"For Viscount Mountfellon, to be delivered by this messenger's hand to his and no other," Whitlowe read with a slow deliberation, and a degree of pride mixed with relief as he reached the end of the inscription without encountering any words that were beyond his capability.

He looked up at Amos.

"But . . .'e ain't here, sir! 'E's away down to London. 'As been for weeks now."

Amos was listening to the boy's thoughts as he spoke, and knew the absolute truth of the bad news the moment he delivered it.

Decisiveness is a wonderful thing at restoring a sense of direction and forward motion, so much so that it can make you feel unstoppable. And that works right up until you smack into an immoveable object.

The flash of horror in Amos's mind made him invade the boy's head without thinking he was going to do it.

Stay there.

Amazingly Whitlowe did. His face went slack and he allowed the dewdrop to reappear without noticing it as he stared out into the night, a night that was free of any sign of Amos.

Amos was around the corner, stumbling towards the Sluagh and the Ghost who were sheltering in the shadows under the outflung canopy of a tall elm.

He could not believe that none of them could have anticipated this most simple and humdrum of obstacles, that Mountfellon might simply not be at home.

We must go to London. He is not here.

The Ghost looked as if she had been hit, swaying in the saddle.

"But . . ." she said.

Amos could see the simplicity of the means by which her plans had been confounded was hitting her too.

"We can go to London, but we cannot enter it," said Badger Skull.

"And you can enter it but not get there in time. There is not enough night left in the sky for even the fleetest horse to make the journey before first light, and at sunrise . . ."

He shrugged and rubbed his throat.

Amos felt the fiery itch at his own neck and tore open the collar. He thrust himself at the Ghost, baring his throat to the moonlight.

How much is gone black?

She stared at him, then dropped her gaze.

"Oh," she said.

Her eyes said more, but none of it offered anything like relief. He could see that the white tattoo had nearly bruised black and joined up into the final lethal band.

You have killed me.

He staggered back and looked up at the moon. He felt as if he were trapped in the hinges of a great and adamantine door closing on the world, crushing him to nothingness, as if he had never even been. All that valuable time he had wasted wondering if he could, if he would kill Mountfellon, only to see the vainglorious, self-deluding presumption of that inner debate: if Mountfellon was in front of him now he would despatch him without a thought. He would do anything to live. Life, especially the brief weeks of early autumnal freedom that he had just stolen for himself, was inexpressibly sweet. It was the most desirable thing imaginable; even the grimmest moments in his curtailed life in the counting-house among his unkind "family" were sweeter than the alternative, because there were still moments when he could imagine future happiness. He knew this now without a moment's hesitation: life was sweet because the opposite was a blank and bitter darkness in which nothing grew, not even hope.

And it was that darkness to which he was now irrevocably condemned, simply because neither the Ghost nor Badger Skull had been able to imagine Mountfellon might not be where they assumed he would so conveniently be.

He looked at them.

You have both killed me.

FOURTH PART

THE DEATH OF WATER

CHAPTER 36

THE DROWNING GLASS

Had he not been able to hold onto the raft of barrel staves, Mr Sharp would have drowned long before the flood rose to the roof of the cave. As it was, he was lifted by the buoyancy of the wood to which he clung, which was just enough to keep him afloat but woefully inadequate at enabling him to keep any part of his body other than his head and shoulders clear of the sapping cold of the water. That chill relentlessly leeched the bodily warmth from him until he felt his numbed and shivering fingers begin to lose their grip on his tiny liferaft, at which point he decided the time had come to jam one hand beneath the belts that held it together, effectively lashing himself to it in order that he would stay afloat even when, as was now inevitable, he drifted into moments of unconsciousness.

He loosened a belt and wedged his left forearm beneath it. Then he awkwardly cinched the buckle tight again, a process that involved more kicking and swivelling in the dark water than he would have liked. The more he moved, the faster his energy would be used up, and since his only hope, so infinitesimally unlikely as to be scarcely worth the name, was in staying alive until and in case the nun returned to the chink above his head and somehow rescued him, he resented every unnecessary expenditure of that dwindling vital spark.

The chill was relentless and worked itself deep into him, a dull bone ache that felt irrevocable. It was the kind of coldness that not only banished warmth, but destroyed the very idea and memory of it.

He tried to keep still. In the dark he hung there, now thirty or forty feet above the bottom of the cavern, in a rapidly decreasing airspace, tightly clenched in the grip of a cold that he knew would ultimately be fatal. He attempted to clear his mind of the fear that was jumbling his thoughts, but he couldn't. Maybe it was an effect of the cold on his thinking, but he changed his mind about conserving his strength because the impotence of just floating and waiting for the inevitable was suddenly claustrophobically intolerable; if there had been something to do, some action, however futile, that would take his attention he would have gladly thrown away that last reserve of energy in pursuing it, but there was nothing more to be done. He heard himself stifle a groan. He would just have to wait.

But then again, what was he saving the candles for? He might have to die, he was going to die, but he didn't have to do so in the dark.

He reached his free hand inside his waistcoat and retrieved one of the candles stored there. He snapped his wrist and lit it while still underwater. It was one of the features of the fire that he was able to raise and hold on the candles that it was unquenchable, and he stared dully downwards at the sudden paradox he had made flower in the stygian darkness.

"B-b-brighter," he croaked, shocked to hear the reedy weakness in his voice.

The submerged flame flared and twisted in the current whirling slowly beneath the surface. He saw its glow reflected and distorted across the walls of the cavern around him and was shocked to see how narrow that circumference of water had become. The level had risen much higher and faster than he had imagined, and because he had risen with it, he had not experienced any sense of velocity. Craning his head back and lifting the candle out of the flood and into the air, he was able to see the roof of the cavern perilously close.

"Damn," he said, and then adding inexplicably, even to himself. "Sorry."

As he floated there, with the candle flame flaring close to his head, he felt something else: the heat of the flame. It felt good.

He could think of no reason to save the other candles now. He would run out of air and drown long before he burnt his way through them. So he clenched his teeth to stop them chattering and began to retrieve candles from his pockets and set about lighting them. He was able to clasp six in the hand lashed to the staves, and hold them there. Then he lit another one but fumbled and dropped it from his shivering hand. He watched the flame tumble away from him into the water beneath, water that was clear enough for him to see it all the way down until it landed on the sunken floor of the cave far below.

The six flames clenched in his hand wavered and flared in front of his face. He felt the welcome heat and held his free hand carefully over them, warming it, trying to loosen the ice-block dullness which had made it so fumbling and clumsy. He smiled, or tried to. It was, he suspected, more of a grimace.

"Well. I shall not die in the dark at any rate."

As the rising water moved, he was being swirled in the slow eddy created by the in-gushing flow beneath so that he spun lazily around and around. It was a mark of how tightly the incipient hypothermia had him in its grip that he watched the chink in the roof swing past him at least half a dozen times before he noticed that something new was happening and that the water had – could this really be so? – stopped rising.

He waited for the slow vortex to spin him round again, and then kicked towards the small hole. It was perhaps seven inches wide at its biggest, just enough to get an arm through, maybe up to the shoulder. It was acting as an overflow for the rising water, which was now spilling healthily over the lip of the hole and audibly splashing down into the unseen space beyond. Sharp felt a flutter of something akin to hope move in his chest. He clamped it down and concentrated on the chink. It was not large enough to jam a head through, certainly not enough to offer any kind of escape route, and yet it was slowing the rise in the water in a way he had been too dulled to realise was a possibility. There was only eighteen inches or so of air pocket left to him, but if the hole kept on providing an outflow for the water as it evidently was now doing, and also providing an inflow of air, things might not end as fast as he had feared. The reason he clamped down on the hope was because this was a delay, not a stay of execution. The cold would eventually do for him as fatally as suffocation, but every second saved was one in which help might arrive. It was the most risibly unlikely of eventualities, his rational mind knew that, but he was discovering that rationality was of limited utility at this furthest extreme of survival and that even the tiniest fraction of hope was worth fighting for.

"Plenty of time to rest when you're dead," he said, thinking again of Cook as he did so, these being the words with which she had turfed him out of his box-bed behind the kitchen range on every morning of his youth, before he graduated to his own rooms on the upper floors of the house.

He reached for the hole which was angled at roughly forty-five degrees, being offset on the arc where the cavern wall swept up to become the roof. His fingers scrabbled awkwardly for a grip on the stone lip, missed, clawed out again and held. He pulled himself into the side, managing to wedge the barrel staves into the hole far enough to be able to hold himself in place against the circular current. He then took his free hand and snatched one of the lit candles from those lashed to the staves, and threw it through the chink.

He saw it bounce and bob in the space beyond. He jammed his face to the hole and peered awkwardly at what was there.

He saw a narrow passage hacked through the rock, like a mineworking, no more than five feet high. The wall opposite was cut into low rectangular galleries walled in by hedges of regularly shaped stones, curiously bobbled and rounded like flints, laid in a repetitive texture that was anomalously somehow like knitting. In the rest of the snatched view he was allowed before the candle he had thrown was carried away by the shallow stream of water flowing off to the left of the chink, he saw a sooty line snaking along the roof, evidence of miners' candles at one time, and just before the light disappeared he saw someone staring at him – and then the candle bobbed around the curve of the wall and the face he had glimpsed was gone.

"Help!" he shouted. "If there is anyone there, please help!"

No one answered.

The only sound was the water flowing through the hole and splashing to the floor of the passage beyond. He scrabbled for another candle, lit it and jammed it through the hole, this time keeping hold as he squinted through the narrowed opening – obstructed as it now was by his arm – his eyes searching for the face glimpsed opposite.

Two black eyes stared back at him, unmoved and unmoving.

"Help!" he rasped.

Then he realised what he was looking at. Not a face, or at least not a face that could respond. Rather he was staring into the underpinnings of a face, into the eye sockets of a skull wedged into the hedge of strangely regular stones opposite. Except now that he had identified the skull, he realised what the "hedge" was really made of. He had after all spent enough time moving similar things and laying them out on the now sunken floor far below his feet to recognise them for what they were. Not stones, but the knuckle ends of human femurs in their hundreds, stacked on top of each other to make a wall of bones, a wall that the skull had been placed in to make a kind of grim decoration.

Not a mineworking then, he thought, staring back into its mockingly vacant orbits. A catacomb.

He felt the water rushing past his chin, flowing out of the cavern into the passage beyond.

Not a passage, he corrected himself. A galleried sepulchre.

As good a place as any to die.

He held on and closed his eyes. The cold was making him sleepy. He was too tired to think straight. Maybe if he just dozed for a moment, maybe if he just let sleep take him briefly, he would awake with a clearer head. Sleep. Just a nap for a minute or two and then he would revive.

He forced his eyes open.

"No" he said.

This was how the cold took you. He'd seen it in the dead of winter, in icily forgotten garrets and unfrequented alleys choked with snow: people died of cold calmly in the end. It wasn't a violent thing. Exposure snuck up on them like a friend, whispered that if they folded themselves in slumber they would be warmer, or at least not notice the chill. Then they closed their eyes and drifted off into the long sleep, quietly and inoffensively, until they just forgot to take the next shallow breath and the heart kicked for the last time, and all was still.

He wasn't going to go like that.

The sound of the water debouching from the narrow chink into the catacomb passage had changed. It was quieter, less gushing. His heart rose again. He had been wrong. The flow was slowing. He had another look through the hole.

The sound had not changed because the flow had slowed. It had changed because the distance the water had to fall had shortened considerably.

The water level in the passage outside was now rising. Simple physics annihilated his last hope: once the passage filled to the top of the chink, he would be stuck on the wrong side, with maybe three inches of head-space, a wafer-thin air pocket that would run out in minutes.

He was dead in the water.

CHAPTER 37

THE STONE SEA BY MOONLIGHT

High on the Steinernes Meer, the rolling limestone karst that tops the central plateau of the Berchtesgaden Alps, a middle-aged woman was screaming at the sky.

It was a clear, crisp night gripped in an unnatural stillness that had in it neither hint nor even memory of wind. The entire lofty and untravelled wilderness of wave-like ridges, gorges and swallow holes was silvered by a high hunter's moon that hung above air so fresh and thin that the bright scrabble of stars overhead seemed close enough to touch.

The woman's screaming was rhythmic and wordless, each primal shriek an outraged howl of denial stabbed into the cold heart of the night. She had left her husband and the boy in the lonely shepherd's hut on the edge of the high summer pasture far below on the Salzburgerland side of the massif and had climbed for nearly two hours to gain the perfect solitude of the Stone Sea in order that she could make this noise alone and unheard. The tracks of her tears glistened in the moonlight and her mouth gaped like a cavern as she howled her grief into the upper void. Her grey hair – which she had unbound from its usual plaited crown – hung loose over her dark loden cloak, and partly hid the swollen goitre that bulged her neck, a small blight disguised by the wide ribbon of the embroidered *Kropfband* she wore like a collar. Goitres were not unusual among the inhabitants of this mountainous part of middle Europe; they were a direct effect of their iodine-deprived diet and were not – as the lowland dwellers often ignorantly and unkindly claimed – a consequence of generations of inbreeding.

She was thus not a comely woman, but the purity of her grief gave her a strange and honest dignity that any observer would immediately have responded to with sympathy and humane fellow feeling. She, however, did not want sympathy or indeed observation, and that is why she had climbed so high before allowing herself to let the nakedness of her pain become visible as she keened into the moonlight, clutching a crumpled letter in her hands as she did so.

It was in one of the gaps between her screams, as she drew breath, that she heard the goat-bell far away to her left.

She swallowed the next scream and listened without breathing.

Once more she heard the distinctive jangle, definitely higher and thinner than a cowbell, though she knew she was at an altitude and on terrain that no mere cow could achieve or even contemplate. Cows never came above the summer pastures far below. Only a goat was nimble or stubborn enough to come this high on its own, and the only reason one would depart from the more usually travelled lower slopes was to escape a predator.

The thought that there might be a wolf or even a bear in the vicinity was one of the reasons the woman was listening now instead of screaming.

The bell jangled on, intermittent and irregular, as if the hidden goat were picking its way across the jumbled ground, slowly getting closer. The woman tucked the crumpled letter into the bodice of her dirndl, swept her hair back and tied it out of her face, then picked up the long alpenstock from the rocks beside her, holding its spiked end forward as she peered towards the approaching goat-bell. She heard a foot scuff and a sudden intake of breath.

Not a hoof scuff.

A foot.

So not a goat. Or not *just* a goat, she thought as she retreated into the shadow of the rock behind her.

And then she heard the child's voice.

"Hansi? Oh, Hansi, where are you, you stupid animal? Father is going to kill me . . ."

The woman relaxed. The mystery was revealed. A child, a girl child, clearly left in charge of the family goats, had lost an animal and was so scared of the consequences that she was still out on the mountain looking for it.

The woman half smiled in relief and wiped her eyes. A child was no threat to her. Indeed somebody else's lost child provided an opportunity for her to distract herself from the sadness contained in the letter she had placed back inside her bodice. She kept still, thinking that if she waited, the goat would stumble into her and she could grasp it before it ran away, and then she could call to the girl and tell her she had the errant animal safely waiting for her. It was no time of night for any child to be out on her own. There were bad things in the dark, things just as happy to prey on little girls as wandering goats.

The animal in question stopped just on the other side of a jagged boulder, about ten feet away from her. She sensed it was listening.

"Hansi? You silly thing, where are you now?"

The girl's voice was still a way off, sounding increasingly strained and desperate. The goat moved a little, making its bell jingle once, but then it stopped.

The woman had enough experience of goats to know it was quite likely to wait until the girl got really close before nimbly eluding her again in a game that could go on until dawn, or until the child fell off something steep and fatal in the darkness.

The woman reversed the alpenstock, thinking to use the crook to hook the goat by the collar should it try to run, and then, holding her breath and concentrating on moving very silently, she eased round the boulder.

The goat was hidden in deep moon shadow on the other side. She heard a faint *tink* from the bell and waited for her eyes to adjust. She could make out a shape that was definitely not rock, and then, just as she realised it was perhaps a rather larger goat than she had imagined, the bell tinkled again and the shape moved, emerging into the moonlight.

"Frau Wachman?"

The goat-bell hung on the end of a hunter's crossbow, just below the steely tip of a very sharp bolt that was aimed right at her.

She did not move, which was a credit to her since a very cold shiver went down her spine, not so much at the sight of it as the sound of the very calm and measured voice of the shadowed man, a man whose voice she had never heard before but who seemed, uncannily, to know her name.

"Frau Wachman?"

"Who are you?" she said, her mouth suddenly dry.

"I am Otto von Fleischl."

The shiver that had gone down her spine reversed and ran back up it. She felt the hairs stand on the back of her neck at the name.

"Von Fleischl? You are—?"

"The *Schattenjäger*. Yes."

True to his name, the figure stayed in the throw of darkness behind the unwavering crossbow stuck out into the moonlight. The woman thought of hurling herself sideways around the curve of the boulder and running, but the barren immensity of the Stone Sea lay between her and the sheltering trees, and she knew the crossbow bolt would find her long before she reached them. She had been right: there were dangerous things abroad in the darkness.

Her bowels felt loose and untrustworthy at the thought of exactly how dangerous. She knew the dark stories of the *Schattenjäger*, the Shadowhunter, and had lived in the mountains long enough to know dark stories were often far truer than the things that people safe in the well-lit flatland towns thought was fact.

"And if the bolt did not reach you, I would," said the little girl's voice right in her ear. The child had somehow come around and behind her without her hearing a thing. Except the voice was different now, older and just as calm as the *Schattenjäger*'s.

She felt a tickle in her hairline and knew without looking that a long and very sharp hunter's knife was resting against the base of her skull, and that any attempt to run would end with one fast thrust between the cervical vertebrae, severing her spinal cord and paralysing her from the neck down. She also knew from the way the unseen knife-holder had read her thoughts that the other part of those dark stories was true, and so she knew who she was too. The girl was the Shadowhunter's Knife.

"You are the *Schattenjägermesser*?"

The girl grunted in what might have been amusement.

"A stupid name. I am just plain Ida Laemmel. Put your hands behind your back, very slowly, please."

The woman thought for a moment about trying to run. She had no doubt that this would end swiftly and badly for her, but though she was terrified, she was not a coward, and she knew that once they had her, they might use her to find her husband and the boy, and just because she was in their clutches did not mean she was powerless: she could still save the others. She would make them kill her.

Yet she did not want to die. Despite the great loss and the grief she had been howling at the moon only moments before, she wanted to live. But she was logical, and she loved her husband. She—

Ida Laemmel hit her astonishingly hard, a small bony fist sledgehammering her in the kidneys. She gasped and dropped to one knee, agonised and winded, her wide mouth gaping. She was unable to resist the girl who gripped her right hand and snapped something metallic tight around her thumb, then used it like a painful restraining lever as she dragged the left hand across and snapped metal over the thumb on that hand, so that by the time she got her first breath her hands were thumb-cuffed behind her.

"Ida—" said the figure in the shadows, a note of light-hearted reproach in his voice.

Ida Laemmel stepped in front of Frau Wachman. She was shockingly young, with two long pigtails, shockingly pretty, even in the moonlight, and most shockingly of all, wearing not a skirt but trousers. Specifically she was wearing *Trachten*, men's hunting costume, the soft and soundless deerskin full-length lederhosen that clung tight to her calves, and a matching short jacket. The soft suede of her costume had been dyed black or dark green, so that she appeared to be clothed in shadow. She had a small crossbow slung on her back, the expected knife in one hand and a thin silvery chain in the other.

"She was about to run," she said. "Her husband is in a summer hut on the high pasture. She didn't want us to know."

Frau Wachman felt a pain worse than the one in her kidneys. Just by thinking of her husband, she had betrayed him to this – this monster who could read her thoughts.

"Monster is an unkind word," said Ida. Tugging gently on the silver chain, which Frau Wachman now realised was attached to the small but horribly effective thumb-cuffs behind her.

"We are not monsters . . ." said the Hunter, emerging into the moon-light.

He too wore the dark deerskin *Trachten* of his accomplice, but where her head was bare, he wore a low-brimmed felt hat above unwavering, flinty eyes and a black beard that jutted down off his chin like a spade.

". . . you know who we are."

Frau Wachman looked from one to the other. And then she spat defiantly.

"I do. And I curse you for what you are doing."

"Curse us all you like in your head, but make a noise to warn your husband and not only will we do what we are doing, but what we do to him will be much, much worse than what we will do if you are quiet," said the Shadowhunter. "And since you know who we are, you know we do not deal in threats. Only certainty."

If they had needed to descend on the Bavarian side of the massif, they would have been in shadow and the going would have been slower as they picked their way off the stony tops and headed back down to the tree line and the high pastures below; as it was, they wound their way towards the upper slopes of the valley on the Austrian side in full moonlight which made their passage easier and faster. Frau Wachman walked between her two captors, led by a chain held by the disturbingly pretty and innocent-looking girl with the knife, at every step conscious of the sharp crossbow bolt aimed at her back by the following Shadowhunter.

Before long they could see a distant light or two far below them on the valley floor, the usual and expected static ones made by the odd, unshuttered farmhouse windows on the winding road towards Saalfelden, and a line of moving lights inching their way along the silver streak of river that cut through the fertile bottom lands. The line of lights caught her attention. Why—?

"You know why," said the girl ahead of her without turning or stopping her nimble-footed descent.

"Because they are looking for monsters in the dark," spat Frau Wachman. "With scythes and pitchforks to cut them into ribbons."

"And guns," said the voice behind her. "They have guns too."

"Just as well they are down there and we are up here then, eh?" said the girl.

The *Schattenjäger* grunted.

"They're not hunting monsters," he said. "Not yet."

Frau Wachman kicked at the shale they were walking across, sending a small landslide skittering down the slope towards the trees below. Maybe the noise would alert her husband. She banished the thought as soon as she had it, hoping the disconcerting girl with the pigtails and the lethal blade was not listening to her mind all the time. She tried to fill her head with something else instead. She thought of food. Of cooking. Of how much she loved the doing of it, the warm kitchen, the steady certainty of preparation, of assembling the ingredients and then measuring and chopping and slicing and mixing, and the heat of the oven and the waiting and checking and seasoning. She thought of her kitchen and her table, and thinking of the table she thought of the faces gathered round it in the glow of the lamp hung from the rafter above, but then she thought of her son and the letter, the letter that had brought her to the Steinernes Meer in the first place, the damned—

"What was in the letter?" said the girl.

Frau Wachman sealed her lips and clenched her teeth together. She would not give them that. She would not tell them of the strange man Dee who stepped out of a mirror to deliver it, and then left the same way before they could read its contents. Her mourning was private. Do what they liked, she would not—

"Who died?"

Frau Wachman kicked another cascade of scree down the slope to their side. The yank on her chain made her gasp in pain as the cuffs bent her thumbs the wrong way and she had to spin round so she was facing backwards to stop her shoulders dislocating. This brought her face to face with the *Schattenjäger* who did, as she had feared, have the crossbow aimed right at her.

"Who died?"

"My son," gritted Frau Wachman. "May you rot for making me tell you. One of my sons. If he were here, you would answer to him for what you do to his helpless mother."

The girl laughed, low and humourless.

"Oh, you are not so helpless as you seem, Frau Wachman. If you try and warn your husband again by kicking scree down the slope, you will be hurt and then you will be carried, and all that is going to happen will happen anyway."

"How did he die?" said the *Schattenjäger*, indicating with a jerk of the crossbow that she should turn and walk on.

The cursed letter from London seemed to burn into her skin below the bodice where she had stuffed it.

"And why do you learn of it in a letter from London?" said the girl. "London is a long way from here. What business would your son have among the English?"

Frau Wachman said nothing.

"It's not important," said the hunter. "Keep silent now."

They reached the trees without further delay. Frau Wachman was helpless: helpless because the uncanny girl could read her thoughts so any plan was useless the very moment she made it, and helpless because the hunter would, she knew, have no compunction in shooting her the instant she tried anything. She did not have to be a mind-reader to know that. It was why he carried a crossbow and not a gun. It would be silent; it would be just as fatal as a bullet over such short range. And he would not miss. None of the old, dark stories ever included a moment where his aim was anything other than fatally true.

Her only hope was that her husband was rested and replenished. They had come to the lonely, high pasture and the unvisited cabin to recruit his failing health. If he was returned to his usual vigour, there was still a chance that, if awake, he might hear them coming and be alert enough to save himself. She, she now knew, was beyond saving. These night monsters had her, and whatever her fate would bring was in their hands.

"We are not monsters," said the voice ahead of her. "We are different from you, that is all. And you are wrong: your fate is in your own hands even now, because if you stay quiet, this need not end quite as badly as you fear . . ."

CHAPTER 38

THE LAST BREATH

"*Ici*," said the nun. She tapped the mirror to her right and then rummaged in her habit, emerging with a short, red candle stub and a tinderbox. The redness of the wax was unexpected, Sara's eyes having become used to the almost monochrome world of the mirrors: it seemed ominous and unchancy, a harbinger of blood and death.

Sara looked at the nun. At the mirror. This was the moment the trap would be sprung, if the old Mirror Wight was lying.

"The moment of truth," she said. The nun lit the candle and then looked up at her. Sara wondered if perhaps she had used the wrong phrase. Maybe it didn't translate into French.

"My whole life is a moment of truth," said the nun with an innocent shrug. "Even when I have been forced to deceive, I have never lied."

This was clearly an important distinction to her. But it was a nicety Sara had neither time nor inclination to indulge in, especially when she had no idea what or who was waiting beyond the mirror in question.

"Sharp is on the other side of that?" she said.

"A passage is on the other side," said the nun. "And in the wall of the passage is a hole that will allow you to see into the cavern in which he is trapped."

Sara thought of questioning her further. But all that would produce was more words, and words without proof were just more tinder for the fires of uncertainty crackling away in the back of her head.

"Good," she said.

The nun smiled, beatific.

Sara sized her up.

"We go through together," she said.

Before she could protest, Sara snaked an arm round the nun's middle and hoisted her unceremoniously off the floor. The nun's feet thrashed in the air. She was as light as a child. Sara drew a knife from her boot-top. The nun stopped kicking.

"Again, if there is an ambush on the other side of that mirror, I will likely cut your head clean off," Sara said conversationally. "I shall most probably do the same if Sharp is not there."

"But I thought . . . I felt . . . you were a kind, a nice person! I thought—" spluttered the nun.

"Then you were mistaken," said Sara, "for I am neither kind nor nice."

And before the nun could confuse things with more words, Sara stepped through the mirror.

She gasped as the water hit her, hip-deep and cold as glacier-melt. The nun shrieked and spluttered, arms flailing and splashing. In the moment before the candle was blown out by this, Sara saw the passage was some kind of bone-stacked catacomb, half submerged in a river, and that they had just emerged from a mirror placed opposite a twin on the other side of the flow.

She hoisted the nun higher to keep her clear of the water.

"Be still," she hissed.

"I did not know," wailed the nun. "This is an accident!"

"Do you still have the candle?" said Sara.

"Yes, but—" began the nun.

"Give it to me," said Sara.

The nun fumbled it into her hand, finding it in the darkness.

"Don't let me go!" she gasped, sensing a loosening of Sara's grip. "I cannot swim."

Something in the dark caught Sara's eye just before she snapped her wrist and lit the candle. She left it unlit.

"Then hold on to something," she said, jamming the nun against the hedge of bones and letting her go.

The nun shrieked and scrabbled at the femurs, trying to find a purchase. Sara turned from her and peered at something just below the surface of the water. She had been right. There was something.

On the other side of what must be the hole of which the nun had spoken, there was a faint and flickering illumination. It was submerged, it was dim, but it was definitely—

"Light," said Sara.

The candle nub in her hand flared into life, and without a moment's hesitation she crossed the passage and plunged it beneath the rising water, stabbing her arm through the opening and into the drowned cavern.

"Brighter," she choked, and began waving her arm backwards and forwards.

Nothing happened. All she felt was the pressure of water as it swirled around the cavern past her outstretched hand.

The only sound was the water flowing out of the narrowed gap she was now partially clogging, a distant roar as it flowed off down some other passage, and the sobbing of the nun.

"Be quiet," snapped Sara.

The nun stifled her weeping.

"You do me wrong," she snivelled.

"I shall do you more than wrong if you have drowned him," said Sara, meaning every word. "How much air space is in there above this hole?"

"Air space?" said the nun. "The hole is not at the top of the cavern, it is a little to one side and a bit lower, how much I can't say – half a metre, maybe a whole one . . ." Sara was saved the chore of explanation by the impact of a leg against her hand. The leg was moving sluggishly with the centrifugal motion of the water in the cavern, and it was disconcertingly lifeless and unresponsive, but without thought she grabbed it and tugged, letting the candle end fall.

Sharp was indeed dead in the water.

If she had not pulled at him, he would have continued his descent into the long sleep, but instead he spluttered awake, banging his head on the rock ceiling and opening his eyes to see the candle that Sara had dropped tumbling down into the depths beneath him.

His first thought was that something was biting his leg, nipping and worrying at it, and he had visions of some kind of subterranean river eel attacking him. He jack-knifed and tried to wrench it free, then stopped when his hands found fingers instead of fangs.

And more than fingers, a glove, and on the glove two rings, rings he knew well, rings he had been looking at his whole life.

The gloved hand released its hold on the trousers, found his hand and gripped it tight.

He took a deep lungful of too-stale air from the thin sliver of breathing space above him, and then let the hand pull him down to the hole. He gripped it and stared blearily through the water.

He could see nothing. There was no light in the passage.

He wrenched his other arm free of the lashing that attached him to the barrel-stave raft and took his last candle from his waistcoat. He lit it.

Sara's heart was thumping dangerously fast.

When the candle blazed and light came through the hole she wanted to shout out, but she didn't. Instead she bit it back behind her teeth and stared down at the familiar features staring blindly at her from beneath the water.

"Jack . . ." she said, hoarse with despair. "Oh, Jack, what have you done?"

On his side he hung there in the flooded cavern, his vision blurred but staring up out at her face suspended in the life-giving air that was so heart-breakingly close yet unreachable above the water beyond the small hole.

It seemed to Sara that they stared at each other for a lifetime, but in reality it was only for as long as the lungful of air lasted, and then he pushed away and disappeared back inside, kicking for the surface and the sliver of air waiting beneath the shallow dome of the cavern.

It was gone.

★　★　★

Sara turned to the nun.

"Is there another way into there?" she snapped.

"Yes, but no . . ." said the nun in horror. "There's a single mirror at the bottom of the raft, but if you go in through it you'll . . ."

"How do I go through it?" said Sara.

"Through the next mirror . . . on the right. But . . ."

The nun's eyes skittered in panic.

". . . but then you'll both die," she choked. "There's a way in, but no way out."

Inside the cavern, Sharp saw silvery bubbles trapped beneath the roof, swirling like mercury, some as big as his hand. This was the very last of the air, trapped in the irregularities of the rock roof. He knew he was done for, but he swam up to them and carefully sipped the air from the two largest ones.

He was going to die now, but where that had seemed unbearable only moments ago, the simple, joyous fact that Sara lived – and now knew he had come into the mirrors to find her – eased his distress more than he would have imagined possible. And though she would now never hear him say he loved her, he felt something of that had passed between their clasped hands and the held glance they had shared across the impassable watery barrier. And more than anything, he had been good to his word. He would die true, and he would die with that truth recognised by the person whose regard he most valued.

That was something to savour as he sipped the last bubbles of air, a thought to soften the pain of parting.

Sara heard none of what the nun had shouted after her. All she could hear was the urgent drumming of her blood in her ears as she emerged back in the mirror-maze. Water splashed off her soaked jacket sleeve, spattering and pooling on the floor as she took one fast pace to the side, sucked in a huge breath and plunged into the next mirror along.

★ ★ ★

Sharp felt something large tumble and churn out of the mirror on the bottom of the raft. He held out the candle and watched as, to his horror, the billowing black cloud that emerged resolved itself into Sara's skirts, and legs and then the unmistakeable thick white snake of her plait as the rest of her followed.

Everything in him screamed in despairing protest at the sight.

He had just made his peace with death.

This shattered that hard-won calm like a sledgehammer dropped through a looking-glass.

Dying was bad enough, but that she should have come to perish with him was a brutal cruelty beyond comprehension. It made a nonsense of everything he had done, all that he had pledged life and heart to.

They found each other's shoulders and stared into one another's faces through the clear water, lit by the flare of the last candle. He shook his head at her, the thin half-lungful left to him beginning to fail and burn with the keen acid pain of oxygen deprivation. There were only moments before his body took over and broke his will and he reflexively sucked in the final treacherous mockery of a breath that would be only water and death.

Sara was gesturing at him, short angry movements of her hand.

Why?

His head was thick and confused. All his brainpower was going to fighting back the fatal final reflex that would lead to that water-filled in-breath.

Her gloved hand gripped his chin and pointed.

She was pointing at the mirror on the bottom of the raft.

The one she had come through.

The one that had no twin to make a passage of reflections through which they could escape.

He felt the reflex begin to spasm his throat, his body unable to believe what his head knew, that there wasn't air outside it, that relief for the burn in his chest wasn't one simple breath away.

He clamped his hand over his mouth desperately.

Bubbles began to escape from his nose, unbidden, the exhalation the harbinger of that final paroxysm.

Sara ripped his hand from his mouth.

His eyes went wide in horror.

His body betrayed him, belching out the held breath, and then, as the reflex took over and he began to breathe in, his mouth filled with air. Sweet air, warm air, not water.

Sara's mouth was clamped over his, and she gave him her final breath, then raised his hand to his mouth and pushed it back into place.

Eye to eye, without words, the message was clear.

Don't waste it.

He wouldn't. He would die with that air in his lungs, sealed in place by the memory of those lips, for the first and the last time locked on his own.

She pointed at the mirror and beckoned.

He shook his head and held up one finger.

There was only one mirror.

He pantomimed a shrug.

They were stuck in here.

She shook her head. No. Held up two fingers. And then did something unimaginable. She took the candle and held it between her teeth, and then with both hands free, she reached over and twisted her wrist.

Her hand, the lost hand that he had been too confused to realise she had clearly been reunited with, came loose.

He was so shocked he nearly opened his mouth and wasted her last breath.

He watched, agog, as she turned and showed him the perfectly flat surface of the cut.

It was a mirror.

She held it in front of the mirror on the bottom of the stave-raft and beckoned him urgently.

He didn't need a second invitation. He launched himself over to her, gripped her by the waist to steady himself and looked into a wavering passage of repeated mirrors reflected there.

Because she had to hold herself steady against the raft with her other hand he went first. Wasting no time, he reached out, kicked hard and swam into the mirror.

Sara saw him go and smiled, her own empty lungs screaming in protest as her heart sang a victorious counterpoint.

Sharp tumbled out into the mirror-maze, gasping for breath. He sucked air and turned to receive Sara.

He stared at the reflection of himself, willing her to break it as she too fell out of the cavern, but the reflection remained unwavering and unbroken.

In the cavern, underwater, Sara reached out to steady herself against the wall. She was going to hold the mirrored stump of her wrist in place to make the passage, and then thrust herself through. She wasn't quite sure how it would work, but she trusted she would go through and her hand and stump along with her.

It was a good plan, but steadying herself against the cavern wall was an unthinking, bad mistake.

Her glove buttoned at the wrist. Her action scraped one of the buttons loose and it fell away. The slit it normally secured gaped open a little bit, and her skin touched the stone.

The reaction was instantaneous and shocking.

She glinted.

The jolt of the past spasming into her sent her eyes wide and her mouth wider.

She gagged and breathed in the water, but was able to do nothing about it.

She saw the cavern.

Still underwater.

But peopled.

A churn of drowning humanity.

Shadows and fragments.

Lit by tumbling candles.

Like a maelstrom of fish.

Seething into a feeding frenzy, but not fish.

Men and women.

Wreathed in bubbles.

Bubbles made by last breaths, drowned cries and curses, pleas and prayers.

Bubbles rising past people sinking.

Eyes wide in horror.

Faces screaming silently.

Hands waving.

Clasping. Clawing.

Punching.

Feet flailing.

Boots kicking.

Shoes falling.

The newly drowned buffeted by the last lashings of the living.

Sara would scream if her own lungs too were not full of water.

Her eyes begin to dim as unconsciousness reaches out and pulls her down.

And then she sees her.

The one woman not flailing for an unreachable surface.

Lithe, strong, resolute – dark hair ribboning out behind her as she swims, head down – purposefully kicking for the cavern floor.

Time jerks.

The swimmer is almost there. A ribbon of bubbles flows back and upwards round her face, bobbling towards Sara.

She is emptying her lungs so she doesn't get pulled up by the natural buoyancy of any air left in her body.

She is killing herself to achieve something.

Her face turns upwards, looking past Sara, reaching for someone above her in the churn of death, and in that moment Sara recognises her and the truth of it slices at her like a knife cutting the last thread of consciousness.

Her mouth tries to speak the name, to shriek at this last moment of awareness what is in fact the very first word she ever spoke

one whole lifetime ago

But she can't because she is now drowning too.

And as the field of her vision irises down into an ever narrowing cone, she sees that the black-haired woman has reached her target, the mirror through which all the drowned and the drowning have been lured, and is kicking at it, using the last spark of her own life to try and break it.

To try and prevent anyone else ever dying in the same trap that has killed her.

Anyone else – even her own daughter – who is of course Sara, the very one glinting all of this.

And dying as she does so.

The darkness wins.

Sharp plunged back into the mirror. Into the cavern. His hand found Sara's body before his eyes could even adjust, and he just wrenched her back out with him before he had time to fully enter the cavern.

They tumbled out onto the mirrored floor of the maze, sprawling like fish on a slab.

Sharp rolled out from under her.

"Sara," he croaked.

Her eyes were wide open. Water dribbled from her slack mouth. Her chest was still and unmoving.

"No," he said. "No."

She was dead.

Sharp rebelled.

NO.

He did not know if he roared this out loud or only in his head.

NO.

He did not care which.

NO.

"I do not accept this death," he gasped. "It will not be so."

He looked down at her face.

"No, Sara Falk," he choked, water dripping from his face onto her unblinking eyes. "No death. Not yours. Not today. And never, ever before mine. I gave my word."

He moved fast, flipping her over onto her side and pressing her chest cavity. Some water spilled out of her mouth. He turned her the other way round. More water trickled out. Then he put her on her back and raised her chin and tried to force the rest out by filling her lungs with air from his own. He worked steadily and urgently, breathing, pressing her chest hard, breathing again and repeating.

He had grown up next to the Thames. He had seen watermen try and revive the drowned on several occasions. Once it had even worked.

He tried to remember what he was doing wrong.

He clamped his mouth to hers and tried again and again to breathe life back into her.

Her lips remained cold and waxy beneath his own.

He was becoming light-headed from hyper-oxygenating. He allowed himself a moment to pause and look down at her face, again rebelling at the sight of her blue lips and the pale face that was now as unnaturally white as her hair.

He shook her by the shoulders.

"Sara!" he said. "Sara, please—"

He wondered if he should hit her. One of the rivermen had slapped the victim he was trying to revive. He tried to remember if that had been the single successful attempt he had witnessed.

He shook her again.

"Sara," he said, preparing to slap her.

She jerked and vomited. Copiously, and comprehensively, all over him.

Never before, and only once again in the future, was he so happy.

He threw his head back and laughed.

Her eyes fluttered and she found – unbelievably – that she had more fluid to heave up.

"Sharp," she gravelled. "Not . . . funny."

She gasped and choked some more.

"No," he said. "Wonderful."

She tried to raise herself. He wrapped his arms round her and helped her to sit.

"Go easy—" he said.

She shook her head.

"No."

She pointed at the mirror next to the one she had just fallen out of.

"We get out of these damned mirrors now."

"Sara," he began.

"Now, Sharp!" she said, voice like a slap. "We must get out now."

They stumbled through the mirror and into the catacomb passage which was still hip-deep in water which flowed strongly past them. Sharp clenched her to his side and looked around by the light of the candle gripped in his other hand.

"She's gone," said Sara weakly.

"Who?" said Sharp.

"Mirror Wight. A nun," she said. "Must have believed me."

"Believed you about what?" he said.

"Said I'd cut her damn head off if she tricked me." She coughed. "Not that she did. Maybe she thought I'd died."

"Dramatic," he said.

She retched out more water and shrugged.

"Meant it when I said it. Which way do we go?"

Sharp pointed left.

"Water's pooling and flowing to the right," he said. "Downhill. So let's go uphill."

"Good thinking," she whispered, wiping her mouth with her sleeve and clinging to his arm. "Up and out and no hanging about."

They ploughed through the water. In about fifteen yards it began to get shallower. In twenty-five yards they were standing on dry stone, looking back at the flooding. She steadied herself against the side of the tunnel, then pulled her hand back as it shifted and clattered, and she saw, as if for the first time, what she was leaning on.

"What is this place?" she shuddered.

"Catacomb," he said. "And the sooner we're out of it, the happier I shall be."

FIFTH PART
THE DEATH OF FIRE

CHAPTER 39

AMOS PASSES

"Do you want to live?" said Badger Skull, looking down at Amos.

Of course.

His heart quickened for a moment.

Can you break this tattoo?

"No. The warrandice is an oath-lock. I told you as I scribed it in your skin. It cannot be broken. Or extended."

Amos slumped and turned away. He began to walk into the night.

Then I am doomed.

"Where are you going?" said the Ghost.

I will do this by myself, by your leave.

All he had left, as inescapable fate crushed in on him from both sides, was himself. If he was to die in the horrible way the Sluagh had described, if the body below his neck was to blacken like a rotten fruit and drop away from his head, he would at least spare himself the added indignity of being observed in that final extremity. As he walked into the blanketing darkness, he wondered if the last laugh might even be his, if he might cheat the warrandice's fell penalty by ending his life before sunrise did it for him. He could at least be master of his own destiny. He questioned whether he could manage to drown himself, for he didn't wish to use one of the tinker's knives to open his veins: that would be letting the murderous tinker have the last (albeit postponed) laugh instead of him. Drowning hadn't been too bad, as he remembered. Not as bad as the bite and tug of a knife and the unstoppable outrush of blood that would follow. His stomach rebelled at the thought again and he retched emptily without stopping walking. Maybe there was a cliff or a quarry nearby? A brief moment rushing through a void of air and then an immediate and bludgeoning subtraction of his consciousness from the tangled chorus of the world . . . But what if he only broke himself and didn't fall hard enough to die? Then he would just lie there in shattered agony until the dawn . . .

"Drowning would do it kindest," said Badger Skull, contempt curling the edges of his words.

Amos turned to find the mohawked chieftain had been following him and clearly watching his mind.

Leave me alone.

"Suicide is not the last laugh," said the Sluagh. "It's a scream of defeat."

If you were defeated as I now am, wouldn't you scream?

"No," said Badger Skull. "If I was as you now think you are, I would at least have tried to take me with you, probably with that clasp knife you carry in your pocket, the one with the nasty, iron-steel blade."

And what would that have done to stop the inevitable?

Amos was tired, more tired than he had ever imagined it was possible to be. Maybe just lying down and sleeping until it was over would be the best thing to do.

"It wouldn't have stopped the inevitable, but I think it would have made me feel better about myself," said Badger Skull. "But that's just me. Knowing someone else was going into the blackness with me. Who knows? Maybe we walk again on the other side. It might even have been company."

We don't walk again on the other side.

This was one of the things Amos had decided a long, long time ago, when sitting through the endless church services enforced at the parish orphanage. There was no heaven, and there was no god, because no god as kind as the fat priests pretended the one they invoked was would allow the misery and suffering Amos saw all around him. The Templebanes were in this respect much more honest than the churchmen, in that they admitted of no higher power than their own human agency, and no interest having a stronger pull on man's activities than self-interest.

"You know nothing, and you remember less," said the Sluagh.

Please leave me. Just leave me now. Please.

Badger Skull spurred his horse and came level with him, leaning out, and slapped him off his feet.

Amos was so shocked at the unexpectedness of the blow that he just sat in the middle of the road.

What?

"What did I tell you of the white tattoo," said the Sluagh.

It is a mark of . . . my subservience and compliance to your will.

"And?"

Amos rubbed his jaw. Bitterness was now beginning to bubble back to the surface.

"It marks and guarantees the vow you made me take to kill Mountfellon and retrieve your flag."

"No. We did ask you to do that, but the warrandice itself was just to ensure you do as we ask, and to do so for a fixed term."

He pointed at Amos's neck.

"Which term is running out very fast."

I don't understand.

"You don't understand because fear is clouding your brain. Which is what fear does. Put fear in your enemies' brains and half the battle is won."

Amos scrabbled to his feet.

Enough lessons. I don't have time or need.

"Again: the oath-lock is to ensure you do as we ask, and do so for a fixed term."

The geometric tangle of tattoos split in a thin smile.

"The thing that'll save you, Bloody Boy, is that we can ask you to do anything. We can tell you to kill Mountfellon for the woman. And then we can change our minds and tell you not to kill Mountfellon. Not yet. And we can tell you to go in there and retrieve our flag instead. Now."

I don't believe you.

"Why would I lie to you?"

Amos grunted, the closest he ever got to an audible laugh.

Because you want the flag. Because nothing is more important to you than breaking the Iron Law. Because you'd say anything to do that.

The Sluagh looked at him.

"I would," he said. "I would lie from now until the end of time to do that. But I am not lying. Think back on the form of words we used and see if this is so."

Amos tried to clear his brain and remember if the precise phrasing had been as described.

"And even if I am lying," laughed the Sluagh, "which I am not, what have you got to lose?"

Not very much, Amos had to admit as he looked around the moonlit fields and the ragged groups of cows being driven towards the top of the hillock behind the gibbet.

Not very much.

Which is why three minutes later he had walked past the Ghost who was still swearing at the Sluagh, demanding they put a new warrandice around his neck to ensure he remained her weapon against Mountfellon, and was looking into Whitlowe's eyes.

You will do as I say. I cannot talk. You will take me to the house. You will help me get into the room where Mountfellon hides his treasures behind ironbound doors. And then you will help me carry something back here. Do you understand?

For a moment he thought he had failed to control the boy's mind, and was kicking himself for his foolhardy conceit. But then Whitlowe's head bobbed, and the shiny dewdrop had fallen off his nose and plashed to the coconut matting lining the tunnelled driveway at his feet.

And a minute after that the gate was open and the two of them were trotting into the wide underground passageway, the arched ironstone ceiling lit by the ring of light from the Running Boy's lantern.

They covered the near half-mile in brisk time, and the boy preceded him up into the covered turning circle outside the sprawling manor house, flitting through the cast-iron pillars supporting the glass roof and – before Amos could stop him – knocking on the door at the top of the steps.

The door swung open after a minute to reveal an irritated-looking footman who had clearly been roused from a deep and dishevelled slumber.

"What d'you want?" he slurred down at Whitlowe. He focused on Amos. "And who's the darkie . . ."

Amos glared into the man's eyes.

Get out.

The man's lip blubbered in incomprehension, torn between the compulsion to obey and revolting at the naked violation of Amos's intrusion into his mind.

Get out. Run away. Now!

The eyes stared at him, wavering. Amos decided he was halfway there. And deduced that he needed a more specific purpose before his subconscious control let itself be guided.

Run to the wall around the estate. Run round it until sunrise. Then you can sleep.

"Yes," said the footman. "Yes, I will."

At once.

"At once," said the footman, and without another word lumbered away into the night. Whitlowe displayed no surprise or qualm at this; in fact, he displayed no sign of having actually noticed.

Who else are we going to meet?

"Old Biles," said the boy. "'E sits up outside the master's study of a night."

Alone?

"Alone 'cept Bessie," said the boy.

Bessie is a woman?

"Bessie is an 'orse-pistol," said Whitlowe.

Amos felt a chill pass through his guts. He decided he didn't have time for that either.

Get me close enough to see his eyes.

Despite the unavoidable urgency of his task and his determination not to let anything delay him, Amos had time to marvel at the height of the cavernous hallway as they crossed its cathedral-like immensity. He looked up at the galleries running around the upper level, and at the strange shapes of the suspended bags covering the chandeliers. He noted the dustcovers draping every piece of furniture, turning the space into a maze of oddly shaped bundles. He listened to the passage of their feet across the marble floor and up the wide staircase. And then as they entered the long passageway that was lined with Mountfellon's glazed collection of cabinets, his mouth, despite himself, hung open. He had never seen such a variety of animals and fish and insects, laid out, dried, or boiled clear of their flesh. There were close-set ranks of every creature he could imagine, from butterflies and beetles to boned-out skeletons of gorillas and humans.

He quailed a little as the lantern caught a skeleton whose head seemed, by a trick of the light, to turn and look at him out of hollow eye sockets, and then his attention was taken by the skin of the man – if it was a man – flensed and dried and cured and then pinned to the back wall of the cabinet behind the scaffolding of his bones, like a tiger-skin trophy. Except the tattoos decorating the body were much more intricate and deliberate than those on a tiger. And then he heard someone move.

He looked round the corner to see a huge footman – Biles, no doubt – getting to his feet and raising a large horse-pistol in a sleepy manner.

"Whitlowe," he growled. "Whitlowe, you stupid boy, I nearly blew your noggin off."

Whitlowe just turned and looked blankly at Amos, who stepped forward.

Mr Biles?

Biles lowered the gun in confusion.

"Er . . ." he said, then, as he realised his confusion was the specific and previously unencountered one of someone talking to him inside the confines of his own head, his brow crinkled. "Oi . . ."

"Er" and "oi" were all he was able to contribute to the evening's conversation because Amos, ever more conscious of the itching round his neck, persuaded him to gently hand over the horse-pistol and then open, by the use of three large keys, the room beyond.

It should have been harder. Later, when the bad thing happened, Amos returned to this moment. If it had been harder, perhaps he would have paid more attention. Perhaps he would have found a deeper well of caution to pause and drink from. Perhaps he would have been able to avoid that terrible consequence after all.

As it was, the box with the flag was easily found, without any need to avail themselves of any more light than that provided by Whitlowe's lantern. A slender ironbound box, eight feet long by a foot on each side, was unusual enough to stand out. The room Mountfellon used as a study had originally been a ballroom, and a generously proportioned one at that. The windows were shuttered and the walls, floor and ceiling were covered by an immense gridwork of iron straps criss-crossing each other at yard-long intervals, making an internal cage that Mountfellon relied on to protect this inner sanctum from the depredations of the uncanny and the supranatural. He had a dark oak banqueting table at the centre of the room that, from the stacks of paper covering it, he clearly used as a writing desk. One end of the room was covered in a huge floor-to-ceiling bookcase, accessible via a ladder, and on the floor beside it they found the flag box.

Biles was persuaded that he wanted nothing more than to help Whitlowe and Amos carry this long and cumbersome object out of the room, down the long stairs and out onto the turning circle. If Amos had not seen a wheelbarrow propped against the tunnel mouth, he would no doubt have persuaded him to help them carry it to the very perimeter of the estate or beyond. As it was, they put the box across the width of the barrow and Amos persuaded old Biles that he was tired and might do well to return to his station and go to sleep, perhaps remembering to forget, when he woke, that he had been party to such a smooth and deceptive act of burglary.

Whitlowe accompanied Amos all the way back to the gate-house by way of the tunnel. The ironbound wheel of the barrow made little noise on the matting as they passed, and the slope was so much in their favour that Amos was running in order to prevent the heavy barrow escaping him by the time they got to the end.

The Sluagh were ranged across the end of the tunnel, beyond the iron gates, waiting.

There was something predatory in their stance, in the way their eyes did not waver from the approaching box, and the almost palpable sense they emitted of being about to pounce.

Amos felt suddenly protective of the sniffing child jogging beside him. He stopped messily, leaning back on the barrow handles and digging his heels in and scraping to a lopsided halt. He reached over and took Whitlowe's chin, turning his face to his. He found his eyes and locked on.

Go inside. Go to sleep. Forget all this. Hurry.

Whitlowe nodded and trotted obediently over to the gate-house and disappeared within. Amos had no idea if him telling the boy to forget this would mean that he would, but there was no harm in trying because the memories wouldn't do much to make the child grow up into a secure and confident young man. He would be stalked with nightmare visions like the line of Sluagh for the rest of his life, always knowing what the night truly contained. Maybe Amos had spared him that.

He bunched muscle and pushed the barrow back into action, wheeling the ungainly box out into the road.

There. Your bloody flag. I've done your will. Take this damned warrandice off me.

He hadn't known he was so angry. He'd been too scared to notice.

The Sluagh – to his surprise – stepped back from the box.

What?

The Ghost pushed through the crowd.

"Ironbound box," she said, voice curdled with scorn. "Poor things can't open it."

Badger Skull threw him a rope.

"Tie it to the handles," he said, attaching the other end to his pony. "We will drag it to the dewpond and you will open the box for us."

"What about Mountfellon?" said the Ghost, tight with anger. "I give you the tool who can enter Gallstaine and get you what you have never managed to regain, and you cheat me?"

"No one has cheated you. It would not have been . . . useful to let the boy die without achieving something rather than nothing," said the chief. "But yes, we owe you a debt."

"Thank you," she said.

"You are welcome," he replied. "The payment is: we will let you live."

She took a half-pace back in shock. Then the import of his words sunk in and her face twisted in rage.

"BUT I DO NOT WANT TO LIVE!" she shrieked.

"Then find a cliff or a river or a blade," shrugged Badger Skull. "Talk to your Bloody Boy. He has ideas about these things . . ."

She caught at his sleeve and bellowed into his face.

"BUT BEFORE I GO, MOUNTFELLON MUST DIE!"

He pushed her away and snapped his fingers at Amos.

"Is it done? Have you tied the rope?"

Amos felt the warrandice twinge around his neck. He found it hard to breathe for a moment, and then he bent and knotted the rope to the handle on the end of the box.

The Sluagh headed up the hill, led by the pony pulling the box across the rough grassland.

Amos followed. As he passed the Ghost, who was standing stock-still in the middle of the road, she clawed out a hand and gripped his arm.

"Mountfellon must die," she said quietly.

I will not kill for you. Not now I do not have to. I will never kill again.

She snatched at him and pulled him close. He found he flinched, expecting her to pour bile on him or shout in his face, but her eyes were both oddly sympathetic and unhinged.

"You will, you will," she breathed. "Even if you won't you will. For are you not the bloodiest of boys?"

He couldn't stay with her so he shook himself loose and hurried up the hill to join the Sluagh.

Amos had seen some bad things in his short life and, as we know, done at least two of them. He had run errands through Smithfield Market and the slaughterhouses attendant on it often enough to be inured to the sounds and smells of common or garden butchery: what he found at the top of the hill around the moonlit dewpond was a different order of thing, though it had superficial similarities. Below the surface, however, coming off it like a hum, he could feel but not hear a deep sense of wrongness and foreboding shot through with a strange mix of despair and exultation. He'd never felt anything quite so strong or so hard to put a name to. It was terrifying, and all the more so for being intangible. It was like one of those unvoiceable screams running around the inside of his skull – like them, but a hundred times more intense, to the point where the mere feel of it made it hard to breathe.

The Sluagh had some power over the herd of cattle they had assembled on one side of the pond, for the animals stayed calm and compliant, even as they were led one by one into the water. The Sluagh had stripped to the waist and removed their boots and, in some cases, their leggings and britches.

Their bare flesh was just as marked as their faces, so that even when near naked they appeared to be garbed in dense intertwined patterns. All the designs were different, the only consistencies being that each one had a perfect black circle placed just off-centre on their chest, favouring the left side, and each had an animal scribed on their back, like a personal totem. A tall Sluagh with a picture of a bull straddling his scapula stood up to his waist in the middle of the pond, among some new hummocks in the flat water, a short crookbacked bronze blade waiting easily in his right hand.

And this is where the bad thing happened, because as one of the hummocks twitched reflexively, Amos realised he was looking at a cow's body. And then he saw the Bull Sluagh reach out a hand to the next cow being led towards him, and then, with a low calming noise, draw it closer. Amos saw the large trusting eyes of the cow reflecting the moon above, and then there was another reflection moving fast, in and out below the cow's throat, and the cow seemed to just cough and shiver a little and then the eyes rolled and it stumbled deeper into the water, and then the Sluagh opened the artery in its throat wider and the blood plumed out and gurgled up through the surface of the water, and the Sluagh was already pushing the body aside and reaching for the next animal.

Why?

Nobody answered him, all eyes too intent on the methodical carnage in hand.

The docile complicity of the waiting cows made it all the more horrific.

Amos staggered between the Sluagh, looking for Badger Skull. He found him standing over the ironbound box, stripped to his breeks, revealing the tattoo of a snarling badger emblazoned among the dense thicket of spiked lines cocooning his back.

You don't have to do this!

Badger Skull didn't waste time looking at him.

"You know nothing of what we must do. We need a blood mirror to open the door to the Other place."

No.

"Open this box," the Sluagh said. "I would see our flags before we send them away and remove the Iron Law warrandiced into them."

He grinned at Amos.

"Please. It is my last request. Our people have not laid eyes on the magnificence of our true flags since long before what your kind call history began. It will be a great thing to be the first living Sluagh to see the majestic sigils of our great days one time before consigning them to the Other. So open the box now, and then the warrandice *you* carry will be discharged, and you will live, Bloody Boy."

I am not the Bloody Boy.

The Sluagh cocked his head at him. Then laughed, a short bark of mirth, and palmed him hard in the chest. Amos stumbled, his heel catching on the edge of the box, and then windmilled backwards into the dewpond. He hit it with a flat smack and a furious splashing and spluttering noise as he went under and tore himself back onto his feet. He swallowed water and spat it out, except it tasted thicker and more metallically rank than water and he looked down at himself and saw why the Sluagh were all pointing at him and laughing.

"You see," said the chief. "You truly are the Bloody Boy. Come and open this now."

Amos was drenched in the blood of the thirty or more dead cows now beginning to clog the dewpond, gory from head to foot.

He spat his mouth clear of the taste as best he could and walked out of the bloodbath and knelt by the box.

He didn't know why he was crying, but he was.

He worked the iron bolts, loosening them and then dragging them back. One stuck and he hammered at it with the heel of his hand, oblivious or uncaring of the pain. The bolt freed and he threw back the lid.

The moonlight slashed over the contents, revealing them in all their ancient glory.

Amos began shaking, his silent sobs doing a disconcerting thing of changing to uncontrolled soundless laughter without warning.

"What?" said the Sluagh, stepping close and looking down.

Amos's blood-covered hand pointed into the box.

See the magnificence of your true flags. The majesty of your sigils.

The box was full of dust and tatters.

"What happened?" said the Sluagh. "What happened to them?"

Time.

It wasn't the right moment for an answer like that, Amos realised this the instant he saw Badger Skull reach for his bronze blade. He flinched away. But the Sluagh just used the blade to sift through the remnants. The rags were so fragile that they went to dust as soon as he stirred them, as if they had been just sitting in the dark waiting for this final indignity.

The Sluagh met Amos's eye, and then his hand lashed out like a snake striking and he had him by the throat.

And then the Sluagh smiled.

"Can you feel it?"

Amos could feel the blade at his neck, no question. He felt the nip and then the sharp bite of the blade, and then a searing, horrible feeling that was both blunt and acute, and he knew the Sluagh had cut his throat while smiling into his eyes.

"Gah," he said, astonished to hear a noise coming from his own mouth, now, after all this time, right at the end. "Gah!"

"It's all right, Bloody Boy," said the Sluagh gently. "It always hurts at the end."

He stood and stepped back, kicking the lid of the box shut with a thump.

Amos tried to hold the blood-slick flaps of his throat closed, but he couldn't find them. All he could find was more blood.

"Gah!"

"You said that," said the Sluagh.

You said you would save me!

"I did," said the Sluagh. "You felt the pain as the warrandice flowed out of you back into my blade. You're free."

Amos scrabbled at his severed throat again. And again he could find no purchase on his wound. And this time he understood that this was because there was no wound.

I thought—

"No, you didn't," said the Sluagh. "You panicked. I told you. You can't do those two things at the same time. Fear kills thought."

You don't mind about the flag?

Badger Skull looked surprised.

"I mind a lot. I would like to have seen it once in my life. But I can do nothing about that. And since the warrandice is still held by the dust of what it once was, the plan is the same. We will open this door and send it out of this world. And then we will be free from the cursed Iron Law."

He grinned, showing a wickedly hooked eye-tooth Amos had not noticed before.

"And that is when we will be free again. And then our enemies will begin to pay for the past. Now, go or stay, for we must get this done before day comes."

Amos began to walk away. And then, not knowing where to go, he just turned and sat and watched. He watched because he had to. He had to see something that made sense of all the placidly dying animals, something that made sense of the blood and the death.

Nothing he saw made the least bit more sense of it for him. But he watched wide-eyed anyway. Maybe, he wondered at some point, he was watching because he was ignobly revelling in the fact he had cheated the death sentence of the warrandice, contrasting his continuing vitality with the deaths of the cattle. He dismissed the thought but the possibility of it remained like a bad taste at the back of his mind. He saw more than fifty cows and one bull led into the pond and watched as their lives were bled out of them. The water became thicker and more viscous with each act of slaughter. The moonlight didn't allow colour, but he could see how thick the blood was by the black stains on the Sluaghs' legs as they walked in and out. When every animal was dead, Badger Skull said something to a Sluagh with a raven totem scarified across his back.

The Raven Sluagh clambered out into the centre of the carcase-jammed pond carrying a bag inside which something was flapping and trying to escape. He pulled out a large crow, maybe actually a raven. Before Amos could blink, he cut its head off and emptied its blood into the pond below. All the other Sluagh gave a loud shout of approval as he did so.

Then he hopped back to the edge of the pool, using the dead cows as stepping-stones. As soon as he was clear of the blood-filled pond, he reached in the bag and pulled out some kind of dark disc with a handle. He angled it flat to the ground and craned his head to look back up at it as he inched it out over the surface of the blood, ensuring it was parallel.

Then he held it there and nothing happened. And nothing kept on happening until his arm began to shake and he screamed and there was a colossal silent impact, as if something had just sucked half the air out of the night in one giant indrawn breath, and then Amos saw what wasn't there any more.

The fatally compliant cattle whose carcases had clogged the three-foot-deep dewpond with ungainly bellies and horns and strangely delicate upturned hooves and hocks had gone. In place of all their slaughtered, bumpy irregularity, there was a perfectly flat mirror surface again, the same as when it had been water but – and this was of course impossible – blacker. And, when he looked closer, also flatter – impossibly flat and unmoving with no hint of a ripple despite the freshening night breeze stirring around them.

And then he realised it was not just the cows that had been sucked into the theoretically non-existent depths of the shallow pond. The reflection of the moon had gone. He had not changed position, but the mirror-like surface was not reflecting it.

And as he began to see the black circle as not a mirror but a hole, Badger Skull and the Bull Sluagh slapped the pony into motion. It leapt forward, snapping the rope tight, as it dragged the flag box into the centre of the pond, where it sat, as if on a sheet of black ice. For a moment nothing happened. And then the blackness reared up and grabbed it and yanked it into itself. The rope whiplashed tight again and before anyone could stop it the pony was brutally somersaulted off its feet and dragged broken-backed and shrieking to the edge of the pond to be grabbed by the dark and snatched down into it as well.

Badger Skull bellowed something at the Raven Sluagh, who threw himself backwards, taking the mirror with him. As soon as the connection between the two black surfaces was broken there was a massive subsonic concussion as if the missing half of the night's oxygen had been blown back into it.

No one moved. Then Badger Skull walked to the edge, and took a handful of liquid. He let it fall, clear and bloodless. Water again.

"It is done," he said.

His eyes found Amos's.

"Still here, Bloody Boy?"

Yes.

He wished he wasn't. He wished he could rub out what he'd seen from his memory, scrub his eyes with lye to bleach out the stain of the night.

"Wash yourself here," said Badger Skull as if he had read his thoughts. "The water is good again. Just a mist pond once more."

He exhaled in relief, showing nerves he had clearly kept in check throughout the previous operation. He caught Amos looking at him.

"It's important to break the connection as soon as you can. Our fathers told us the black mirrors weren't always black. Once they were bright. Then the Wildfire was taken from whatever lies beyond, plunging it into everlasting dark. And so that darkness hungers for the fire, and if the way between our worlds stays open too long, who knows what will come through seeking the lost fire? And who can say what harm that hunger and hatred would mean for all of us?"

He shrugged and shook himself, a little like a dog drying off.

"Throw me your knife."

My knife?

"Your damned iron-bladed knife."

Amos found it in his pocket and did so.

The Sluagh caught it. Every eye on him. He didn't flinch. He carefully unfolded the blade. And laid it flat on the soft skin of his wrist. He laughed softly. He stuck his tongue out and laid the blade on that. He grinned.

The other Sluagh roared in excited approval.

He snapped the blade shut and looked across at Amos.

"Iron no longer has power over us. And so we rise again."

He held up the knife.

"I think I will keep your blade," he said. "I will need to get used to this dull grey metal that holds such a fine edge."

Amos shrugged.

It wasn't mine anyway. It never brought me luck.

"Luck is made, not brought," said Badger Skull. "But for what you have done for us, I wish it for you."

"Wait," said a voice. The Ghost stumbled up the hill.

"Our business is done," said Badger Skull.

"No," said the Ghost. "I have just been inside Gallstaine. You need to see it. And now that iron cannot bar you, you may."

Badger Skull crinkled his brow, then looked a question at Amos.

"Do I need to see inside the Hall?" he said. "If Mountfellon is not there, what can there be of interest?"

Amos didn't answer. He was done with them.

"Bones," said the Ghost. "There are bones you must see."

Amos squatted on the hill and waited while they went down the tunnel. He didn't want to go until he saw which direction the Sluagh were headed, so he could go the other way. And he really wanted to sleep.

The Ghost and Badger Skull were gone a long time. And when they returned, she was smiling and the Sluagh was seething. He carried something wrapped in a hide, a hide covered in tattoos. Amos realised with a sick lurch that it was the bones and skin of the Sluagh from the display cabinet. Badger Skull's knuckles were cut and bleeding.

He held up the skin and bones.

"He flayed one of us, and displayed his bone cage to the world. Manacled with iron in a glass case for all to see."

The other Sluagh roared disapproval.

"I have left him a surprise," said Badger Skull.

He looked one last time at Amos.

"And they say we are the monsters . . ."

And with no more ceremony than that he snapped his fingers and within a minute Amos and the Ghost were alone on the hill among the cowless fields.

Where do you go now?

He felt exhausted. But he knew he needed to put miles between him and this place before the countryside woke up.

"London," she said. "If Mountfellon is there, then it is in London he must die."

She set off without more ceremony, heading for the high road.

He caught up with her.

"Are you coming to help me, Bloody Boy?" she said as they crossed the ditch and stepped on to the moonlit strip ribboning south.

Maybe, he lied.

In almost every way imaginable, London was the last place he wanted to go. But she had told him about the Free Company which opposed the Sluagh. He had spent too many nights thinking the Sluagh had killed him with the white tattoo to be well disposed to them, and they had worked a different kind of magic on his mind too, making him begin almost to feel a kinship with them as time had gone on. But then they had come to Gallstaine, and he now realised it must have been a way they had of keeping him docile on the road. Because after what he had seen, he was sure he had nothing in common with them. He couldn't possibly have. And now after what he had witnessed, every night would be filled with the fear of them.

Perhaps finding those who could fight them could end the nightmares he knew were coming.

CHAPTER 40

THE LAST ROOM

Sharp and Sara staggered through the endless low tunnels that snaked through the catacomb. They were weak and soaked and shivering badly with the cold, too chilled to talk, too fatigued to move faster than a dogged shamble. It was all they could do to keep moving. Sara kept one hand clenched on his arm, and the other held protectively across her body: partly this was to try and hug whatever remaining warmth there was in the core of her body, but mainly she knew she was keeping her hand clear of the bone piles they were hemmed in by. Even though she was wearing her gloves, she didn't want to touch them. The pull of the past was all around her and if she glinted again she thought she might never find her way back from that past to the present. Glints did go mad if they were unable to escape the visions, and she had no intention, after all she had gone through, of losing what was left of her rational mind.

The stacks lining the passage were the ordered-looking walls of femurs and tibias laid end out, but the candlelight shed enough illumination into the recesses behind the regular bone hedge to see that all the other smaller bones had been tumbled behind them in an unending, disordered jumble. The people who had laid the ossuary had, perhaps as an attempt to relieve the innate grimness of their trade, on occasion indulged in flights of macabre decorative whimsy, and every now and then the bone hedge was broken up by designs made of carefully placed crania, inlaid into the knuckle ends: they passed crosses, diamonds and heart shapes made from grinning skulls, and one skull placed piratically atop a pair of crossed bones. They came to forks in the tunnels and, without needing to discuss it, always took the tunnel that seemed to rise.

They passed several dead-ended chambers, each again decorated in their own individual manner in the style of cathedral side-chapels, with bone altarpieces and freestanding pillars wrapped in mosaics of skeletal remains. They did not linger on these morbid cavities, but shuffled onwards.

Eventually, just when Sharp was beginning to think he would have to carry Sara, and was wondering if his remaining bodily strength would allow him to do so, they stumbled into a wider space, like a low-built hall. At the centre of it was a sturdy pillar made from tiers of bones, interspersed with bands of skulls, like a grotesque barrel-shaped layer cake.

They stopped and stared at it. Sara's legs sagged and she clasped herself tighter to his arm. In the strangest way, he took strength from her need and reached around her to support her.

"This is a bad place," she said.

"Of course," he said.

Her hand flexed, and she shivered.

"No," she said. "Not because of the poor dead ones piled here. Something truly bad happened in this room."

He saw her eyes becoming glassy and felt her beginning to sag again.

"Come," he said, and walked her to the door on the other side of the pillar. She seemed to drag her feet, almost as if she did not want to leave, as if the horror of it was exerting a powerful magnetic pull.

They ducked under a low lintel and found, to Sharp's enormous relief, that they had stepped down into another room, a wedge-shaped space that was entirely free of bones. Something eased in him and he paused for a moment.

"Where are we?" she said, looking round at the smooth-hewn walls.

He turned and looked back at the doorway they had just emerged from. It was an ominous black maw into which his candle was seemingly unable to cast much light. There was writing incised into the lintel above it in deep capital letters:

ARRETE! ICI, C'EST L'EMPIRE DE LA MORT.

"The Empire of Death," said Sara quietly.

"I don't think we are under London," said Sharp.

She shook her head. Her eyes dropped from the writing to stare back into the darkness beyond the door.

"No," she said. "No, we are not."

He pulled her away towards the rising passage at the far end of the wedge. She craned her head backwards, watching the door into the catacombs until the circle of candlelight moved too far for her to see it. He thought he felt something relax in her, and after a hundred yards he noted a renewed vigour in her stride. She gently slid out from under his arm and walked under her own steam. They picked up speed and soon felt something new. The candle flickered and a fresh breeze winnowed down the passage, cold air from above. Sharp turned a corner a pace before she did and stopped.

A ladder had been nailed to the wall, and thirty feet above their heads he saw daylight through a metal lattice.

"We're free," he said, turning with a smile. "We can go home."

Motes of dust seemed to be falling down the chimney-like shaft, and as he turned his face upwards some of them began to land on his face and melt. He held his hand out in wonderment.

"Sara," he said. "Snowflakes. It is snow. It isn't winter. How can that be . . . ?"

He turned to look at her. She was not looking up at the snow. She was looking back down the dark tunnel.

"Come," he said, making room for her at the bottom of the ladder. "You go first; I will follow close in case you miss your hold."

"No," she said. "No. I cannot go. Not yet."

"Yet?" he said, dumbfounded.

She nodded and walked back into the dark passage.

"Sara," he said, reaching for her arm. She shrugged him off and kept striding down the slope.

He followed her, this time grasping her shoulder and not allowing her to shake him off. She turned her face to him. Her eyes were wide and despairing, but her jaw was set.

"I have to go back into that last room. I have to enter the Empire of Death and touch the walls—"

"No. Absolutely not," he said. "I will not allow it."

Something hardier than despair glimmered into her eye and replaced it.

"It is not yours to allow."

"I am sworn to pr—" he began and stopped, shocked to find her gloved fingers on his lips. She shook her head sadly.

"You do protect me, Jack. You have always protected me and I have always known it and esteemed you for it, even when you think I have not noticed you doing so, and especially when I have seemed to resent it most. But there is one thing you can never, must never protect me from . . ."

"Death," he said.

"No," she said. "Duty."

She smiled up at him, face tight.

"Death? Death you are more than welcome to protect me from any and all the time. I'm no martyr, Jack. But duty? Never. Whatever else we are, we are first and most importantly The Oversight. Others rely on our protection."

She turned and strode off.

He followed.

"Sara," he began.

"I have to go in there and glint," she said without slowing down. "I have to. I need to . . ."

"You are weak," he said. "You are too weak – let us get out of here, get dry, warm, eat, sleep and then maybe—"

"In the cavern," she said.

"What?"

"In the cavern. Under the water. Alone. Before you came back through the mirror and plucked me out. I . . ."

Her voice faltered but her stride did not.

"What?" he said. She cleared her throat.

"In the cavern. I touched the wall. I glinted."

Her voice was ragged.

"That's why you didn't follow me," he said.

He saw her nod her head. She cleared her throat again. He knew enough not to stop her and turn her. The rawness in her voice was clue enough as to why she would not thank him for seeing her face as she spoke.

She cleared her throat for a third time and took a deep breath.

"I saw the moment of the Disaster. I saw what happened after all those good . . . those good, misguided hearts went into the mirrors via the damned Murano Cabinet, all those long years ago, thinking that they were going to save us all. I saw it. I saw a churning cavern full of water and the dead and drowning trapped in it. I saw them all, the lost ones, the faces you and I grew up with. I saw them in the final moment no one should witness."

The pain in her voice was unbearable to listen to.

"I saw them dying."

"Sara," he said again.

"I saw my mother die," she said. "She tried, she fought to the last, and then she tried to break the mirror so no one else would come through it and be trapped and die as they did. If we had not needed to escape through it, I would have shattered it for her. Even in the teeth of her own death she did her duty. How can I do less?"

She stopped and turned and looked him straight in the face, unashamed of the tears streaking down her cheeks.

"And I need to know why there is something in that hellish chamber that wants me to touch it."

He stared back at her.

"I know all the things you want to say to stop me doing it – that it's dangerous, that I am weak after our ordeal, that it's your job to think straight when I can't – but—"

"Do it," he said. "You must do it."

Her eyes widened in surprise.

"But I'm coming with you," he finished.

She nodded slowly, then grinned through eyes too bright to be just smiling. She wiped them.

"So I should damn well hope."

He handed her the candle.

"Lead on," he said. "And hurry up. That candle's nearly done."

She began to run, moving into the darkness in her own circle of bobbing light.

"It'll be all right," she said, breath coming in short jerks. "I saw the Disaster. I saw her die. Nothing could be worse than that."

CHAPTER 41

THE DYING BOY

The boy is dying. He can feel it. He's lying helpless on his back, and the great weight on his ribcage is squashing him down into the thin mattress so hard that he can feel the stones beneath the straw digging into his shoulder-blades. He feels the compression on his lungs, that his ribs must start snapping like dry firewood if the thing sitting on him does not raise itself and let him inhale.

Only he knows that the thing will never let him inhale again. The thing told him this. It told him to breathe in deeply, because it would all be over in one short breath, and all he had to do was be still and breathe out only one last time, and then sleep. The thing had said sleep, but the boy knew it had meant death. And so the boy had fought. He had struggled and scratched and hit and bit, and then the thing had punched him, knocking all the wind from his lungs, and then, when he had taken his first deep breath, it had clamped its hands over his mouth, hands that smelled strongly of tobacco and chicken shit, and it had pinched his nostrils closed and pushed him back onto the thin mattress.

The boy screamed silently in his head for his mother and father, the parents he knew now he would never see again, and then the thing leant over him, kneeling on his chest.

The thing now bent about him looked like a man, a grey, bearded man whose skin and pale eyes were as devoid of pigment as his hair, drained of all colour and vitality, leaving him with the slack and silvered fish-belly pallor of a lifeless thing. And he was a thing, not the man whose shape he appeared to have. The boy knew this. He was one of the monsters which people the dark, the shadow things from the fairy tales, the ones that were spoken of to frighten young children.

The boy was frightened. Scared to death. And now that the fight had been knocked out of him, he was dying. He was dying because the thing leant down and stretched its mouth wide, placing it over both the boy's nose and mouth, clamping over them as it pressed down. At first the boy had tried not to breathe out, and had resisted the burn as lactic acid flooded his oxygen-deprived lungs, but then the thing had readjusted its bony old-man's knees on his chest as if settling in for a familiar and welcomed ritual, and the boy had breathed out into the thing's mouth.

Even over the defeated gagging noise that accompanied his final surrender, he felt the thing swell and purr. It gurgled with a nasty, liquid noise of exultation as he felt it grow warm on top of him. It shivered and pressed down even harder, like a greedy drunk squeezing the last drops from a wineskin. The boy's lungs were shrieking with pain, and his last tears were literally jumping from his eyes, like water under pressure. He felt them splash back down on his face. He tried to think of God, to ask forgiveness for all and any of his childish sins, knowing he was going to Judgement now, but all he could think of was his mother and father. Maybe there was no God. He panicked, thinking this was a terrible thought to die on . . .

. . . he didn't hear the door open. But he felt the cool breeze on his cheek.

He heard a new voice.

"No!" It was a woman's voice. Screaming a warning.

He felt something fly across the room and throw the thing off him with a hard chunking noise, like a sharp axe biting into seasoned oak.

As soon as the thing's mouth was ripped from his, he opened his eyes and tried to breathe.

He couldn't.

Nor could he make sense of what he was seeing above him.

The thing was struggling with a stick that seemed to have pinned it to the wall beside the mattress, a stick that had gone through its neck with enough force to nail it to the untreated wood planking. It was a crossbow bolt, the feathers now slick and glistening with the blood that had turned the old-man's beard red and dripping.

The boy turned his head to look across the room.

A hunter stood inside the door. A woman – the thing's wife – lay on the ground, half in and out of the hut, unconscious, and another hunter – or at least a girl in hunter's leather, a girl with two dark pigtails and a very large knife – crouched over the prone body.

He gagged at her, soundless, unable to get a breath.

"Lungs collapsed!" said the hunter. "Ida!"

The girl moved fast, so fast she seemed to shift between time and space, not through it. One moment she was checking the woman was unconscious; next moment she was at the boy's side. Her eyes sparkled in the dying glow of the fire on the stone hearth beside the dead thing pinned to the wall.

"It's all right," she said. "It's all right."

And she leant down, pinched his nose gently and kissed his mouth. Her lips were soft and the air that she breathed into him was sweet. She breathed out, long and hard, until her lungs were empty and his were suddenly full and there was a pain and a kind of crackling feeling in his chest, and then she lifted her mouth from his and he coughed and spluttered and gasped in again and again, amazed that he could breathe.

"Easy," she said. "Breathe easy. It's over. And you do not need to be so greedy of the air now, young Peter."

The hunter crossed the room and pulled the old man from the wall. There was a sucking noise as he slid him off the crossbow bolt and dropped him unceremoniously to the floor. The hunter then set about working the bolt out of the wall.

The boy looked from one to the other, listening to his breaths becoming normal again.

"Take your time, Peter," said the hunter. "You have a lifetime of breaths ahead of you again. You don't have to use them all up right now."

The hunter's face was grim but kind. The girl had left the boy and was with Frau Wachman on the floor in the doorway. She pulled a letter from the unconscious woman's dirndl and crossed back to the fire where she unfolded it and looked at the writing in the red glow. She sucked her teeth and looked at the hunter, who was now using a short knife to ease his bolt from the wall.

"Not good," she said.

"Who are you?" the boy said quietly.

"Frau Wachman knew who we are," she said, looking at the prone figure at her feet. "She knew all about monsters in the dark."

"You're not monsters," he said.

"No," she replied. "She and her husband, they're the monsters. And we hunt them."

"So who are you?" he repeated, realising even as he asked that he knew, because the old stories were not just about dark things, but also about heroes.

The girl folded the letter and stowed it inside her jacket, then came over and sat by him. She smoothed his cheek with a surprisingly cool and soft hand. Her eyes were, in contrast, warm.

"We are *Die Wachte*, little Peter."

The man grimaced as he pulled the crossbow bolt from the wall.

"We are the Shadowhunters."

"The monster-killers," said Peter, in awe.

The girl shrugged and passed her hand gently over his eyes. He experienced the merest feather of alarm at the back of his mind, perhaps remembering the thing becoming hot as it breathed in his last breath, but the soft voice calmed him and made him feel pleasantly tired.

"If you will. But by the time we have taken you back to your family, you will forget all this and only remember that you walked in your sleep and woke to find yourself alone and wandering in the dark, lost on the

Berchtesgaden road, where my friend and I found you crying in a ditch."

She lifted her hand from his eyes. He was asleep.

Otto looked at her.

"You could have waited until he walked off the mountain."

She shook her head.

"He was too tired to walk."

"And now I have to carry him!" he said.

She shook her head, reached down and lifted the child onto her own shoulders.

"No," she said, pointing at the unconscious figure on the threshold. "You have to carry Frau Wachman."

"I thought—" he began.

"No, you didn't," she said. "Law and Lore. We only kill to save life."

"They stole the child," he began.

"They stole the child, but she didn't do it to kill him. She wanted to take him back to Berchtesgaden and raise him as her own. She lost a child, and was replacing what was lost. Even Alps go mad with grief."

"And how do you know this?" he said, beginning to drag the dead Alp from the hut.

"How do I know what she was thinking?" said Ida, raising an eyebrow. "You're really wasting breath asking me that question."

"But he was killing the child," he said, grunting with the effort of moving the deadweight of the Alp's corpse.

"He had less control of his needs than she. He was older, he hungered for the vigour, the life the child would bring him. He was a man. He was weaker. What do you want me to say? They must have both been strong at one time to live as normal people without drawing attention to themselves. They were chicken farmers. I'd guess they were feeding on the death breaths of their hens and not touching people at all, until this."

"This . . ." he said. "And what is that note?"

She held up the letter.

"This is something to do with London. Someone there wanted the services of another one of their sons, the previous one having . . . disappeared. And he wasn't there to kill chickens."

"And that's why I have to carry that fat woman down the mountain?" he said.

She was silently reading the rest of the letter. She came to the signature and swore under her breath.

"Ida?" he said. "What?"

She showed him the letter, pointing at the signature.

"Maximilien de what?" he squinted. "I can't make it out."

She told him.

"No," he said. "No, Ida. He is dead. Long dead. They killed him for perverting the Paladin as much as for prosecuting the Terror. He is dead."

"A regular access to Alps can prolong life a lot," she said, looking at Frau Wachman.

"But—" he said.

"We'll take her back to Lichtenberg," she said. "We can show the others the letter and ask her questions. But I think I need to go to London without delay and warn our brothers and sisters in The Oversight that something very wicked is in their midst."

"You, Ida?" he said. "Why should it not be one of the older members?"

"Because none of the others had a Scottish mother," she said. "And I speak English."

"Right. If you leave in the morning you could be there in three days," said Fleischl grudgingly.

"I will be back within the week," she said. "And there is little urgency in our hunting for now. We have found our Alps."

The *Schattenjäger* nodded.

"And Herr Wachman?" he said, looking at the body on the mattress.

"There's a perfectly good — and very deep — ravine behind the hut," she said. "And if I leave tonight I can be in London in two and a half days."

CHAPTER 42

THE NAME OF THE ENEMY

The candle had burnt down to less than half a thumb's length when they paused at the entrance to the catacomb, looking up at the warning carved into the lintel.

"What?" said Sara.

"*L'Empire de la Mort*," said Sharp. He was aware that he was futilely trying both to postpone and lighten the coming moment. "Very French, no?"

"Histrionic?" she said.

"No," he said. "I mean yes, possibly that too, but I meant making death feminine."

"Well," she said, "we all come into the world through a woman: birth's feminine. Only right that a woman should hold the door on the way out."

"And where does that leave room for us murderous men?" he said.

"Holding the candle," she replied, passing him the dwindling nubbin of wax and working quickly at the buttons on her glove. She peeled it back, revealing the pale elegance of her hand. The look she gave him stilled any more conversation.

"I need to get this over with," she said quickly. And before he could prevent her, she squared her shoulders and plunged into the room beyond, striding straight up to the barrel-shaped pillar of bones and splaying her naked hand right on the shiny nut-brown forehead of the nearest skull.

"Sara!" he said, the word escaping despite himself.

Her back arched, the long white braid of her hair snapped like a whip and she was no longer in the present with him.

She was deep in the past, screaming silently as it cut viciously into her and burnt its images on eyes that she no longer had the power to close, leaving her helpless to shut out the incoming horror.

The chamber – lit by a circle of tall church candles arranged around the pillar.

Men make a second circle outside the candles.

The clothes of the last century. Of the French Revolution. The fashions of the Terror: britches. Tight, high-collared jackets. Some in the red Phrygian caps and tricolour cockades of the sans-culottes.

All staring at the pillar.

A prisoner is brought in.

Thrown to the stone floor.

Writhing in pain. As if the iron shackles on his ankles, wrists and neck are burning him.

As if the iron chains twisted around his nakedness are scorching him.

But the marks on his body are not burn marks.

They are tattoos. Twisting and coiling around him like creepers.

He is Sluagh.

Three men enter behind him. Two pick him up and spread-eagle him on the pillar, face first. Arms spread. Like a profane crucifixion.

The third man is older. Face dinted with pox. Eyes merciless.

Carries a black stone knife.

Says something to the Sluagh.

The Sluagh writhes and tries to rip himself off the pillar, head twisting to look out at the ring of men behind him.

One of the two men holding him nods at the pockmarked man.

"Citizen?"

The Sluagh wrenches the manacles.

The Citizen seems frozen in a moment of anticipatory ecstasy, eyes closed and face smiling. As if he can smell the blood to come.

"Citizen Robespierre?"

The eyes open. He moves.

The Sluagh's cheeks bulge. Teeth clenched. He's trying to keep the pain inside. Trying not to scream.

The Citizen hooks a short brutal punch into his unprotected belly.

He exhales in a panicked *whoof* of air.

Mouth gapes wide.

The Citizen moves, reaches in to the mouth, grabs the tongue.

The other hand has the knife in motion.

Time slices.

Sara gasped.

The Sluagh hangs slack on the pillar.

Black blood ribbons from his mouth, filling a bucket held there by one of the two men.

The Citizen is jamming something meaty and dripping into the gaping teeth of one of the skulls on the pillar.

Time slices.

The Citizen dashes the pail-full of blood onto the pillar and shouts something high-pitched and unintelligible.

Time slices.

The pillar rotates. The different strata of bones crushing round in opposite directions.

Like grindstones in a mill.

But they are not producing flour or oatmeal.

They're milling darkness.

It's trickling from the gaps between the bones.

Now it's pouring from the eye sockets and the mouths of the skulls.

Streaming down the pillar, cloaking its irregularities with a thick layer of black, like tar.

The darkness pools out across the floor.

Climbs each candle.

Coating it black.

Reaches the flames.

Turns the light red.

The watchers step back. Screaming.

The red light pulses black.

The watchers fall to the ground and are still.

Only the three men remain on their feet.

The Citizen strips off his shirt.

Nods.

They plunge their hands into the blackness and then smear it below his jaw-line, daubing it in a thick band around his neck. He roars with pain but holds himself steady through will alone.

His eyes are staring wide. And quite, quite mad.

Time slices.

The two helpers are on the floor. One broken against the pillar, which is still.

The other halfway to the doorway, face down.

The Citizen is hunched over him, jerking the obsidian knife from his back.

He stands and looks around at the stuttering candles. The dead audience. The broken Sluagh.

He smiles.

He is ringed in black from shoulders to jaw.

He puts his shirt back on.

Calm as if at home.

Time slices.

He has tied his stock around his neck. He shrugs into his coat.

He tosses the blade over his shoulder as he leaves.

It skitters its way across the floor. Into the black puddle.

It stops but does not slow down, spinning on its axis.

Sending out a cyclone of sprayed darkness that spatters the prostrate corpses.

Sara screams.

The knife starts to rise off the ground, sucking the blackness with it, like an invisible hand lifting a cloth from the centre.

The bodies are dragged inward. The candles tumble and are melted into the rising cone of dark.

The flames remain, rippling round the rising shape like a diaphanous shroud.

The shape is becoming a figure that seems to suck in everything dark to build itself.

The whirling knife sits atop what is now almost a veiled head, like a spinning crown.

There are shoulders now, arms, a waist.

The outline of powerful legs beneath the dark mantle of liquid black.

The arms rise, hands and fingers poking their shapes into view, reaching for the spinning knife—

The only thing left on the floor is a body.

Naked.

The Sluagh.

It shudders.

The dark tattoos peel off its corpse like black lace and hang in the air for an instant, before being sucked into the growing figure, leaving the Sluagh lying on the ground, pale and lifeless.

The figure carefully raises its fingers to the spinning knife – tentative – perhaps trying to stop it.

The knife sends black finger joints flying. Like carrot tips.

And the whole dark figure splashes to the floor and is sucked straight back into the pillar

Dropping in an instant.

So fast she nearly missed it.

Would have missed it in a blink.

If she'd been able to blink.

The chamber empty but for the bleached Sluagh's body.

No movement other than the blackness seeping back into the pillar through every available chink and hole.

And a black knife that spun in the air and moved inexorably towards Sara's neck. Spinning with intent. As if it could see her.

As if the knife

In the past

Could see Sara

In the future

And had been waiting for her.

She wanted to duck. Couldn't. Tried to hang on to the fragment of normal that told her she was just glinting.

That this was just a vision.

That the blade couldn't possibly hurt her.

The last ribbon of black was sucking into the eye socket of a skull when the skull jerked and exploded and the blade bit into her neck

and then whatever had burst out of the blackness hit the blade in an eruption of oily black feathers

And the glinting stopped dead.

And she fell to the floor.

Sharp leapt across the space between them and caught her before her head dashed itself on the stone.

Her eyes rolled back and then forward and then they focused and found his.

"Sara," he said.

"I know," she choked. "I'm all right. It was just a vision . . ."

"I know," he said. "But where did that blasted Raven come from?"

The Raven fluttered to his shoulder and pecked his ear.

She stared in disbelief.

"And what's that cut on your neck?"

CHAPTER 43

COMINGS AND GOINGS

The house on Chandos Place was not normally a busy one. The solitary habits of Mountfellon and his guest dictated that, and the household matters went attended to by only three taciturn and mildly threatening manservants. It was one of these who slid back the bolts and opened the door to the messenger from the north. The messenger was Biles, the footman, and he seemed to have brought a large acreage of Rutlandshire with him, since his greatcoat and horse were heavily spattered with mud.

"Is he in?" he said. His face was gaunt and hollow-eyed from exhaustion.

The manservant looked him up and down.

"You ain't bringing that mud in here, Mr Biles, for I'm the one as will have to clean it—"

Biles pushed past him, leaving a muddy smear on his livery as he went. He thumbed over his shoulder.

"Look after the horse, pretty boy. He's blown and needs a good rubdown and feed."

Mountfellon could not initially believe what the bemired messenger was telling him. And then he spat his mouthful of breakfast kedgeree the length of the table as it hit him.

"Stolen?!" he shouted, staggering back from the table and upending his chair. "The flag?"

"Dunno how but it's gone, sir," said Biles. "And all your display cabinets smashed, and the cattle from Home Farm vanished like the devil spirited 'em away. Tracks all lead to the dewpond behind the gibbet, and then they just stop. Like it swallowed 'em."

"What the blazes do I care for damned cattle?" roared Mountfellon. "Do I look like a farmer?"

Biles shook his head.

"They got into my room," said Mountfellon. "And none of you addle-pated incompetents noticed?"

Biles shook his head again.

"No, sir. It's a proper enigma and no mistake."

Mountfellon reached for him, then controlled himself and withdrew his hand.

"If you are hiding anything, Biles, I shall gut you, do you understand? Gut you and likely flay what remains."

He staggered from the room.

"Get my carriage ready to leave immediately. I must go and see what else is awry."

He had never felt so assaulted. All the care he had taken in building an unassailable sanctum swept away in an instant, and all the surety he felt about his work gone too. The room was locked, ironbound and guarded.

Someone would hang for this.

Ten minutes later, the viscount's carriage had left at speed.

Fifteen minutes after that, Coram Templebane appeared at the side-door and asked for Mountfellon. He had walked across town to do this, and on the way had been thinking of the plan he was about to betray. Part of him, the wiser part, hoped Mountfellon would confront Templebane, because then his side-plan of implicating the unfortunate Abchurch would come into play and Coram's life and fortunes would brighten as a result. And the other part of him was becoming increasingly interested in seeing the full destructive force of his plan in motion: explosions, fire, rivers of molten sugar and more conflagration would be a heady spectacle and something to remember.

He was perturbed when the servant told him that Mountfellon was out of town. He had been about to leave disappointed when a thin but commanding voice from down the passage told the servant to let him in if his name was truly Templebane.

A minute later he found himself in the most extraordinary interview. He was in a dark room with a light reflected off a brass disc aimed at him so he could not make out the face of his interlocutor. The man spoke with a foreign accent, but made it clear that he could speak to him as if he were the viscount himself, and that in turn whatever he said was to be taken as the noble lord's wishes.

Coram explained that he was coming to warn Mountfellon, as instructed, of Issachar's plans regarding The Oversight. When these were explained, the voice behind the light interjected:

"The plan is their complete eradication, you say?"

"Root and branch, bag and baggage, burnt out," said Coram. "I thought 'is Lordship should know."

There was a silence from the other side of the light. The Citizen was weighing up his inclinations against his host's instructions, his high-handed instructions about not destroying the contents of the Red Library. Mountfellon would, he knew, have objected in the strongest fashion.

"Thank you," said the voice. "We approve. What time will the unfortunate accident occur?"

"Eleven o'clock sharp tomorrow morning," said Coram. "Timed so the day shift is at their tea-break, so as to avoid unnecessary casualties."

"Very commendable, very humane," said the voice. "Thank you for your information. Eleven o'clock. Very good. We are obliged."

CHAPTER 44

AMERICAY

Lady of Nantasket had berthed in the Pool of London for two days before the message of its arrival came to the Safe House, the result of the dock-master who had undertaken to alert them having been indisposed and so not on station when she dropped anchor. So it was with some dispatch that Caitlin set out to find Captain Tittensor and his wife and set about retrieving the Factor's baby.

As had become habitual, Lucy went with her, and since no opportunity to learn on the job was to be squandered, they were set the task of getting there without being seen by Charlie or Hodge who would not only be shadowing them, but had the goal of getting wherever they were going first, while being able to tell Cook what route the two girls had taken when they all returned for a late tea.

Cait had let Lucy choose the route but had made it clear she wanted no long detours since the main object was to retrieve the baby before the *Lady of Nantasket* refilled her cargo-hold and set off back to America.

They made good time, and Lucy was sure they had also evaded their shadowers.

So it was a bit galling to find Jed wagging his tail at the dock gates, while Charlie and Hodge leant against the fortress-like wall looming high above them, annoyingly innocent smiles on their faces. Hodge was puffing on a pipe and Charlie was coolly twining a piece of yellow ribbon round and round his fingers, as if butter wouldn't melt in his mouth.

"Nearly lost us the second time you crossed Ratcliffe," said Charlie.

"Business now, gloating later, Charlie boy," said Cait. "Come on, Lucy. You keep a bit away from me as if we don't know each other and watch the conversation, see if you pick up anything that might be useful, or I might miss."

She put a hand on Lucy's arm and walked her under the forbidding gate. Lucy knew she had done this to spare her Charlie's teasing, and to give her something to do that didn't really need doing since the prospect of Cait missing anything was unlikely.

Hodge – via Jed – watched the girls disappear into the boiling mass of dockworkers, stevedores, porters and sailors milling within the dockyard. Then he relit his pipe and looked at Charlie, who was also trying to keep track of them in the multitude.

"The ribbon," said Hodge.

Charlie had again forgotten that Hodge shared Jed's eyes and could see what the dog, sitting at Charlie's feet and innocently wagging his tail, could see. He stuffed it back in his pocket self-consciously.

"It's nothing," he said.

"Not Lucy Harker's ribbon, I'd say," said Hodge.

"No," said Charlie after a bit.

"Good," said Hodge.

"Why?" said Charlie.

"Dunno," said Hodge. "None of my business, really."

"But," said Charlie.

"But she'd got an edge to her, that one," said Hodge, "and The Smith ain't got it figured yet."

"Well, I don't much care what The Smith makes of her," said Charlie defensively. "She's my friend, and she's brave and she's all right."

He surprised himself at his vehemence.

"Sure that's not her ribbon, are you?" said Hodge, the edge of his mouth twitching upwards in a particularly irksome smile.

"Yes," said Charlie. "It's nobody's ribbon. I got given it."

"Wouldn't have thought yellow's your colour no more than it's Lucy's," said Hodge. His smile was really annoying now.

"I was just given it by someone. At the fair," said Charlie. "Don't know why it's still in my pocket. Stupid really."

And suddenly his whole life before London seemed a million miles away. His childhood friend Georgiana Eagle had given it to him. But she had given scores of them to other people, men and women, on the day of her father's humiliation, as if wearing the yellow was like showing support for the Eagle family. It had been a vain, silly thing to do. He didn't know why he still kept it. It wasn't like he was going to use it for anything. He looked down to see Jed was looking at him strangely, his head cocked to one side.

"Love ain't stupid," said Hodge. "Inconvenient and embarrassing often enough, but not stupid."

Charlie felt defensive. The gentle voice which Hodge spoke in, quieter than his normal gruff rasp, was unexpected and a little unnerving.

"Never apologise for who you love, Charlie," he said. "Because it's not who you love that matters anyway. Having love in your heart and not being true to it, that's the crime. That's worth apologising for. But don't apologise for loving someone who isn't what you think others might see as . . . appropriate."

"It's not that," said Charlie. "It's stupid because I know she's not quite . . ."

He trailed off, unable to put words to it.

"Interested?" said Hodge. "Available?"

"Kind," said Charlie. "She's lovely. But I'm not sure she's kind. Or quite . . . good. I mean she's not bad. But she's somewhere in between."

"Amoral?" said Hodge.

"Don't know what that means," said Charlie.

"Means her conscience works for her, but not for other people."

"That's it," grinned Charlie.

"Ah," said Hodge as if that explained everything. "A heartbreaker."

"Yeah," said Charlie. "Yeah, I think she will be."

"And seeing that clearly, you're still holding onto her ribbon," said Hodge.

Charlie nodded. "Told you it was stupid."

"Love is a bugger," said Hodge, slapping him on the shoulder. "And a sight more complicated than ratcatching."

He nodded across the road to a food stall.

"Let's have us a whelk."

Cait found her way to the *Lady of Nantasket* by asking directions and then threading her way through the crowded dockyard beneath the jungle of masts and spars that overlooked it without needing to ask twice, which was, thought Lucy as she trailed after her, no mean achievement. She also thought the docks were the biggest thing she had ever seen, other than London itself. It was a vast teeming machine and it felt dangerous, not through malice but because everybody knew what they were doing except her: unloading, loading, carrying huge loads or swaying nets of cargo in and out of the waiting boats with little regard for anyone who did not know precisely where they should be. The risks of getting knocked over, squashed, mangled or accidentally tipped off a quay and drowned seemed very real.

But eventually Cait found the clipper in question, a handsome tall-masted ship besieged by workers trying to cram as much cargo aboard as possible, and by any means necessary. Lines of stevedores proceeded up and down the two gangplanks with teeteringly improbable loads on their backs or heads, while two cranes worked in a kind of competitive ballet, lofting bulging nets of goods off the dock and down into the bowels of the cargo-hold.

And overlooking all this was a tall man with a spade beard, a captain's hat and a salt-stained pea-jacket.

Cait approached him directly, while Lucy observed from a distance, hoping she could remain unnoticed and unsquashed while she did so.

"Captain Tittensor?" she said.

He turned and looked her up and down and, as with most men who met her full smile and clear green eyes, clearly both approved of what he saw and was more than a little pleased to be engaged in conversation by such a bracingly attractive young woman.

"You have the advantage of me, ma'am," he said, bowing a little, his hand unconsciously smoothing his beard as he did so, "but it is a pleasure nonetheless to make your acquaintance . . ."

Her eyes glittered with an engaging flash of mirth as she bobbed her head in response to his gallantry. Lucy could see that it was in this combination of refreshing wholesomeness with just a hint of playful mischief, as of a joke shared but never voiced, that a great deal of Caitlin Sean ná Gaolaire's power over men lay. Lucy saw this, and felt an hook of something disconcertingly like jealousy tug at her.

"I have a message for your wife," said Cait.

"Ah." He smiled. "Well, you'd as like be better giving it to me, for she's far away back in Boston."

"With your daughter?" said Cait.

His eyebrows raised in surprise.

"Yes, ma'am –" Lucy saw Cait take the unwelcome news without any visible sign of frustration. If anything her smile increased in intensity. "– but you really do seem to have the advantage, since you know about my family and I still don't know your name," he said.

"Arrah, now there's me with my country manners," she smiled. "I am Caitlin Sean ná Gaolaire, and the pleasure of meeting is mine, I'm sure."

"And you have a message for my Prudence," he said, "which, if it is in written form, I would be happy to take back for you."

"No," said Cait, ducking as a bale of cargo swung over their heads onto the *Nantasket*. "No, no, it is the young lady from whom you adopted your baby—"

"Emelia," he said, and his eyes stuttered a little.

"Emelia, sure and isn't that a pretty name for a beautiful girl," said Cait. "Well, I'm sorry indeed to be the bringer of unwelcome news, but the young lady sends her apologies and fears she must disappoint you both in the matter of providing a sibling for little Emelia—"

"Thank God," he said, his eyes steadying in unexpected relief.

And now Lucy saw surprise pass over Cait's features.

"Thank God, sir?" she said. "Why, pardon my surprise, but you're taking it powerful well, for I thought I was in for a sticky conversation here and no mistake!"

He grinned at her.

"Emelia has not only brought us the joy of parenthood, it seems she has unblocked the well of my wife's fecundity."

"She's having a baby?" said Cait.

"My Prudence is with child," he smiled. "Eight years without a hope, and then the moment we adopt—"

"Well, I've heard it can go like that," said Cait. "And joy of it to you both, 'tis a miracle, so it is. And in Boston too . . ."

The musing way she said it caught a nerve in the momentarily happy sea-captain, and he bristled a little.

"Our fine city of Boston is no less likely a spot for miracles than anywhere else, Miss ná Gaolaire—"

Cait reached out and put a hand on his arm, with all the air of an unconscious gesture of apology.

"No, no, no, Captain Tittensor, I know you're right about that, for don't I have family there myself – no, I was saying that because it's to Boston that I was hoping for passage."

His feathers visibly unruffled as he felt the reassuringly warm pressure of her hand on the salt-stained pilot cloth of his pea-jacket and found himself rather pleasantly drowning in the clear green water of her eyes.

"Well, we're not the most comfortable of vessels for a passenger, but I'm sure we could—" he began.

"Sure now and don't you think I'd be the loveliest nurse to help your dear Prudence with the babies . . . and don't you think it'd be the nicest thing to find room for me on the long passage back across the cold grey sea? Why, you could let me work my way by helping your sea-cook with some cooking of my own, maybe some washing and mending and who knows what other comforts of home on the long evenings . . ."

She dropped her hand from his arm. He sneezed twice and looked at her as if momentarily confused.

"I'm sorry, Miss ná Gaolaire. I, er—"

"I was just wondering when you are sailing and if you might have a space for an enterprising and diligent girl such as myself to work her passage, if that's not too bold," she said. "Or failing that, I was interested in the fare you might be—"

His face lit, as if a wonderful idea had just arrived out of nowhere.

"No, no, no. If you are truly bound for Boston, I have a proposal for *you*—"

And that simply, without the good captain ever thinking he'd been worked on, the deal was done. The *Lady of Nantasket* was to heave anchor and leave the Pool of London on the turn of the tide at noon the next day, and if Miss ná Gaolaire would be on board by ten at the latest, she might work her passage in the mildest and least demanding of ways. Hands were shaken, leave was taken and moments later Lucy had joined her as they walked back out of the dock gates.

"See, the poor captain and his wife have money and a fine boat and a good life, but the wanting of the one thing they didn't and couldn't have made them vulnerable to the changeling filth," said Cait. "Remember that, and take it as my last bit of a lesson to you: wanting is always a weakness. It lets others put handles on you and try and run you off your own path. But if you can make do with less, you travel lighter and freer, so you do."

Lucy was, for some reason, offended by the spring in her companion's step.

"Well now, that's me off to Americay," Cait said, "and there's a sight more travel and time in this job than I'd anticipated, I'll tell you that for nothing. Still, the captain's wife is with child and that's a big bonus, for I won't feel half so bad reclaiming the Factor's baby, knowing they have their own flesh and blood for consolation. He seems like a nice enough feller, and I'm sure his Prudence is a good sort."

"You're really going?" said Lucy.

"Turn of the tide tomorrow, on board by ten in the morning," said Cait.

"You're leaving us," said Lucy. She knew she sounded stupid. She said it anyway. It filled a hole opening up inside her.

"I was always going to be leaving you," said Cait. "There was no secret there."

She looked questioningly at her as they approached Charlie and Hodge who were leaning on a wall beside a whelk stall. Jed sat at their feet looking uncharacteristically self-conscious. Someone had tied a yellow ribbon around his neck.

"Don't look so glum. You'll be safe here with your Oversight, while I'll be far and away over the deep water, where I'll probably be sold into slavery or have all my lovely red hair scalped off me by some wild Red Indian brave—"

"America," said Lucy glumly. "I don't know anything about it."

"Me neither, girlie," grinned Cait, quickening her pace towards the others. "And that's what'll make it such an adventure."

CHAPTER 45

ON THE RAILS

Late at night, The Smith walks the streets of London as Emmet watches over the girl on the Isle of Dogs. The Smith has walked these streets since they were fields and woods, and he has seen many strange things. Some of them he has stopped. Some he has laughed at. Some he has taken part in.

Strange is not something The Smith is unused to.

What he is unfamiliar with is the large block of ice that seems to appear just behind his breastbone, stopping his breath when he sees what is in front of him as he crosses the East London Railway tracks in the moonlight.

It just stands there and grins, as if waiting for him.

Its laugh cuts through the clean quiet of the night like a dirty knife.

And then it stoops, and for a moment The Smith wonders if it is bowing, performing some obscene, mocking kow-tow of abasement to him. And then he realises the Sluagh (for it is impossibly a Sluagh that is standing on top of the iron rails without a qualm or quaver) is licking the metal.

The Sluagh then stands and puts its hat on its matted hair.

It is Fore-and-Aft, the one who berated him on Hackney Marsh.

"I had always wondered what the cursed iron tasted like, Smith." He smiled, a savage ruin of a grin, teeth rotted and akimbo. "It tastes like blood."

He waved a derisory farewell.

"No wonder you like it so very much. Sleep well."

It takes a long time for that block of ice to melt enough for The Smith to breath properly again and turn back to the Isle of Dogs. He begins to walk faster and faster, breaking into a jog. The three advantages he had told the others they could rely on even at this lowest ebb in their fortunes – the fact they were still a Hand, the power of the Wildfire and the unshakeable protection of the Iron Law – are crumbling around him as he moves. The one thought giving him strength as he absorbs the new rules of his world, and the reduction of his paltry trio of strengths to a mere pair is that the Isle is surrounded by running water. Whatever else he has done wrong, whatever else The Oversight has overlooked, that is one thing he got right. The Isle is safe ground.

Sleeping London is a whole other thing.

CHAPTER 46

SHIPS IN THE NIGHT

Sharp and Sara had emerged from a grating in the shadow of a tall city wall. The surrounding streets were filling with snow, and the pedestrians hurrying home were too concerned with not slipping to make much of the two people emerging from the depths. The first person Sharp accosted affirmed that yes, this was Paris, the Montparnasse district specifically and, more than that, they had emerged in a square appropriately known as the Place d'Enfer.

Sara's lips were blue with cold.

"Hadn't thought hell would be this damn chilly," she said, and proceeded to interrogate the man further in reasonably fluent but shivering French.

Within half an hour, thanks to that and the gold sovereigns she carried in her belt as a matter of course, they had a room in the station hotel by the Montparnasse terminal with a roaring fire and a hot bath, brandy and food, and thirty minutes after that, Sharp gone back into the city and had determined there was a train to Rouen leaving from the Embarcadère des Batignolles at St Lazare which a hansom cab – already engaged – could take them to directly. He had also confirmed there was a corresponding fast coach to Dieppe to connect with a steam-packet that would put their feet back on English chalk by five in the morning.

He ran back to the hotel with the good news through a pall of thickening snow and explained the itinerary.

"And then by locomotive to London, where we should arrive by ten-thirty," he said, shaking the flakes off his shoulders.

"You are a marvel of organisation," said Sara, hidden from him by a screen erected around the copper bath in front of the fire. She had, as he had left, announced that she intended to stay in the hot water until hell froze over, and wondered hopefully if that was the reason behind all the unseasonable weather outside. He put her unaccustomed levity down to relief and the brandy she had fortified herself with.

"Should you ever require another string to your bow, you would make a very effective dragoman."

The pink foot he had glimpsed hanging over the edge of the bath made him very aware of the screen and what was unguarded behind it. He cleared his throat.

"We don't need more strings," he said. "We need more bows . . . And more time. I'm afraid we should leave now. I have a carriage waiting."

"Right now?" she said. "You're sure?"

"I checked the timetables and the connections in a convenient book at the ticket office at the Montparnasse Station."

"Books," she said with a sigh. "They should be banned."

There was a decisive splash and gurgle from behind the screen and he realised that she had stepped out of the bath. He looked away. And found the Raven sitting on the bed rail, cocking its head at him.

"I read a book. A novel in fact. A diversion," she said.

"You?" He laughed despite himself. "A novel?" He turned. Her face was looking steadily at him over the top of the screen as she dried herself briskly. She inclined her head in assent, almost defiantly.

"Me," she said. "Guilty of a novel. We spend so much time dealing with the dark realities of the world that I thought I might take a short holiday from the harshness of dry actuality and read a confection, a fantasy if you will. The story was written by a very bright and clever woman and interestingly, though clever, she had taken as her subject the supposedly trifling matter of love: it concerned a long and mutually frustrating courtship between two principled people who allowed their respective pride to prejudice their joint happiness."

She ducked out of sight and he realised she was now pulling on clothes as fast as she could. The thought unsettled him.

"And were you diverted?" he said. Increasingly conscious of the thinness of the screen and what lay beyond.

"I was enthralled and impressed by the author's perspicacity," she said, "but ultimately I was struck by how much of what amused me depended upon the convenient device upon which she propped so much of her artifice, that of otherwise admirable characters lacking the sense to speak and act plainly with each other. I found I was taking pleasure in watching people whom I esteemed being tortured by too much restraint and false modesty. I will have no similar false modesty between us, Jack."

And then she stopped his heart by stepping out from behind the screen, theoretically dressed but actually scandalously not yet buttoned up as to her blouse and jacket, which she worked on as her eyes held his.

"I love you," she said. "And in the matter of loving you I have no pride. It is simply what it is: true, as true in fact as the truest thing I know. Which happens to be your heart and your friendship."

"Sara—" he said.

"Is that understood?" she said, eyes steady on his. "For it is true to the bone and the bedrock of my life."

"Understood and returned tenfold, my—"

"Good," she said, and she reached up and stopped his mouth with a kiss.

It also seemed to start his heart again, for he was conscious of it pounding unusually rapidly, and then he kissed her back, which she allowed for an instant, and then pushed him gently away.

"Not in front of the Raven," she said, perfectly straight-faced. "And not now. We have a train to catch. I have a sense of dread on me and every minute away from London makes it worse."

She looked around the room.

"One day it might be pleasant to spend time in a place like this, with a fire and fine brandy and a comfortable feather bed and no cares in the world. But I'm afraid that is for another life."

Sharp nodded. Then stopped and wondered what exactly she had meant by that. Her face was unhelpfully unreadable on the subject. She held out a hand. The Raven hopped aboard from its perch on top of the armoire and climbed to her shoulder.

"Lead on," she said. "Time and tide wait for no man . . ."

The Raven clacked its beak in her ear.

"Or woman."

CHAPTER 47

RUDDY GLUE

It should have been a jolly last meal.

Cait announced her plans for the morning, and though her departure was regretted, it was decided that the timing couldn't have been better in one respect, in that Cook had that very day acquired a carcase of salt-marsh lamb from the meat market, and had spent a happily energetic afternoon with her heavy Chinese hatchet and boning knife, jointing it and putting up the resultant cuts in the cold larder. As a result, chops were on the menu for a lavish farewell meal and, as the topper, she had taken delivery of a large and much anticipated basket of Westmoreland damsons.

Lucy was set up with a darning needle, pricking lots of holes in the purple-blue skin of each small and astringent plum, which she then dropped into the wide neck of a wicker-wrapped five-gallon demijohn on the floor beside her.

"Damson gin," said Cook. "What you're making now will warm us through next winter. You'll be glad enough of it then, I imagine. Winters aren't getting any hotter, I've noticed, and these things go in cycles."

Charlie was set to help Cook prepare the supper's dessert.

"Men should learn to cook properly," said Cook. "Then they might learn to be a little more independent. Put an apron on or you'll end up with sago all down your front."

"What are we making?" he said, resigned.

"Ruddy Glue," she said. "It's a beautiful old pudding with a bit of bite to it, just like me. Take two pints of those damsons, and get them on the fire in the same amount of water, then shake in a pint of crushed sago. You'll find a sack of it next to the oatmeal over there."

She looked at Lucy, who was scowling over her chore.

"What's making you so cheery?" she said.

"Nothing," said Lucy, jabbing the fruit in her hand and wincing as she went through and pricked her thumb.

"I can see that," said Cook, her eyes flicking to the door out of which Cait had just passed in order to pack her bag for the ten o'clock embarkation in the morning. "Well, when you've chewed it over, spit it out or swallow it."

She pulled up a chair and joined her in preparing the damsons. Charlie was kept stirring his pot until the stones broke free of the fruit, at which point he was to skim them off and crack them (with a hammer on the back step), splitting the sweet kernels out and placing them back in the pot with the fruit and sago, which by now was becoming stained vermilion.

"Sugar it," said Cook without looking up. "And maybe give missy here a spoonful, because she's still looking very sour."

Lucy finished pricking a damson, dropped it in the demijohn and then carefully laid the needle on the table and left without a word.

"That wasn't needed," said Charlie.

Cook didn't reply. Just carried on jabbing with even more intensity. Five damsons later she looked up at him.

"I know," she said with a sigh. "Truth is, Charlie Pyefinch, that I'm an imperfect vessel. Wish I'd bitten my tongue, but I didn't. I've just had this feeling something bad's coming for the longest time. Sometimes I say things and the worry and meanness comes out by mistake. I'm no bloody saint. Show me the pot."

She peered inside.

"Good," she said. "Now pour it into one of those oven dishes, the deep one with the yellow glaze, and put it in the range to bake. It'll be lovely."

It was lovely. But the farewell meal wasn't quite jolly. What had become an easy association between the six of them, in which conversation and laughter had begun to run freely became, this last time, too stilted and self-aware to be comfortable, as if the shadow of the future departure was casting a pall into the present.

And then The Smith of course deepened the shadow tenfold by taking a breath and telling them about the Sluagh on the iron rails. Lucy felt a shiver of horror go through her at the thought of Sluagh in the city. The others couldn't believe it, not at first. Cook swore quite a lot.

"Cold iron's been our ally long as there's been an Oversight," said Hodge. "It's not possible."

"It's like the sun turned into the moon," said Cook. "It's all different now."

She swore some more in a language Lucy didn't recognise.

"You must be mistaken," said Hodge. Jed whined and nuzzled his hand. He didn't notice, his blind eyes pointed towards The Smith.

"No," said Cook. "I felt something changed in the air. The cream in the pantry all went sour overnight."

"This'll be bad as the Great Fire," said Hodge.

"Worse, probably," agreed The Smith. "Worse because normal people won't notice the boundary's shifted because they never knew it was there in the first place. When things go bad and they're being preyed on they won't know by what. They'll think it's each other. The fire just destroyed buildings. Breaking the bonds that glue society together, that's harder to repair."

"Worse than the Disaster, I shouldn't wonder," said Cook. "But we survived that too, didn't we? And those that go on surviving have to eat. Just because the world's going to hell in a handbasket doesn't mean we can't have a nice sustaining supper to see us on our way."

The mood remained sombre despite her bravado, but the food was delightful and abundant. The whole Last Hand sat in the cluttered warmth of the kitchen, faces lit by the candle in the five-wood wreath at the centre of the table, and having enjoyed the chops and the trimmings

Cook piled on with them, they cleared the course and watched as Charlie brought the baking dish to the table. The sago had disappeared, the whole vermilion mush having darkened to a deep crimson gum that looked very handsome in the gold glaze of the earthenware dish. Cook put a jug of cold milk and a bowl of crushed sugar on the table next to it.

"Damsons?" said Hodge, nose crinkling hopefully.

"Ruddy Glue," said The Smith. "Your favourite."

Lucy looked at the sugar and then caught Cook looking at her.

"I spoke unkindly this afternoon, Lucy Harker," she said, swallowing. "And though it was just words, they can hurt more than anything else, especially if they come from one whom you've every right to trust as a friend."

Looks were exchanged across the table. The Smith opened his mouth to speak.

"I want to trust you," said Lucy.

The Smith closed his mouth and just looked a question at her instead.

"But you can't," said Cook. "Or rather, you can't let yourself."

"It is a want that comes from the weakness in me," said Lucy, not looking away from The Smith's anvil-hard eyes. "And I have not survived on my own for so long by being weak."

"But you are not alone now," said Cook. "You're part of us. Part of The Oversight."

"And that makes me safer?" she replied, still looking back at The Smith.

"It makes you part of something bigger," he said.

"I am already part of something bigger," she said. "I am part of the world. And the world is large and I can get lost in it. I can survive and prosper, unnoticed and unremarked by any ill-wishers. In the wide world, I can live free and move fast. I can plot my own course."

"You are too young and inexperienced to understand about courses," snapped The Smith.

Lucy was pleased he showed some anger. It frightened her just enough to put steel in her resolve.

"And you are too old to notice the world changing anew," she said. "Or to know where it might be headed."

"You—" he began, half rising out of his chair.

"Let her speak," said Cook, and though she spoke quietly, the edge in her voice cut through the suddenly heightened tension and dropped him back into his seat without finishing the sentence. Lucy swallowed and tried not to look at Charlie who was staring at her, trying to send signals she didn't want or have time to read.

"The Oversight is sinking," she said carefully. "It is more than sinking. This is not news to anyone round this table. It is being attacked and targeted. So it is not merely dwindling and failing, it is being destroyed by hostile forces. Joining it does not make me safer. It draws attention to myself. It makes me a target."

The room was very quiet, only the fire crackling and the spatter of windblown rain against the windows answering her declaration. Cait looked at the ceiling. Cook sniffed and then blew her nose.

"You feel we have harmed you?" she said. "You think we have not had your best interests at heart after all we have—?"

"No," said Lucy. She took a deep breath, risked a glance at Charlie, but he was leaning back and studying the ceiling beside Cait. "No. I think you believe that you are rescuing me from the sea where you found me rowing my small boat. And I think you want to help me by bringing me aboard your larger ship. But I think that you have all been on your ship so long that you do not understand it is holed, fatally damaged below the waterline. You don't really believe it can sink, that it is in fact sinking under you right now, sinking fast."

Cook glared at her. Charlie and Cait remained fascinated by the ceiling, and The Smith just stared at her with eyes as worn and unyielding as the blunt face of his hammer.

"You don't believe in us," said Charlie.

The "us" slipped in beneath her guard and bit sharply at her resolve. It spoke of his loyalty but felt like the worst betrayal at the same time. Maybe he knew this. Maybe that was why he kept his eyes on the beams overhead.

"I would like to," she said, "but that is the same weakness as wanting to replace the family I lost."

"Wanting a family is not weakness," said Cait. "For one thing, it is the essence of motherhood, and if there's a stronger thing in the world than a good mother, then I've not yet seen it."

And again that, coming from her of all people, was another betrayal. But then Lucy felt in a way which she knew was irrational that Cait had already betrayed her that afternoon.

"Wanting is *always* a weakness," said Lucy, turning her words neatly back on her. But as she did so, she felt the unpleasant twist of the weapon as her low blow slid in. She knew she had won the argument, at least on her own terms, but she'd done it ignobly. Still and all, despite the silence around her, she'd won. She was not as interested in being noble as being safe.

It was hard to get the ring off her finger. It did not seem to want to move, but once she had so visibly started to try and divest herself of the talisman, she felt she had to keep tugging and twisting until she could take it off and slide it back towards The Smith.

She didn't see him move, and flinched as his hand found hers, then relaxed as she realised he was going to help her take it off. But he just stopped her hands from moving at all.

"Keep the ring," he said. "However you make your choice, keep the ring. Oh, and this—"

He reached into his pocket and pulled out a thin gold chain, from which hung a little cage.

"For your heart-stone," he said. "As we discussed."

And now it was her turn to feel on the receiving end of a low blow. The sad generosity in his eyes was insupportable to her.

"You don't need to explain any more," he said. "I see that it is done."

"I do want to fight the shadows," she said. "I wish to be strong, but I wish . . . I think I need to be a different kind of strong. There is a strength in numbers – sometimes – but there is also a strength in solitude."

She looked across the table for support, but Cait was still looking at the ceiling, avoiding her eyes.

"She wants to be like Cait," said Cook.

"A venatrix," said The Smith.

"A free hunter," said Lucy.

"Alone," said Cait, finally lowering her eyes and looking at her. In her own way those eyes were as adamantine and unreachable as The Smith's had been before he accepted her decision. "A true *fiagaí* is always alone . . . whence the freedom."

Lucy looked at them all.

So. Alone then. She was to have neither quite what she wanted, nor what they wanted. Just alone. She would do it with as much dignity as she could. Her voice felt like it had to sidestep something uncomfortably lodged just behind her larynx.

"I will always owe you a great debt," she said, hoping her eyes were not glistening.

"But you will not stay," said Cook.

"NONE of us should stay," said Lucy. She nodded at The Smith. "You said it. You taught us the history, you said when the Last Hand fails, as it has in the past, whoever is left separates and scatters and only returns when enough new blood is found to rebuild."

"You are new blood, Luce," said Charlie.

"I am not enough," she said. "And you should all scatter. If not for your own safety, for the safety of The Oversight . . ."

"If you go, you go," said The Smith. "It is not your job to then tell us what to do. But if the Last Hand is no more, then the steps that are to be taken will be taken methodically, not in panic. Seeing what I have seen, a Sluagh on iron, I would have done that anyway. Hodge will want to ensure the Tower remains safe and will stay there. Cook and I will plan itineraries and divide up the country, then go and look for any who might join us and refresh our numbers. Charlie, if he would be kind enough, might go to his parents and ask them if they would reconsider."

"I don't know," said Charlie. "I think they're going to find it hard enough that I've joined. But I'll give it a go, course I will."

They all sat with their own thoughts. Lucy felt the long silence was as bad as anything they might have said to her.

Cook turned a spoon in the crimson paste.

"Ruddy Glue. Looks lovely but can't stick a damn thing together."

It should have been a jolly last meal.

CHAPTER 48

No Goodbyes

Cait was striding towards the docks, her carpet-bag in her hand and a bright face on to greet the day. She was whistling for the joy and luck of it, the tune she chose being the sea shanty known as "Fare thee well, my own true love". It seemed the right tune for a day when she was setting off on a voyage across the ocean to America.

Her passage drew smiles from those she passed, for she looked blithe and bonny, and the whistling also made it easy for her stalker to keep track of her in the morning crowd.

As she neared the dock gates, Cait ceased whistling and when she walked under the arch she stopped in its shadow and spoke to no one in particular.

"You should have said farewell."

The crowd milled past.

"Did you hear me?" she said.

And part of the crowd broke away and walked up to her. It was Lucy, and she had a bag over her shoulder.

"I did. Last night. You were there," she said. "How long have you known I was following?"

"Since we left the house," said Cait. "You should have said farewell."

"I did," she repeated.

"To Charlie Pyefinch," said Cait, walking into the dockyard. "He's been a good friend to you, girl."

"I left him a note," said Lucy, jogging to keep up. "He was gone ratting with Hodge by the time I woke."

"Hmm," said Cait, not breaking her long stride. "Goodbye in a note is no kind of a goodbye at all: it's at least half of a cowardly thing. I expect more of you."

Lucy walked behind her as they wove through the stevedores and dockers. Then Cait turned and looked directly at her with an exasperated sigh.

"Lucy Harker."

"Yes?"

"I don't like girls."

Lucy's face flushed.

"What?"

"Not in that way."

"I don't know what you—"

"Sure you do," said Cait. "And there's nothing wrong with it, see. There's enough pain and loneliness in the wide world that you'd have to be a rank fool, and an unkind one at that to say any kind of love was bad."

Lucy knew her face must look very hot. A memory flashed into her head of Georgiana Eagle, very close to her face, looking at her in growing horror. It made her wince.

"Look, I still don't know—"

Cait rolled her eyes.

"All right then, try it the other way: sure you *don't*. Or maybe you do. Or maybe, just maybe it's what you might call a "mash". I had a terrible fierce mash on an older girl when I was a slip of a thing. I think I confused wanting her with wanting to be her. But I had a mash on, all right, and it felt realer than real, to be sure. But I do like men, *acushla*. Not many, not often, because finding a good one's a rare thing. I fierce liked that Mr Sharp, but he didn't like me, and truth is he didn't make me laugh, when I thought about it. See, a good strong feller who can make me laugh, that's my poison, and find me one of them and I'm as big a fool for the love as anyone. D'you see now?"

Lucy nodded, miserable.

"And I work alone. Venatrixes work alone."

Lucy's chin came up.

"But you had a teacher. You told me. A mentor, you said."

Cait stared at her, face giving nothing away as a stevadore who seemed to be carrying a small house on his back staggered past between them.

"If you're right," said Lucy, once the obstacle had lurched away towards the warehouse. "If you're right and what I'm feeling is wanting to *be* you and not . . . not the other thing . . . then show me how."

Cait looked away, up at the sky. The world kept walking past them, and all Lucy could see was the curve of Cait's neck and the line of her jaw.

"Cait," she said.

Cait shivered.

"There's cold weather coming in."

"Cait," said Lucy. "Please!"

"I'll give you one year, same as I had. Then you're on your own," said Cait briskly.

Her eyes dropped and found Lucy's.

"A deal?"

"A deal."

"Take your glove off then," she said.

"Why?"

"Because lesson one is do what I say," said Cait.

Lucy peeled off her right glove and began to remove the other.

"That'll do," said Cait.

She spat in her own right hand and looked at Lucy.

"Go on then."

Lucy spat in her own hand and they slapped skin to skin, gripped firmly and shook.

"One year," said Cait.

"Thank you," said Lucy.

"Lesson two," said Cait, pointing at her carpet-bag on the pavement. "You carry the luggage."

CHAPTER 49

THE RAT KING

Whether or not the Last Hand was done, some things would continue, and the most important, according to Hodge, was his routine. So while the rest of London stirred itself from its various beds and began to think about breakfast, Charlie was deep beneath the north end of the White Tower listening to Jed yipping in unprecedented excitement. Hodge was not with them, having decided Charlie would learn more by ratting on his own, while he boiled the tea and fried the bacon in his quarters, claiming the very blurry shapes he was just beginning to be able to make out through his less ruined eye made this not only possible but "good practice".

Charlie and Jed had patrolled the usual corners and crannies, and found nothing but a dead pigeon that had somehow got stuck in the cellar stairwell. And then, just as Charlie had decided it was time to go and see if Hodge had remembered to save him any bacon, Jed went mad.

The normal excited barks had quickly changed to something Charlie hadn't heard before – a fiercely rising crescendo of sharp, high-pitched yips – and then, as he bent and peered forward beneath the low roof, pushing the bull's-eye lantern ahead of him to try and see the dog, the noise stopped.

"Jed!" he shouted. "Jed!"

The sudden silence was the nastiest thing he had yet encountered while underground in the dark. It made his heart race.

"Jed!" he shouted.

More silence answered him. Silence from the darkness beyond the light of his lantern.

Charlie didn't hesitate. He liked the dog, and more than that, they were a team. He didn't really need to think at all. He was on his hands and knees, crawling forward as fast as he could and somehow he had managed to draw his knife and hold it between his teeth, ready for whatever had silenced the terrier. The floor rose towards the roof as he went, pressing down on him and turning his crawl to a squirm, and then just as he thought he could go no further, a growling, screaming ball of something hurled out of the darkness ahead. It hit him and scratched and bit its way around his body, knocking the lantern from his hand and extinguishing it, and in the moment before his world went black he saw a nightmare fragment of rats – giant rats, wrong rats – and teeth and tails and fangs and fur fly past.

He stayed there stunned, scrabbling for the lantern. He felt wetness and glass. The lens was shattered, the fuel was spilled. Trying to relight it would start a small fire that would burn or asphyxiate him.

He heard a terrible noise of howls and snarls and screams interspersed with a brutal sound of metal bashing against stone from the void behind him. Again he froze, trying to make sense of what he was hearing.

And then something grabbed his ankle.

He lashed out with his boot.

"Hoi!" said a familiar voice. "Less of that!"

It was Hodge. He dragged Charlie free of the cramped squeeze-point and they both scrambled back into the cellar. Hodge had left his lamp on the floor and in its light Charlie saw three things.

A blood-stained shovel. A nearly as gory Jed, lying panting on the stone flags, covered in bites and scrapes, but wagging his tail proudly. And in front of him, in a spattered puddle of blood, the rats, seemingly laid out in a circle.

And now they were dead Charlie could see what was wrong with them. As they had gone past him, he had snatched a glimpse of some running forwards and some seeming to run backwards. That's what hadn't made sense. Now he could see why: they were more than twenty in number and their tails were snarled together, twisted and plaited and glued in place by their own droppings and dried blood and filth. It was a wheel of rats.

"What is it?" said Charlie.

"It's a fucking harbinger is what it is," spat Hodge.

Charlie had never heard him swear before. It was the second most shocking thing he had experienced today. It was almost as bad as that horrible silence in the dark.

"Pardon my French," said Hodge. "But that's a Rat King, and Rat Kings mean bad trouble's coming sure as a gunshot means a bullet's on the way. Sluaghs walking the iron rails, the Last Hand threatened and now a f— a bloody Rat King for breakfast. Batten down the hatches, Charlie, cos there's an anvil dropping out of the sky and it's got our name on it."

He spat at the Rat King.

"Let's get Jed patched up and then we'll go and tell everyone the lovely news and see how they take it."

Because they had been underground, muffled by rock, earth and masonry, they did not hear the explosion. The first they knew of the new disaster was when they saw the dark smoke pluming into the sky to the east.

Jed spotted it first and barked.

And then they ran.

CHAPTER 50

DOWNFALL

If Ida Laemmel had not been a trained hunter, she would have walked right up to the door of the Safe House and announced herself. As it was, she had taken passage on a fast ship from Zeebrugge which had brought her right up the Thames and deposited her a short walk from Wellclose Square. She had picked up her woollen pack and a violin case, and gone straight there. She had taken up position in the centre of the square against the wall of the Danish Church and was now observing it to find the lie of the land: as a hunter she wanted to acclimatise herself to the local terrain and ensure all was as it seemed before she made herself known, not least because for all she knew The Citizen may have made his move already and those in the Safe House were dead, imposters or — as he had done with the Paladin — turned into his puppets.

The Paladin had been as ancient a Free Company as The Oversight or *Die Wachte*, and he had perverted them in a handful of years. They had been numerous too, and his cunning had almost destroyed The Oversight, from what she had heard. If they were as reduced in number as rumour had it, then they would be hanging on by their fingertips, and he would find them much easier to pluck than their French counterparts had been.

So she wrapped herself in her long *loden* cape and went shadow-still, and just watched the square from beneath the deep overhang of her hood.

She had seen a young man leave and head towards the Tower of London. He had worn a ring.

Forty minutes later she had seen a striking redhead leave, swinging a carpet-bag and whistling cheerily as she went. A moment or two later, a girl had slipped out of the house with a small bag over her shoulder and followed the redhead in a furtive, swift way that Ida the hunter recognised only too well. The first girl had not worn a ring. The stalker had worn a ring and gloves. A Glint perhaps. Her behaviour was odd, and so Ida stayed in the shadows and watched both everything and nothing in the way she had learned, staying open to both patterns and breaks in patterns.

She spotted the other watchers by the sugar factory. They looked like loafers but they had a focus she could feel: though they tried to be subtle about it, they loafed with intent, and all that intent was focused down the slope at the Safe House. They did not wear rings, and one scarcely had a chin.

A subtle change in sensibility that she knew well came over her as she went from watching for anything to watching something: the loafers broke the pattern because they were doing nothing, but looking agitated and stressed about it.

Then she saw them relax. A wagon pulled up outside the Safe House. It was piled with barrels. The driver put the brake on, and then did not go to the door and knock but walked away up the hill. As he passed the chinless loafer without pausing or seeming to see him, the loafer winked at him, and the wagoner gave a thumbs up with his hand held low at his side.

The wagoner stopped beside a hansom cab parked on the corner. Ida saw a flash of the interior, a waiting man with a face that had the pallor of a toad's belly, his arm held in a sling across his chest. She got a better look at his face as the door closed and he reappeared at the window, peering hungrily at the Safe House. Then he looked quickly at the loafers and made a sign with his hand.

The loafer with a chin reached into a bag and handed the chinless one what looked like a large black pomegranate.

And now Ida knew she had been right to wait. Something bad was about to happen. She loosened the knife in her belt and then reached down and quietly pushed back the hooks on the lid of her violin case.

She heard a metallic bouncing noise, and her head whipped back to look at the sugar factory in time to see the chinless loafer roll the second grenado.

"*Scheisse!*" hissed Ida, throwing off the cloak and pulling the crossbow from the violin case in the same movement. She was still wearing her hunting clothes, dark suede *Trachtenjacke* and the shocking, men's lederhosen. As she ran, she ratcheted the bow and slapped a bolt in place.

She was torn between two options – catch the loafers or warn The Oversight.

She saw a tall, caped coachman in an old-fashioned tricorne hat walk out of the Safe House to look at the wagon parked outside.

The first grenado exploded, a deep shattering concussion that nearly knocked her over as the doors blew off the sugar manufactory. She saw a house-high vat split and slowly tilt forward and then she stopped thinking and started acting.

She turned and yelled at the coachman as she pointed at the ruined factory and the slowly toppling vat.

"FIRE! FIRE IS COMING!"

Then without waiting to see if he understood, she whirled and looked for the bomb throwers.

The chinless one was climbing up next to the driver on the hansom cab; the other one had opened the door and was about to get in.

Ida shot him, almost without aiming.

The crossbow bolt blew out Coram's knee and knocked him shrieking into the gutter.

Her hands worked fast so that by the time the second grenado blew she was loaded and firing. The bolt chunked through the back of the cab.

Then she was running. A thin river of flaming sugar was starting to roll down the street towards the Safe House and the wagonload of barrels.

She fired a last bolt, then turned to outrun the fire stream.

Issachar Temblebane stared in shock at the two arrowheads stuck through the wall of the cab facing him.

"Arrows?" he said. "ARROWS?" And then he slammed his hand on the roof.

"GO!" he screamed. "GO!"

As the cab lurched into motion, he caught a glimpse of Coram writhing in the gutter, clutching his leg. His face opened in a yell, eyes staring at Issachar's as he passed.

"Father!"

And then he was gone. Issachar slumped back as the cab sped away, staring in controlled horror at the bolts which protruded through the seat back in front of him.

"Who the hell uses arrows?"

Ida was pleased the coachman had run back in the house.

"Get out!" she shouted as she ran in the door he had left open in his haste.

"Everybody out! Fire is coming!" she yelled as she followed him in at speed.

She was just thinking that she'd done a stupid thing running into a house that was about to get hit by a river of fire without knowing where the back door was when she skidded to a halt at what was obviously the kitchen door.

A large, red-faced woman with a scar running down her face was swearing like a trooper and fighting to free herself from the undignified position she found herself in, which was over the coachman's shoulder.

"Emmet, you effing lump of mud, what the bloody hell are you doing manhandling me like this?"

"He's trying to save you!" said Ida.

Cook registered her in shock.

"Who the buggery are you?"

"Friend," said Ida. "No time. The factory's blown up, there's a river of burning sugar headed this way and—"

Outside, the sugar-lava hit the wagon and ignited the barrels of turpentine. The wagon, the barrels and bits of unfortunate horse blew in the windows at the front of the house.

Pots and pans and kitchen paraphernalia rained from the hooks and rails on the ceiling, jolted adrift by the concussion.

"Right, got it – put me down," said Cook.

Fire began to glow angry red in the passage behind Ida as the burning sugar began to find its way into the basement.

Cook snatched a hatchet and a cutlass from the debris, stuck the cutlass through her apron strings and snatched the candle and the five-wood wreath from the centre of the pine table. She looked wistfully at the kitchen and then found Ida's eyes. She pointed at a box covered in Chinese writing.

"Right," she said. "You, Trousers, grab that box and follow me. Time to abandon ship. Emmet, grab the table, block the door, stop the fire as long as you can, so's we can get this damned Wildfire to safety."

Emmet lifted the table and looked at Ida. She realised she was in the way. She ran after Cook. He smacked his arm down and chopped the huge table in half, then ran at the door and slammed the table over the opening just as the first wave of burning sugar splashed into it. He leant against it, wedging back the tide as flames licked hungry fingers round the edge, leaking into the doomed kitchen.

Ida followed Cook as she ran down the passage to the back of the house. Cook stopped herself with one hand, catching on one of two pillars halfway down.

"Emmet," she shouted. "Come now, and drop the roof as you go."

"Anyone else in the house?" said Ida.

"No. But there's a lot of irreplaceable— Bugger, yes. Maybe. A girl," said Cook.

"Redhead?" coughed Ida. Smoke was beginning to curl in from the kitchen end, twining towards them across the roof.

"Glint," said Cook. "I mean she is a—"

"She left," hacked Ida. "And we need to too."

"I'm with you," said Cook, eyeing the smoke. She opened a door to another passage. "This way. Takes us uphill, towards the Tower. Away from the flow."

"I need to get back on the street fast," said Ida. "I shot one of them. Hobbled him. I can find out who he is. Or follow his blood trail to his lair."

"Trousers," said Cook, "don't know who the bloody hell you are, but I like your style."

"I'm Ida Laemmel."

"Maybe," grinned Cook, a dangerous spark in her eye, "but you'll always be Trousers to me."

She seemed to be getting an unaccountable burst of energy from the mayhem, almost as if it were her element. "We'll take the side tunnel to the Sly House."

There was a crash and a *whomp* of flame as a fireball curled out of the kitchen, eating its way along the ceiling as it bellied towards them like a hungry snake.

Cook grabbed her shoulder and yanked her through the door, slamming it shut.

"But Emmet—" said Ida.

"He's a golem. Hard to kill," said Cook.

Behind the door, a burning figure walked determinedly through the flames, knee-deep in molten sugar that was now coursing ahead of him as it searched for the quickest way down to the river.

He reached the pillars, his clothes burnt off him and hanging in fiery tatters as he stretched across the width of the passage and pulled them. They didn't move. And still he pulled, the fire river lapping his thighs, every ounce of strength fighting the downward force of the building above. His mouth was open and screaming silently, and then with a jolt and a thud the pillars buckled inwards and, as he staggered forward, it was as if the whole of the Safe House came crashing down behind him, sealing the passage and pitching him face down into the fire.

CHAPTER 51

DEVASTATION

Sharp and Sara arrived in London after an astonishingly speedy night crossing from Boulogne by the new South Eastern & Continental Steam-Packet Company that had eaten up the Channel and ejected them onto the quayside at Folkestone in time for the first train to London.

It had been an uncomfortable and uneventful passage, except for one moment mid-Channel when Sharp had woken to find Sara looking at him.

"What?" he said.

"I never thanked you for coming into the mirrors for me," she said.

"Nor I you, come to think of it," he said.

The boat churned on through the night.

"When I was restored to my hand and found you had gone, two things were immediately apparent," she said, as if describing the results of an experiment. "The first was that although my hand and heart-stone were an integral, necessary part of me, I was still not whole."

She looked out at the moon.

"The second thing," he prompted.

"You know the second thing, Jack," she said, pulling her collar tight round her neck and closing her eyes. "Don't be obtuse. It's the same reason you went into that damned glass maze."

And he watched her fall asleep. And he might have been wrong, but before she did he would have sworn he saw the very edge of her mouth tic up in a quickly suppressed smile.

He watched her until they docked, and then they followed the mail to the railway station and arrived in the city before nine-thirty, having travelled through a dawn that revealed in its crisp first light a landscape almost magical with snow. On arrival the Raven flew ahead, and they engaged a sleepy hansom cab driver to take them to the Safe House. The cab squelched through slush and ice that was distinctly unmagical, but made good time despite that.

They heard the clocks strike ten as the cab paused at the bottom of St George Street, just below Wellclose Square. When it didn't make the expected turn, Sharp stuck his head out the window.

"Sorry, guv," said the driver, pointing with his whip. "Some bugger's lost a wheel."

A cart carrying what looked like carboys of turpentine had got stuck on the turning, and three very angry carters were trying to replace a wheel that had broken on the high kerb without tipping the cart into the street.

"We can walk," said Sara.

They paid the driver and made their way up the short street to Wellclose Square.

"Home, Sharp! We're home. And I feel not a minute too soon!" she said, squeezing his arm. "Come on. I can't wait to see Cook's face when we walk in!"

And she dragged him into what developed quickly into a laughing race up the slope through the snow.

He let her lead, and so when she stopped at the top of the street he saw the stutter-step and then the stillness hit her as the laughter died on her lips.

"Sara," he said. "What—?"

And then he saw it too.

The Safe House was gone.

It had disappeared as if plucked from the face of the earth.

Where he should have been looking at the familiar back wall, he was seeing straight through to the Danish Church beyond the house in the centre of the square, and beyond it another absence where the sugar factory had been.

"But . . ." said Sara. "But . . ."

His arm went round her shoulders, keeping her on her feet as their eyes tried to make sense of what they were seeing.

One side-wall of the Safe House remained, a smoke-blackened cliff with the outlines of the once hidden rooms clearly visible on it. Of the rest of the house there was nothing recognisable. A huge pile of charred rafters and cross-beams had been made in one corner of the now vacant lot, and facing it there was a brick pile where the debris had been sorted and moved out of the way. Whatever had happened had happened a long time ago.

"But this can't . . ." she said. "This isn't . . ."

"Sara," he said. He felt like he was being repeatedly hit in the stomach. "Time. Time in the mirrors is unreliable. The nun, Dee, someone warned me: it flows differently."

"Oh, Jack," she said. "Oh, Jack. What happened here?"

He looked around the street. There were no familiar faces. Just a girl and a boy running across the square, preceded by a dog that he for a brief, excited, moment thought was Jed but now saw was not, being a puppy instead.

"I'll find out," he said. "I'll go to Bunyon's, the Sly House . . ."

"No," she said. "I'll do it."

He felt her stiffen and straighten her back and walk towards the looming wall, peeling off her glove as she went.

"No, Sara," he said, running after her as he realised what she was about to do. He grabbed her arm. "Please. If they are dead we shall find out soon enough, but you do not have to witness it."

"Yes, I do," she said. "Yes, I damn well do. Let me go."

He didn't.

"Mr Sharp," she said, voice and eyes suddenly icy as a midwinter wave. "Unhand me, please."

He didn't. Nor did he know what to do next.

The running girl paused in front of them.

"Mr Sharp?" she said, eyes bright and face pinked from the exertion of her run.

"Do I know you?" he said.

"Not a bit," she said. There was a clipped, foreign intonation to her accent. His head was spinning and sick with dread, but there was something familiar about her. "I am Ida Laemmel. Thanks be that you are both alive."

"Miss Falk!" said the boy, skidding to a halt. Sharp had never seen him before, but there was something familiar about him too.

Sara's eyes left Sharp's face and found his. And the midwinter wave crashed and the ice melted and her knees buckled for an instant and then she straightened.

"Pyefinch?" she said. "Charlie Pyefinch?"

He brushed his hair out of his eyes and grinned in embarrassment. And Sharp saw the familiar thing. He wore a bloodstone ring. As did the girl Laemmel.

"The Raven found us at the Tower," said Charlie. "I was teaching Ida and Archie to rat . . ."

He pointed at the terrier puppy happily worrying the cuff of his trousers. He beamed at Sara.

"You're bloody alive!" he said. "Sorry. Swearing. But this is the first good news . . . well, it's the first good news, apart from Ida here poling up, since this—"

He suddenly looked stricken as he pointed at the devastation behind him.

"Since this happened."

"What happened?" said Sara. "Exactly what?"

Sharp saw her tensing as if making ready to receive a blow. He stepped up close behind her and put an arm round an unyielding shoulder.

"Long answer's a bit complicated," he said, stumbling a little.

"The short answer is Templebanes," said the girl.

"Charlie Pyefinch," said Mr Sharp, voice raw, "I know your parents and like them greatly, but if you don't tell us what has happened to Cook and Hodge and The Smith and Emmet, I am going to have to strangle you."

"And the girl Lucy Harker?" said Sara.

A look flew between Ida and Charlie.

"I think we better let the others tell you," he said. "Those that remain. They're at The Smith's on the Isle of Dogs . . ."

"You won't like it when they do," said Ida.

Sara stared at the ruin of her only home.

"I already don't," she said.

Only now did she let herself bend and sag against Sharp for an instant.

"I'm here," he said quietly into her ear. "Bone and bedrock."

"Good," she breathed back, her eyes looking to the east to where the low winter sun was still rising. Then he felt her straighten again.

"Because we have some building to do and vengeance to take . . ."

Epilogue

BACK BAY, BOSTON, MASSACHUSETTS

Prudence Tittensor does not normally curse, either in or out of polite company, in both of which situations she is equally comfortable and equally likely to be found. She is a sea-captain's wife and a prosperous trader in her own right, given to travelling with her spouse on his voyages to Europe and beyond. She has only done one bad thing in an otherwise blameless life, the fruits of which should have been grizzling in the empty and silent Crandall's Patent Baby Carriage at her side in the room overlooking the dock beyond.

She had told herself no one would know, and persuaded herself that if she had not made the agreement the vendor would likely have disposed of the child by dropping it in a sewer or leaving it to die in the streets. And she had known that the warning sense she was suppressing all the time was that the girl selling her the baby, as her own, for adoption, was no girl at all, but older than she was, and was a changeling. Smell alone should have alerted her. But she had been in extremis herself, her faculties dulled, her scruples suppressed, and the prospect of the child had made her husband so very happy. And she loved him.

And then later she felt the quickening of her own belly, and could no longer hide from herself what she had done. And so she had sent her husband away in order that she could engineer a discreet solution to her problem. She had allowed a childless couple from Marblehead to adopt the child. They were kind, young and determined to build a new life in the West, away from families that both found too cloistering for comfort. And they had headed to the new territories with their optimism buoyed by the prospect of a future happiness promised by the happy two-year-old that Providence, and Prudence, had provided for them.

She could never tell her husband the real reason she had done it, for to do so would be to disabuse him of certain illusions both about how the world was constituted in general, and what Prudence's abilities were in particular. So she had determined just to tell him God had told her to share their fortune by giving Emelia to a deserving couple of fine upstanding moral character in order that he and she could concentrate their love and attention on the coming child who would be blood of their blood and flesh of their flesh. Using God — who he deeply believed in — as an excuse for her less explainable rashnesses always worked, and was quite consequence-free for Prudence who no more believed in a god than her husband believed in changelings or Wendigos or any of the lesser manitou. Or even Skinwalkers like his wife.

The reason she swore like the basest wharfie was that she had come down to the dock to meet the Lady of Nantasket *and greet her beloved. She was steeled to finesse the bad news about Emelia and glaze it with a thick sugar-coating of good news about the progress of her own pregnancy.*

What she was not steeled for was the tall redhead stepping off the gangplank ahead of her husband whom she immediately registered, as of a fierce vibration in the air, as fiagaí, *nor was she in any doubt of why the girl following her was wearing gloves on such a mild winter's day.*

She wondered if they were here to contact the Remnant, perhaps to search for Emelia. Stranger things had happened.

One thing was certain: they were two things.

Abled, as she was.

And trouble.

ACKNOWLEDGEMENTS

A word on the Rat King's appearance in the preceding pages: it didn't just come unbidden out of the deep darkness beneath the White Tower to surprise Charlie and Jed. It crawled from The Stewpot, out of the Gumbo. A while ago, when I was thinking about stepping outside my screenwriting comfort zone to venture a first novel, I conspired to interview Terry Pratchett for a Sunday supplement over a long and very – on his part, towards me – indulgent dinner in Edinburgh. I was of course hoping to pick up some tips from the master. (The best way to learn about something is, in my experience, to interview an expert in the field.)

Somebody had recently come up to him at a signing having seen an illustration of Ponder Stibbons (in *The Last Hero*) and snarkily pointed out that he'd obviously been , er . . . "inspired" by the then young Harry Potter, and that by association perhaps Unseen University itself was "stolen" from Hogwarts. Terry just very calmly mentioned that the first Harry Potter book was published a year after *The Last Hero* and left it at that. This led us into to a general discussion about inspiration and where ideas come from, and Terry outlined his theory of the Gumbo, or The Stewpot: everything that's ever been written *and* everything you write gets thrown into a big pot, and everyone one can pick different bits and pieces out of the stew and use/remix them as ingredients in their own recipe. The only crimes against The Stewpot are to either pretend it doesn't exist, or that you own it. It's a rational, robust and generous rule, and in that is like my experience of Terry himself. He was a great inspiration, hard-edged about the process of creativity, truly funny and righteously angry about all the embuggering™ pretence, venality and self-delusion in the world. I hate the fact we will have no more books from him, and I'm profoundly grateful for the ones we have, the ones I've enjoyed and stolen from: the Rat King is a fragment I speared out of The Stewpot which originally creeped me out in his *The Amazing Maurice and His Educated Rodents*.

The other thing I particularly remember from the dinner had nothing to do with being a writer and everything to do with being a dad: we talked about video games and, in the course of enthusiastically recommending *Thief* as a profitable and enjoyable aid to Writer's Procrastination, he spoke of his daughter. Just for a moment the public Terry dropped his guard and revealed a flash of deep and gruff pride. I didn't put that in the article then, but I'd like to mark it now, perhaps because I never found a way to thank him properly for his indulgence and inspiration. He created strong, courageous and independent-minded women in a range that went from young Tiffany Aching to Granny Weatherwax, and though I'm pretty sure he was confident enough in his own art to be proud of them, I'm equally certain that the one he was most proud of was not a fictional character at all, and that her name begins with R.

Many thanks to Orbit/Little Brown, especially to Jenni Hill and Will Hinton, my excellent editors at Orbit on either side of the pond, to Joanna Kramer for her exemplary copy-edit which makes me seem much smarter and less repetitive that I really am. Thanks also to Lauren Panepinto for contriving another lovely cover. I'm very grateful to and for Karolina Sutton, my agent at Curtis Brown, and to Michael McCoy at Independent whose work on the other side of my writing street gives me confidence and time to spend on these books. None better.

Thanks to Hugh and Anne Buchanan for the Austrian hospitality that led to my fictional forebears emerging out of the dark, high on the Steinernes Meer.

Ave atque vale to our neighbour and friend who was one of the two main inspirations for Cook, who sadly died between *The Oversight* and this book: I said it at her funeral, and I'll say it again: you have to admire a woman whose collection of swordsticks outnumbers her handbags.

Finally, thanks to my family for their support, inspiration and indulgence: to my mother for her enduring gameness and youthful outlook, to Jack and Ari for making your mother and me laugh so much, and to D herself, first and best reader and all round one-woman inspiration machine . . .

extras

orbit

meet the author

Photo credit: Domenica More Gordon

CHARLIE FLETCHER is the author of the internationally acclaimed *Stoneheart* trilogy. He also writes for film, television and as a newspaper columnist. Charlie lives in Edinburgh with his wife and two children.

introducing

If you enjoyed
THE PARADOX,
look out for

SKYBORN

Seraphim: Book 1

by David Dalglish

The last remnants of humanity live on six islands floating high above the Endless Ocean, fighting a brutal civil war in the skies. The Seraphim, elite soldiers trained for aerial combat, battle one another while wielding elements of ice, fire, and lightning.

The lives of their parents claimed in combat, twins Kael and Breanna Skyborn enter the Seraphim Academy to follow in their footsteps. There they will learn to harness the elements as weapons and fight at break-neck speeds while soaring high above the waters. But they must learn quickly, for a nearby island has set its hungry eyes upon their home. When the invasion comes, the twins must don their wings and ready their blades to save those they love from annihilation.

PROLOGUE

Breanna Skyborn sat at the edge of her world, watching the clouds drift beneath her dangling feet.

"Bree?"

Kael's voice sounded obscenely loud in the twilight quiet. She turned to see her twin brother standing at the stone barricade that marked the end of the road.

"Over here," she said.

The barricade reached up to Kael's waist, and after a moment's hesitation, he climbed over, leaving behind smoothly worn cobbles for short grass and soft dirt. Beyond the barricade, there was nothing else. No buildings. No streets. No homes. Just a stretch of unused earth, and then beyond that… the edge. It was for that reason Bree loved it, and her brother hated it.

"We're not allowed to be this close," he said as he approached, each step smaller than the last. "If Aunt Bethy saw…"

"Aunt Bethy won't come within twenty feet of the barricade and you know it."

Wind blew against her, and she pulled her dark hair back from her face as she smirked at her brother. His pale skin had taken on a golden hue from the fading sunlight, the wind teasing his much shorter hair. The gust made him stop, and she worried he'd decide to leave her there.

"You're not afraid, are you?" she asked.

That was enough to push him on. Kael joined her at the edge of their island. When he sat, he sat crossed legged, and unlike her, he did not let his legs dangle off the side.

"Just for a little while," he said. "We should be home when the battle starts."

Bree turned away, and she peered over the edge of the island. Below, lazily floating along, were dozens of puffy clouds painted orange by the setting sun. Through their gaps she saw the tumultuous Endless Ocean, its movement only hinted at by the faintest of dark lines. Again the wind blew, and she pretended that she rode upon the wind, flying just like her parents.

"So why are we out here?" Kael asked, interrupting the silence.

"I was hoping to see the stars."

"Is that it? We're just here to waste our time?"

Bree glared at him.

"You've seen the drawings in Teacher Gruden's books. The stars are beautiful. I was hoping that out here, away from the lanterns, maybe I could see one or two before..."

She fell silent. Kael let out a sigh.

"Is that really why you're out here?"

It wasn't, not fully, but she didn't feel comfortable discussing the other reason. Hours ago their mother and father had set them down beside the fire of their home. They'd each worn the black uniforms of their island of Weshern, swords dangling from their hips, the silver wings attached to their harnesses polished to a shine.

The island of Galen won't back down, so we have no choice, their father had said. *We've agreed to a battle come the midnight fire. This will be the last, I promise. After this, they won't have the heart for another.*

"It is," Bree said, wishing her half-lie were more convincing. She looked to their right, where the sun was slipping beneath the horizon. Nightfall wouldn't be long now. Kael shifted uncomfortably, and she saw him glancing behind them, as if convinced they'd be caught despite being in a secluded corner of their small town of Lowville.

"Fine," he said. "I'll stay with you, but if we get in trouble, this was all your idea."

"It usually is," she said, smiling at him.

Kael settled back, sliding a bit further away from the edge. Together they watched the sun slowly set. In its glow, they caught glimpses of two figures flying through the twilight haze. Their mechanical wings shimmering gold as they hovered above a great stretch of green farmland. The men wore red robes along with their wings, easily identifying them as theotechs of Center.

"Why are they here?" Kael asked when he spotted them.

"They're here to oversee the battle," Bree answered. She'd spent countless nights on her father's lap, asking him questions. What it was like to fly? Was he ever scared when they fought? Did he think she might ever be a member of the Seraphim like they were? Bree knew the two theotechs would bless the battle, ensure everyone followed the agreed-upon rules, and then mark the surrender of the loser. Then would come the vultures, the lowest ranking members of the theotechs, come to reclaim the treasured technology from the fallen.

The mention of the coming battle put Kael on edge, and he fell silent as he looked to the sunset. Bree couldn't blame him for his nervousness. She felt it too, and it was that reason she couldn't stay home, cooped up, unable to witness the battle or know if her mother and father lived or died. No, she had to be out there. She had to have something to occupy her mind.

They said nothing as the sun neared the end of its descent. As the strength of its rays weakened, she turned her attention to the east, where the sky had faded a deep shade of purple. The coming darkness unsettled Bree. Since the day she was born, it had come and gone, but it was rare for her to watch it. She much preferred to be at home next to the hearth, listening to her father tell Seraphim stories, or their mother reading Kael ancient tales of knights and angels. Watching the nightly shadow only made her feel...imprisoned.

It began where the light was at its absolute weakest, an inky black line on the horizon that grew like a cloud. Slowly it crawled, thick as smoke and wide as the horizon itself. The darkness swept over the sky, hiding its many colors. More and more it covered, an unceasing march matched by the sun's fall. When it reached to the faintly visible moon, it too vanished, the pale crescent tucked away, never to be seen until the following night. Silently the twins watched as the rolling darkness passed high above their heads, blotting out everything, encasing the world in its deep shadow.

Bree turned her attention to the setting sun, which looked as if it fled in fear of the darkness complete.

"It'll be right there," she said, pointing. "In the moment after the sun sets and before the darkness reaches it."

Most of the sky was gone now, and so far away from the lanterns, the two sat in a darkness so complete it was frightening. The shadow clouds continued rolling, blotting out the field of stars that the ancient drawing books made look so beautiful, so majestic and grand. But just as she'd hoped, there was a gap in the time it took the sun to vanish beyond the horizon and for the rolling shadow to reach it, and she watched with growing anticipation. She'd seen only one star before, the north star which shone so brightly that not even the sun could always blot it out. But the other stars, the great field...would they appear in the deepening purple?

Kael saw it before she did, and he quickly pointed. In the sliver of violet space the star winked into existence, a little drop of light between the horizon and the shadows crashing down on it like a wave. Bree saw it, and she smiled at the sight.

"Imagine not one but thousands," Bree said as the dark clouds swallowed the star, pitching the entire city into utter darkness so deep she could not see her brother beside her. "A field spanning the entire sky, lighting up the night in their glow…"

Bree felt Kael take her hand, and she squeezed it tight. Blind, neither dared move, instead remaining perfectly still as they waited. It would only be a matter of time.

It started as a faint flicker of red across the eastern horizon. Slowly it grew, spreading, strengthening. Just like the shadows, so too did the fire roll across the sky, setting ablaze the inky clouds that covered the crown of the world. It burned without consuming, only shifting and twisting. It took thirty minutes, but eventually all of the sky raged with midnight fire, bathing the land in red. It'd last until daybreak, when the sun would rise, the fire would die, and the smoky remnants would hover over the morning sky until fading away.

A horn sounded from a watchtower further within their home island of Weshern. The blast set Bree's heart to hammering.

"They're starting," she whispered.

Both turned to face the field where the two theotechs hovered. The horn sounded thrice more, and come its halting, the forces of Weshern arrived. They sailed above the field in v-formations, their silver wings shimmering, powered by the light element that granted all seraphim mastery over the skies. Hundreds of men and women, dressed in black pants and jackets, armed with fire, lightning, ice, and stone that they wielded with the gauntlets of their ancient technology. Despite her fear, Bree felt an intense longing to be up there with them, fighting for the pride and safety of her home. Sadly it'd be five years before she and her brother turned sixteen, and could attempt to join.

"Bree..."

She turned her head, saw her brother staring off into the open sky beyond the edge of their island. Flying in similar v-formations, gold wings glimmering, red jackets seemingly aflame from the light of the midnight fire, came the Seraphim of Galen. The two armies raced toward one another, and Bree knew they'd meet just above the fallow field, where the theotechs waited.

Bree pushed herself away from the edge of the island and rose to her feet, her brother doing likewise.

"They'll be fine," she said, watching the Weshern Seraphim fly in perfect formation. She wondered which of those black and silver shapes was her mother, and which her father. "You'll see. No one's better than they are."

Kael stood beside her, eyes on the sky, arms locked at his sides. Bree reached for his hand, held it as the armies neared one another.

"It'll be over quick," she whispered. "Father says it always is."

Dark shapes shot in both directions through the space between the armies, large chunks of stone meant to screen attacks as well as protect against retaliation. They crashed into one another, and as the sound reached Bree's ears, the battle suddenly erupted into bewildering chaos. The seraphim formations danced about one another, lightning flashing amid them in constant barrages. Enormous blasts of fire accompanied them, difficult to see with the sky itself aflame. Blue lances of ice colored purple from the midnight hue shot in rapid bursts, cutting down combatants with ease. The sounds of battle were so powerful, so near, Bree could feel them in her bones.

"How?" Kael wondered aloud, and if he weren't so close she wouldn't have heard him over the cacophony. "How can anyone survive through that?"

Boulders of stone slammed into the fallow field beneath, carving out long grooves of earth before coming to a stop. Bree flinched at the impact of each one. How did one survive? She didn't know, but somehow they did, the seraphim of both islands weaving amid the carnage with movements so fluid and beautiful they mirrored that of dancers. Not all, though. Lightning tore through bodies, lances of ice with sharp tips punctured flesh and metal alike, and no armor could protect against the fire that washed over their bodies. Each seraph that fell wearing a black jacket made Bree silently beg it wasn't one of her parents. She didn't care if that were selfish or not. She just wanted them safe. She wanted them to survive the overwhelming onslaught that left her mind baffled on how to take it all in.

The elements lessened, the initial devastating barrage becoming more precise, more controlled. Bree saw that several combatants were out elements completely, and were forced to draw their blades. The battle had gradually spread further and further out, taking them beyond the grand field and closer to the edge of town where Bree and Kael stood. Not far above their heads, two seraphim circled in a dance, one fleeing, one chasing. They both had their twin blades drawn. Bree watched, entranced, eyes wide as the circle tightened, and the combatants whisked by each other again and again, slender blades swiping for exposed flesh.

It was the Galen seraph who made the first mistake. Bree saw him fail to dodge in time, saw the tip of the sword slice across his stomach. The body fell, careening wildly just before making impact with the ground. The sound was a bloodcurdling screech of metal and snapping bone. Bree's attention turned to the larger battle, and she saw that many more had drawn their blades. The number of remaining seraphim was shockingly few, yet they fought on.

"No one's surrendering," Kael said, and she could hear the fear threatening to overtake him completely. "Bree, you said it'd be quick. You said it'd be quick!"

The area of battle was spreading wildly out of control. Galen seraphim scattered in all directions, loose formations of two to three people. The Weshern seraphim chased, and despite the nearing town, they still released their elements. Bree screamed as a pair streaked above their heads, the *thrum* of their wings nearly deafening. A boulder failed to connect with the fleeing seraphim, and it blasted through the side of a home with a thundering blast.

"Let's go!" Bree screamed, grabbing Kael's hand and dashing toward the barricade. More seraphim were approaching, seemingly the entire Galen forces. They wanted to be over the town, Bree realized. They wanted to make Weshern's people hesitate to fight with so many nearby. As the twins climbed over stone barricade, the sounds of battle erupting all about them, it was clear their seraphim would make no such hesitations. Lightning flashed above Bree's head, and she cried out in surprise. She ducked, stumbled, lost her grip on her brother's hand. He stopped, shouted her name, and then the ice lance struck the cobbles ahead of them. It shattered into shards, and Kael dove to the ground as they flew in all directions.

"Kael," Bree said as she scrambled to her feet. "Kael!"

"I'm fine," he said, pushing himself to his hands and knees. When he looked to her, he was bleeding from several cuts across his face and neck. "I'm fine, now hurry!"

The red light of the midnight fire cast its hue across everything, convincing Bree she'd lost herself in a nightmare and awoken in one of the circles of Hell. Kael pulled her along, leading her toward Aunt Bethy's house, where they were supposed to have stayed during the battle, waiting like good children for their parents to return. Hand in hand they ran, the air above filled with screams, echoes of thunder, and the deep hum of the seraphim's wings.

When they turned a corner, they saw two seraphs flying straight at them from further down the street. Fire burst from the chaser's gauntlet. It bathed over the other, sending her crashing to the ground. Kael dove aside as Bree froze, her legs locked in place from terror. The body came to a halt mere feet away from her, silver wings mangled and broken. Her black jacket bore the blue sword of Weshern on her shoulder, and Bree shuddered at the sight of the woman's horrible burns. High above, the Galen seraph flew on, seeking new prey.

"Bree!" her brother shouted, pulling her attention away. He'd wedged himself in the tight space between two homes, and she joined him there in hiding.

"We have to get back," Bree insisted. "We can't stay here."

"Yes, we can," Kael said, hunkering deeper into the alley. "I'm not going out there, Bree. I'm not."

Bree glanced back out of the narrow alley. With the battle raging above the town, Aunt Bethy would be terrified at their absence. They were already going to be in trouble for not coming in like they were supposed to in the first place. To hide now, afraid, until who knew when it all ended?

"I'm going," she said. "Are you coming with me or not?"

Another blast of thunder above. Kael shook his head.

"No," he said. His eyes widened when he realized she was serious about going. "Bree, don't leave me here. Don't leave me!"

"I can't stay," Bree said, the mantra overwhelming her every thought. "I can't stay, Kael, I can't stay!"

She dashed back into the street, racing toward Aunt Bethy's house. As strongly as Kael wanted to remain hiding, Bree wanted to return to their aunt's home. She wanted to be inside, in a safe place with family. Let him be a coward. She'd be brave. She'd be strong.

A boulder crashed through the rooftop of a home to her right then blasted out the front wall. Bree screamed, and she realized she wasn't brave at all. She was frightened out of her mind. Fighting back tears, she turned down Picker Street, where both they and their aunt lived. Five houses down was her aunt's home, and Bree's heart took a sudden leap. Her legs moved fast as they could carry her.

There she was. Her mother was safe, she was alive, she was...

She was bleeding. Her hand clutched her stomach, and Bree saw with horrible clarity the red gash her fingers failed to seal. She lay on her back, her silver wings pressed against the door to Aunt Bethy's home, a dazed look on her face. Beneath her was a pool of her own blood.

"Bree," her mother said. Her voice was wet, strained. Tears trickled from her brown eyes. "Bree, what are you...what are you doing out here?"

Bree didn't know how to answer. She fell to her knees, felt her pants slicken from the blood. She reached out a trembling hand, wanting so badly to hold her mother but fearing what any contact might do.

"It's all right," her mother said, and she smiled despite her obvious pain. "Bree, it's all right. It's..."

Her lips grew still. She breathed in pain no more. Her hand fell limp, holding back her sliced stomach no longer. Bree touched her shoulder, shook her once.

"Mom," she said, tears rolling down her cheeks. "Mom, no, mom, please."

She buried her face against her mother's chest, shrieking out in wordless agony. She didn't want to see any more, to hear any more. Bree wrapped her arms around her mother's neck, clutching her tightly, not caring about the blood that seeped into her clothes. She just wanted one more embrace before the vultures came to reclaim her wings. She wanted to pretend her mother was alive and well, holding her, loving her, kissing her forehead before flying away for another day of training and drills.

Not this corpse. Not this lifeless thing.

A hand touched her shoulder. Bree pulled back, expecting to see her brother, but instead it was a tall Weshern seraph. Blood smeared his fine black coat. To her surprise, the surrounding neighborhood was quiet, the battle seemingly over.

"Was she your mother?" the man asked. Bree could barely see his face through the shadows cast by the midnight fire. She sniffled, then nodded.

"Then you must be Breanna. I...I don't know how else to tell you this. It's about your father."

His words were a dagger to an already punctured heart. It couldn't be. The world couldn't be that cruel.

"No," she whispered. "No, that can't be right."

The seraph swallowed hard.

"Breanna, I'm sorry."

Bree leapt to her feet, and she flung herself at the man, screaming at the top of her lungs.

"No, it can't. Not both, we can't lose them both, we can't... we can't..."

She broke, collapsing at his feet, her tears falling upon his black boots. She beat the stone cobbles until she bled, beat them as she screamed, beat them as high above, the midnight fire burned like an unrelenting pyre for the dead.

introducing

If you enjoyed
THE PARADOX,
look out for

AGE OF IRON

Iron Age: Book 1

by Angus Watson

LEGENDS AREN'T BORN. THEY'RE MADE.

Dug Sealskinner is a down-on-his-luck mercenary traveling south to join up with King Zadar's army. But he keeps rescuing the wrong people.

First, Spring, a child he finds scavenging on the battlefield, and then Lowa, one of Zadar's most fearsome warriors, who has vowed revenge on the king for her sister's execution.

Now Dug's on the wrong side of the thousands-strong army he hoped to join—and worse, Zadar has bloodthirsty druid magic on his side. All Dug has is his war hammer, one small child, and one unpredictable, highly trained warrior with a lust for revenge that might get them all killed...

CHAPTER 1

"Mind your spears, coming through!"

Dug Sealskinner shouldered his way back through the ranks. Front rank was for young people who hadn't learned to fear battle and old men who thought they could compete with the young.

Dug put himself halfway in that last category. He'd been alive for about forty years, so he was old. And he wanted to compete with the young, but grim experience had unequivocally, and sometimes humiliatingly, demonstrated that the young won every time. Even when they didn't win they won because they were young and he wasn't.

And here he was again, in another Bel-cursed battle line. Had things gone to plan, he'd have been living the respectable older man's life, lord of his broch, running his own seaside farm on Britain's north coast, shearing sheep, spearing seals and playing peekaboo with grandchildren. He'd been close to achieving that when fate had run up and kicked him in the bollocks. Since then, somehow, the years had fallen past, each one dying with him no nearer the goals that had seemed so achievable at its birth.

If only we could shape our own lives, he often thought, rather than other bastards coming along and shaping them for us.

Satisfyingly, the ragtag ranks parted at his request. He might not feel it, but he still looked fearsome, and he was a Warrior. His jutting jaw was bearded with thick bristle. His big head was cased in a rusty but robust, undecorated iron helmet. His oiled ringmail shone expensively in the morning sun, its heaviness flattening his ever-rounder stomach. The weighty warhammer which swung on a leather lanyard from his right hand could have felled any mythical beastie.

He'd been paid Warrior's wages to stay in the front rank to marshal the troops, so arguably he should have stayed in the front rank and marshalled the troops. But he didn't feel the need to fulfil every tiny detail of the agreement. Or even the only two details of it. First, because nobody would know; second, because there wasn't going to be a battle. He'd collect his full fee for a day standing in a field, one of thousands of soldiers. One of thousands of *people*, anyway. There were some other Warriors – Dug knew a few of them and had nodded hello – but the rest were men and women in leathers at best, hardly soldiers, armed with spears but more used to farm equipment. Quite a few of them were, in fact, armed with farm equipment.

What, by Camulos, is that doing here? he thought, looking at a small, bald but bearded man holding a long pole topped with a giant cleaver – a whale blubber cutter, if he wasn't mistaken. He hadn't seen one of those for a while and wanted to ask its owner what it was doing so far inland. But an interest in fishing equipment wouldn't help his battle-hardened Warrior image.

He pushed out into the open field. Behind Barton's make-shift army, children in rough wool smock-frocks ran across the bright field, laughing, fighting and crying. The elderly sat in groups complaining about the army's formation and other things that had been better in their day. To the left, sitting in a heap of rags and shunned by all, was the inevitable drunken old druid, shouting semi-coherently about the imminence of Roman invasion, like all the other dozens of drunken druids that Dug had seen recently.

Over by the bridge were those others who escaped military service – Barton's more important families. A couple of them were looking at Dug, perhaps wondering why their expensive mercenary was taking a break.

He put his hands on his hips in an overseer pose and tried to look like he was assessing the line for weaknesses. *Very important, the rear rank of a defensive line*, he'd tell them if they asked afterwards.

Dug hadn't expected to be in the Barton army that sunny morning. He'd been stopping in Barton hillfort the day before when word came that the cavalry and chariot sections of King Zadar of Maidun Castle's army would be passing on their way home from sacking the town and hillfort of Boddingham.

Boddingham was a smaller settlement than Barton, forty miles or so north-east along the Ridge Road. It had stopped paying tribute to Maidun. Perhaps Boddingham had felt safe, a hundred miles from the seat and capital of King Zadar's empire, but along good metalled roads and the hard chalk Ridge Road, that was only three days' journey for Zadar's chariots and cavalry – less if they pushed it. It would have taken much longer to move a full army, as Dug well understood, having both driven and hindered armies' movements in his time, but everyone Dug had spoken to said that Zadar's relatively small flying squad of horse soldiers was more than capable of obliterating a medium-sized settlement like Boddingham. If that was true, thought Dug, they must be the elite guard of Makka the war god himself.

The Maidun force had passed Barton two days before, too set on punishing Boddingham to linger for longer than it took to demand and collect food, water and beer. Now though, on the way back, swords bloodied, slaves in tow, the viciously skilful little company might have the time and inclination to take a pop at weak, underprepared Barton.

"You!" A man had shouted at Dug the night before. So courteous, these southerners.

"Aye?" he'd replied.

"Know anything about fighting?"

You'd think his dented iron helmet, ringmail shirt and warhammer might have answered that question, but southerners, in Dug's experience, were about as bright as they were polite.

"Aye, I'm a Warrior."

And that was how he'd ended up at the previous night's war council. He'd actually been on his way to sign up with Zadar's army – finally fed up with the strenuous life of a wandering mercenary – but he saw no need to mention that to the Barton defenders.

Fifty or so of Barton's more important men and women, the same ones who weren't in the battle line, had been packed into the Barton Longhouse for the war council. Calling it a longhouse was pretentiousness, another southern trait that Dug had noticed. First, it was circular. Second, it was only about twenty paces across. At most it was a mediumhouse. It was just a big hut really, made of mud, dung and grass packed into a lattice of twigs between upright poles. Four wide trunks in the middle supported the conical reed roof. Dug could have shown them how to build a hut the same size without the central supports, thereby freeing up space. Perhaps the hall predated that particular architectural innovation, but there was a wood at the foot of the hill and plenty of people, so rebuilding would have been a doddle.

This tribe, however, was clearly neither architecturally diligent nor building-proud. One of the support posts leaned

411

alarmingly and there was a large, unplanned hole in the roof near the door. At the end of a long hot day, despite the hole, the air inside was thick and sweaty. It could have done with double ceiling vents. Dug could have shown them how to put those in too.

King Mylor of Barton sat on a big wooden chair on a platform in the centre, rubbing the back of his hand against his two remaining rotten teeth, staring about happily with milky eyes at his visitors and hooting out "Oooo-ooooh!" noises that reminded Dug of an elderly seal. He looked like a seal, now Dug came to think of it. Smooth rings of blubber made his neck wider than his hairless, liver-spotted skull, which was wetly lucent in the torchlight. Whiskers sprayed out under his broad, flat nose. Dug had heard that Barton's king had lost his mind. It looked like the gossipy bards were right for once.

Next to Mylor sat the druid Elliax Goldan, ruler in all but name. You didn't cross Barton's chief druid, Dug had heard. He was a little younger than Dug perhaps, slim, with tiny black eyes in a pink face that gathered into a long nose. Rat-like. If you could judge a man by his face – and Dug had found that you could – here was an angry little gobshite. Dug had seen more and more druids as he'd migrated south. There were three basic types: the wise healer sort who dispensed advice and cures, the mad, drunk type who raved about dooms – almost all Rome-related these days – and the commanding sort whose communes with the gods tended to back up their plans and bolster their status. Elliax was firmly in this latter camp.

On Mylor's left was the druid's wife, Vasin Goldan. Her skin was shiny and mottled. Big eyes sat wide apart, far up her forehead, very nearly troubling her hairline. Frog-face, Dug had heard her called earlier. *Spot on*, he mused. Seal-head, Rat-nose and Frog-face. Right old menagerie.

Behind Elliax and Mylor were four Warriors in ringmail. It was never a great sign, Dug thought, when rulers needed protection from their own people.

Elliax silenced the hubbub with a couple of claps, interrupting Dug's explanation to a young woman of how he'd improve the hut's roof. "The meeting is convened!" he said in a surprisingly deep voice. Dug had expected him to squeak.

"Could we not do this outside?" asked Dug, pulling his mail shirt away from his neck to get some cooler air down there. Spicily pungent body odour clouded out. The woman he'd been talking to shuffled away. Blooming embarrassment made Dug even hotter.

"Barton war meetings take place in the Barton Longhouse!" Elliax boomed, also reddening.

"Even when it's hot and there's plenty of room outside? Isn't that a bit stupid?" Several people around Dug nodded.

"Hot-t-t-t-t!" shouted King Mylor.

Mylor, it was said, had lost his mind along with Barton's wealth and position ten years before, when he'd bet his five best against King Zadar's champion. The champion, a massive young man called Carden Nancarrow, had slaughtered Barton's four best men and one woman in a few horrifying moments. Barton had paid painful taxes to Maidun ever since.

By persuading Mylor to accept the five-to-one combat rather than defend the highly defendable fort, Elliax claimed he'd saved Barton from annihilation. Over the following decade he'd continued to serve his town as Zadar's representative and tax collector. Zadar's taxes would have starved Barton in a couple of years, said Elliax, but he was happy to mislead Maidun about Barton's assets and collect a little less. All he asked in exchange were a few easy gifts like land, food, ironwork or the easiest gift of all – an hour or so with a daughter. While others became steadily malnourished, Elliax thrived, his wife fattened, and unmarried girls bore children with suspiciously rodent faces. Anyone who complained found themselves chosen by Elliax's druidic divinations to march south as part of Zadar's quarterly slave quota.

"We have nothing to fear," Elliax continued, ignoring Dug and King Mylor. "I have seen it. We pay our dues and it's in Zadar's interest that we keep paying them. He will not attack."

"But Zadar can't be trusted to act rationally!" shouted a young woman at the back. "Look what he did to Cowton last year."

Dug had heard about Cowton. Everybody had. Zadar had wiped out the entire town. Men, women, the elderly, children, livestock…two thousand people and Danu knew how many animals had been slaughtered or sold to Rome as slaves. Nobody knew why.

Elliax looked sideways at King Mylor. The king was picking at the crotch of his woollen trousers.

"Who is your chief druid?" Elliax asked. Nobody had an answer. Elliax smiled like a toad who'd caught a large fly. He held out his arms. "This morning, on the wood shrine, I sacrificed a seabird from the Island of Angels to see its tales of the future. As the bird quivered in death, I was distracted by a sound. I looked up and saw a squirrel hissing at a cat. The cat passed by, leaving the squirrel unharmed." Elliax looked around smugly, eyes finishing up on Dug's.

Most people looked at each other and nodded. More often than not the gods' messages were too cryptic for Dug to grasp immediately, but he got this one.

"Can't argue with that!" said a stout man.

"Yeah, if it was true. Ever heard a squirrel hiss?" muttered a woman behind Dug.

"No one would dare lie about something like that!" whispered a man who, by the frustration in his voice, Dug took to be the woman's husband.

Elliax continued. "I looked into the bird's viscera and found Danu. She told me we had nothing to fear from Zadar. Next I found Makka. He outlined our strategy. The weather has been dry, so Zadar will leave the Ridge Road and take the quicker lowland road, as he did on the way to Boddingham. Makka told me that we should gather everyone on the valley floor and form a spear and shield line between the two curves of the river on the other side of the bridge. Cavalry and chariots cannot charge a spear line."

"Unless the spear line breaks," said Dug. He wouldn't have usually challenged any god's proclamations, especially Makka's, but these people didn't know battle and needed to be told. A few older voices murmured agreement, which encouraged him to continue: "In which case you might as well have a row of children holding wet reeds. Why not bring everyone up into the fort? Do a bit of work on the walls overnight – sharpen the angles, tighten the palisade, few spikes in the ditch – and they'll never get in."

"And leave all our farms, homes and crops to the whims of Zadar's army!" Elliax spat, his voice becoming steadily higher. "You're as stupid as you look, northman! You shouldn't be in here anyway. You're not from Barton. There's no reason for a spear line to break. I think two gods know a little more than some shabby has-been Warrior. And actually I have the advice of three gods, because further into the guts of the bird, I found Dwyn."

"Pretty crowded in that bird," said the woman behind Dug. Her husband shushed her again.

Elliax ignored the interruption. "That cunning god perfected the plan. He told me to send a rider to Zadar to tell him that we'll be lining the route to celebrate his passing with a ceremonial battle line. We'll defend our land with something that looks like a show of respect. That's the sort of strategic thinking you won't have seen much of where you're from."

"Are you sure that's what Dwyn told you?" Dug had never questioned a druid before, but Elliax's plan was madness. "Forewarned, as most kids where I'm from know, is forearmed."

Elliax sneered. "We have slings, many more than Zadar can possibly have. His troops will be on horseback and in chariots, we'll be behind shields. If Zadar tries to attack, our shields will protect us and we'll send back a hailstorm of death. Zadar is not stupid. He will not attack! He knows how futile it would be. Besides, the gods have spoken to me. Perhaps if you'd listened to them more, you wouldn't be walking the land begging for work. At your age too. It's shameful."

Dug's ears were suddenly hot. Elliax turned away from him and outlined his plan in detail. Irritatingly, thought Dug, the jumped-up prick's idea made some sense. Charging a line of spears on horseback or in a chariot was indeed suicide. Horses knew this too, so it was also near impossible. He was right about projectile weapons as well. Barton's more numerous slingers and shields should neutralise any projectile threat.

Geography also favoured Barton. To get from Zadar's likely route to most of Barton's land, you had to cross a river. The only bridge for miles was in the centre of a long bend. The best way for cavalry to beat a line of spearmen was to gallop around and take them on the flank or from behind. With the army bracketed by two loops of the river's meandering course, that would be impossible. But there was still one big, obvious flaw.

"Why don't we stay this side of the bridge?" Dug asked. "We can hold the bridge with a handful of soldiers, protect most of the land and you can still have your wee procession. If Zadar attacks and your long line of bakers and potters doesn't hold, which it probably wouldn't, then we're trapped between him and the river and in all sorts of bother."

Elliax grimaced as if someone had just urinated on a relative's funeral bed. "Still you challenge the gods? They know, as you don't, that there's valuable property just the other side of the river."

"This property wouldn't happen to be yours, would it?"

"Why don't you shut up and stop embarrassing yourself? We share property. It's *everyone's* land, you northern fool." Elliax stared at him furiously, but then, as if recalling a pleasant memory, smiled. "Or maybe you'd like a stronger reading? Why don't you come up here and we'll see what your spilled entrails say about Zadar's intentions? We'll see the next ten winters in your fat gut! Bob, Hampcar, why don't you find out just how much this know-it-all knows about fighting?"

Two of the four guards stood forward and slid swords a couple of fingers' breadth from scabbards. They were both big men. One had a long face with a pronounced muzzle and drawn-back lips showing uncommonly white teeth. The other was beardless, with a scar soaring redly from each corner of his mouth into his shaggy hairline. That injury was caused by making a small cut at each corner of a person's mouth, then hurting them; an iron auger screwed between wrist bones was one method Dug had seen. The victim would scream, ripping his or her flesh from mouth to ears. If the wounds healed and they didn't die of infection, they were left with a smile-shaped scar. Way up north this was called a Scrabbie's kiss, after a tribe keen on handing them out. Men generally grew beards to cover the scars, but this guy had shaved to show them off. It was, admittedly, quite effective, if you were going for the scary bastard look. His mate looked even tougher.

Dug decided not to take them on.

"Are you coming? Or are you a coward?" Elliax sneered.

Dug stared back in what he hoped was a cool, Bel-may-care manner. He didn't need to take on four Warriors to prove a point. Or even two. Besides, if Dwyn, god of tricks, Makka, god of war and Danu, mother of all the gods, had all been involved in the planning, who was Dug to argue? He might as well negotiate a decent fee for standing in the line, then leave the following evening a richer man with his guts still in his belly.

"Are you coming, I said?"

"I'll stay here."

"Stupid, fat and cowardly too. Some Warrior!" Elliax looked around triumphantly and seemed to grow a little. "Ignore this oaf's ignorant comments. I have been shown the way. The plan is made and King Mylor agrees." Mylor looked up and smiled at hearing his name, then returned to plucking at his genitals. Elliax continued: "Have no fear. Zadar hasn't got where he is today by attacking against impossible odds. We are completely safe."